THE ANGEL

a novel

JAMES H. PENCE

Kregel
Publications

The Angel
© 2006 by James H. Pence

Published by Kregel Publications, a division of Kregel, Inc., P.O. Box 2607, Grand Rapids, MI 49501.

Library of Congress Cataloging-in-Publication Data
Pence, James H.
The angel : a novel / by James H. Pence.
      p. cm.
         1. Women physicians—Fiction. 2. Euthanasia—Fiction. 3. Serial murderers—Texas—Dallas—Fiction. 4. Dallas (Tex.)—Fiction. I. Title.
      PS3616.E53A85 2006
      813'.6-dc22   2006003464

ISBN 0-8254-3472-6

Printed in the United States of America

06 07 08 09 10 / 5 4 3 2 1

To all the PALS and CALS* out there who have learned that every day we live is a gift from God. Instead of *dying* from ALS you are *living* with it. Your courage is an inspiration.

(*PALS* is an acronym for a person with ALS; a *CALS* is a caregiver for someone with ALS.)

ACKNOWLEDGMENTS

Writing a novel is a solitary task; bringing it to publication is a group effort.

Thanks to everyone who had a part in bringing this story to life.

Special thanks go to Steve Barclift, my managing editor, for his great patience with me through the whole process. Dave Lindstet, thanks for an awesome job of editing. Paul Ingram, my hat is off to you for catching those eleventh-hour glitches. My family deserves kudos for putting up with me as I retreated to my recliner to crank out the various drafts of this novel. And special thanks to my wife, Laurel, for helping me with page-proof reviews. I couldn't have done it without you.

As always, any mistakes that remain are my own.

PROLOGUE

Mercy Hospital
St. Louis, Missouri

The woman hovered between life and death.

One day after her thirty-third birthday, MariBeth Wilson, mother of three young children, suffered a massive stroke. Quick work by an EMS team kept her alive; severe brain damage kept her in an irreversible coma.

Her husband, Rick, sat beside the bed, staring at a photograph in his hands, virtually in a coma of his own.

The third-year resident assigned to the case watched silently from the corridor. He was jarred back to reality when the nursing shift supervisor nudged his arm. "He hardly ever moves," she said, shaking her head. "He won't eat, won't talk. I told him if he didn't eat, he'd turn into as much of a vegetable as she is."

The resident's anger flashed white and hot. "Don't say 'vegetable' around me and certainly not around him." He jerked his head in Rick's direction.

"I'm sorry, doctor," the nurse replied, a hint of annoyance in her voice. She had, after all, been an RN when he was in diapers. She didn't say it though. Not to his face. She knew better.

"Bring me a cup of coffee," he ordered as he stepped into the room.

The nurse drew herself up. "Doctor, you can get your own—"

A look from the resident cut off the retort. She turned on her heel and strode angrily down the hallway.

The young physician crossed the room and circled around to the far side of the bed. He held out his hand. "Good morning, Mr. Wilson."

Rick kept his head down, gazing at the photo. His black hair was matted and unkempt, and judging by the stubble on his face, he hadn't shaved in days.

The resident pulled up a chair and sat down. "I hear you're not eating."

No response.

"Is that your family?" the resident asked, gesturing toward the picture.

Rick nodded weakly, his eyes fixed on the photograph.

"May I see it?"

Rick hesitated, then offered the picture to the resident.

"Nice family," the resident said. "Three children?"

The grieving husband looked at the resident through red-rimmed eyes. He swallowed and nodded. A tear fell from the corner of one eye, traced its way down his cheek, and disappeared in the stubble on his face.

"Those kids are going to need you, Mr. Wilson." The resident's voice was gentle.

Rick put his head in his hands and ran his fingers through his hair in one slow motion. "I can't do it."

"Doctor?" a voice broke in from the doorway.

The resident looked up. The nursing supervisor stood in the doorway, frowning, a paper cup of coffee in her hand. He motioned her to bring the coffee to him.

"What can't you do?" the resident asked as he took the steaming cup from the nurse's hand. He motioned toward the door with the back of his hand, dismissing her. She sighed disapprovingly and left the room.

"I can't handle this," Rick said, his eyes sweeping MariBeth's still form on the bed. "They said she could go on like this for—" He choked.

"—for a long time," the resident finished for him. He handed Rick the coffee. "Here, you look like you could use this."

"Thanks," Rick said absently, taking a sip from the cup. For the first time since he'd entered the room, the resident thought he saw the man make an effort to turn awareness toward him and what he was saying.

A tiny ceramic angel, about the size of a person's thumb, sat on the table next to MariBeth's bed. Trying to draw Rick in a conversation, the doctor pointed to the angel. "Yours?"

Rick picked up the angel and handed it to the resident. "Her mother gave it to her when she was little. Told her the angels would always be watching over her." He shrugged. "She always kept it at her bedside at home. I don't know why I brought it. The angels forgot about her."

In bed after an endless shift, the resident couldn't sleep.

Thoughts of the young husband with three children to care for tore him up inside. He kept trying to put himself in Rick Wilson's place. If it were *his* wife lying there, he'd want to do something about her condition. If he couldn't, he'd want someone else who could help to step in.

The man's final lament kept playing in his head. "The angels forgot about her."

A thought had been lurking in the recesses of his mind and now crept to the fore—*Maybe they haven't forgotten.*

He mulled over an idea for a long while. His resources were limited, but he had a supply of insulin, left over after his mother's recent death from complications of diabetes. It was one of the many things he hadn't gotten around to taking care of after she died. Now he understood why he'd held on to it.

It would be quick, easy, painless.

Almost certainly Rick Wilson would refuse to allow an autopsy. Even if he did permit a post mortem, the insulin would be difficult to detect if they weren't looking for it. Chances were good the medical examiner would take no notice. Why should he? MariBeth's death was a certainty at some point anyway.

It was late on one of the resident's rare nights off when he walked quietly down the hall and into the darkened room. Rick had gone home to be with his children. All the nurses were occupied and a resident's presence was so commonplace as to go unobserved. It didn't matter. He was assigned to this patient and nobody would think about him being in her room at any hour.

Nevertheless, he was risking everything. But he could not stand by while this young husband suffered. No matter the consequences, he would—he *must*—release him.

Going through the motions of checking MariBeth's vitals—in case someone walked in unexpectedly—the resident pulled the syringe from his lab coat pocket.

After inserting the needle in the IV port, he slowly depressed the plunger, injecting an overdose of insulin. He felt a shiver up and down his spine as the fluid disappeared into the IV tubing. The hair on the back of his neck prickled and he could feel his heart pumping. Was he afraid—or was this exhilaration something else?

When the syringe was empty, he pulled it from the IV port and capped the needle, slipping the syringe back into the pocket of his lab coat. It would not be long before the comatose woman went into insulin shock. After that, her condition would deteriorate rapidly.

He turned to leave the room, then stopped and went back to the bedside. He picked up the ceramic angel and looked at it again. It was milky white and some type of glitter had been embedded in the glaze. The angel's delicate wings stretched out behind it. Its tiny hands were pressed together in a childlike expression of prayer. Its face was turned upward toward heaven.

He looked from the angel to MariBeth's expressionless face, rotating the tiny figure in his fingers. Then he slipped it into his pocket.

He opened the door quietly, looking down the hall to make sure no one would observe his departure. Quickly, quietly, he exited into a stairwell.

The next morning, he learned that MariBeth Wilson had gone code blue at about three thirty in the morning. The crash team had worked on her for forty-five minutes before the attending physician pronounced her dead at 4:18.

MariBeth's death hadn't raised any suspicion at the hospital. The resident was certain he was in the clear. But he needed to observe

MariBeth's family, see how they responded to her passing. He wanted to make sure he had done the right thing. He decided to attend her funeral. He chose a seat near the middle of the church and sat down.

Rick Wilson still looked grief-stricken, but he showed visible signs of relief. His ordeal was over. Though he still had a rough road ahead of him, at least now he could get on with his life.

As the young resident watched the family comforting each other in the front row, he knew that he'd done the right thing. More than that, he knew he'd found his true calling in life.

He would dedicate his life to setting people free.

Part One

ISIDORE

ONE

Sentinel Health Systems
Dallas, Texas

Ruthie Jacoby wheeled her husband along the beautiful path toward Sentinel Health Systems' main building. Pausing for a moment, she closed her eyes and inhaled the sweet fragrance of roses. Although Isidore no longer recognized her, Ruthie knew that he loved these walks through Sentinel's gardens. The little detour might make them late for check-in, but Ruthie could not resist bringing him here. She rolled the wheelchair up to a rose bush blanketed with scarlet blossoms. Gently plucking a newly opened rose, she crouched down and brought it close to her husband's nose.

"Isn't it beautiful, Poppie?"

Isidore stared straight ahead, his vacant eyes showing no recognition. A thread of saliva trailed from his chin to his rumpled shirt. Ruthie could hardly bear to look at him anymore. Once handsome and robust, her Poppie was now pitiful and frail, and no longer remembered any of their wonderful forty-two years together.

Ruthie tucked the rose into the breast pocket of Isidore's sweater. Blinking back her tears, she hesitated a moment, hearing her sister's concerned voice in the back of her mind. *Why don't you put him in a nursing home, Ruthie? He's too much for you to take care of. You need a life. It's not as if he'd miss you, for heaven's sake. Isidore doesn't even recognize you anymore.*

Ruthie pulled a tissue from her purse and dabbed away the saliva that trickled from the corner of Isidore's mouth. She still felt horror at her sister's suggestion. *"I won't allow my Poppie to shrivel away in one of those awful places. As long as I can take care of him, I will."*

"And what will you do when you can't take care of him any longer, Ruthie? What will you do then?"

Ruthie hadn't answered.

That was three years ago. Since then, Ruthie's sister had died, but Ruthie was going strong and Isidore was still hanging on. Granted, she faced her own share of health problems. A slight stroke two years earlier had left her weak on the right side, but she was left-handed and had adjusted quite well, thank you. An ongoing battle with glaucoma threatened her vision, but the progress of the disease had been arrested. Even her diabetes was under control.

Ruthie Jacoby was a fighter.

But Ruthie was also weary, though she wouldn't admit it to anyone. Isidore required constant care, and their home-health coverage had reached its limit a year ago. With no family to help—they'd never been able to have children—she had to rely on friends for those few moments each week when she got out to go grocery shopping and have her hair done.

Ruthie looked into Isidore's blank eyes. "It's so hard sometimes," she said. "You understand, don't you Poppie?"

Isidore's eyes didn't meet hers. He stared blankly into space, looking at nothing. Fighting to maintain her composure, Ruthie rose to her feet and began pushing the wheelchair toward the building.

Her voice husky, she said, "I love you, Poppie."

———

Ruthie wheeled Isidore's chair through the sliding glass doors into Sentinel's atrium. In her opinion, the atrium was at least as beautiful as the gardens. Sentinel's four main buildings stood at the atrium's four corners. Clear glass walls connected the four buildings and a thirty-foot-high glass ceiling stretched across the entire span, creating a giant greenhouse. Palm trees and other tropical plant life thrived inside the climate-controlled room. The spacious, crystalline structure also housed a generous collection of newsstands, gift stores, coffee shops, and restaurants.

A young woman, dressed in a smart-looking blue and gold outfit, stood behind the reception desk, just inside the sliding doors. She smiled as she greeted Ruthie and Isidore.

"Hello again, Mr. and Mrs. Jacoby. May I see your room pass, please?"

Ruthie rummaged through her purse and handed the woman a sheet of paper.

The woman quickly glanced over it and pressed a button on the podium. "Very good. You'll be in room D477."

Immediately a tanned young man with neatly cropped, jet-black hair and a bodybuilder's physique walked up and stood beside the receptionist. She handed the paper to him and said, "Tony, take good care of them."

"You can count on that," Tony said with a broad smile. He walked behind Isidore's wheelchair and pushed it toward the elevators.

Years ago, when the hospital had opened, Ruthie and Isidore had been delighted at the opportunity to become charter members of Sentinel Health Systems, the ultimate in patient-friendly HMOs. One of Sentinel's latest innovations was a streamlined admissions process that allowed patients to do most of the paperwork online. Ruthie found this particularly helpful because she had her hands full just getting Isidore *to* the hospital. She didn't want to be bothered with paperwork. With SHS, she didn't need to be. Sentinel's automated verification system checked the necessary references and e-mailed an admission pass directly to her. The pass even included Isidore's room number. All she needed to do to check Poppie in was present his pass at the front desk. It was easier than making airline reservations. Ruthie smiled when she saw the familiar banner engraved into the dark marble over the reception desk.

"Quality health care for all God's children."

———

Room D477 was more like a nice hotel room than a hospital room. Everything from the warm lighting to the wall-sized mural of a river flowing by an old mill felt comforting to Ruthie. Soft recliners, coffee tables, and computer desks had replaced the utilitarian furnishings of most hospital rooms. A refreshing hint of cherry vanilla wafted through the room, masking the typical hospital smell. Not that a hospital room could ever really be like home, Ruthie mused, but Sentinel came as close as possible.

"There you go, Mr. Jacoby," said Tony as he helped Isidore out of his wheelchair and into a plush recliner. "Would you like to watch some television?"

Ruthie sat in a chair beside her husband's recliner. "He likes the Food Channel," she said.

"Ah, a closet gourmet." Tony touched the remote beside Isidore's chair and the TV screen came to life. Isidore took no notice.

After he turned down the bed, Tony walked over to a computer terminal set back in a niche in the wall and touched a spot on the screen with an attached stylus. The computer beeped and instantly the colors on the monitor changed as Isidore's medical chart was displayed. Tony surveyed the screen. "Looks like everything's arranged for Mr. Jacoby's procedure. Dr. Westlake should be checking in within the next hour or two. And Dr. Galloway will be dropping by, too." Tony touched the screen with his stylus again, and the computer made some more beeping noises.

"Dr. Galloway? I don't think I know him."

"Dr. Galloway is head of our hospice service," replied Tony. "He likes to make a courtesy call on cases where the patient is—" Tony stopped himself and shifted awkwardly on his feet.

"Is what?" Ruthie challenged. "Dying? My husband is *not* dying, young man."

Tony flushed with embarrassment. "I'm sorry, Mrs. Jacoby. That was a bad choice of words." He picked up the TV remote control and handed it to Ruthie. "Do you need me to help you get Mr. Jacoby changed and into bed?"

"No, thank you," Ruthie said more curtly than she had intended. "Poppie and I have a routine and he's more relaxed if we stick to it."

"All right, then. I guess I'll be on my way. If you need anything, just press the Call button on the remote. Someone will be right in."

"I know," she replied.

Tony laughed, lightening the mood. "I keep forgetting. You know this drill so well, you could probably fill in for me on my day off." He patted Isidore on the shoulder. "You take good care of this lovely lady, Mr. Jacoby, or I might just steal her from you."

Ruthie blushed as Tony left the room and closed the door behind him.

Isidore stared vacantly into space.

TWO

"You look done in, doctor. Why don't you call it a day and go home?" Katherine Bainbridge asked from the doorway to Barnabas Galloway's office.

Dr. Galloway checked his watch and raised his bushy gray eyebrows. "Katherine, when have you ever known me to leave work at 4:20 in the afternoon?"

Katherine put her index finger up to her lips. "I promise I won't tell a soul."

"My day won't be finished till well after eight. But *you've* put in a good day, Katherine. Why don't *you* take off early?"

Dr. Galloway took off his reading glasses and rubbed his eyes.

"You really need to go home and get some rest," Katherine said.

Galloway laughed. "That's exactly what Margaret would have told me," he said, nodding toward the portrait of his wife that hung on his office wall. "She was always after me to take time off. Now that she's gone, I just find more reasons to work late."

"She was quite a woman," Katherine said.

Katherine had never met Margaret Galloway, but based on the doctor's descriptions of his late wife, she had not only been stunningly beautiful but wise and gracious as well. Judging by the size of the portrait of her that hung in Dr. Galloway's office, her death had left a huge void in his life. Margaret had also served as Dr. Galloway's assistant until the cancer had taken her just before their fortieth anniversary.

Dr. Galloway had relocated to SHS Dallas a year after her death.

Galloway opened the file folder that Katherine had given him a few hours earlier. He tapped the papers inside the folder with his finger. "Not to change the subject, but I've glanced through your report."

"What do you think of my conclusions?" she asked.

Dr. Galloway chewed on the end of his reading glasses. He leaned back in his chair and motioned toward an empty chair by his desk. "Close the door and have a seat."

When Katherine was seated, the doctor leaned forward onto his desk, now alert. "Do you think someone's euthanizing patients here?"

"Don't put words in my mouth, doctor," Katherine said, shifting uncomfortably. "I never said *euthanize*."

"Perhaps not," Galloway replied, "but your findings certainly point to that possibility."

"All I'm saying is that in the last five years several of our hospice patients died before they were expected to, and there doesn't seem to be any reason."

"But Katherine, hospice patients *are*, as a rule, terminal."

"But these patients expired well before their diseases had run their course."

Galloway nodded. "So, what are you suggesting we do?"

Katherine didn't miss a beat. "I wouldn't have brought this to you if I didn't think we need to investigate further."

"If word got out, an investigation would generate an enormous amount of negative publicity, don't you think? How would you recommend we handle that?"

Katherine blushed. "Doctor, I don't think it's my place to make that determination."

Galloway laughed. "All right, all right, I'll let you off the hook. But you *do* realize that I can't go off half-cocked and start making allegations without proof."

"Dr. Galloway, if you'll take the time to study that report, I believe you'll find plenty of proof."

"All right then," he said. "I'll give your evidence a fair reading, and if I think it has merit I'll pass it on to the proper authorities."

"Promise?"

"Promise." His careworn face crinkled in an indulgent smile.

"I'll be going home, then," Katherine said. "Call me if you need anything."

"I will, Katherine. And close the door behind you, please."

Barnabas Galloway watched his office door close. He leaned back in his chair, absent-mindedly flipping through the pages of Katherine's report. After about five minutes he flipped the file folder closed, went over to his door, and listened for a moment. Not hearing any movement in Katherine's office, he turned the lock. Returning to his chair, he swung around and opened the oak cabinet behind his desk, revealing a large combination safe. He twirled the tumbler back and forth and pulled down on the gold-plated lever. The safe's door popped open. Reaching inside, he pulled out a bottle of vodka and a shot glass.

After filling the tiny glass, he held it up toward his wife's portrait in a silent toast. Then he drained it in one gulp. He refilled the glass and drained it a second time.

Leaning back in his chair, he closed his eyes, waiting for the deadening rush of the alcohol to hit his system. After a few minutes, he returned the bottle and glass to the safe and picked up Katherine's file folder again.

"I'm sorry, Katherine," he said as he slipped the folder into the safe and gave the tumblers a spin, "but we can't afford the publicity."

Dr. Lori Westlake held her tongue as Nina Ware lit a cigarette. Smoking wasn't allowed in the Sentinel Health Systems complex, but considering the news this young mother was about to receive, she wouldn't nitpick.

She pushed a half-empty coffee mug across her desk toward Nina.

"I'm sorry, I don't have an ashtray. Maybe this will work."

The thin young woman pushed her dirty blonde hair away from her eyes. Her hand trembled as she took a drag. "I don't guess I should be doin' this," she said, waving the cigarette. "They got signs all over sayin' I can't smoke in here." She shook her head. "It's just a nasty habit I ain't never been able to break."

Lori smiled and shook her head. "Don't worry about it."

Nina shrugged, "I really oughta quit, at least 'fore Dakota gets old enough to take on my bad habits." She nodded toward a dirty-faced toddler who was sitting on the floor playing with Nina's car keys. The little boy squealed as if in agreement.

A stab of sorrow shot through Lori's heart. Ten years of practice had not made it any easier to give a patient bad news. And the news she had to share with Nina was the worst.

She looked down at the folder on the desk in front of her. "Nina, your test results aren't what we'd hoped for."

Nina put the cigarette to her lips and inhaled deeply, closing her eyes. She held the smoke in for several seconds, almost as if everything would go away if she just held her breath long enough. Finally, she released the smoke with a shuddering breath. "It's cancer?"

Lori bit her lip and nodded. "In the pancreas."

Nina did nothing for a moment. As the tears welled in her eyes, she blinked and looked toward the ceiling. As if on cue, Dakota grabbed her pant legs and pulled himself up beside her. Nina dropped her cigarette into the coffee mug and swept the child into her arms. She held the wiggling boy close to her as tears streamed from her eyes.

Lori knew that the adage "Silence is golden" applied in moments like these. You could do more harm than good by offering empty words of comfort. Instead, she left the seat behind her desk and moved to the chair beside her patient. She put her hand on Nina's shoulder, sitting quietly as sobs racked the young woman's body.

Dakota threw the car keys to the floor and tried to wriggle free from his mother's grasp.

After several minutes, Nina spoke softly. "How long have I got?"

Lori shook her head. "We're going to fight this with everything we've got. Cancer of the pancreas is serious, but some of the new treatments available are improving chances of re—"

"No." Nina waved her hand. "No chemo. I saw what it did to my mama. I'm not havin' it."

Lori nodded, "That's certainly your choice to make, of course. But I'd still like to refer you to an oncologist—a cancer specialist. He'll be able to advise you of your options."

Nina shook her head. "No, I don't want that."

"But Nina—"

Nina stood up. "Dr. Westlake, my mama died from pancreatic cancer. So did my brother and my uncle. I seen what they went through and told myself a long time ago that I wouldn't let that happen to me. I ain't goin' through it."

"Nina, please," said Lori. "Think of Dakota."

Nina's voice hardened. "I am, Dr. Westlake." She hoisted the young boy onto her hip and walked out of the office, bumping into a man in a crisp pair of Dockers and a pullover sweater as she went through the door.

"Pardon me," he said as she brushed by him. Nina ignored his apology as she hurried down the hallway. The man turned to Lori and raised his eyebrows. "Was it something I said?"

"No, it was something *I* said. Come in, Drew."

Drew Langdon sat down in the chair that Nina had just vacated. Handsome and athletic, with thick brown hair in tight ringlets that would make most women jealous, Drew could have worked as a model if he'd wanted. Instead, he'd chosen to spend his life as a grief counselor, working with families of terminally ill patients.

"What's up?" he asked.

Lori rested her head in her hands. "Oh, nothing much. I just had to tell a young mother that she probably won't see her baby's next birthday."

Drew shook his head. "Hmm, I'm sorry. It's never easy, is it? Do you think she's open to talking about it? I'd be happy to work her in."

Lori shrugged. "Right now, she's not even willing to get treatment for the cancer. I doubt counseling is high on her list of priorities." She stood up and moved back behind her desk. Swiveling her chair toward a credenza beside her desk, she poured herself a cup of coffee from a thermal carafe. "Like some coffee?"

"Thanks, no. I'm on caffeine overload already."

"So what brings you down to my neck of the woods?" she asked.

Drew shrugged and gave Lori a sheepish look. "Actually, I was hoping to take you out to dinner tonight. That is, if you don't mind being seen in public with a humble grief counselor."

Lori sighed. "I don't know, Drew. I don't think I'd be very good company."

"Lori, if I may give you a bit of unsolicited counsel," Drew offered, "you can't let yourself get dragged down every time you have to give a patient bad news. You'll go nuts if you do. Besides, as I often tell people I'm counseling, getting out for a meal is a good way to restore balance and perspective."

Lori took a sip of her coffee. "It's not just that. I already promised Kate that I'd have dinner with her tonight."

Drew smiled. "Yeah, right. I've heard *that* story before. But you might want to check your calendar again, doctor."

"What do you mean?"

"Just that every time I ask you out, you have some 'previous engagement,' usually with your sister." He reached into his pocket and pulled out a folded piece of paper, pushing it across the desk toward Lori. "Well, this time I did some reconnaissance before I got here."

Lori unfolded the sheet of paper and noticed the familiar-looking handwriting:

> *This is to certify that my sister, Dr. Lori Westlake, has no previous plans with me for the evening.*
>
> *Katherine Bainbridge.*
> *P.S. Sorry, Sis, I cannot tell a lie.*

"I'll get her for this," Lori threatened as she crumpled the paper and tossed it into the wastebasket beside her desk.

"When do you get off?" Drew asked.

Lori held up her hands. "Not so fast, Romeo. Tomorrow's Isidore Jacoby's surgery."

"Lori, you're not a surgeon. Dr. Johnston's doing the procedure. I'm sure he has everything under control. Now when can I pick you up?"

"I'm not the surgeon, but I'm still going to check on Mr. Jacoby before I leave. I'm still hoping to talk his wife out of it."

Drew shook his head. "You're really into self-punishment, aren't you?"

"Meaning?" Lori asked.

"Meaning Dr. Johnston will have a fit if he knows you're trying to interfere—again."

Lori held up a finger. "Don't even go there, Drew. Mr. Jacoby is *my* patient. If anyone is interfering, it's Johnston."

Drew raised his hands in surrender. "I'm not saying any more. But you know that if you and Johnston go head-to-head, you're going to lose."

Lori shook her head and sighed. "I've already lost."

"Which is exactly why you need a change of pace. I'll be by here to pick you up at six sharp." Drew stood and went to the door. "You've been hiding behind your sister for almost a year. Even *she* wants to see you get out once in a while. Six o'clock. Don't be late."

"Make it eight. And pick me up at Kate's house," Lori replied. "I've got self-defense class tonight."

"Confucius say, 'Never argue with a woman who can break boards.' Eight o'clock it is." He smiled as he walked to the door, closing it behind him as he left.

As soon as he was gone, the grin faded from Lori's face. "Thanks a lot, Kate," she muttered.

THREE

Charles Hamisch had dreaded this day for months. If there had been any way to avoid it, he would have. He held out hope that an emergency call would come in, requiring his attention, but he knew that would never happen. He had been put on desk duty a month ago, and his partner had been reassigned. Charles hated it, but he also understood.

A cop who can't fire his weapon isn't much use to anybody.

Charles opened and closed his right hand, then wiggled his fingers. That's where it had all started. Practicing at the weapons range. At first, he had noticed he was having difficulty pulling the trigger on his service revolver. Then his hands had felt weak and crampy, and his fingers had developed an annoying twitch. He hadn't paid much attention to it because he hadn't been out to the range in a while, and firing a weapon correctly wasn't child's play.

Then he had started dropping things—a file folder, a pencil. It was annoying, but nothing major. But he began to worry the day he shattered his favorite coffee mug on the floor of the break room. It had just fallen out of his hand.

Not long after that, he began stumbling when there was nothing to stumble over. Then he tumbled down a short flight of stairs and nearly broke his neck. Things had gotten to the point he knew he had to go to a doctor and get checked out. He would never forget the chill that had bolted through his system when the doctor offered the diagnosis: Amyotrophic Lateral Sclerosis. ALS. Lou Gehrig's disease.

Charles wiggled his fingers again and ran them through what was left of his coal black hair. He felt fine today. That's what drove him crazy. Each day was different. Some mornings he woke up feeling strong and on top of the world. Other days, just climbing out of bed required a Herculean effort.

What would he do when he no longer *could* climb out of bed?

He had decided to go on disability while he still was able to do some things for himself. He had always prided himself on his self-sufficiency, but it wouldn't be long before self-sufficiency would be a thing of the past. A thirty-nine-year-old bachelor with no family or support system, Charles wasn't sure *what* he'd do when that moment came.

"Detective Hamisch?"

Charles looked up. Shea Lockwood, a young female officer fresh from the Academy, stood in the doorway.

"Yes?"

"We have a little problem in the break room and we were wondering if you could help us with it."

Charles resisted the temptation to roll his eyes. Because Shea was "low man on the totem pole," she had been awarded the task of luring him into the break room for his "surprise" retirement party. He had known about it for a week and would have avoided it if he could find a plausible excuse. Nevertheless, he didn't have to make it easy on her.

"Sure. What is it?"

"Sir?" Shea asked, nonplussed.

"The problem. What is it?"

"The problem? Oh. Uh—" She looked at the ceiling, then down at the floor. "Well, the candy machine is jammed and we thought you—"

Charles interrupted. "You thought I could fix it?"

"Yes, we thought you could fix it."

Charles shook his head. "I'm lousy with mechanical things. Better find someone else." He turned his attention back to his paperwork.

"But—but you've got to come!"

A man's voice broke in, rescuing Shea from her dilemma. "Go on back, Officer Lockwood. *I'll* take care of Detective Hamisch."

Looking deeply relieved, she made a hasty retreat.

David Bachman sat down on the edge of Charles's desk, shaking his head. "It's not nice to mess with a rookie's mind."

Charles kept his eyes focused on his paperwork. "Not nice, but eminently satisfying."

"Maybe," Bachman answered, "but that's not why you did it."

Charles glanced up at his best friend and former partner and shook his head. "Maybe not."

David reached over and picked up a small mahogany carving from the desk. He turned it over in his hands, examining it as if it were a piece of evidence. The exquisitely detailed interpretation of Albrecht Dürer's *The Praying Hands*, could easily have fetched hundreds of dollars from a collector. It certainly was out of a homicide detective's price range—unless the homicide detective was the artist who had carved it.

David placed the sculpture back on his friend's desk. "You know I hate this as much as you do, Charles, but there are a lot of people back there who are going to be awfully disappointed if you don't show."

Charles worked his jaw muscles and returned his gaze to the pages in front of him. "I can't do it, David."

"What's to do? You go in there, eat some cake, let them sing 'For He's a Jolly Good Fellow,' pat you on the back and tell you how much they'll miss you."

"It'll be like going to my own funeral." Charles looked up from his reports and stared at his partner. He pushed himself awkwardly up out of his chair. An oak cane lay on the floor beside his desk, but he ignored it. His gait unsteady, he walked over to the window and looked out, leaning against the frame.

"Charles," said David, "those people care about you. They want to say good-bye."

"That's what would happen at a retirement party," Charles answered. "But not at *this* party. They'll talk about the weather, about the Cowboys game, about work. The whole time, they'll walk on eggshells trying to avoid talking about the thing that's on *everybody's* mind—the elephant in the living room."

"Charles—"

Steadying himself with one hand on the windowsill, Charles turned to face his partner. "I'm not retiring, David. I'm dying. It might be six months or six years before this thing gets me, but it's going to happen."

"They all know that," said David.

"Of course they do," Charles shot back. "And have you noticed how they avoid me now? How they suddenly find something else to do when I walk into the room?"

"Not all of them."

"No, not all of them," Charles agreed. "But *enough* of them." He looked at the floor. "Can't do it, David. I'm going home." He made his way cautiously back to his desk and crouched down to pick up his cane.

When he stood back up, he saw Shea Lockwood standing in the doorway again. This time, she was carrying a cake. Charles could see "We love you, Charles" written in frosting on the top. Shea came into the office, followed by Charles's other coworkers. Some carried cups, others plates and plastic forks. One burly officer carried in a bowl full of punch. Others brought in gifts and cards.

Charles stood where he was. He tried to swallow but his throat was dry.

David Bachman broke the uncomfortable silence. "Do you remember three years ago when I caught that bullet on a drug bust and didn't know if I'd ever walk again? Every person in this room was pulling for me, but especially you, Charles. You stood by me; you wouldn't let me give up. Every battle I fought, you fought.

"That's what we want *you* to know, partner. You're right. This isn't a retirement party, but it's not a funeral, either. We're with you. We're going to stand beside you and help you fight this thing all the way. You can count on that."

Charles sat back down in his chair. He had no choice. His legs couldn't hold him up a moment longer.

After the party, David Bachman walked Charles to his car.

Late afternoon rain had left the steps and sidewalk wet and slippery. David stayed close to his former partner's side, trying not to be too obvious that he was prepared to catch Charles if he stumbled and fell.

"Do you need help getting home?" David asked. "Roads are slick."

A cool mist blew through the air, punctuating his words.

Charles leaned against the open driver's side door of his Mazda RX7, holding his keys in an unsteady hand. "I'm tired, David, but I think I'll be okay. One thing's for sure, though. I won't be able to drive this thing much longer. I can hardly get in and out of it."

He smiled ruefully. "I remember when I had to take the car keys away from my dad. He'd had three minor accidents in as many weeks. He didn't speak to me for a month. Deep down, he knew it was time to quit, but he just couldn't accept it. It'll be the same with me," Charles said as he eased himself down into the driver's seat and lifted his legs one by one into the car.

"Knowing when to quit won't be the problem. The problem will be accepting it."

David Bachman closed the door for his friend. He watched as Charles carefully negotiated his way out of the crowded parking lot and into Dallas's busy rush-hour traffic. Charles was already driving like a ninety-year-old.

"Don't take too long, my friend," David said.

FOUR

Isidore Jacoby, wearing pajamas bearing the Sentinel Health Systems monogram, reclined in his bed as Ruthie finished making him presentable. "We can't have all those doctors and nurses parading through here and finding you a mess, now can we?"

When she had finished combing Isidore's silken gray hair, she gently kissed him on the cheek.

"Almost done, my love." With a twinkle in her eye, she added in a stage whisper, "I almost forgot the most important part." She went over to the small nightstand and pulled out a bottle of Old Spice cologne. Dabbing a little bit under each of Isidore's ears, Ruthie said, "Do you remember what we were doing the first time you ever wore this?"

He looked up at her, not comprehending.

Ruthie smiled. "It was our first date. You were all of sixteen and had just started shaving. You borrowed your father's cologne, but you didn't know how to use it." She muffled a giggle with her hand. "There you were, hair slicked down, a corsage in your hand, and smelling like you'd bathed in Old Spice. My mother never told you, but she could smell you from fifty feet away."

She sat on the edge of Isidore's bed and took his hand in hers. Even though almost all the muscle tone was gone, his hand felt warm and comforting. She held it to her cheek and gazed into the depths of his chocolate brown eyes. "I fell in love with you that very moment, Poppie. That very moment."

Isidore blinked and appeared to turn his attention to the television set, though his gaze was still blank.

Ruthie sat down in a chair beside the bed, still holding her husband's hand. Sometimes she wondered whether he understood anything she said or did for him. Had Alzheimer's taken him away completely? Was there some corner of his mind that still knew her, still remembered their years together, still loved her?

Over the last three months, his decline had been steep. It was almost as if he had decided to give up. At the beginning, even when Alzheimer's had erased most of his memory, he had still talked to her. He'd still eaten her cooking—and loved it. He had enjoyed her company, even though he often didn't know who she was. But then it all started to change. He interacted less and less, withdrawing into himself. Now he'd stopped eating. Ruthie's throat tightened at the idea, but she feared that her Poppie was trying to leave her. He was starving himself to death.

Ruthie couldn't let him die that way.

———

When Lori Westlake rapped lightly at the door to room D477, Ruthie was sitting in the large recliner and had nearly fallen asleep.

"May I come in?" Lori said.

Ruthie smiled and started to push herself to her feet to greet her. "Dr. Westlake. I'm sorry. I must have dozed off."

"Now, now, don't get up. I just wanted to stop by and check on Mr. Jacoby before I left for the night." She walked over to Isidore's bed and patted his hand. "How are you doing this evening, Mr. Jacoby?"

Isidore's eyes flicked over to Dr. Westlake and he studied her for a moment. Then he gently put one hand on top of hers and a hint of a smile came to his face. Just as quickly, the smile faded and he returned his attention to the television.

"Dr. Westlake, you're about the only one who can get a reaction out of him anymore," Ruthie said. "He doesn't even smile for *me* now."

"I'm flattered," Lori said with a smile. Turning to face Ruthie, she said, "Dr. Johnston has Mr. Jacoby's procedure scheduled for first thing in the morning. Usually we would have admitted him on the morning of the surgery, but Dr. Johnston wanted to make sure that your husband got a good night's sleep. He's ordered a sedative, and someone will be by to administer it a bit later. You should feel honored," she said to Isidore. "It's not often that you get to spend the night *before* your surgery in this splendid hotel."

Turning back to Ruthie, she continued, "Dr. Galloway, the head of Sentinel's hospice service, should also be stopping by soon. Since Mr. Jacoby's having a feeding tube inserted, I asked him to stop by and make sure that you understand all the options that are available to you and your husband."

"Options? What do you mean by 'options'?"

Before Lori could answer, a tall woman with frizzy blonde hair pushed a cart into the room. She came over to the bed and patted Isidore's hand.

"Hello, Mr. Jacoby," she said. "I'm Faye. I'll be your nurse tonight. I'm just here to make sure you're all prepped for your procedure tomorrow." Faye came around the bed and shook Ruthie's hand. "This shouldn't take too long, ma'am. Would you mind stepping out for a few minutes?"

Lori offered Ruthie her arm and helped her stand up. "Come on, Mrs. Jacoby. Let's take a walk while Faye tends to your husband. He's in very good hands. Faye's the best."

Looking back at Isidore as if he might not be there when she returned, Ruthie followed Lori into the corridor.

———

"I'll be with you in just a minute, Mr. Jacoby," Faye said.

Using a stylus, she quickly logged on to the computer and called up Isidore's chart. "Mm-hmm," she said as she reviewed the items that had already been checked off. "I see they've already done your blood tests. And your IV's been started. I just have to check your vitals and get you prepped and you'll be ready to go."

Isidore offered no resistance, no reaction at all, as Faye checked his blood pressure, pulse, and respiration. "So, Mr. Jacoby," she said as she carefully unbuttoned his shirt, "I hear that you and your wife have traveled all over the world." She watched his eyes for some reaction, but there was none. "Tony—he's the man who checked you in—he tells me that you ran for the state senate a long time ago." She gently washed the area where the feeding tube was to be inserted. "Sounds like you've had a very busy and full life."

She continued making small talk as she shaved a large area of his chest surrounding the place where the feeding tube would be surgically implanted. Isidore sat calmly, clear-eyed but unresponsive.

Standing in the hallway outside Isidore's room, Ruthie asked Lori, "What did you mean by 'options,' dear?"

"Mrs. Jacoby, I just want to make sure that you're prepared for the possibility that, even with a feeding tube, your husband may not live much longer." She waited for a response but Ruthie offered none.

"And," Lori continued, breaking the uncomfortable silence, "I know you want to make his passing as comfortable as possible."

Ruthie remained stone-faced.

"Our hospice service exists for just this type of situation. We want to stand beside you and help you."

Ruthie's brow furrowed. "And how do you propose to do that?"

"Why don't we discuss it over a cup of coffee," Lori replied. She took Ruthie by the arm and led her down the hallway toward a waiting room with a small coffee kiosk. After helping the older woman settle herself at a table, she poured coffee for both of them and sat down across from her.

"Mrs. Jacoby, it's obvious how much you love your husband. The sparkle in your eyes when you look at him tells me that there's no other man on the planet for you.

"When someone you love is as ill as Mr. Jacoby, it's hard to let go. We don't even like to think about the possibility of that person dying."

She put her hand over Ruthie's.

"Mrs. Jacoby, inserting this feeding tube may buy your husband a little more time. But have you considered that it might not be in his best interests?"

"Not for a minute, young lady." Ruthie's voice was firm.

"But what quality of life will he have?" Lori asked.

Ruthie's eyes flashed. "The same quality of life we've had over forty-two years of marriage." The elderly woman drew herself up and glared at Lori. "You think quality of life is all about things being normal? Dr. Westlake, my husband has stood beside me through every high and low of our lives.

"He was there when I miscarried three children. He never knew what to say, but he was always there. He stood by me when I was diagnosed with breast cancer. He held my hand through every chemotherapy treatment." A quaver crept into her voice. "After the surgery, when I thought I was no longer attractive, that he wouldn't love me anymore, he brought me roses and told me I was lovelier than ever.

"When we married, Dr. Westlake, we married for better or worse. I will not abandon him simply because things have turned worse."

"Mrs. Jacoby," Lori replied, "no one's telling you to abandon your husband. We're just suggesting that by prolonging his life, you might be unintentionally prolonging his suffering."

"I am *not* prolonging his suffering—or his life, Dr. Westlake. I am *feeding* him. And no one is going to change that. Not you. Not your Dr. Galloway. No one."

Ruthie stood up. "I need to get back to Isidore. I've been away from him too long as it is."

———

Faye Renaud took a wireless laser scanner from her pocket and ran it over the bar code on Isidore Jacoby's armband.

The terminal beeped and data filled the screen.

Name: Isidore M. Jacoby
Address: 731 Pin Oak Lane, Richardson, Texas
Phone: 972-555-3481

She scrolled down the screen, reviewing his previous admits and treatments. Glancing over her shoulder, Faye quickly pulled a tiny jump drive from her pocket and plugged it in to the computer's USB port. A dialog box on the screen said, "Copy?"

She clicked Yes. A lime green LED on the small device flickered on and off as the computer wrote data to it. A few seconds later, she pulled the thumbnail drive from the port and slipped it back into the pocket of her lab coat. Seconds later, Ruthie and Lori entered the room.

"All done," Faye remarked. "He's good to go."

"Thank you," said Ruthie.

"I'm afraid I have to leave now, too," said Lori. "I'm sure that Dr. Galloway will stop by later."

"If he is only going to give me more of the same lecture," Ruthie answered, "he needn't bother. Tell him that for me—and for Isidore."

"I'll be sure to pass it on," said Lori as she turned toward the door. But before she could leave, a short woman, whom Ruthie would have kindly described as "full-figured," peeked in. Straight black hair with streaks of gray framed her round face. Her smile was broad and infectious. She flashed an awkward grin at Lori. "Hi, Sis."

"I'll talk to *you* later," Lori said as she left the room.

The woman shrugged and nodded in Lori's direction. "My little sister. Good evening, Mr. and Mrs. Jacoby. I'm Katherine Bainbridge, but everyone around here calls me Kate. I'm Dr. Galloway's assistant. He was going to visit you this afternoon, but he got tied up, so he asked me to welcome you."

Ruthie's reply was stiff and formal. "Dr. Westlake has already explained the 'options' to me."

"That's interesting," said Kate. "What options did she explain?"

"She said you would try to talk me out of having Isidore's feeding tube inserted. That I should just let him die. Well I won't do that, Ms. Bainbridge. I simply won't do it."

"Mrs. Jacoby, that's not why I'm here. Dr. Galloway and I just want you to know that we're here to help you and your husband in any way we can. Hospice is about providing care and pain management, about making things as easy as possible for you and your husband. We're not going to dictate treatment options for Mr. Jacoby."

"Well...," Ruthie said, dabbing at her eye with a linen handkerchief.

"My sister has her own views on death and dying. I'll speak to her about it."

Ruthie nodded. "Thank you, Ms. Bainbridge."

Kate turned to leave. "You try to get some rest now."

Ruthie waited until she was sure that Katherine Bainbridge wouldn't return. Then she sat on the edge of her husband's bed and took his hand. She ran her fingers through his gray hair and caressed his cheek with the back of her wrinkled hand. A hint of gray stubble made Isidore's face feel like fine sandpaper.

Tears filled her eyes as she gazed at the shrunken shell her husband had become.

"It's going to be all right, Poppie."

She drew a shuddering breath. A teardrop traced its way down her cheek and fell onto Isidore's hand.

———

With practiced speed, the man at the computer terminal entered his code name into the log-in window: *Quinn.*

He typed in his password: *Peace.*

His eyes quickly scanned the display that came up on the monitor. His name was the only one that appeared at the bottom of the screen. Nobody else had checked in yet.

His eyes flicked over to the digital clock in the screen's right-hand corner. It was still a few minutes before six.

He was early.

As an active member of the Circle of Peace, Quinn was expected to log in to the Circle's chat room at a prearranged time once a week. During those few minutes, he and the other members would discuss any intervention requests received that week.

When someone requested an intervention from the Circle, a carefully choreographed process went into effect. One member would personally evaluate the patient. That person would then make a recommendation to either proceed or decline the request. Then the other Circle members would log on to a special Web address and evaluate the case. Finally, they would all access a chat room and vote on whether to become involved. Sometimes they went months without accepting any cases. Other times, they might find four or five valid cases in as many weeks. If that happened, they would prioritize the cases according to need. The Circle members had agreed to take only one case at a time. Too much activity in too short a time increased the probability that their work would be noticed.

Once a case was accepted, the senior member of the Circle— Malachi—would assign it to someone. That person would then carry out the intervention within twenty-four hours. The Intervention Agent, or IA, was given specific instructions about how to carry out his or her task. Everything must be done precisely according to plan, so as not to endanger the Circle or its work.

The mission of the Circle of Peace was inherently dangerous. They all knew that it was impossible for them to totally avoid risk.

However, by following procedure, they could significantly reduce exposure.

Quinn's laptop emitted a short beep, and a new line of text appeared at the bottom of the chat room window.

Malachi has entered.

Seconds later, the computer beeped twice more as Zoë and Copper logged in.

There was a slight pause before another line of text appeared on the screen.

> Malachi: Greetings, fellow members. We have one case to consider today. Zoe, would you fill us in on the details?

Quinn rolled his eyes at Malachi's stodgy language. It didn't take a PhD to figure out that none of these people ever spent time in a chat room. They didn't have a clue how to talk. One of these days he was going to have to give them lessons.

After a pause, Zoë's response appeared on the screen.

> Zoë: Case #11034. Alzheimer's patient, male, seventy-five years old. Admitted to SHS today for insertion of a feeding tube. Tube is being inserted at his wife's request. Patient is lethargic and disoriented. He shows no recognition of his wife or surroundings. According to his wife, he has stopped eating. Hence, the request for the feeding tube. Prognosis: terminal. Intervention request made five days ago. I recommend we proceed.

> Copper: Who made the request?

> Zoë: The patient's nephew.

Quinn was concerned. One of the Circle's ironclad rules was that an intervention request could only come from the patient—or, in special cases, from an immediate family member. In this case, the patient obviously could not have asked for the Circle's help, so by rule only his wife should have done so.

Quinn typed a question on his keyboard and hit *Enter*. A few seconds later it appeared on the chat room screen.

> Quinn: A nephew's not immediate family. Why the exception?

> Zoë: The patient has no children and the nephew functions as an immediate family member.

> Copper: What about the man's wife? Why didn't she make the request?

> Zoë: According to the nephew, the patient's wife is part of the problem. Apparently the patient is starving himself, and the wife wants to prolong his life.

> Copper: Then the wife is *not* in agreement with the request?

> Zoë: Correct.

Quinn shook his head in disgust. The intervention request should never have made it to this point. He fired off a question and hit the *Enter* key again.

> Quinn: Why are we even discussing this? If the patient's wife is not in agreement, we *can't* intervene.

> Zoë: Why not?

> Malachi: Policy, Zoë. We do not intervene against a patient's or family member's wishes.

> Zoë: I think we should make an exception in this case.

> Copper: Why?

> Zoë: The patient is clearly trying to end his own suffering, and his wife is interfering with his wishes. The nephew understands and wishes us to act on his uncle's behalf.

Quinn leaned back in his chair. He didn't like the way this was going. It was too risky.

> Quinn: I don't like it. What if the wife demands an autopsy?
>
> Zoë: If the intervention is done correctly, there's no reason she should suspect anything.
>
> Copper: I agree with Quinn. What we're doing is too important to risk on a questionable case.
>
> Zoë: What we're *doing* is giving people a choice. We're giving them control over the last moments of their lives. Sometimes risk is necessary to do the right thing.
>
> Quinn: Perhaps. But we must also weigh the benefit to one patient against the possibility of compromising our overall mission. My vote is that we decline the request.
>
> Copper: Agreed. I also vote no.

Quinn watched his laptop screen, waiting for Malachi's response. If Malachi sided with Zoë, causing a tie vote, then the case would be held for reevaluation one week later. If he sided with Quinn and Copper, the case would be declined—with no possibility of reconsideration.

The screen remained blank for a long time. Finally, Malachi's response appeared.

> Malachi: My sympathies are with the nephew, but we must consider the greater good. Since the spouse is not on board, we cannot violate procedure. If we were to be exposed, many would suffer. To me, that outweighs benefit to the patient. The request is denied.

Quinn's computer emitted the digital sound of a door closing. At the bottom of the screen, a new line of text appeared.

> Zoë has left the chat room.

And Elvis has left the building, Quinn quipped to himself. *Don't go away mad, Zoë. Today wasn't your day.* He flipped his laptop screen closed.

Lori walked through the sliding doors leading from her office building into Sentinel's atrium. Cutting through the atrium was not the most direct route to the parking garage. It would be quicker to take the elevator to the basement and follow the underground tunnel to the physicians' lot. But Lori had a thing about dark, enclosed places, and she preferred walking through the always-populated atrium rather than navigating the dismal, claustrophobic corridors beneath the SHS complex.

When she heard Dr. Johnston's voice calling after her, Lori realized that, at least this time, she should have braved the basement.

"Dr. Westlake, I'd like a word with you."

Lori suppressed a groan as she turned to face the one person at Sentinel Health Systems she truly disliked. Judging from his expression, the feeling was mutual.

Lori forced a smile. The man was loathsome, but he *was* head of surgical service and next in line to be chief of staff.

"Yes, Dr. Johnston?"

He stormed up to Lori and stood so close that she instinctively took a step backward. He enjoyed invading others' personal space, she had observed.

It's probably one of his winning-through-intimidation techniques. That, and suffocating adversaries into submission by wearing too much aftershave.

Every conversation with Dr. Johnston started the same way—with Lori taking a step backward.

Of course, she thought, *he needs all the advantage he can muster.* Measuring in at a disappointing five-foot-five and possessing a physique roughly comparable to that of a pear with legs, Dr. Johnston hardly presented an imposing presence. He had plastered what was left of his steel gray hair across the top of his head in a futile attempt to hide his bald pate. Several facelifts had left his facial features pulled so tight that he looked like a male Norma Desmond.

"Dr. Westlake," Johnston said, "I just received a telephone call from Mrs. Jacoby. She says you were in to see her husband."

Lori resisted the temptation to roll her eyes.

"Yes, Dr. Johnston," she said, a slightly patronizing edge creeping into her voice. "Mr. Jacoby is, after all, one of my patients."

"Not for *this* procedure," Dr. Johnston retorted.

Lori took a deep breath and paused before she answered. "Well, doctor, if you hadn't talked Mrs. Jacoby into it, her husband wouldn't be *having* this procedure."

Dr. Johnston took a step closer and Lori took another step backward. "Ruthie Jacoby came to see me on her own initiative because *you* refused to give her a referral. Isidore Jacoby is *my* patient now and you have no business interfering."

Lori shook her head. She valued her job, but there was no way she intended to kowtow to this jerk. She took a step forward, invading *his* space for a change.

Moving as close as she could to take full advantage of her height advantage, she said coolly, "Dr. Johnston, I said it in ethics committee, and I'll say it now: What you are doing is *wrong*. You have no business keeping that man alive against his will."

Dr. Johnston yielded no ground. He pointed a finger at her. "Just stay away from my patient *and* his wife."

Lori turned and began walking away.

"Dr. Westlake."

She stopped and looked back over her shoulder.

"You'd better hope that I don't become chief of staff. If I do, I'm going to clean house. And I'll start with you."

Lori could think of several snappy retorts. But opting for discretion, she shook her head and walked toward the parking garage.

FIVE

The Metro Mall parking garage wasn't much better than SHS's. Lori held her car keys in her hand as she scanned the nearly empty parking garage. She was weary and hadn't wanted to bother with self-defense class today, but she couldn't let Jackie Palermo down. So, after her encounter with Dr. Johnston, she had driven over to the mall where Jackie had her martial arts school. No matter how many times she walked through this parking garage, it gave her the creeps.

She scanned the dimly lit garage and listened for footsteps. The first lesson she had learned in self-defense class was to be aware of her surroundings; the second was to keep her keys in her hand. The keys served two purposes. Obviously, they would enable her to unlock her car and drive off. But a ring of keys could also be a useful weapon in a pinch. Held between the fingers with the points sticking out, a set of car keys might disable an attacker long enough to buy an opportunity to escape.

She kept her eyes moving as she headed toward the mall entrance. The eerie clicks of her heels echoing off the walls made her feel like she was in a tomb. She had never felt so alone.

Ten feet to go. Home free.

Silent and swift, the attacker came out of nowhere. He grabbed Lori from behind in a bear hug, pinning her arms to her side. Her car keys clattered to the floor.

So much for being prepared.

Without time to think through a plan of action, she switched into autopilot. As Jackie had taught her, she scraped her right heel down the man's shin and slammed her foot down on his instep. For a split second his grip weakened. She threw her head backward into her attacker's face. He groaned and released his hold.

Seizing the advantage, Lori put her right hand over her left and used strength from both arms to drive her left elbow backward into the man's midsection. He stumbled backward, doubled over in pain. In a flash, Lori wheeled around and kicked his knee, dropping him to the ground.

Scooping her keys from the floor, she ran to the door leading into the mall.

Before she opened it, she stopped, turned, took a bow, and said, "So how did I do?"

Jackie Palermo and the other class members gave an enthusiastic round of applause.

"Excellent. Excellent," Jackie said, pulling the attacker to his feet. Dressed head to foot in red protective padding, the man looked like a giant, sunburned version of the Pillsbury Doughboy. "Thank you, Sam."

Sam threw Jackie a salute and lumbered back into the shadows.

"How did it feel, Lori?" Jackie asked.

"Terrifying. Even though I knew it wasn't real."

"That's why I asked mall management for permission to hold these drills in the parking garage. You can practice the techniques in a class, but if you've never used them in a realistic situation, it's easy to blank out and forget them when you need them the most. Very good, Lori," said Jackie. She turned to the rest of the class. "Okay. Who's next?"

After the parking garage drills, the class returned to the classroom for some practice on the heavy workout bags. Jackie Palermo stood behind the bag and braced it as each student rehearsed a series of kicks and punches.

When Lori's turn came, she stood before the tall, hanging bag in a ready stance. Jackie wasn't putting much of her weight into steadying the bag. Lori had the reputation of being a wimpy puncher when she worked out on the heavy bag. In her first class at Metro Martial Arts, she was timid and still bearing the bruises of an abusive relationship. She had tapped the bag as lightly as she would pat a young child's head.

"What was *that*?" Jackie had asked in disbelief.

Lori had shrugged, raised her eyebrows, and answered quizzically. "A punch?"

"Oh, honey, you gotta do better than that," Jackie had said. "Hit the thing."

"I'm not mad at it," Lori had responded.

Jackie's green eyes had flashed with annoyance. "Then *get* mad at it. Pretend it's the guy who gave you those bruises."

Since that day, whenever Lori approached the heavy bag, she imagined that Philip, her ex-husband was standing there.

It helped.

But as Lori stood in front of the bag today, all the day's frustrations roiled together: her unexpected date with Drew; the confrontation with Dr. Johnston; and—most frustrating—her helplessness in the face of Nina Ware's cancer.

She squared off and delivered a roundhouse kick that shook the bag's metal support frame and knocked Jackie backward a step. Before her teacher could recover, Lori attacked the bag with a fury she'd never before demonstrated in class, unleashing a flurry of punches followed by kicks and more punches in such rapid-fire succession that Jackie was barely able to hang on.

When her energy was spent, Lori stopped. Breathless, she stood in front of the bag, trickles of sweat rolling down her face and dripping from the tip of her nose.

Jackie looked at her, wide-eyed. The other students had gone quiet.

"Rough day?" Jackie asked.

Lori caught her breath and said, "You have no idea."

"Anything you want to talk about?"

Lori shook her head.

"O–*kay*. Ladies, today we're learning how to escape from choke holds. Line up in pairs, please."

SIX

It is impossible to describe the adrenaline rush that comes with holding someone's life in the palm of your hand. Knowing that you possess the power to spare that life or extinguish it like a candle—having the ability to determine who will live and who will die. The Angel had discovered that the power of life and death is the ultimate narcotic.

According to some, this power belonged only to God.

They were wrong. The *right* to take a life might belong to some deity, but the Angel also had the *power*.

The Angel cruised the dark streets of downtown Dallas in an old, burgundy Toyota Corolla. Just a few blocks away, Dallas nightlife was in full swing. Restaurants, clubs, and theaters lined the neon-lit streets. On other streets, a different nightlife raged. This nightlife, fueled by crack cocaine, heroin, cheap liquor, and a host of other vices, was carried on in the shadows. In one part of downtown, people pursued pleasure; in the other, people fled from life.

The city council had made panhandling illegal, and the homeless were no longer quite as easy to find. But one who knew where to look could find them. They didn't leave; they merely became more elusive. "Stealth" panhandlers, you might call them. Instead of setting up camp on a particular corner all day—as if working a regular job—they rotated territories.

They also teamed up to stay one step ahead of the police. Scouts watched for police cruisers while their partners held "Homeless and

Hungry" signs. When scouts spotted a patrol car, a sophisticated signaling system alerted the "beggar of the day," enabling him to close shop before he was ticketed or arrested. At the end of the day, they divided the spoils between the scouts and the panhandlers. It wasn't ideal, but it worked. Panhandling laws were a nuisance that could be circumvented.

The laws certainly had not made the Angel's work more difficult. There were so *many* out there who needed his help, too many. The Angel had no delusions of grandeur. He knew he couldn't save the world, or even all of Dallas. The best he could do was to reach his own little corner of the world. And to do that, he had to make friends with the people he wanted to reach.

So one or two nights a week he cruised the streets of Dallas, getting to know the homeless. Sharing food. Bringing coats. Hearing their stories. Winning their confidence.

At first, they were wary. Now, at his approach, they streamed like ants attacking a sugar bowl from deserted buildings, ramshackle tenements; and from under bridges and overpasses. They all wanted the Angel's gifts. That's how they knew him—an anonymous angel of mercy. Someone who cared.

As the Angel rolled through a dark intersection near the southeast corner of downtown Dallas, one of his regulars waved and ambled toward the car. The Angel pulled over and rolled down his window as Shadowman walked up to him.

"Eddie, how are you?" The Angel flashed his warmest, most compassionate smile.

Shadowman's hands trembled like a patient with advanced Parkinson's. Even in the dim light, the Angel could see his reddened eyes. Shadowman blinked, sniffed, and rubbed his nose with the back of his hand. He left behind a slug's trail of mucus across his cheek and on his wrist. "Okay, I guess."

Cynicism crept into the Angel's smile. Shadowman was *anything* but okay. He wore dirty green slacks with holes in the knees and a navy sweatshirt two sizes too large that was torn in at least five places. Shadowman—so named because his dark clothes and darker skin enabled him to blend into the shadows—was a crack addict.

No one who saw him would believe that Eddie Shoemate held an MBA from the University of Houston and had been a Fortune 500 wonderboy who single-handedly brought three companies back from Chapter 11 bankruptcy before his thirtieth birthday. A professional turnaround CEO, he had specialized in taking companies on the brink and making them profitable. He could overcome any problem.

Almost any problem.

His gambling addiction was one problem he couldn't turn around.

What started as an innocent vacation in Las Vegas had ballooned into an obsession. Casinos. Horses. Cards. Football. It didn't matter. When the authorities caught up with him, Eddie had been funding his habit by cooking the books of his latest company. His world collapsed. He was indicted for embezzling more than half a million dollars from his employer. A jury convicted him and he spent ten years enjoying the accommodations of the Texas Department of Criminal Justice, Institutional Division.

When the state released him, Eddie Shoemate was a broken man. Forty-three years old. Twice married; twice divorced. One child from either marriage. He hadn't seen or heard from either child in at least ten years. A gambling rehabilitation program did no good. Eventually, he ended up on the streets. Eddie Shoemate became Shadowman.

The streets were filled with human refuse. Drug addicts. Prostitutes. Thieves. Rapists. Murderers. People who had devoted their lives to harming others. The Angel had no use for them. He sought out those who had lived generally good lives but who had stumbled, those worthy of redemption but who had come to the point where they could not function in decent society.

The Angel provided a way out for these worthy ones. When he looked at Shadowman, the Angel's heart swelled with compassion. It was for people like Eddie that he had come.

The Angel reached for a brown paper sack on the seat beside him. He handed it through the open window, and Shadowman took it. "Good stuff today, Eddie. Roast beef on pumpernickel, a Red Delicious apple, a giant chocolate chip cookie, and a bottle of cherry cola."

Shadowman's eyes filled with gratitude. "God bless you," he said in a rasping baritone. He turned and went in search of a dark corner in which to eat his only good meal of the day. The Angel smiled as Eddie dissolved into the darkness.

"Hang on, Shadowman," he whispered. "It won't be much longer. You'll be free soon."

SEVEN

The late afternoon sun had just dropped below the horizon when Charles Hamisch pulled into the parking spot of his apartment. The handicapped space in front of his building was at least twenty feet closer to his apartment, and he could legally park there now. On his doctor's insistence, he had filled out an application for a handicapped permit to hang from his rearview mirror.

He'd applied just to keep his doctor happy. The permit was buried somewhere under a pile of old newspapers and unopened junk mail. Charles had never used it.

The handicapped space remained vacant.

Charles would need it someday.

He removed his key from the ignition and tugged on the door handle, but the car door wouldn't open. He checked to make sure he'd unlocked it.

He had.

After a few more futile attempts, he leaned sideways, pushing with his shoulder until the door finally popped open. Nudging the door all the way open with his knee, he carefully lifted each leg out of the car. It felt like his shoes were encased in concrete.

He kept his cane alongside the driver's seat in easy reach. Although he stubbornly refused to use the cane at work, he allowed himself to use it at home, though not without a good deal of grumbling. With no banister or stair rail to steady himself, he could not negotiate the seven steps up to his front porch without the cane. The last time he'd tried, he had tumbled sideways and landed in some holly bushes.

On a good day, the trip from the car to his front door took two or three minutes. On a bad day, the trip took up to ten minutes. A year ago, he would have traveled the distance in under fifteen seconds.

Holding the cane in his right hand, he worked his way up one step, then a second, then a third. His every movement was sluggish and deliberate, as if he were in a video being played in slow motion.

He hadn't given the mechanics of walking a second thought since he'd been about fourteen months old. Now he had to concentrate on every motion, every step. He didn't like to think about how long it would be before he needed a walker—or a wheelchair.

Arriving at his front door, he pulled his keys from his pocket, holding on to them with a death grip. ALS made simple movements difficult, and something as minor as retrieving a set of dropped keys could pose a major problem.

The brass key slid into the keyhole easily enough but the lock felt like it had been stuffed with bubble gum. Charles knew there was nothing wrong with the lock.

Droplets of sweat formed on his forehead. He glanced over toward the leasing office. A beat-up white pickup sat in one of the parking spaces. The maintenance man hadn't gone home yet.

"I will *not* call maintenance," he muttered.

He jiggled and twisted the key repeatedly. It went nowhere. He tried to force it to turn. He felt like he was arm wrestling a giant.

"Come on." He urged the lock as if it could hear him. "Come on."

His heart pounded. A droplet of sweat trickled into his left eye. He shook his head, trying to blink away the burning sensation.

At last the key turned and the lock released with a muffled click. Charles pushed open the door, dropped his keys and cane, and stumbled into his recliner halfway across the small living room. He left the front door ajar.

He sat in the soft chair, as breathless as if he'd just run a hundred-yard dash—several times. The muscles in his arms and legs twitched. His heartbeat thrummed a staccato rhythm.

Once he caught his breath, he became aware of the delightful aroma of spaghetti and meatballs drifting from the kitchen. Then he felt something rubbing on his ankles. He leaned forward and looked down. At his feet sat a dirty tan and white cat that had no tail and looked about as scruffy as twenty-year-old shag carpet.

⸻

By the time Drew Langdon arrived to pick up Lori, she had showered and dressed in a pair of faded denim jeans and an oversized Dallas Cowboys sweatshirt. She had taken time to blow-dry her long curly hair but hadn't invested much energy in applying makeup. Her sister might be able to corner her into a date with Drew, but that didn't mean she would encourage him. And it *definitely* didn't mean she had to go out with him more than once. This would be a one-shot deal, particularly since Kate was obviously avoiding her until after her date.

She hadn't been suspicious when Kate didn't show up for self-defense class. It wasn't unusual for her to put in extra hours at the hospice. But when Lori got home and Kate had left no message, she knew her sister was lying low until her date was over. Well, Kate would hear about it when Lori got home from dinner. *That* much was certain.

On the other hand, part of her *was* looking forward to this evening out, although she'd never admit it to her sister. She hadn't gone out with a man since she'd left Philip more than a year ago. The physical scars had long since healed; the emotional ones still felt raw. But for the first time since she'd moved in with Kate, Lori found herself almost willing to admit that she missed the companionship of a man. But she didn't know if she could allow herself to trust, to be vulnerable, ever again.

Maybe that's why she had been avoiding Drew.

When she heard the doorbell ring, her stomach lurched. She momentarily considered not answering it, but she relented and went to the door.

Drew Langdon looked like he was on his way to a wedding. His crisp, navy blue pin-striped suit, robin's egg blue shirt, and gold silk necktie starkly contrasted Lori's Saturday-afternoon-at-the-carwash outfit.

"Guess I look a bit shabby," she said, moving away from the door. "You'd better come in while I go put on something more appropriate."

"Don't worry about it," Drew said, stepping inside. "You don't need to change a thing."

"Right," Lori quipped. "And you can tell people you found me on the street holding a 'Please Feed Me' sign."

Drew laughed. "Tell you what. I know this little Italian place where they keep the lights low. I'll take off my coat and tie, we'll eat by candlelight, and nobody will be the wiser. Deal?" He offered his hand.

Lori shook hands with him. "Deal."

Maybe this wouldn't be so bad, after all.

———

"Go away," Charles said to the disorderly mass of fur at his feet.

Ignoring him entirely, the cat rubbed its head on Charles's trouser cuffs and shoes, then hopped into his lap, purring. It put its feet on his stomach and stood nose-to-nose with the newly retired detective.

"Listen closely, because I'll only say this once," Charles said to the intruder. "I—don't—like—cats."

Purring even louder, the animal started to massage Charles's stomach with its front paws. Charles reached up and scratched behind the cat's ears. His new acquaintance responded with more ecstatic kneading, digging its claws into his midsection.

Charles winced. "Okay. You just wore out your welcome." Cradling the cat under his left arm, he pushed himself to his feet and worked his way over to the front door. He set the cat down on the welcome mat.

"Thanks for the visit," he said. "You can go home now. Come back when you can't stay so long." He swung the door closed.

Turning back to his one-bedroom apartment, Charles decided to explore the aromas drifting from the kitchen. Thankfully, the combination kitchen-dinette was only a few steps away.

The sparsely furnished, handicapped-accessible apartment—another of Charles's grudging concessions to his condition—was much easier to manage than the split-level, four-bedroom house he'd lived in until recently. He'd bought the house anticipating a future when he would be married and have a host of children to occupy those bedrooms. But the years had passed and Charles never married. He'd kept the big house anyway. He liked his space.

Things changed after he learned he had ALS. He'd tried to think of ways he could keep the house but ultimately decided that it had to

go. Besides, since the mortgage was paid off, he would need the proceeds from the sale to pay for more important things, like a motorized
wheelchair, a modified van, and maybe a ventilator.

A low-wattage bulb in the vent over the stove cast a dim light
across the tiny kitchen. Someone had placed a large pot on one of the
stove burners. The burner was turned off, but the heavy pot was still
warm. A yellow sticky note on the pot's lid explained everything:

*Apartment clean. Spaghetti and meatballs in the pot—enjoy! David and I
will drop by around 7:30 for your workout. Love, Pam.*

Charles groaned. When David hadn't mentioned the workout earlier, Charles had hoped that maybe his partner had forgotten about
it. He glanced at the clock over the kitchen sink. 6:25. He'd better get
started with dinner. At his current pace, it would take him close to
an hour to eat.

———

Drew and Lori sat at a table for two in a secluded corner of Tony's
Italian Cuisine. Despite her qualms about going out, she had to admit
that she was enjoying his company.

"So, how does a nice girl like you wind up a black belt in karate?"
Drew asked.

Lori laughed and shook her head. "I'm not a black belt. I'm not
any kind of belt. It's just a women's self-defense class." She took a sip
of chardonnay. "The funny thing is, I really didn't want to take the
class in the first place. Kate pushed me into it, and I was *so* angry with
her. But I've gotten to where I look forward to going."

"So why'd she push you?"

Lori shrugged. "Let's say that my ex-husband didn't approve of
my leaving him. He made some threats; even stalked me—at least I
think it was him."

"What happened?"

"Someone followed me home a couple of times. Whoever it was
never tried anything. But I have no doubt that I was followed. I
assume it was Philip."

"Ever had to use your martial arts?" Drew asked.

Lori shook her head. "Not yet, but . . ." Her voice trailed off.

"But what?"

Lori waved it off. "With my marital history, you never know
when it might come in handy. Philip got his jollies from using me for

a punching bag. I don't really like talking about it. That part of my life is over."

"I'm sorry," said Drew.

There was something about the way Drew said "I'm sorry," something in his eyes that told Lori he really *was* sorry, that he wasn't just mouthing empty platitudes. She liked that.

"Anyway, Kate wanted to make sure I'd be prepared in case Philip came calling again. She insisted that I enroll in the self-defense class *and* that I take firearms training and get a license to carry a gun."

"You're *armed*, too?" Drew held up his hands. "I surrender. You're one lady who will definitely have my respect."

Lori laughed and took another sip of wine. "The gun—which *Kate* bought—lies unloaded and safely buried under a pile of clothes in my closet. And the only reason I keep it is so that she won't fuss at me."

"Sounds like she loves you and wants to protect you."

Lori rolled her eyes. "There's a fine line between protecting and smothering. What about *you*?" asked Lori. "What got you into grief counseling?"

Drew shrugged. "Seemed like the thing to do. My father was a minister, but that life never appealed to me. I still wanted to help people, you know?"

Lori nodded.

"I wanted to be a surgeon. Graduated from medical school. Started a residence in a prestigious hospital . . . the whole nine yards."

"I didn't know you were an MD," said Lori.

Drew shook his head. "It didn't last. I washed out during my residency."

"What happened?" Lori asked.

Drew sipped his wine and gave her a wry smile. "I like talking about that about as much as you like talking about your ex."

Lori smiled. "Understood."

"Let's just say I didn't have what it takes. I dropped out and went back to grad school, mostly because I couldn't decide what else to do."

"That brings me back to my question," said Lori. "How'd you get into grief counseling?"

Drew finished his drink and waved his empty glass at the waiter.

"I was a grad student in 1995 when Timothy McVeigh bombed the Murrah Federal Building in Oklahoma City. A bunch of us went over there to do what we could. As I worked with grieving family members and friends—I don't know—it just felt right, like I'd found my niche. I've been in grief counseling ever since."

Lori gazed into her nearly full glass. "I could have used your services this afternoon."

"The young mother?" he asked.

Lori nodded.

"She looked pretty broken up," Drew said.

"She had every right to be."

"Don't you wish you could somehow just push a magic button and make it all go away? Make everything better?" Drew said.

"It would be nice. But there's not much we can do to help her. Not legally, anyway."

—

Charles Hamisch carefully rolled the last of his spaghetti onto the fork and brought it to his mouth. Although the process was slow, at least he wasn't having trouble eating yet. He knew the day would come when the disease would weaken his jaw, tongue, and throat muscles. Sometimes that happened early on with ALS patients. In his case, the symptoms began in his extremities—his hands and feet. Nevertheless, sooner or later he would have difficulty chewing and swallowing. When that happened, every mouthful of food he took would carry the possibility of choking to death. His food would have to be pureed. When he was no longer able to swallow, he'd need to decide whether to have a feeding tube surgically inserted in his abdomen or let himself starve to death.

Of all the symptoms that accompanied Lou Gehrig's disease, Charles dreaded this more than anything else, although he wasn't sure why. There were more humiliating things than not being able to eat. As ALS progressively ravaged his body, someone would ultimately have to dress him, bathe him, help him go to the bathroom. But as embarrassing as these things were, he didn't dread them as much as not being able to eat or even take a sip of water when his mouth was dry.

Maybe it was because he'd always enjoyed food. He was not a gourmand by any means, but he did like the taste of a good steak. He would miss ice cream, his morning cup of coffee, even the occasional stale doughnut left overnight in the station's break room. But none of these things explained his dread.

When you got right down to it, he guessed that he dreaded losing his ability to eat because eating was more than just sustaining life. Eating was part of life.

Eating had been a delight. Now it was work. Soon it would be an impossibility. And when he could no longer eat, death would not be far away.

He set his fork down and flexed his fingers. His hand ached and painful muscle spasms racked his upper arm. He closed his eyes and massaged his bicep with his left hand.

After a few minutes, the pain subsided enough for Charles to carry his plate and fork over to the sink. As he turned on the water to rinse the plate, he heard the front door open.

"Anybody home?" a woman's voice called.

"Come on in, Pam," Charles answered.

Pam Bachman came into the kitchen and gave Charles a peck on the cheek. When she spotted the clean dishes, she scolded him. "Hey, what's going on here? If you wash the dishes, I'm just going to have to sit around and be bored while you and David do your thing."

Charles smiled and nodded toward the stove. "I left you the big cooking pot. Where is the old slave driver, anyway?"

"Right behind you."

David Bachman carried a large box and Charles could tell by the aroma drifting from it that the box contained more food.

Pam pointed to a countertop near the refrigerator. "Put that over there, David. Then both of you can get to work."

"In other words, 'Get out of the kitchen,'" David said. "I can take a hint." He kissed his wife and then shook Charles's hand. "It's work-out time, partner. You ready?"

"No, I've got a full stomach," Charles answered. "Just finished eating your wife's cooking."

"And you're still standing?"

Pam gave her husband a playful swat on the rump and pointed toward the living room. "Out. Both of you."

Charles's cramped living room did not offer an ideal workout space, but neither did any of the other rooms in the apartment. David pushed the leather recliner up against one wall and scooted a coffee table toward the other, leaving enough room on the floor for Charles to lie down.

Charles used the coffee table for a prop as he went down on one knee, then sat on the floor. He pointed to a small blue pillow that lay on the sofa. "Toss me my pillow."

David handed him the pillow. "You're sure you wouldn't be more comfortable doing this on your bed?" asked David.

"I won't be comfortable doing it anywhere. Let's get it over with. Legs first."

Charles put the pillow on the carpet behind him. He lay back and David knelt on the floor beside him. He took Charles's left foot, holding his other hand underneath the calf, and gently lifted it up, bending it at the knee and pushing the knee toward the chest.

Charles winced at the pain but said nothing.

Slowly returning Charles's leg to a resting position, David counted, "One."

"Twenty-four to go," said Charles. Then he sighed. "I hate this."

<hr />

The waiter cleared the dinner plates from the table.

Drew's brow furrowed. "You said that there's nothing you can do *legally* to help your patient. What did you mean?"

"That's just my frustration talking. Sometimes you know that no matter what you do, your patient is going to die. Despite all the chemo and radiation and alternative medicine in the world, that young lady has no hope of recovery. She knows it, and I know it. Now she's refusing treatment because she knows it won't help in the long run. I have to encourage her to pursue it, but I can't really blame her. Treatment or no, she's condemned to a lingering, unpleasant, and painful death."

"So, what's the alternative?" Drew asked.

"Sometimes I just wish we had a few more options."

"Such as?"

"Ways to help people avoid the inevitable suffering that comes with incurable disease."

"You mean like trying to mitigate the suffering? Pain management?"

Lori shook her head. "It's a start, but it's not effective for everyone. Administering enough pain medication to control pain in end-stage cancer patients often requires a nearly lethal dose. Many physicians don't want to take the risk, so they won't order the larger dosage."

"So what other options are there?" Drew asked.

"How about letting people decide when they've had enough suffering?"

"Physician-assisted suicide?"

"It's working in Oregon," Lori said. "When the law was being considered, the naysayers all predicted it would be the proverbial 'slippery slope,' but it hasn't worked out that way. There hasn't been a rush of depressed people wanting to commit suicide. They haven't bred a crop of 'death doctors.' Legal controls are in place. The system works."

Drew looked skeptical. "Some people might say that the end doesn't justify the means."

"So," Lori shot back, "it *is* right to stand by and watch people suffer, knowing you can do something to stop it?"

Drew held up his hands. "Whoa. I didn't say that's what *I* thought. I'm just playing devil's advocate."

Lori relaxed. "Look, all I'm saying is that now we have the ability to prolong life. But prolonging life should not involve prolonged suffering. We're supposed to be about ending suffering. About healing."

"I agree with you in principle," Drew said. "I just don't want to see you damage your reputation."

"What do you mean?"

"Lori, come on. You created quite a stir at the last meeting of the ethics committee."

Lori's eyes flashed. "If you're referring to my comments about the Jacoby case, *somebody* had to say something. It's criminal to insert a feeding tube in a man in Mr. Jacoby's condition."

Drew nodded. "And it would have been fine if you had stopped there. But word around the hospital is that you practically suggested we euthanize the man."

Lori heaved a sigh. "I don't know who your sources are, but I *said* that we should let Mr. Jacoby make his own choice, and it would be nice if we could help him along the way. Seems to me that he's making

his choice by not eating. Instead, we're allowing our treatment decisions to be influenced by a family member who can't let go."

Drew held up his hands again, surrendering. "I don't want to get
into it all over again. Just try to tone down the rhetoric a bit. SHS is
a very conservative system and you're dangerously close to making
enemies you can't afford to make. I don't want to see you lose your
job here."

"If you're referring to Dr. Johnston, I appreciate your concern.
But I think it's too late. We're not exactly on good terms."

Drew reached across the table and took Lori's hand.

Reflexively, she pulled her hand back.

Drew pretended not to notice. "Just watch your back. Johnston
plays hardball."

Charles pushed himself to a sitting position and grabbed a towel
that Pam had placed on the sofa. "I'm not into this today," he said as
he wiped the perspiration from his face.

"We're not even half done," said David. "You need to finish."

"Do I?"

"Every day that you skip your range-of-motion exercises, you lose
ground."

"I lose ground whether I do these stupid exercises or not." Charles
glowered at him. "I can't stop this, David. No matter how much I
work out, no matter how hard I try, it's going to get me. I'm tired of
fighting it."

"You *have* to fight it."

Charles balled up the towel and threw it on the sofa. "Oh, really?
Why? I don't have any relatives. I'm not married. I don't have any
children. Give me one good reason I can't quit."

"How about Pam and me? *We* care about you."

Charles's voice grew soft. "Do you have any idea what you're asking, what it's like to face something like this?" He paused and looked
off into space. "If I live another hundred years, I'll never forget a
single detail of the doctor's office the day I learned I had ALS." He
looked over at Pam and tapped the side of his head. "Every single
detail. Right here."

He glanced over into a corner of his living room. "I can see the peeling wallpaper on the left corner wall behind the doctor's desk, the cobwebs clinging to the ceiling fan." He closed his eyes and inhaled. "I can even smell the cheap cinnamon air freshener they used to cover up the 'doctor's office smell.'

"ALS was a possible diagnosis from the beginning. I knew that. But I kept thinking there would be a different outcome—one that didn't include a death sentence." Tears filled his eyes as he looked up at David and Pam. "I asked the doctor how long—"

He paused for a few seconds, trying to gain control of his emotions. Finally he continued, his voice unsteady. "The bottom line is that I am going to die by inches. Day by day, I'll get weaker as ALS destroys my brain's ability to talk to my muscles. Eventually I won't be able speak or swallow. At the end I'll probably suffocate. But you know what really scares me?"

David and Pam shook their heads.

Charles tapped his temple again. "What scares me is that my mind will remain sharp and alert to the very end."

Tears spilled from his eyes and ran down his cheeks. His hands trembled. His jaw muscles worked furiously. He looked back up at David. "Do you have any idea how horrible this is? How unfair?" He grabbed a plastic water bottle from the coffee table and hurled it across the room. It bounced off the wall and spilled its contents on the floor.

Pam's voice came from behind him. "So you just want to quit?" Her voice was soft, gentle. She sounded hurt.

Charles wiped his eyes with the back of his hand. "If I had heart disease, they could operate. If I had cancer, at least I'd have a fighting chance. But with ALS, no matter what I do, the disease is going to win. The scoreboard's already flashing the final score: ALS 21, Charles Hamisch zip.

"I can fight. I can resist. I can take riluzole to slow it down. I can do range-of-motion exercises dawn to dusk. But nothing will change. It may take a little longer, but in the end, I still lose." He rested his head in his hands. "I'm just tired of fighting. That's all."

"Charles," said David, "don't throw in the towel. Not yet."

Charles didn't even look up. "God threw it in for me when he gave me ALS."

David and Pam stood at the front door of Charles's apartment. He was sitting in his recliner, dressed for bed with his feet up.

"You're sure you don't need anything else?" David asked.

Charles shook his head.

"Good enough, then," David said. "Pam will bring supper tomorrow evening. I'm on duty. If you change your mind about the exercises, someone from the church or an off-duty officer will be happy to come by and help."

"I won't change my mind." Charles's voice was soft, resigned.

David opened the front door but Pam went back to Charles's chair and planted a kiss on top of his head. "We love you," she said.

As she turned away, Charles caught her hand. Pam looked back at him.

His eyes were rimmed with tears. "Thank you."

Pam nodded and patted his shoulder. Then she followed her husband out the door.

Charles heard the engine of David's Ford F-250 pickup roar to life, then diminish into the distance.

"Stupid," he muttered to an empty room. "They were only trying to help. If you keep driving people away, you're going to be in a fix when things really get rough."

Deep down, though, he knew he hadn't driven them away. He had never had a more faithful partner or a better friend than David. He and Pam wouldn't give up on him, even if he gave up on himself. The thought comforted him as he lay in his recliner and began to doze off.

He was almost asleep when something punched him in the stomach. He opened his eyes and found himself nose-to-nose with the scruffy, tailless cat.

"How did *you* get back in here?"

The cat simply gazed at him, began purring, and curled up on Charles's stomach.

He stroked the cat's thick fur. "Just for the record," he said, "as soon as I get up from this chair, you're outta here."

They fell asleep together.

EIGHT

Ruthie Jacoby sat beside Isidore, watching television with the sound muted. He had fallen asleep a few minutes before. She held his hand as he quietly snored. The door opened and Nurse Faye came through, carrying a small bundle.

"Mr. Jacoby," she said in a sing-song voice, "it's time for your ba—" She stopped as Ruthie sat up and put a finger to her lips.

"He just dozed off," Ruthie whispered.

"I came to give him a sponge bath," Faye whispered back, holding up the bundle.

"I can do that a little later, if you don't mind," Ruthie said. "It would give me something to do, and it would take a little of the load off for you. I'm sure you're busy."

"I can't argue with you there," Faye said. "I'll just leave this over by the sink."

Ruthie smiled and nodded as Faye laid the bundle on the countertop next to the washbasin and quietly left the room. For a moment, she thought that Faye had forgotten something, because the door began to open again almost as soon as it had closed. Instead, a tall, thin man wearing a white lab coat and an attractive gold silk necktie came in. His silver hair, hugging his head in tight waves, reminded Ruthie of her nephew Jacob. The man had an intriguing face, both distinguished and kindly. He came over to Ruthie and shook her hand. When he spoke, it was with a soft, gentle voice, just above a whisper.

Ruthie thought he had a hint of a British accent. "I'm Dr. Galloway. I'm sorry that I'm dropping by so late. It appears I missed the opportunity to introduce myself to your husband."

"He's resting, and that's good," Ruthie said. She ran her hand gently over Isidore's arm. "Changes unsettle him."

Dr. Galloway pulled up a chair and sat down beside Ruthie. "Is there anything you need? Anything I can get for you? A cup of tea or something from the cafeteria perhaps?"

"No, thank you," said Ruthie, shaking her head.

"I won't take up much of your time," Dr. Galloway said. "I'm the head of our hospice service here, and—"

Ruthie interrupted. "Your assistant has already been by to visit."

A broad grin spread across Dr. Galloway's face. He chuckled. "Ah, Katherine is a jewel. I don't know how I'd get on without her." When Ruthie didn't reply, he continued, "Well then, it appears that Mr. Jacoby is all set for his procedure tomorrow, so I won't disturb you any longer. I just wanted to drop by and introduce myself. I'm sure that Katherine has explained that we want to be available to help you whenever you need us."

He stood up and moved toward the door.

"Thank you, Dr. Galloway," said Ruthie.

Dr. Galloway smiled and nodded toward Isidore. "I'm confident your husband's procedure will go well. Dr. Johnston is one of our best surgeons."

"I know," said Ruthie. "I've known him for years."

After Dr. Galloway left, Ruthie sat motionless for a while, considering Dr. Galloway's final words. She truly *hoped* that Isidore's procedure would go well.

NINE

In the shadows of the canyon created by Dallas's immense skyscrapers, the Angel walked down a narrow alley, searching for Shadowman. He had parked his Corolla several blocks away in a hotel parking garage. Better to walk than to risk being seen in something that was identifiable, something that could be traced.

The sedative he'd used to spike the cherry cola should have taken effect by now. If it had, he would find Shadowman sleeping peacefully in some quiet corner. Hopefully, it hadn't worked too quickly or he might have a difficult time finding his patient.

Shadowman normally slept near a Dumpster behind the loading dock of a downtown restaurant. It was a good place to camp out because it afforded him first dibs on any food the restaurant management decided to throw out.

The Angel made his way down the dark alley toward the Dumpster. Shadowman lay curled up in his usual spot against the trash bin, his head resting on a pile of cardboard boxes. The remnants of the sack lunch the Angel had given him were scattered on the concrete. Shadowman still held the empty bottle of cherry cola.

Good.

Shadowman wouldn't be providing any unexpected surprises.

The Angel checked Shadowman's pulse. It was strong. He apparently had the constitution of a horse.

The Angel prodded the sleeping man's shoulder.

"Eddie? You awake?" he whispered.

Shadowman's eyes fluttered open but there was no recognition in them. They were dull and lifeless. He was completely out of it.

"Relax, Eddie. I'm here to help."

Shadowman blinked, then closed his eyes.

The Angel donned a pair of latex examination gloves and rolled up Shadowman's right trouser leg. He didn't bother checking the man's arms. He already knew that they were much too scarred from years of heroin usage. He would never find a usable vein there.

Wrapping a tourniquet around Eddie's calf, the Angel palpated down near the man's ankle.

No luck.

He quickly unlaced Shadowman's worn sneaker and pulled it off. Shadowman wore no socks.

The Angel's fingers probed along the top of Shadowman's foot, searching for the telltale bulge. Perfect. He pulled from his trench coat pocket a syringe loaded with undiluted potassium chloride and injected it into the vein.

Within seconds, Shadowman's muscles tightened. He gasped twice, then relaxed.

The Angel pressed his fingers to Eddie Shoemate's neck. No carotid pulse. In the dim glow cast by the Angel's tiny flashlight, Shadowman's face looked peaceful, serene.

"There you go, Eddie," the Angel whispered, caressing the man's forehead. "You're free now."

The Angel reached into his trench coat pocket and pulled out a small bottle of Valium pills. The pills had been taken in a recent—and unsolved—burglary at a downtown pharmacy. The bottle still bore the prescription number and patient's name. He placed the bottle in Shadowman's right hand and pressed his fingers against it. Then he tucked the nearly empty bottle into the dead man's trouser pocket. When an overdose of Valium showed up at autopsy, it would provide a plausible explanation of his death.

Reaching once more into his trench coat, the Angel produced a small ceramic angel. He placed it on the ground behind Shadowman among a pile of the dead man's meager belongings.

Shadowman was with the angels now.

TEN

When Charles Hamisch awoke, the cat was still curled up on his stomach.

"Okay, Felix—or whatever your name is—party's over. Time for you to go back out into the cold, cruel world."

He stood up and for the second time that evening placed the cat outside on the welcome mat. "Been nice knowing you," he said as the shaggy feline fixed him with a sorrowful gaze. He closed the door and shuffled his way down the short hallway toward his bedroom.

Orange light from the parking lot's sodium vapor lamps filtered through the open window blinds, sketching warm slats across strange shapes in Charles's bedroom. On first glance, a visitor walking into the room might think that he had walked into an artist's studio instead of a bedroom. A drafting table with an assortment of colored pencils sat near one window. Nearby, a large palette filled with pools of mixed oil paint colors decorated another table. An assortment of wood carving tools lay beneath the table. An easel stood in one corner of the room with an unfinished oil—an autumn scene—resting in the easel.

Art had always been Charles's safety valve. When things got too stressful at work, he would draw or paint or carve. It didn't seem to matter which. They all relaxed him. Were he to wear a blood-pressure cuff as he created, he knew he would be able to watch the pressure drop when he picked up his carving tools.

Charles had no aspirations of being a great artist. He'd never sold a single piece. For that matter, he'd never tried. He preferred to give his work away rather than sell it.

He shuffled up to the easel and took a brush in hand. With no paint on the brush, he guided the bristles across the canvas as if in the process of painting a masterpiece. He made another swipe, but his fingers cramped and the brush clattered to the floor. He picked up another brush and tried again. This one too slipped from his grasp as a cramp caused his hand to spasm.

He backhanded the canvas, sending the easel crashing to the floor. Limping over to his bed, he sat down, resting his head in his hands.

On a nightstand beside the bed lay a brochure that Charles had been ignoring. He'd nearly thrown it away a few times. The cover displayed a picture of an attractive elderly woman, who Charles thought looked a bit like Barbara Bush. The heading read, "Hospice Care: Making the Final Journey Easier." He had read the brochure so many times that he practically had it memorized. He ripped the brochure in half and threw it into the wastebasket.

"No one can make *this* journey easier."

———

Drew pulled his car into Katherine Bainbridge's driveway and killed the engine.

He shifted in his seat and turned to face Lori. "I had a nice time tonight," he said. "Thanks for going."

"Me, too," Lori agreed. After a pause, she added, "It's been a long time."

"Too long," Drew said.

Lori nodded. "Too long."

"Do you think that maybe you'd like to go out again?"

Lori had seen this coming and had been dreading it. She shook her head. "Drew, it's not that I don't like you. I'm just not ready to get into a relationship again. Not yet."

Drew grinned. "You know what a grief counselor would say about that?"

"Probably that when you fall off a horse, you need to get right back on," Lori said.

Drew laughed. "Well, I'd couch it in more sophisticated terms, but basically, yes."

A pained expression darkened Lori's face. "It was really bad with Philip," she said softly. "It's going to take me a while to climb back on that horse—if I ever can."

Drew climbed out of the car, then walked around and opened Lori's door. As he held out his hand to help her out, he asked, "Is it okay if I wait?"

"Might be a while."

"I'm a very patient man."

Lori stood at the curb and watched as Drew drove away. As she walked up the steps to the house, she noticed that Kate's car was gone.

"Thought she'd be sitting on the porch steps waiting for a report," Lori muttered.

When she checked her voicemail, there was only one message. It was from Kate. Her voice sounded slightly tinny and scratchy, as if she were calling from a cheap cell phone.

"Hi, Sis. Dr. Galloway asked me to take care of some things for him at the last minute. Looks like I'll be working late. Have the coffee ready when I get home, and we'll have a good long talk. Hope you and Drew had a good time."

ELEVEN

Ruthie Jacoby placed the washcloth back into the basin and kissed her husband's forehead. A few minutes later, Faye came in to administer a sedative. Dr. Johnston wanted to make sure Isidore slept well, she said. Now his bed had been laid flat again, and Poppie was resting peacefully.

Ruthie sat for a long time, just looking at him, remembering happier times.

"Do you remember our first anniversary, Poppie?" Her voice was soft, almost a whisper. "We were so poor. You worked two jobs just so we could make ends meet. You wanted our first anniversary to be so special, but we could hardly afford to eat, let alone go out.

"So you made supper all by yourself. Wouldn't even let me in the kitchen. You even wrote up your own menu, just like at a real restaurant." A smile creased her face.

"But you couldn't cook to save your life. We both knew it was the worst meal we'd ever had. But we choked down every bite." She caressed his wrinkled hand. "I loved you before that day, of course, but when I saw what you did for me—just to show your love—I fell in love with you all over again."

As Ruthie's eyes fixed on Isidore, a tiny tear trickled down her cheek, gently tracing its way down through the wrinkles. She lifted his hand to her lips, kissed it, and pressed it against her cheek.

"You're my prince. You always will be."

She kissed his hand once more.

"I love you, Isidore Jacoby."

She laid his hand down on the sheet and shuffled toward the door. Before she left the room, she turned around and blew her husband a kiss.

———

Malachi checked his wristwatch. It was 2:30 AM.

He glanced up and down the corridor before entering room D477. All clear.

The only light in the room was a dim fluorescent at the head of the bed. Subject was sleeping soundly. Vitals had been checked fifteen minutes earlier. No interruptions expected.

Malachi moved quickly, but not *too* quickly. Mistakes could be costly. He examined the subject's IV tubing. Everything looked good. He removed a syringe from the pocket of his lab coat.

Wearing latex gloves, he pushed the needle into the man's IV port. He depressed the plunger slowly, forcing the syringe's contents into the IV tubing. When he finished, he withdrew the needle and capped the syringe. Then he slipped it back into his coat pocket.

Malachi opened the door of room D477, making another quick check of the hallway. The coast was clear.

Mission accomplished.

The patient was no longer suffering.

Part Two

THE CIRCLE

TWELVE

The irritating chirp of her cell phone jarred Lori out of a sound sleep. It took her a moment to remember where she was. The phone continued its chirping and increased in volume. She fumbled in the darkness until her fingers found the little phone. She pressed the answer button.

"This is Dr. Westlake."

"Dr. Westlake, this is Faye Renaud over on Four East."

"Yes? What's the problem?"

"You'd better come over. Mr. Jacoby passed away."

Lori was instantly alert. "When did it happen?"

"I found him at about three thirty. He was unresponsive and had no pulse or BP. I called a code, but it was too late. Dr. Franklin pronounced him at about four."

"Have you called Mrs. Jacoby?" Lori asked.

"I wanted to call you first," said Faye.

"All right. Call her nephew and tell him that Mr. Jacoby has taken a turn for the worse and that we need him to bring Mrs. Jacoby down right away. The number's in Mr. Jacoby's records. You'd better call Dr. Johnston and let him know."

"I already called Dr. Johnston," said Faye. "He's going by Mrs. Jacoby's house to break the news personally. Then he'll bring her over to the hospital."

Jealousy pierced Lori like a spear. "You called Dr. Johnston *first*?"

"Yes. Mrs. Jacoby insisted that he be called if anything happened. She said he is an old family friend. I didn't think you'd mind."

"That's fine," said Lori, biting her tongue. "I'll be in as soon as I can."

Lori hung up the phone, quietly fuming. Dr. Terrence Johnston had been horning in on this case from the beginning. He was the one who had suggested that a feeding tube be inserted. Once he had sold Ruthie Jacoby on the idea, she would not consider other options. Dr. Johnston had suggested it, and she was going with his plan no matter what. Lori had insisted that the matter be brought before the hospital ethics committee, but she lost the brief heated debate. Dr. Johnston had been with Sentinel since its inception and the decision makers accepted his opinions far more readily than those of a newcomer like Lori. Since the debate, her relationship with Dr. Johnston had been tense at best.

As she threw on some clothes, her thoughts returned to Ruthie Jacoby. She felt a pang of sadness for the poor woman. She disagreed with her decision about the feeding tube, but there was no doubt that this woman dearly loved her husband. Losing him would devastate her.

Lori didn't know whether Dr. Johnston would have thought to call a minister or rabbi. Somebody certainly needed to be there for Mrs. Jacoby. She picked up her cell phone and keyed in a number. After a few rings, a groggy voice responded at the other end.

"Yeah?"

"Drew, this is Lori."

"What time is it?" he asked.

"Four thirty," Lori said. "I'm sorry to bother you, but we've got a situation at the hospital, and I think you can help. Isidore Jacoby passed away early this morning. Can you come by in case Mrs. Jacoby needs you?"

Concern replaced the groggy irritation in Drew's voice. "I'm sorry. She know yet?"

"No. That's why I'd like you to be there."

"Be there in fifteen minutes."

Lori flipped the phone closed and put it in the pocket of her slacks. She considered waking Kate but decided against it. Dr. Galloway had kept Kate working late again and she needed her rest. Instead, Lori wrote a short note telling her sister where she was, plopped it on the kitchen table, and rushed into the garage.

When she flipped on the light, she stopped short.

Kate's car was still gone.

———

A hint of frost covered the perfectly clipped grass on the dark SHS campus as Lori wheeled her metallic teal Mustang convertible toward the physicians' parking garage. Sodium vapor security lights bathed the landscape with an anemic orange-yellow tint, perfectly reflecting Lori's funereal mood.

She wasn't sad that Mr. Jacoby had died. She was quietly nursing a feeling of satisfaction that Johnston's plan had fallen through. Mercifully, Isidore Jacoby had been spared an unnecessary surgery. She felt sorry for Ruthie, of course, but the outcome was inevitable; it was only the timing that was unfortunate.

How much better if they had been able to make arrangements in advance, if they could have planned for the foreseeable progression of Mr. Jacoby's Alzheimer's. He had lived a good life. He should have had the option of quietly and peacefully ending his life instead of being forced to suffer for so many years. Of course, in this case it never would have happened because the surgeon, Dr. Terrence Johnston, was a family friend.

Lori pulled into her parking spot and shut off the engine. She closed her eyes, took a deep breath, and exhaled. Occasionally in Jackie Palermo's self-defense class they had practiced board breaking. The object of the lesson wasn't to show off but to show the students that they were stronger than they thought. When a young woman who might weigh ninety-eight pounds soaking wet split a one-by-twelve board with a palm strike, it often proved to be a life-changing experience.

Lori looked forward to the board-breaking sessions, although they didn't do it very often. It provided a welcome release of tension and frustration, not to mention an exquisite feeling of satisfaction. At the moment, she wished she had a line of five or six boards to break, and perhaps a concrete block or two. It might help her avoid saying something she would regret when she met up with Dr. Johnston.

Inside, she headed for the small prayer room that occupied a corner of the fourth floor. She knew that this is where they would have Mrs. Jacoby wait until they were ready for her to see her husband. Knowing that Mrs. Jacoby did not like "no" or "wait" as answers, Lori expected the prayer room to be more like a war zone. In keeping with the SHS motto, "Quality Health Care for All God's Children," the architects designed the hospital complex with a prayer room on every floor. About the size of a small private room, each prayer room was lit with soft, incandescent table lamps. Like a surgical waiting area, the prayer room had been furnished with comfortable sofas and chairs and an outside telephone line. Unlike a waiting area, however, the room had been designed to turn visitors' minds to spiritual matters. There was no television or radio and no outside window. A faux stained glass window—lit from behind with fluorescent tubes—allowed streams of red, green, and blue light to trickle in while maintaining a subdued atmosphere. Copies of the Koran, Torah, Book of Mormon, and the Bible lay neatly arranged on a coffee table in front of a small flower-patterned love seat. SHS didn't care which faith you came from. If you were one of "God's children," they would accommodate you.

When Lori entered the room, she found Mrs. Jacoby sitting on a large brown leather recliner across from the love seat. Dr. Johnston had brought in a small secretary's chair from the nurses' station and had pulled it up beside her. He sat there, holding the newly widowed woman's hand.

Ruthie stood up as Lori entered the room.

"Please, Mrs. Jacoby," Lori said, "you don't need to get up."

Nevertheless, the little woman took both Lori's hands in her own. Her smile was radiant, although tears rimmed her brown eyes. "Thank you for coming." She drew a shuddering breath. "My Poppie isn't suffering anymore," she said through her smile. Then tears spilled from her eyes and she broke into sobs. As Mrs. Jacoby's knees began to give way, Lori caught her by her elbow and held her up. Dr. Johnston quickly rushed to her other side and helped Lori guide Mrs. Jacoby back to the recliner. Then he nodded to the door.

"Ruthie," Dr. Johnston said in his deep baritone voice, "Dr. Westlake and I will check and see how long it will be before you can see Isidore." He handed her a tissue.

"Thank you, Terrence," said Ruthie.

—

"I'm sorry you had to come in," Lori said as they walked toward Isidore Jacoby's room. Her words were terse and clipped.

"No inconvenience," Dr. Johnston said. "Ruthie's nephew is in England on business. He's been notified and is catching the first plane back. Until he gets here, I'm the unofficial 'next of kin.' Besides, I'd have come in pretty soon anyway."

"Quite a disappointment for you," Lori said as they passed by the nurses' station.

Dr. Johnston stopped and turned to face her. "And what is that supposed to mean?"

"Well, you fought so hard at ethics committee for the right to insert that feeding tube, I just figured you'd be disappointed that Mr. Jacoby died before you had a chance to prolong his life."

Dr. Johnston's face reddened. "Dr. Westlake, we've been through all this several times. I see no need to hash it out again, especially with *you*." He turned and walked away but Lori followed right on his heels.

"Mrs. Jacoby had no interest in having a feeding tube inserted in her husband until you convinced her," said Lori. "She was content to let him slip away quietly."

Dr. Johnston whipped around and pointed a finger at Lori. "And *that*, doctor, must have disappointed *you* immensely. If you'd had your way, you would have just euthanized him and been done with it. What's your preferred method? Gas? Lethal injection?" He shook his head. "Too bad the electric chair's not politically correct anymore. You could have sent the man out with a bang."

Now it was Lori's turn to get angry, but she had no intention of being baited into a shouting match. Not here. Not now. She brushed past the surgeon and headed for Isidore Jacoby's room.

"Just stay away from my patients in the future and we'll get along fine," she muttered under her breath.

Faye Renaud was combing Isidore Jacoby's baby-fine silver hair as Lori entered the room, followed by Dr. Johnston.

Mr. Jacoby appeared to be asleep. Indeed, were it not for his color, Lori might have wondered if she'd been called in by mistake. He lay flat on his back with the covers neatly arranged and his hands folded on his chest. The room had been straightened up and the body was ready for what was virtually a funeral home viewing. This was one of

Dr. Galloway's innovations. As head of hospice, he made every effort to represent death as a natural part of life. Arranging the deceased and allowing a special visiting time before the body was removed was one way, he said, to reduce the trauma for those who were left behind.

"Is everything ready, Nurse Renaud?" Dr. Johnston asked before Lori had a chance to speak.

"Yes, sir," she said, not looking up.

"Good," he said. "I'll go get Ruthie."

After Dr. Johnston had gone, Faye said, "I'm sorry, Dr. Westlake. I know I should have called you first, but Dr. Johnston would have had my head if he hadn't been the first one notified."

"He *asked* you to call him first?"

Faye nodded. "I've been working here fifteen years and I've learned that there are certain people you don't cross if you plan on a long employment. He's one of them."

Lori sighed and shook her head. "Let's pull that chair over close to the bed in case Mrs. Jacoby needs it."

Lori and Faye each took a side of the recliner and scooted it across the floor toward Isidore's bed.

"Dr. Johnston is a shark," Faye said. "He's very good at what he does, but getting in his way can be hazardous to your health."

"I've already gotten in his way," Lori said. "And I plan to continue getting in his way if he keeps interfering with my patients."

Faye smiled. "I prefer to fly under the radar," she said.

Before Lori could answer, the door opened and in came Ruthie Jacoby, assisted by Dr. Johnston and Drew Langdon. Drew nodded to Lori as they walked past her toward the bed.

Ruthie stood at her husband's bedside, supported by both men. She stretched out a wrinkled, trembling hand and smoothed his hair. Tears streamed down her cheeks, yet a peaceful smile creased her face. A smile of relief. A smile that now saw the end to years of toil and suffering.

"He looks good, doesn't he, Terrence?"

Dr. Johnston smiled and nodded. "He looks good, Ruthie."

Drew spoke up for the first time since they'd entered the room. "Would you like to sit down, Mrs. Jacoby?"

"I'm fine, young man," she said softly. She patted Isidore's hand one last time. "Good-bye, Poppie." She looked up at Dr. Johnston. "I'm ready to go home now, Terrence."

"I'll take Mrs. Jacoby home," Dr. Johnston said to Drew. "Arrangements with the funeral home have already been made. They'll be by to pick up Mr. Jacoby later this morning."

Drew nodded, but Lori broke in. "Shouldn't the medical examiner be notified?"

Mrs. Jacoby's response was a sharp and sudden "No!" The worn and frail old woman's eyes flashed with anger.

"There's no need for an autopsy," Dr. Johnston said.

"Excuse me," said Lori, "but Mr. Jacoby died in the first twenty-four hours of his hospital stay. The medical examiner should be notified."

Dr. Johnston was about to speak, but Ruthie drew herself up and walked over to Lori. "Young lady, do you have any idea who I am and who my husband was?"

Lori backpedaled. "Mrs. Jacoby, I didn't mean to suggest—"

"I am a respected member of this community. My husband served as an advisor to two governors and has been entertained at the White House. An autopsy is one indignity I will not permit. He will be buried today."

Dr. Johnston put his arm around Mrs. Jacoby's shoulder. "Don't worry about it, Ruthie. I'll make sure nothing is done." To Lori he said, "The medical examiner will be notified. And there will be *no* autopsy. Come on, Ruthie. I'll take you home." With that, he ushered Mrs. Jacoby out of the room. On his way out the door, Dr. Johnston looked back at Lori. "I'll deal with *you* later."

"I'm looking forward to it," Lori shot back.

Lori, Drew, and Faye stood in silence for what seemed like an eternity.

"Guess they won't be needing me," said Drew. "Would you care to join me for runny eggs and soggy bacon in the cafeteria? I'm buying."

Lori smiled and shook her head. "Sounds tempting but I'm going to go home for a little while. Kate must have pulled a double. She wasn't home when I left."

"Does she pull double shifts often?" Drew asked.

Lori shook her head, a concerned expression on her face. "Almost never."

THIRTEEN

Charles Hamisch's face was hot. He lay in bed, trying to ignore it, but as droplets of sweat began to trickle from his forehead down the side of his head, he knew it was no use. His plan on his first day of "retirement" had been to sleep for as long as he could. What else did he have to do? But he had forgotten to close the blinds on his east-facing window, and a beam of sunlight was focused directly on his head. It felt as if someone had turned on a theatrical spotlight and pointed it at him.

Now that sleep was no longer an option, the question was how his body would respond today. The aching sensation in his hands and legs foretold a bad day. His fingers had curled up during the night, making his hands look like little claws—a sign of progressing muscle atrophy. He slowly opened and closed his fingers, working the stiff, unresponsive muscles, trying to force them to life. The comforter felt heavy to throw off, as if it was filled with concrete.

"Welcome to retirement," he said to himself.

He willed his legs to move. They obeyed—sluggishly.

He pushed himself to his feet and stood where he was for a moment, making sure that his legs weren't going to give out before he could take a step. He had forgotten to put his cane near the bed last night and would have to get by without it until he tracked it down.

When he was fairly certain he wouldn't lose his balance, he shuffled haltingly toward the bathroom door. Walking used to be such an uncomplicated process. Not anymore. He had to concentrate on every step or risk a fall from which he might not be able to get up.

Using the furniture to prop himself up, he was able to make it to the windowless bathroom, but when he switched on the light he wanted to throw up. Standing in front of a full-length mirror, wearing only boxer shorts, he found his reflection nauseating.

He had prided himself on his physique. He was no Arnold Schwarzenegger, but he *had* worked hard to keep in shape. Now his body was deteriorating before his eyes. His emaciated arms and upper body made him look like a poster boy for world hunger. His stomach, once hard and flat, now sagged like a beer belly. In only a few short months, ALS had transformed him from a man of vitality into a physical shipwreck, a skeleton with skin. Eventually this horrible disease would reduce him to nothing more than a brain in a shell.

"It's not fair," he exclaimed as he slammed his hand against the light switch, throwing the bathroom into darkness. At least he didn't have to look at himself while he was in there.

When he was finished in the bathroom, he made his way back to his bed and sat down.

"*No one* should have to die like this." He looked toward the ceiling. Tears welled in his eyes. He whispered, his voice thick and husky. "I do *not* want to go out by inches."

He pulled open the nightstand drawer. In it lay a worn, leather Bible and a .38 caliber revolver. He'd turned in his service piece when he left the Department. He had purchased *this* gun the day after he'd been diagnosed with ALS.

Just in case.

He took out the revolver and spun the cylinder, making sure it was loaded.

It was.

———

Lori sat at the kitchen table, nursing her fourth cup of coffee. Bright sunlight streamed through the lace curtains that sheltered a bay window on her right. She watched the sunbeams bounce off an etched crystal sun-catcher, exploding into filaments of red, green, and blue light. The happy colors did *not* reflect her mood.

It was seven thirty in the morning, and she'd been sitting there for nearly an hour, waiting for Kate to get back from her night shift.

She had been carefully planning a confrontation with her interfering sister, but if Kate didn't get back shortly it would have to wait for later. Lori would have to leave for work soon.

Lori dearly loved her sister and didn't want to hurt her. But Kate needed to realize that Lori was thirty-five years old and perfectly capable of managing her own life.

Granted, Lori owed her sister big time. It wasn't stretching things to say that she owed her life to Kate. Kate had rescued her from Philip, arranged for Lori to move in with her, and even pulled some strings to land her a job with Sentinel Health Systems.

When Philip started making threatening phone calls and stalking Lori, Kate had gone on the offensive. Although Lori had refused to press charges against her husband, Kate had contacted a lawyer who got a restraining order issued. If the jerk came anywhere near Lori, they could have him arrested.

Lori was broken physically, mentally, and financially when she came to Kate for help. However, with Kate's support and encouragement, she had made a strong comeback. Over the past year she'd regained her self-confidence and managed to put Philip behind her. She was a respected—albeit new—staff member at Sentinel. The self-defense class had helped complete her transformation from a cowering wimp to a self-assured, assertive person.

But Kate was stuck in mother hen mode.

Lori was pouring her fifth cup of coffee when she heard the garage door opener kick on. She pulled a mug from the cabinet above her head and poured an extra cup for Kate.

Lori finished filling Kate's mug as a squadron of butterflies flew kamikaze missions in her stomach. Knowing that her sister was a gracious but formidable personality, the kind of person you usually didn't say no to, Lori had rehearsed her speech until she could have recited it in her sleep. Nevertheless, she felt distinctly unprepared as she waited for Kate to come in from the garage.

"It's showtime."

―――

Charles sat on the edge of his bed with the pistol in his lap. He ran his fingertips over the cold steel as tears spilled from his eyes. It would be so easy. Just one quick flash, a burst of sound, and it would all be over. No pain. No long decline. No paralysis. No humiliation. But as he considered this convenient escape, his eyes fell on the Bible in the drawer.

He reached over and picked it up.

The book's leather corners were worn rough. Gold leaf around the edges had long since worn away, leaving the pages dirty and mottled. On the cover's lower right corner a name was barely visible: Bradford Taylor Hamisch.

Charles flipped through the pages and allowed the binding to fall open to the book of Psalms. A laminated news clipping slid out from the Bible and into his lap. The picture in the clipping was of a man who looked very much like Charles. Lines under the picture identified the man as Officer Brad Hamisch.

Charles heaved a sigh and closed the Bible. He laid it gently back in the drawer and pushed the drawer closed.

Then he turned his attention to the revolver once more. He popped open the cylinder and gave it another spin. Six bullets.

It would only take one.

Lori took the two steaming coffee mugs to the table near the bay window and sat down to wait for Kate.

She didn't have to wait long.

Lori forgot her prepared speech the moment she saw her sister.

Kate came through the door looking like death warmed over. Lori expected her to look tired. Her sister *was* coming off a double, after all. But the lines on Kate's face reflected something more than weariness, although Lori couldn't put her finger on what it was.

"Kate, what's wrong?" Lori asked.

Kate sat down across the table from Lori. She kicked off her shoes and took a long sip from her coffee mug before answering. "Long night, Sis," she finally said.

"Long night for me, too," said Lori. "Isidore Jacoby passed away sometime around two thirty."

Kate looked up sharply, instantly alert. "What? What happened?"

Lori shrugged. "No explanation yet. He just coded."

"Any idea as to cause of death?"

Lori shook her head. "Not yet. And if Dr. Johnston has his way, there won't be an autopsy. All I know is that the moment I mentioned it, Mrs. Jacoby went ballistic. Johnston backed her all the way. As well-connected as she and her husband were politically, I have no doubt she'll get her way.

"By the way," she added, "why'd you have to pull an extra shift? Somebody call in sick?"

Kate hesitated for a moment. "I don't know if I should tell you."

"Tell me what?"

Kate gazed into her half-empty coffee mug as if she were reading tea leaves. She breathed a quiet sigh and looked back at Lori. "Something's not right, Lori."

"What do you mean?"

Kate didn't answer right away. For a moment, she glanced out the window. Then she drained her coffee mug and placed it on the table. She looked back at her sister and the weariness returned to her face. "People are dying at Sentinel. People who *shouldn't* be dying."

"What are you talking about?" Lori asked.

"You want to know why I didn't come home last night? I didn't work a double. I spent most of the night in Medical Records researching cases."

"And . . . ?" Lori prompted.

"And things are not adding up," Kate replied.

"Like what?"

"An awfully high number of patients have died of 'natural causes' in the past few years."

Lori was perplexed, and her face reflected it. "Natural causes? You lost me."

"Look," Kate said, "a patient, Isidore Jacoby for instance, is admitted to SHS for treatment or some kind of surgery. The patient has a serious but not immediately life-threatening condition. But within a few days after the patient is admitted, he dies for no apparent reason. The death is usually attributed to the disease or to natural causes. Because the patient had a serious or chronic illness, everyone considers the death a 'blessing,' and nobody calls for an autopsy. But when you look closely at the case, there's no reason the patient should have died."

"And so . . ." Lori urged her sister on.

"So I'm beginning to think that somebody's killing them."

"You think somebody's euthanizing patients?" Lori asked.

"I've found at least fifteen suspicious cases over the past few years. Whenever I can steal a few minutes, I go down to Records and access the database. I'm finding new ones all the time. The only explanation I can come up with is that we've got a doctor or nurse murdering patients."

"Have you discussed it with anyone?"

Kate nodded. "I put a report together and gave it to Dr. Galloway." She shook her head. "He's skeptical." She stood up and took her coffee cup over to the sink. "Isidore Jacoby's case may be the break I've been looking for, if I can look into it before the evidence gets cold."

Walking past the table, she kissed Lori on the top of her head. "G'night, Sis." Before she exited the kitchen she stopped and glanced back. "By the way, how'd your date with Drew go?"

The butterflies returned. Lori was careful to keep her voice soft and carefully measured. "Actually, I'd wanted to talk to you about that."

Kate grinned and waved her off. "No need to thank me. I had a feeling you just needed a nudge. You two'll be great together."

"But—" Lori protested, but Kate's back was turned and she was plodding up the staircase in the back of the kitchen toward her bedroom on the second floor.

Lori sighed. "Right, Kate. We're a real pair, Drew and I."

She dumped the rest of her coffee into the sink.

Calling an emergency meeting of the Circle of Peace was dangerous, but Quinn felt it was necessary. Every member had the right to call such a meeting but those who did so frivolously risked expulsion from the Circle. Nevertheless, Quinn had to make sure it was simply an unfortunate coincidence and not because a Circle member had violated protocol. Zoë's abrupt exit from the last meeting made him nervous. The last thing the Circle needed was a renegade member.

Quinn pulled out the prepaid cell phone given to him by the Circle. Every member had one, exclusively for Circle business. Because the phone required no contract, and minutes could be added without the use of a credit card, it provided a reasonably secure means for the Circle members to stay in touch.

All the members knew each other, but they were forbidden to dis-cuss Circle business by e-mail, over the phone, or face-to-face. They met only in temporary online chat rooms and used screen names rather than their real names. Not perfect security by any means, but it was *something*.

Using the text-messaging feature, Quinn keyed in a series of numbers—211.0.9.12—and sent them to Malachi, Zoë, and Copper. Along with the numbers, he sent a meeting time: 12:12 PM. At twelve minutes past noon, the other members of the Circle would have to log in to a chat room to give an accounting of their activities over the past twelve hours.

If Zoë had started freelancing, Quinn wanted to know about it.

FOURTEEN

Despite the brightness of the morning, the back alley was still veiled in shadow as Angelica carried a plastic trash bag toward the Dumpster. Same routine, day after day. Or night after night, actually. Go through the whole building. Clean all the offices. Pick up the trash. Then wrap up the night's work by hauling off the gringos' garbage. And for this she didn't even make the minimum wage. She didn't dare complain, though. Without a green card, there was no one she could complain to without finding herself on her way home to Mexico.

She snorted with contempt when she saw the rail-thin black man stretched out on the concrete near the Dumpster. *Un borrachín.* A drunkard.

She took her broom from the cart and swatted at the man's feet.

"*Levántate. Vaya.*"

The man didn't move. Angelica looked closer. The man's eyes were half-open. Glazed.

"*Madre de Dios.*" Angelica crossed herself.

———

David Bachman parked his car behind the coroner's van and walked down the alley. The officers who responded to the initial call had already secured the area around the Dumpster with crime scene tape. David showed his ID to the officer standing near the scene and stepped underneath the tape.

"What have we got?" he asked the officer in charge.

"Black male. Looks like an overdose."

"Who called it in?"

The officer shrugged. "Anonymous tip. Hispanic woman is all we know. She didn't speak much English."

"Did 9-1-1 get an address?" David asked.

"Didn't call 9-1-1. She called the main number."

"Witnesses?"

"Haven't found any yet," replied the officer.

"Figures," David said, walking over to the corpse. "Any ID on him?"

A young crime scene tech kneeling beside the body shook her head. She handed David a numbered plastic bag containing some small pills. Another bag held a bottle. "We've got some Valium here."

"Valium?" David remarked, holding up the bag. "Interesting drug of choice for a street person."

The tech shrugged. "You get what you can get, I guess."

"What else have you got?"

"Remnants of a sack lunch. A few personal possessions. That's about it."

"What kind of possessions?" David asked.

"Trinkets mostly. An old pocketknife, a photo, a few coins. A little ceramic angel. Not much else."

David raised an eyebrow "An angel? Let me see it."

The tech handed David another plastic bag. He took it and held it up to the light, squinting at it through the plastic.

The angel was about the size of a man's thumb. There was nothing extraordinary about the workmanship. It was the kind of thing you'd find in most dollar stores. Virtually impossible to trace.

David breathed a quiet prayer. "Please, God, no."

"What?" the tech asked. "Did I miss something?"

"No." David handed the angel back to her. Then he added under his breath, "Unless the homeless community of Dallas has started collecting these, we're dealing with a serial killer."

FIFTEEN

Charles struggled to maintain his grip on the black Sharpie marker but the unrelenting cramps in his fingers and arms made the effort all but futile. In frustration, he threw the pen across the living room and knocked his yellow legal pad to the floor.

"Can't even write a lousy suicide note," he grumbled.

He leaned back in his recliner, still exhausted from washing and getting dressed—a process that had taken him nearly an hour to perform. He'd wait a while before making a second try at writing the note.

Charles carried two things with him from the bedroom: his Bible, and the pistol. The pistol lay on the end table beside his chair; the Bible was in his lap.

His stomach growled. He'd had no breakfast, even though Pam Bachman had left several days' worth of premade breakfasts in the fridge. Seeing himself in the mirror earlier, he had lost his appetite—for everything. Now he sat in the threadbare recliner trying to figure out how to tell his dearest friends why he'd decided to check out early.

He wasn't exactly sure why he'd brought his Bible with him. He knew he'd never find justification for suicide in its pages. Perhaps subconsciously he wanted to bring it along to make him think—slow him down. On the other hand, maybe he wanted them to see it in his lap when they found him. It might give them some hope that he hadn't abandoned his faith. He still believed. He'd just had enough. That was all. And he didn't see the point in fighting a battle he was sure to lose.

He fingered the Bible again and flipped through its pages. His gaze bounced back and forth between the pistol and the book.

He'd just begun to doze off when a knock at the door jarred him awake. He blinked his eyes and shook his head, trying to clear away the cobwebs as he clambered out of the soft chair and made his way toward the door.

"Coming," he muttered, but not nearly loud enough for anyone outside to hear. "I'm coming."

His fingers felt like rubber as he tried to work the one-way deadbolt's handle. He winced at the pain. It felt like an eternity before the latch popped free from the doorframe. When he went to unlock the second deadbolt, he noticed that it was already unlocked. He pulled the door open and found Pam Bachman standing there with a key in one hand and Charles's lunch in the other.

"I'm sorry, Pam," he said. "I forgot there's no keyhole for the top deadbolt. I don't know where my mind is these days. Come on in."

"Don't worry about it," she replied as she walked past him and into the kitchen. "I didn't have to wait long." She opened the refrigerator and put the sack containing Charles's lunch inside. "And," she said, turning back toward him, "if I got hungry, I could have eaten your lun—"

The smile faded from her face, replaced by a look of horror.

"What's the matter, Pam?"

He didn't need to wait for an answer. All he needed to do was follow her gaze to the pistol on the end table.

___

Twelve-year-old Scott Oaks pulled off his shirt and hopped up onto the examining table. He pushed his ash-blond hair out of his eyes as he and his mother waited for his doctor to come in. Like most kids, Scott didn't like going to the doctor. But in this case he was willing to make an exception. For the last few days, whenever he swallowed anything, it felt like razor blades going down his throat. Besides, Dr. Westlake was pretty cool—for a doctor.

He only wished he had been able to talk his mother into staying out in the waiting room. He was old enough to see Dr. Westlake by himself and it was beginning to embarrass him to have his mother with him all the time. But she'd insisted on being there, and he was feeling too rotten to argue. Of course, he couldn't have given her much of an argument, even if he'd wanted to. Even talking hurt. He probably hadn't said twenty words all day. As he sat with his mother in Dr. Westlake's examining room, he just hoped they didn't have to wait too long.

Turns out, they didn't; Dr. Westlake came in after only about five minutes.

"Hi, Scott." She smiled at him and spoke in that bright, cheery voice he liked. "I hear you're not feeling so good."

He nodded and managed a weak smile in return.

"Well, I'll see what I can do to get you up and running again." Dr. Westlake turned and shook hands with Mrs. Oaks, but then turned right back to Scott. He liked that. Dr. Westlake treated him like *he* was important, instead of just talking to his mother.

"Okay Scott, let's see if we can figure out what the problem is." Lori took her stethoscope and pressed it to his chest. The cool plastic against his skin sent a shudder through him. He felt goose bumps coming up on his arms.

"Give me a deep breath."

Scott inhaled and blew it out.

She moved the stethoscope. "Again."

Scott complied.

After asking for a few more breaths, Dr. Westlake moved the chestpiece to his back and repeated the process. Then she took her stethoscope out of her ears and put it back in her lab coat.

"Well, your lungs are clear. That's good. Let's see what's happening up here." She reached out and began feeling Scott's neck.

Dr. Westlake's brow furrowed and her lips curled down in a tight frown as she pressed her fingers against the back of his jaw. She didn't say anything but Scott could tell she didn't like what she was feeling.

She took out a tongue depressor and her pen light.

"Almost done. Let's have a look at what's happening inside."

Scott hated this part. It always made him feel like he was going to throw up. Nevertheless, he opened his mouth and allowed Dr. Westlake to press down on his tongue as she looked with the flashlight.

She let out a low whistle. "Swallowing isn't fun, is it?"

Scott shook his head.

She tossed the wooden stick into a small container marked "Bio-hazard" in red letters.

"You, sir, appear to have a nasty case of strep throat. We'll need to get a culture to be sure, though."

Scott looked worried, and Dr. Westlake smiled.

"It's no big deal. The nurse will come in with an extra long cotton swab. She'll grab a few of those germs from your throat and we'll see if you've got strep swimming around in there. Then we'll know what kind of medicine to give you. Sound like a plan?"

Scott nodded and smiled.

"Great. You can hop down and put your shirt back on," she said.

Dr. Westlake raised her hand and Scott gave her a high five.

"Now," she said, "if I hurry, I think I may actually get fifteen minutes for lunch." But almost before she finished speaking, her pager beeped. She looked at it, sighed, and said, "Well, so much for lunch." On her way out the door, still smiling, she said, "See you later, Scott."

───

"What is *that* for?" Pam Bachman demanded.

Before Charles could come up with a plausible reason why a revolver was beside his chair, Pam looked at him with mixed anger and hurt.

"No. You don't have to tell me. I *know* what it's for. Charles Hamisch, how could you even *think* of such a thing?"

"Pam, listen—"

"No, I will *not* listen." Angry tears welled in her eyes and her face flushed red against her dark brown hair. Her voice trembled. "Did you take time to think who would find you? Did you?"

"Pam—"

"It would have been me." Tears streamed down her cheeks. "Well, Charles, if you're *that* cowardly, you just go ahead. I'm not going to stop you." She brushed past him on her way to the front door. Standing halfway out the door, she looked back at Charles and pointed to the pistol. "But I'll tell you this. I'm not going to be the one to come in here and clean up the mess. Nobody should have to do that more than once in a lifetime."

She slammed the door so hard it rattled the drinking glasses in the dishwasher. Stunned, Charles just stood there in the wake of her fury, not really knowing what to do. Finally, he made his way back to the recliner and sat down.

This was certainly not the reaction he'd expected. He had halfway prepared himself for someone discovering his plans. He'd even taken some time to think through how he might explain why he wanted to take his own life—just in case David or Pam found the gun. But he had prepared himself to defend against arguments, not unbridled rage.

He sat in his recliner, feeling more alone than ever.

How was he going to make it right with Pam when she was so angry, when she wouldn't even listen to him?

Maybe I don't need to. Maybe it was all for the best.

After all, when she cools down, she'll probably call David, and he'll send some officers to check on me. If the job's done by then, she won't have to be the one who finds me.

Charles picked up the .38, felt its weight in his palm.

It'll be quick. Then no more pain.

He noticed that his heart was beating faster and that a cool film of perspiration had broken out on his face. His hand felt clammy.

His finger curled around the trigger, but before he could pull it, he heard a crash in the kitchenette, followed by the sound of shattering glass.

"Pam?" Charles called out, but it couldn't be her. She could not have gotten back inside without him seeing her. Who else could have gotten in?

Still holding the pistol, Charles pushed himself to his feet. "Who's there?"

No response.

Not really in any condition to handle an intruder, he supposed that he should be moving *away* from the sound, not toward it. But he also figured he didn't have anything to lose, so he continued to inch toward the kitchen.

Another rustling sound. Someone was definitely in there.

At a distinct disadvantage because he couldn't move quickly, Charles struggled to maintain his balance as he entered the small kitchen. The element of surprise was definitely not his.

As it turned out, he didn't need it.

He saw the source of the noise as he entered the kitchen. On the counter beside the kitchen sink, the scruffy white and tan cat was busily working on a sack of potato chips. All that Charles could see was the cat's rear end sticking out of the large bag. On the floor in front of the sink, the remains of a broken water glass lay scattered.

Charles rolled his eyes and set the gun down on the counter. He pulled the cat from the bag of chips. It came out reluctantly, still grasping a chip between its two front paws. He held the cat up and turned it to face him.

"You don't take no for an answer, do you?"

Still licking its lips, salt and chip fragments clinging to its whiskers, the cat closed its eyes and purred. Charles shook his head and carried the cat back to his recliner. He brushed the potato chip debris from the cat's face.

The cat curled up and went to sleep in Charles's lap.

He stayed in his recliner, gently stroking the cat's fur.

The gun stayed in the kitchen.

Lori didn't recognize the telephone number on her pager but that wasn't particularly unusual. Ever since she had started working at SHS, she'd found her life getting busier and busier. It was not uncommon to get calls from an ever-increasing number of patients and potential patients. That's what she loved about being in general practice. Her patients came from all backgrounds, all with different needs. It was never dull or routine. One day would bring the sadness of a patient in Nina Ware's condition; the next would bring a bright, irrepressible boy like Scott Oaks. Lori knew that her decision not to specialize had been the right one. She loved family practice.

Back in her office, she keyed in the number on her cell phone.

"Dr. Westlake. I'm glad you returned my call," a man's deep voice responded almost instantly.

"May I help you?" Lori asked.

"I hope so," the man answered. "This concerns one of your patients. Nina Ware."

"Is she all right?" Concern edged into Lori's voice.

"She's fine. Or at least as fine as she can be under the circumstances."

Lori thought she smelled a lawyer. "What exactly is your connection to Ms. Ware?"

The man chuckled. "I can't tell you that over the phone."

"And why is that?" challenged Lori.

"Certain matters are best discussed in person, Dr. Westlake, not over unsecured airwaves."

Definitely a lawyer.

"Look, I don't know who you are, but if this is about a lawsuit, just bypass me and go straight to my attorney."

The man chuckled again. "There's no lawsuit involved. And just to ease your mind, this isn't an extortion attempt either. However, it does have to do with your patient's welfare. And I believe you will want to hear what I have to say. Please give me fifteen minutes of your time. That's all I ask."

"Where and when?" Lori asked.

"In the gardens. Now. If you're not there in five minutes, I'll take it that you're not interested. But if you don't come, you'll miss out on a chance to truly help your patient."

"How will I know you?"

There was no response. The mystery man had already disconnected.

Lori looked at her watch. From where she was in the SHS complex, it would take nearly the entire five minutes to walk to the gardens. The clock was running but Lori wasn't sure it was worth the trouble to try to beat it. The guy could be a crank or a con man. On the other hand, if this guy had some means of helping Nina, Lori was certainly willing to risk fifteen minutes to hear him out.

She went over to the desk and pressed a button on her intercom. "Shelley," she said, "I'm going to be out for a few minutes."

———

Charles and the cat were still in the recliner when a knock came at the door. A second later, the door creaked open and Pam Bachman peeked in. Her eyes were red and she had a tissue in her hand.

"May I come in?"

Charles nodded.

She stepped inside and closed the door behind her.

"I'm sorry I went off on you like that," she said as she walked across the room. She dabbed away a tear that trickled from her eye.

"Pam," said Charles, "tell me about it. What happened?"

"I'd rather show you," she said. "Will you go for a ride with me?"

"If you'll take my new roommate into the kitchen and give him a bowl of milk."

Pam was surprised. "I didn't know you had a cat."

Charles looked at the mass of fur curled up on his lap. "Neither did I."

SIXTEEN

In the brief time she had worked at Sentinel, Lori had come to love the SHS gardens. They were not only the focal point of the complex, but a tourist attraction in their own right. Often described as a cross between the Japanese Tea Gardens of San Antonio and Fort Worth's Water Gardens, the SHS gardens were always populated by a fair crowd of visitors.

A maze of winding ramps, pathways, and staircases led downward through cascading streams, tranquil pools, and waterfalls. Meticulously kept rose bushes and vines accented the walkways with splashes of intense reds, pinks, oranges, yellows, and countless variations.

Carefully placed benches along the paths offered the opportunity to sit quietly and enjoy all that nature had to offer.

The gardens were a favorite spot for young couples looking for a romantic setting, and scores of weddings were held there each year.

The gardens were a peaceful place.

A place to meditate. A place to relax.

A place to be invisible.

She strolled down a staircase and into the heart of the gardens. Her caller had not specified a meeting place, only a time frame. So rather than waste time trying to find him, Lori just decided to walk— and let him find her.

She didn't have to wait long.

"Dr. Westlake. I'm glad you decided to come." The voice came from behind her. Lori recognized it as the voice from the phone conversation.

She turned and faced the man who had called her. Short and balding with a neatly trimmed crescent of black hair above his ears and a matching mustache, the man was not what she expected. Based on his voice, she'd expected a fairly young man. However, judging by his hair, facial wrinkles, and paunch, she guessed that this fellow was in his late fifties. He wore wire-framed trifocals that reminded Lori of her high school biology teacher.

The man's outfit screamed *tourist*—Bermuda shorts, a bright yellow pullover shirt, comfortable walking shoes, and socks pulled up nearly to his knees. He carried a small paper bag, presumably full of bread crumbs for feeding the birds and fish. Capping off the ensemble, an expensive digital camera hung from his neck. He even had a hint of sunburn.

"I almost *didn't* come, Mr.—"

"Doe," the man answered. "You can call me John."

Lori raised an eyebrow. "John Doe. Not a very imaginative name."

He smiled and held out his hands. "What can I say? I didn't have imaginative parents."

"You said you could help Nina Ware. How?"

The man laughed. "You get right to the point. I like that." He nodded toward the staircase. "Walk with me."

They made their way down the stairs and turned aside to a path that led toward a pool of brightly colored koi. John Doe leaned on the railing and gazed into the pool as if the fish fascinated him. Then he opened his paper bag and tossed in a few bread crumbs.

"If your patient really wants to avoid the suffering associated with her terminal illness, there is a way."

"What do you mean?"

"Doctor, your views on the issue of physician-assisted suicide are a matter of record around Sentinel. I think you *know* what I mean."

Lori nodded. "I know what you mean. But last time I checked, Jack Kevorkian was still in prison. Has someone else picked up the baton?"

John Doe shook his head. "Kevorkian took an 'in your face' approach. He wanted to force a change in society's views by direct confrontation. The Circle is more patient."

A chill ran down Lori's spine. Was it possible that this was the solution to Kate's mystery?

"The Circle?"

"The Circle of Peace. Let's just say they're a group of people who share your viewpoint. The Circle exists to help patients such as Nina Ware—patients who want a solution that is currently not quite legal."

"So you're into helping people die, not confrontational social change. Is that it?"

"Make no mistake about it, Dr. Westlake. Physician-assisted suicide and voluntary euthanasia *will* eventually be accepted and legalized. It's simply a matter of time. But we're wise enough to realize that the time is not *now*. Nevertheless, our work is important. Confrontation with the authorities would be counterproductive at this point. So until society comes to its senses, we're committed to providing a discreet alternative."

"That's interesting," Lori replied. "But why me? Isn't it a risk even approaching me?"

John Doe tossed some more bread crumbs into the pond. "Every now and then we discover someone of influence who sees things our way—someone like you. When that happens, we give that person the opportunity to join us."

"Ah, I see. You need another physician to assist in your *efforts*. I can't say that I disagree with what you're doing. But agreeing with you and joining you are totally different things. You're asking me to risk my license, to risk prison. I'm not sure that I'm ready to do that."

John Doe dumped the rest of the bread crumbs into the pond, then crumpled the bag and put it in his pocket. "I'm not asking you to," he replied. "Not right away at least."

The man's remark caught Lori off balance. "I thought you were here to recruit me."

"In a way, I am. But we must protect ourselves in the process. A person becomes involved in the Circle of Peace slowly. By degrees, you might say."

"What sort of degrees?"

"At the beginning, you'll be asked only to refer people to us. Nothing more. Eventually, as you become more comfortable with us and we are convinced of your trustworthiness, you may be given the opportunity to help in more substantial ways."

Lori considered his words for a moment. "How do I know that this isn't some kind of sting? For all I know, you could be with the FBI, fishing for doctors who are willing to cross the line."

"That's a fair question," said John Doe. He stretched out his arms. "Check me for a wire if you want."

Lori waved him off. "Mr. Doe, I'm sorry. But I don't see the point—"

"Don't make a decision yet," he broke in. "Wait until you talk to our people at Sentinel."

"You already *have* people here?"

"I *told* you, doctor, we're well placed. Do you have something to write on?"

Lori nodded and pulled a pen and pad from the pocket of her lab coat.

"Write down this number," he said. "Two-forty-nine, dot fifteen, dot twenty-four, dot one-twenty-five." Lori wrote the number in her pad. "Is this a phone number?"

"It's an IP address. Internet Protocol. Type it into your Web browser at exactly seven o'clock this evening. Enter the user name *Servant*. Your password will be *Goshen*. You will be admitted to a chat room. There you will meet people who can answer your questions about the Circle."

Lori shook her head. "I don't know anything about chat rooms."

"Don't worry about it," he said. "None of them do either. It's just a convenient way to communicate."

"What about you? Can't you answer more of my questions?"

The man looked at his watch. "No time. This is the first, last, and only time you'll ever hear from me. I don't live in the Dallas area, so don't try to track me down. I flew in this morning and I'll be gone before afternoon happy hour."

"Just how big a network do you have?" Lori asked.

"Visit the chat room, Dr. Westlake. Your questions will be answered there." The man turned and began walking up a ramp leading away from the pond.

"By the way," he said, stopping and turning again to face Lori, "the chat room will only be open from seven to eight. If you don't log in, the server will be disabled and you'll never hear from us again." He shrugged and held out his hands. "Security." Then he turned and disappeared around the corner.

———

Pam had been driving for nearly an hour and a half. In that time, Charles had watched the concrete and glass of the Dallas-Fort Worth metroplex gradually morph into the rolling hills and piney woods of East Texas. As they traveled, the roads withered from the broad, fast-paced I-20 to a bumpy, pothole-filled, dangerously curvy county road just outside of Longview. As Pam drove the van to the crest of a hill, Charles noticed a small, plain white building with old clapboard siding, built as a perfect square. The building was the focal point of a tiny private cemetery. A sign over the cemetery's gate read Franklin Heights Cemetery.

Pretty place, thought Charles. *Kind of place I'd like to be buried in.*

The little cemetery overlooked hundreds of acres of trees and pasture. Judging by the number of headstones, Charles guessed that there couldn't have been more than a hundred graves in the little place.

Pam drove her van through the front gate, pulled up to the old chapel, and parked. She got out and walked around to open the door for Charles. "Here we are," she said. "I hope the drive didn't tire you out too much."

"Not at all," he said, putting on a brave face. Even if he were on the verge of collapse, he wouldn't tell Pam. She needed to talk. And he felt so guilty about what had happened earlier, he was determined to let her say whatever she needed to say.

"It's over there," Pam said, pointing toward a small cluster of granite headstones about fifty yards away. She held out her arm to escort Charles. A month earlier, he would have rejected such an offer of help as demeaning.

He took her arm.

They approached a small marker made of polished black granite. A photograph of a handsome young man who bore a striking resemblance to Pam was embedded in the stone. The name on the marker was Jonathan Keller. Born November 21, 1970. Died April 17, 1992.

"Jonathan was my younger brother," Pam said.

"He looks a lot like you," said Charles.

Pam nodded. "Sometimes brothers and sisters fight when they're growing up. Jonathan and I weren't like that. I can't remember us ever having a disagreement."

She laid a white carnation in front of the headstone.

"What happened to him?"

"What happens to too many teenage boys. He had a car that was too fast and he couldn't resist a challenge to race."

"He was killed in an auto accident?" asked Charles.

Pam shook her head. "No, but he wished he had been. He was street racing one evening and a little girl came out of nowhere and walked in front of him. He swerved to miss her, lost control, and hit a tree." She paused for a moment, fighting back tears.

"After the accident, the doctors said that he'd never walk again. When they told him he was paralyzed, he didn't get angry, didn't shout. Didn't even cry. He just shut down. He was like a candle that someone had just snuffed out. He was still there, but all the light was gone."

A tear pushed its way out of Pam's eye and traced its way down her cheek. She didn't try to wipe it away.

"We tried everything to encourage him. Counseling. Support groups. Getting angry with him. Anything. He just wouldn't respond." She dropped her head. "Not even to me."

Charles broke in, "Pam, I—"

Before he could finish his sentence, Pam took a deep breath and let it out with a sob. "I came home one day and found him in his wheel-chair. He'd gotten one of my father's handguns out." She buried her face in her hands as another sob escaped.

"Pam, you don't have to do this."

She looked down at the headstone and wrapped her arms around herself. Her voice was barely more than a whisper. "He was so cold when I touched him."

She turned to face Charles. She seemed to have aged a lifetime in those few moments. Her haunted expression exposed raw grief, undi-minished after sixteen years.

"I'm sorry, Pam." Charles couldn't think of anything else to say.

She took both of his hands in hers. Her hands were cold and Charles could feel them trembling. "I can't go through that again. Promise you won't make me."

He felt like he'd been sucker-punched. For a moment he couldn't answer. He'd expected a lecture on the evils of suicide, not an object lesson about its effects on the survivors.

"Pam, you're asking too much. You have no idea what I'm going to have to go through."

"Neither do you," she said.

He nodded and turned away, looking back up the hill at the other graves. "You got that right." Still looking up the hill, he said, "I can't promise anything."

"Just take it one day at a time. That's all I'm asking."

"I'm tired," said Charles. "Maybe you'd better get me home."

SEVENTEEN

At five minutes past noon, Quinn sat at his office desk with his laptop computer open before him. He was the first person to log in to the chat room, as was expected. The Circle member who called an emergency meeting was required to be present before anyone else and to act as a moderator.

He would have preferred to set up his laptop in Sentinel's atrium and enjoy the beautiful autumn day as it unfolded. His laptop was wi-fi equipped and the atrium was well supplied with hot spots where he could get online.

Unfortunately Circle meetings could not take place on a wireless Internet connection. The possibility that the signal could be intercepted was too great. And then, of course, there would be the problem of explaining what he was chatting about to any friends who happened by. Thus, for the duration of all Circle chats, Quinn remained tied down to an old-fashioned cable.

His laptop beeped and a text line appeared at the bottom of the screen.

Malachi has entered.

In quick succession, both Zoë and Copper logged in.

Malachi: Your meeting, Quinn.

Quinn: WC all.

Malachi: In English, please.

Quinn: Sorry. Welcome, everyone. In reference to case #11034. As you all know by now, the patient expired early this morning.

Copper: We know.

Zoë: What's the purpose of this meeting? Certainly not to tell us something we already know.

Quinn: I want to be sure that nobody violated protocol.

Zoë: What are you saying?

Quinn: We decided not to intervene in this case but the subject is dead. Is this an unfortunate coincidence?

Zoë: I think it's a blessed coincidence. The poor man isn't suffering anymore.

Quinn: But did you help him, Zoë? You weren't pleased with the decision.

Copper: That's not fair, Quinn.

Zoë: I resent that.

Quinn: I haven't seen an explanation yet.

Zoë: For what?

Quinn: For how or why the subject died.

Zoë: And you won't. At least not from me. I had nothing to do with it.

Malachi: Quinn, your questions are out of line. Every member has made a commitment to abide by the group's decisions. It's the only way we can function.

Quinn: Commitments can be broken.

Malachi: No one here would do that.

Quinn: Don't you think it's a strange coincidence
that someone for whom intervention was requested
turned up dead the same night?

Copper: It happens, Quinn. People die for all sorts of
reasons. You know that.

Quinn: I need assurance that none of us is freelancing.
If we can't trust each other, the Circle is doomed.

Copper: For what it's worth, I am not freelancing.

Zoë: Whether you believe me or not, I had nothing to
do with the patient's death.

Malachi: Nor did I. Is that sufficient?

Quinn: I suppose I'll have to live with it.

Zoë: What about you, Quinn? How do we know that
you didn't slip in and do the job, and now you're trying
to cover your tracks?

Quinn: Don't be absurd.

Malachi: We could spend the day arguing about this. It
boils down to trust. We must trust one another. It's the
only way our work can proceed.

Copper: Regarding work proceeding, a new member
is being recruited. We're scheduled to meet tonight to
answer her questions.

Zoë: Is that wise? So soon after the subject's death?

Quinn: You said there was nothing unusual about his
death. Care to change your story?

Malachi: Enough bickering. Log back on at seven
sharp. Like it or not, we have a recruit to interview.

Quinn: CYA.

Quinn's laptop beeped as Zoë, Copper, and then Malachi left
the chat room. He knew the identity of the recruit. She would be a
welcome addition to the Circle of Peace.

Lori sat at her office desk, trying to wrap up her paperwork for the day. Several patients' folders lay on her desktop. She opened one and flipped through its pages, looking at the forms but not seeing the words.

Her digital desk clock read 4:10 PM. Still about three hours until she could log in to the Circle of Peace chat room and learn what this group was all about.

Her mind raced with questions and possibilities.

What was the Circle of Peace? A government sting operation? A fellowship of people who shared her views on euthanasia and were willing to risk everything to put those views into practice?

What about Kate? Had her sister stumbled onto the Circle's activities? If so, should she help her penetrate the group?

The problem was, Lori wasn't certain that she *wanted* to help Kate investigate the Circle of Peace. If they really were trying to put their beliefs into practice, she gave them credit for their courage. She wasn't sure she was ready to cross the line and join them, but she wouldn't necessarily want to see them stopped.

She flipped the folder closed and rubbed her eyes, trying to drive off the headache that had begun pounding her forehead.

One thing was certain. If she *were* to join the Circle, or even protect them, Kate wouldn't like it.

Lori loved her sister, but for most of their lives they had been polar opposites on almost everything. If Kate said black, Lori said white, and vice-versa. Kate was a homebody; Lori liked to socialize. Kate liked vanilla ice cream; Lori had a passion for rocky road. Kate was overweight; Lori kept herself trim. Kate had never married; Lori had been married—and divorced. Kate abhorred the idea of euthanasia and physician-assisted suicide; Lori would practice both if they were legal.

Lori shook her head and stacked the file folders on her desk. She knew there was no use trying to do any more work today.

She wouldn't be able to concentrate on anything until after she met with the Circle of Peace.

EIGHTEEN

Comfortably dressed in an oversized sweat suit, Lori took a sip of coffee and sat down in front of her computer. She glanced at her watch for what must have been the fiftieth time in the last ten minutes. It was still 6:55 PM. Five minutes until the chat room opened, and she still was carrying on an internal debate about what to do.

Common sense told her that she should run—not walk—away from this so-called opportunity. She was just asking for trouble if she got involved. Yet if these people were legitimate, if they really were trying to do the *right* thing, as opposed to the *legal* thing, she could miss out on a once-in-a-lifetime chance to be part of something important. This could be a step toward changing society. People who changed the world had to be risk-takers.

Lori desperately wanted to choose the risk.

Her digital watch chirped. Seven o'clock.

She opened her notepad and looked at the numbers she had written down. Carefully, she keyed them into her Web browser's location bar.

249.15.24.125.

She hit the *Enter* key.

The screen went blank.

Lori waited for what seemed an eternity. She began to fear that the computer had locked when a small window popped up on her screen.

User name?

Lori entered the word *Servant*.

The screen went blank again. Then another prompt appeared.

Password?

Lori typed in her password: *Goshen*.

The screen went blank again.

Lori reflexively looked at her watch. Four minutes after seven. The screen was still blank.

She grabbed her coffee cup, just so that her hands would have something to hold while she waited.

Her watch now read 7:06.

Why was it taking so long?

A tiny "lock" icon appeared at the bottom of her Web browser. Lori was not a particularly savvy Web surfer, but she knew that this meant she had entered a secure site. Finally, a window opened and flashed a warning.

"While you are in this chat room, please do not identify yourself by name. Use code names only. Failure to do so will result in immediate dismissal from the chat room."

When the warning disappeared, four names appeared at the bottom of the chat room window: Malachi, Quinn, Zoë, and Copper.

Almost immediately, a greeting popped up. It was from Malachi.

Malachi: Hello, Servant. Welcome to our Circle.

———

After being dropped off by Pam Bachman, Charles spent the rest of the afternoon sleeping. Fatigue had invaded his body like a cancer, sapping all his strength. Now as he sat on the edge of his bed, willing his legs to cooperate, he began to wonder how much more time he might actually have.

Before he had much opportunity to muse on his own mortality, his new roommate entered the bedroom and sat down at his feet. The scruffy cat looked up at him and meowed—loudly.

"What do *you* want?"

The cat rubbed up against his feet, purring.

"Yeah, yeah. You want food. Well don't expect *me* to get it for you. It's every man for himself around here." Charles looked at his hands. They had curled up like claws again while he slept and now lay limp in his lap. "Look at these things. I'm going to have a tough enough time getting food for myself, let alone *you*. Well, here goes nothing."

He put one hand on his bedside table to steady himself and rose carefully to his feet. Immediately he knew that standing up had not been a good idea. Before he could even take a step, his knees buckled and he tumbled forward. He tried to catch himself but his withered hands would not cooperate.

His forehead cracked against the floor and all went black.

Lori felt a chill run down her spine as she read Malachi's greeting. She already knew that she was about to take a step that would have far-reaching consequences, but seeing the word *welcome* drove home the magnitude of her actions. Part of her wanted to jerk the computer's plug from the wall and get away; another part couldn't resist the allure of the Circle and the need to know more, if for no other reason than to learn if they were the mercy killers Kate was investigating.

Lori noticed that her palms had suddenly become sweaty. She wiped them on her sweat pants and typed in a reply.

> Servant: Hello.

> Quinn: We're glad you decided to join us.

Lori keyed a response.

> Servant: I'm not sure that I'm joining you yet. I'm just investigating.

> Zoë: That's what we're here for, to answer your questions.

> Malachi: Nevertheless, we can't take unnecessary risks. Until we're sure of your commitment, we must address your questions with generalities.

> Quinn: What are your questions, Servant?

> Servant: What is the Circle of Peace all about?

Copper: We're about helping people.

Quinn: We charge no fees.

Zoë: Everything's voluntary.

Malachi: We assist no one without their express consent.

Quinn: Or if they are incapacitated, that of their family.

Copper: They must seek us. We do not seek them.

Lori broke in to their sales pitch.

Servant: How do they find out about you?

Malachi: As with any specialist.

Quinn: Physician referrals.

Servant: Then you're all MDs?

Malachi: Not necessarily.

Zoë: Our network includes concerned individuals of all sorts.

Servant: How do you conduct business?

Quinn: Same as now, through a secure chat room.

Servant: Internet addresses can be traced.

Copper: We change servers and IP addresses every two weeks.

Malachi: And there are other means of communication that we will not go into here.

Servant: How'd you find out about me? Why invite me to join?

Copper: You haven't hid your views, so finding you was easy.

Malachi: We invited you to join because we're always looking for like-minded individuals to help us expand our network.

Servant: So what are you asking me to do?

Quinn: That should be obvious. We want you to join us.

Servant: I believe in what you're doing but I'm not certain I'm ready to cross that line.

Quinn: We're not asking you to.

Zoë: Not yet.

Copper: New members are asked merely to be in referral network.

Malachi: When you find a case you think merits our services, you recommend the person to us.

Zoë: Then we evaluate it and decide whether to take action.

Quinn: If we decide to intervene, we contact the patient directly.

Servant: So I don't actually have to assist with your interventions?

Malachi: Not exactly.

Quinn: To become a member of the Circle, you are required to assist with one case.

Servant: You said I wouldn't have to.

Copper: You don't have to perform the service, only assist.

Zoë: It puts you in a position to lose as much as we do.

Malachi: If we go down, you go down.

Quinn: It's called "mutually assured destruction."

Servant: Who would my case be?

Malachi: We cannot discuss that here.

Quinn: You'd be notified by some other method.

Servant: What method?

Malachi: You'll know when we contact you.

Servant: And if I choose not to participate?

Zoë: Your involvement with the Circle is terminated.

Quinn: Permanently.

Malachi: No chance to change your mind. And you will not be contacted again.

Lori looked at her watch. The display read 7:13 PM. She entered another question.

Servant: And I would not be required to assist after that?

Malachi: At first, all we need from you are referrals. Eventually you would be free to expand your involvement, if you so chose.

Servant: How do I refer people?

Zoë: You learn that after you commit.

Servant: So no trial period? No window of opportunity to change my mind?

Malachi: This is your window of opportunity . . . right now.

Copper: You know what we stand for. John Doe told you. Either you believe in what we're doing or you don't.

Malachi: You're in or out. If you're on the bubble, we don't want you.

Zoë: One minute.

One minute is not enough time to weigh the possible consequences of a life-changing decision, Lori thought. But these people were putting into practice an ideal she had only talked about, only wished for. They were giving people control over the final moments of their lives, putting the decision back where it belonged, in the hands of the people who were dying. Lori believed in this. She wanted this.

Quinn: Time's up.

Malachi: What's your decision, Servant?

Zoë: In or out?

Lori took a deep breath and typed:

In.

———

Charles awoke with a splitting headache. But he hardly noticed the headache because every muscle in his body was screaming in pain. He blinked and tried to turn his head to survey his surroundings, but moving didn't seem to be a good option at the moment. Instead he flicked his eyes back and forth. The barren decor and antiseptic smell told him all he needed to know. He was in a hospital room; there was no doubt about that. He moved his fingers around, trying to feel for a call button. But his arms felt like they were made of lead. As he strained to lift his arms, he heard a voice off to his left.

"Need some help?"

Charles smiled. "Hi, David."

David Bachman stood up from the chair where he'd been sitting and came over to the side of the bed.

"You owe me one. Big time," he said.

Charles gave him a weak smile. "You the one that found me?"

"Pam was worried about you. Seemed to have this crazy idea you might do yourself in. She called and asked me to check on you after I got off work. Found you on your face in a puddle of blood. For a second, I thought I was too late. Then I realized you couldn't have eaten a bullet."

"Why not?" Charles asked.

"Pam swiped the gun after she brought you home. You were so tired, you didn't notice."

"So where did all the blood come from?" Charles asked.

"You had a pretty nice gash on your forehead. And you know how head wounds bleed."

Charles reached up and felt his forehead. Even through the bandage his touch shot sparks of pain through his head. He winced and then said with a small laugh, "Should I press burglary charges against your wife, Detective Bachman?"

"I think a slap on the wrist will be enough this time," David replied. "I'm pretty sure she won't become a career thief. Assuming you don't buy any more weapons, that is. If you do, she'll probably sneak in and carry those off, too."

"I didn't know about her brother," Charles said.

"She doesn't talk about him much. It's one of those situations where she functions well ninety-nine percent of the time but certain things will set her off."

"Like people contemplating suicide?"

"Exactly."

A bitter expression clouded Charles's face. "And so I'm expected to press on with a brave face and fight ALS with all I've got, because if I decide to check out early it's going to traumatize your wife."

David looked away. Charles knew he'd struck a nerve as he watched David's jaw muscles working. He was sorry, but he really didn't feel like being a "good patient." And he didn't like people telling him what to do with what little life he had left. He knew it would be like rubbing salt in an open wound, but he decided to push further.

"What if I don't want to fight this thing? What if I want to quit?"

A voice, sounding breathless and winded, came from the door. "Then you're giving up too easily."

Charles turned his head slowly toward the door, where a man in a motorized wheelchair was sitting. The man looked frail and emaciated, yet his eyes were bright. But it was his winsome smile that intrigued Charles.

"May I—come in?"

When the man spoke, he delivered his words slowly and deliberately, as if he had to concentrate on every word. His speech was slurred slightly, but Charles had no difficulty understanding him.

Charles gave a nod. "Please."

The man slowly lifted his hand over a joystick control in the wheelchair's armrest and the chair surged forward into the room.

David adjusted the controls on the bed and raised Charles up to a seated position. He patted him on the shoulder. "I need to take off, partner. Got some work I need to do."

After David left, the man guided his chair over to Charles's bed and held out a claw-like hand. "My name is—" he paused to take a breath, "Kenton McCarthy."

Charles took it. "I'm Charles Hamisch. What can I do for you?"

"I'm a PALS."

"A what?"

"Person with ALS. It's the ALS support group."

"I see. And how did you find out about me?"

"Pam Bachman called me."

Great. As if I weren't depressed enough already. She has to send me previews of coming attractions. Thanks a lot, Pam.

"Look, Mr. McCarthy, I appreciate you taking the time to come here and encourage me. I really do. But I'm not looking to get involved in a support group."

"That's okay." Kenton paused again to catch his breath. "I'm not here—to sign you up."

Charles's brow furrowed. "Then why are you here?"

"Mrs. Bachman said—you were thinking—about hurting yourself."

Charles turned his head away and looked out the window. "So? What if I do want to hurt myself? I'm not afraid of death. I worked as a cop for twenty-seven years. I faced the possibility of death every day. I never shrank from it. If God wants to take me, then he can take me quickly. I prefer a quick exit to wasting away like—"

"Like me?"

The question caught Charles off guard. He felt his face flush. He turned back toward the man in the wheelchair. "That's not what I meant." His voice was soft, the defiance gone. "How do you manage? How do you keep going? It must be awful just sitting around waiting to die."

"Who said—I'm just waiting to die?"

Charles rolled his eyes. "I did it again, didn't I? Okay, I don't mean it that way. But, look. You can't work. You can't take care of yourself. What do you do to feel useful?"

A twinkle came into Kenton's eyes. "I'm a pastor."

"You mean you *used* to be a pastor."

"No, I *am* a pastor."

"You're still working? How?"

Kenton smiled broadly. "I can't keep up—the same routine—as before ALS." He stopped to cough. The coughing fit lasted an uncomfortably long time. "And I get tired easily." He stopped again and drew a breath. "But I do—what I can."

"Do you still preach?"

Kenton shook his head. "It would take—too long—too much energy." Then he grinned. "My congregation thought—I was long-winded—*before* I got ALS."

Charles laughed. "So what do you do?"

"I visit." Kenton paused. "I listen." Another pause. "And I pray."

"How do you get around?" Charles asked. "You can't drive anymore, can you?"

"My wife—takes me."

Charles looked in amazement at the shrunken form before him. Kenton's wheelchair almost appeared to be swallowing him. Yet this withered man continued to stay active, seemingly undaunted by the horrors of ALS.

"Aren't you afraid?" asked Charles.

"Sometimes," Kenton admitted. "But then I remember—I'm not alone."

"What do you mean?"

Kenton closed his eyes. Then he took a deep breath and said, "Yea, though I—walk through the valley—" He stopped, winded and breathless.

Charles finished for him, "—of the shadow of death, I will fear no evil: for thou art with me." He thought that at that moment Kenton's face simultaneously revealed deep weariness and great strength.

"Every day—is a gift," Kenton said. "May I—pray for you?"

Charles nodded.

A new instruction flashed onto Lori's screen.

> Your permanent code name is Servant. Password is Goshen. You have fifteen seconds to memorize this information. Do NOT write it down.

A digital countdown timer appeared on the screen and worked its way down from fifteen to zero. When the counter reached zero, the screen went blank for a moment before another window opened.

> In a few days you will receive a prepaid cell phone. It is the property of the Circle and will be your primary link. Keep it charged and in your possession at all times. When a meeting is called, you will receive a text message with the IP address for the chat room. Use this phone for nothing other than Circle business.

Lori scarcely had time to read the notice when the window closed and was replaced by another.

> Welcome to the Circle of Peace. You are now a member of the Outer Circle. Your dealings with Inner Circle members must always be anonymous. Use only the IP address in contacting the Inner Circle. Do NOT attempt to make contact in any other way. Do NOT attempt to discover the identities of other members. After a probationary period, you will be admitted to the Inner Circle. Then you will be permitted to know who your fellow Circle members are. This is for your protection as well as ours.

> Soon you will receive notification about the case in which you will assist. Memorize and destroy any correspondence you receive related to the case.

The screen disappeared and a final window opened:

> We applaud your courage. You are doing the right thing.

"I hope so," Lori said to herself.
The monitor went dark.

NINETEEN

Need drove him.

And every day his need grew.

The Angel had tried to dissipate the tension by beginning his work among the homeless. He had to admit there was satisfaction in ending the suffering of society's off-scourings, but he hated being forced to lurk along back alleys, enduring the smell of rotting garbage, the stench of waste and vomit, and the reek of humans who were rubbish themselves.

He wasn't certain when the change began—when the desire to show mercy had become a need, a compulsion. But it seemed that every killing merely poured gasoline on a burning fire within him.

And when his unfulfilled hunger became insatiable, he would liberate someone. Carefully. It must always be done carefully.

The Angel wanted to make sure he had a long career.

———

Now that Charles was in Kenton McCarthy's capable hands, David Bachman decided to take the rest of the afternoon to do a little investigating on his own time. He sat at a table in the police department's property room with fifteen case files in front of him. The ceramic angel found with the body of Eddie Shoemate lay on the table in an evidence bag.

He took the top folder and flipped open the cover. The file contained the reports and data about a case he had worked on several months earlier: a homeless man found dead in an abandoned warehouse. He remembered the case because it turned out that the victim, Arthur Thompson Harris, had once been a prominent Texas politician. After a scandalous fall from power, Harris had dropped off the map. For years, no one had had a clue where he was.

When Harris's body was discovered inside an abandoned warehouse, David and Charles had been called to the scene. To all appearances, the death was just another homeless druggie who had OD'd on heroin. David hadn't thought much about the ceramic angel found on a makeshift table next to the body. He remembered hoping that the little guardian angel reflected the deceased man's genuine, though probably weak, faith. Perhaps somewhere in the man's past he had found faith in Christ; maybe he had been struggling to come back to God.

That was what David had hoped, not what he'd expected.

When the coroner ruled that Harris's death was an accidental heroin overdose, David had closed the case and forgotten about the little angel. Then he found an identical angel near the body of Eddie Shoemate, another apparent overdose, another man fallen from grace.

Now he sat with the case files for every suspicious death that had occurred among Dallas's homeless in the past two years. In those fifteen files, he hoped he might find something that would either put his mind at ease or confirm his worst fear.

It could simply be a coincidence. Maybe one of the downtown missions had given out angels for Christmas or as prayer reminders. However, if more angels had been found near the deceased, probably nobody had made a connection between the cases because nothing seemed unusual about the deaths.

David had asked the medical examiner's office for a detailed tox screen on Shoemate. Depending on what they found, he hoped to convince his superiors to reopen the Harris case and maybe exhume the body in hopes of finding something. So far, no results had come in from the medical examiner's office, and the powers that be were less than enthusiastic about reopening an old case. They would not risk panicking the public by suggesting to anyone that a serial killer might be at large. Since Arthur Harris's family remained prominent and powerful, David didn't have much chance of getting cooperation at headquarters.

The Angel looked at his watch and then gazed through the plate glass window of a small storefront. The late afternoon sun sent orange-gold beams through the buildings of Dallas's downtown canyon. Gargantuan neighboring high-rises kept his tiny emporium in the shadows.

It was a simple place. A slightly faded sign out front invited all who needed help to come inside and get their lives back on track. Inside, the approximately three hundred square feet of space, leased in the name of the Dallas Free Counseling Clinic, was sparsely furnished. A few folding tables lined the back wall and about twenty metal folding chairs were arranged in a semicircle. The tables and chairs, purchased at a church rummage sale, were covered with nicks and paint splatters. Posters advocating a drug-free and alcohol-free life covered the walls.

A drip coffeemaker spewed out steam and made irritating slurping sounds as it finished brewing a pot of strong coffee. Three dozen fresh Krispy Kreme doughnuts sat invitingly in a box beside the coffeemaker.

The Angel detested coffee and had never allowed himself the frivolous luxury of eating doughnuts. He wanted to remain healthy and fit. Caffeine, sugar, and fat worked against his goals. The refreshments were for his patients.

The goodies offered varied, depending on the time of year. On cool spring or fall days, he provided coffee and doughnuts. In bitter winter weather, he added hot chocolate to the menu. Dallas's summer inferno warranted lemonade, soda, Gatorade, and sometimes sandwiches.

The Angel opened his clinic twice a week: Saturday afternoons and Wednesday evenings. Word of the free snacks spread quickly through the homeless community, and within a week of opening he had a regular clientele. They knew him only as Doc. No first name; no last. He hung no degrees or certifications on the wall, and for all his patients knew or cared, his doctorate was in mechanical engineering.

His patients asked no questions. They were grateful for help.

The Angel asked a *lot* of questions.

They would be arriving soon, and his search would begin anew.

David closed the cover of the last folder and rubbed his eyes. His review of the files had led him to four other cases over the past two years. All in Dallas. All homeless men. All apparently natural or accidental deaths. All found with ceramic angels watching over them. Each case was slightly different but the ceramic angel was a common thread.

On a frigid January morning almost two years ago, a homeless man named Willis Crawford had been found under a bridge, apparently frozen to death. A list of items found with the corpse included one small ceramic angel.

Then for five months, nothing.

In June there was another angelic visit. Trash collectors found the body of Jefferic Emory in an alley, overdosed on crack cocaine. This time the medical examiner found an angel in the corpse's right trouser pocket.

Last Christmas Eve, another angel had witnessed the death of Ramón Caldera. A Catholic priest found Caldera in some bushes behind a nativity scene outside the church. Caldera had apparently drunk himself to death. A paper bag containing an empty bottle of whiskey and a ceramic angel was found beside the body.

Three months later, Odell Taylor and another angel turned up on a park bench near White Rock Lake on a beautiful March morning. Discovered by joggers, Taylor's death appeared to be from heart failure. Investigators found Odell's angel when they sorted through the contents of his shopping cart. The tiny angel lay buried among the flotsam and jetsam of his shipwrecked life.

Electric utility workers found Arthur Harris on a blistering June day. His body had been in an abandoned warehouse on Industrial Boulevard for nearly two weeks before the odor of decomposition drew attention.

David remembered well his arrival on the scene. In fact, he doubted that he would ever forget it. Nausea had swept over him like an avalanche when he stepped inside the ovenlike building. Never before had David tossed his lunch on a DB call. There was a first time for everything.

Another reason David would never forget the day they found Arthur Harris was that it was the last case he had worked with Charles. The next day, Charles had received his diagnosis of ALS and was taken off the streets.

Now it was October. Charles had retired on disability. And the latest victim—Eddie Shoemate—had just joined the party. As with the others, Shoemate's angel was among his personal belongings. Also, as with the others, his death appeared to be from natural causes. Or at least as natural as a street person's death could be.

Six dead homeless men. Six angels.

Four of the angels had long ago been thrown away or returned to family members with personal effects of the deceased. And there didn't appear to be any other tangible evidence linking the cases. Only the angels.

With each victim, there were no witnesses or fingerprints. There was no useful trace or DNA evidence. Nothing here would convince a prosecutor to file charges, even if there was someone to file charges *against*. Nothing helped David connect the cases.

Or was there?

On the surface, one might expect that a killer would choose to victimize the homeless because they were largely nonpersons in the eyes of the world. Invisible, anonymous creatures that nobody cared about. Without clear evidence of a homicide, the cases would quickly be closed and the victims forgotten.

But every "angel" victim had been successful in life before hitting the skids. There were no career criminals or lifelong bums among the victims.

Arthur Harris: once a politically connected investment banker.

Eddie Shoemate: professional CEO.

Ramón Caldera: former major league ballplayer.

Odell Taylor: powerful corporate attorney.

These were not victims who would be totally forgotten.

And then there were the angels.

David knew that some serial killers included a "signature" in their murders—something that somehow fulfilled a private need in the killer's mind.

It might involve staging the scene, posing the victim, or some type of mutilation. David would be willing to bet his next month's salary that the ceramic angels were the killer's signature.

They might also be the killer's downfall.

━━━

The Angel surveyed the ragtag group of men sitting in a semicircle on rickety folding chairs. Some held foam cups filled with scorching

hot coffee. All were munching on doughnuts. They had come for their
weekly therapy session with Doc. Most of the men who came through
the door were not serious about rehabilitation. This was a good place
to kill an hour and get some free food.

Only six had shown up today, but that was how it went sometimes. One day the attendance would be standing room only, the next
time it would be slim pickings. Still, each week the Angel conducted
his "therapy" sessions with the homeless men, hoping that somewhere
amid the mass of human refuse he might find at least one man he
could cultivate, one who might prove worthy.

Things did not look promising today. Most of these men were
regulars, already eliminated from consideration.

Devouring his fourth or fifth doughnut, sat Jones. Doughnut
crumbles and glazing littered his unkempt beard but he didn't appear
to notice or care. A short, skinny black man who weighed maybe
110 pounds dripping wet, Jones never said much. But he came every
week, perched himself on the edge of a chair and ate one doughnut
after another, chased by an occasional sip of coffee. Every so often
he'd nod, smile a toothless grin, and add an "uh huh" or an "amen"
to the general discussion. Judging by his uneven, graying Afro and
virtually white beard, the Angel guessed that Jones was in his early
sixties. Other than that, the man was an enigma, largely because of
his relationship to the giant who sat beside him.

As if on cue, Jones broke off half of his doughnut and handed it
to Griffin. That wasn't his real name, as far as the Angel could tell.
As of yet, the Angel had not gotten a word out of him. At six-four and
about three hundred pounds—most of it muscle—Griffin looked like
he could play offensive line for any NFL team. But Griffin was one
of a legion of people who were homeless because of untreated organic
mental illness. He never accepted any of the Angel's gifts unless they
came through Jones. No coffee. No doughnuts. No Gatorade. Nothing. Somehow, he and Jones had worked out a symbiotic relationship
in the hazardous world of street people. Jones looked after Griffin
and in return Griffin protected the little man from the dangers of
the street. You never saw one without the other. Also, you didn't act
aggressively or unkindly toward Jones without risking serious bodily
harm. For that reason alone, the Angel had removed both Jones and
Griffin from his "A" list.

Several chairs away from Jones and Griffin, Jesse sat shivering with his arms wrapped around himself. He had only come a few times but the Angel had already diagnosed him as an incurable heroin addict. Jesse was, perhaps, in his early twenties. Brittle blond hair with the consistency of straw framed his long, haggard face. He had blue eyes rimmed by weepy red lids and accented by dark rings, and a constantly dripping nose. Looking into Jesse's eyes was like peering into a deep cavern, a haunted, hollow emptiness.

One chair over from Jesse, looking bored, sat Spencer, a handsome black man in his mid-thirties. Spencer claimed to be diabetic so he usually skipped the doughnuts and drank his coffee black. Of course, that all depended on the day. Some days he gobbled everything in sight—including the little sugar packets. Spencer's tale was simple. He had been in and out of jail and prison since he was eleven. Didn't finish school. Didn't want to. His current stint on the street was a brief interlude between prison sentences.

The one other regular was Javiér, a tough Hispanic man in his early twenties. Javiér was from El Paso and had been on the streets ever since being caught stealing from his employer several years earlier. He'd skipped town before his trial. He was hoping to hook up with a local gang but had not yet made the right connections.

The only newcomer for the day introduced himself as Toby. Unkempt black hair streaked with gray hung down across his field of vision, obscuring world-weary eyes. An old scar traced its way from his upper lip across his right cheek and behind his ear. Toby's hands shook with Parkinson's-like tremors. He could only fill his coffee cup half full without spilling it everywhere.

"I'm glad you all came today," said the Angel. "Those of you who have been here before already know me."

"Um-hum. Tha's right," Jones chimed in, nodding and grinning.

The Angel smiled at Jones and nodded toward the newcomer. "Everybody around here just calls me Doc. We're just here to discuss whatever you want—or need—to talk about. Let me toss out a question just to get us started. Why are you living on the street?"

"Can't get no job," Spencer said. "Don't want one neither."

"You got that right, *hermano*," Javiér added. "They just rip you off anyway. Chew you up and spit you out."

"Who's that?" asked the Angel.

"The Man," Javiér answered. "You know what they're like, Doc. You been around."

The Angel nodded. "I have indeed, Javiér."

A soft voice broke in. "I screwed up."

The Angel looked toward Toby. He was looking at the floor, his hands—still shaking—resting on his knees.

"I'm sorry," said the Angel. "I didn't catch that."

Toby peered at the Angel through his salt-and-pepper hair. "I said, I screwed up. Got no one to blame but myself."

"What happened?"

Toby shrugged. "I had everything going my way. Gorgeous wife. Three beautiful kids. Great job in the IT industry. American dream, you know?"

The Angel nodded sympathetically.

Toby pushed his hair out of his eyes. "Started innocently enough. Parties. Social events." Toby paused.

Spencer tried to finish for him. "Drinking?"

Toby shook his head and mumbled something that was practically inaudible.

"Dude, quit mumblin'," Spencer growled. "Can't hear a thing you're sayin'. If it weren't drinkin', what landed you on the street?"

Toby looked Spencer in the eye. His voice was clear, crisp, and emotionless. "Manslaughter."

The Angel eased back in his chair and smiled.

Things were looking up.

TWENTY

David Bachman wheeled Charles Hamisch up to his front door. "Home at last," David said. "After two days in Parkland Hospital, I bet this place looks more appealing than it used to."

Charles fingered the bandage that covered his forehead and said nothing. David noticed that Charles had been glancing from side to side as they rolled up the handicapped ramp toward his apartment. What Charles saw—or didn't see—appeared to be troubling him. The place appeared to be just as Charles had left it.

The apartment door opened before David could even get the key in the door. Pam stepped outside and quickly closed the door behind her. "I've been waiting for you two. You're late. What did you do, take a detour?"

She bent down and gave Charles a peck on the cheek, then gave David a more lingering kiss.

"All right, you two. Save the smooching for later," Charles said. "It's chilly out here."

"Chilly?" said Pam, with a wink. "I didn't notice."

"Mmmm. Something smells great," David said. "What's on tonight's menu?"

"I thought a special occasion like this deserves a special dinner. Linguine with clam sauce sound good?"

"Sounds wonderful," said David.

Pam opened the door and motioned them inside. Charles noticed that all the lights in the apartment had been turned off.

"What special occasion?" he asked. "I hardly think that getting out of the hospital after tripping and knocking myself silly qualifies as a special occasion. And why are the lights off? Did you forget to pay my electric bill?"

Pam and David smiled and exchanged knowing looks as David pushed the wheelchair over the threshold.

"Surprise!" a chorus of voices called out as Pam flipped on the lights.

Charles blinked as a series of camera flashes illuminated the room. Through spots left by the flashes, he saw that someone had decorated his living room for a party. Colored streamers hung from the light fixtures. A bright banner stretched from one end of the living room to the other. On one end was a large graphic of a magnifying glass. On the other end was a Sherlock Holmes hat and pipe. In bright red letters were the words, "Happy *Un*-Retirement, Charles!"

Charles looked around the room. Several officers who had attended his retirement party just a week earlier had managed to squeeze into his tiny apartment. "I—I don't understand," he said.

"We thought maybe your retirement was a little premature," David said.

"But the Department. . . . I can't—"

"Okay, so you *can't* work for the Department," David interrupted. "That doesn't mean you can't work. Your body doesn't work so good, but your mind's still sharp and you still have all those years of experience to draw on, right? Here's what I'm saying: At least until they give me another partner, I could use your help with my backlog of cases. And Pam's already volunteered to be your assistant."

"Look over here," said Pam, moving through the crowd of people who were pressed into Charles's living room like it was an overstuffed elevator.

The crowd parted, revealing a computer desk—wheelchair ready—and a brand new, state-of-the-art computer system with flat panel monitor. A brass nameplate had been bolted to the front of the desk. It read, "Charles Hamisch, Investigative Consultant." A bright red ribbon with a large bow in the middle had been stretched across the front of the computer desk. Beside the desk, in a wheelchair of his own, sat Kenton McCarthy. A giant pair of scissors lay in his lap.

Kenton said, "David, if you will bring—the guest of honor—over here for the ribbon cutting."

David began to push Charles toward the computer desk, but Charles put out his hand. "Wait."

A hint of worry clouded Pam's face as Charles slowly began to push himself up. It was a slow process, but finally he stood up. Still, he looked unsteady on his feet. He turned to David and said, "My cane?"

David smiled and said, "Coming right up." He retrieved the hand-carved cane from its resting place in the dinette and handed it to Charles. Charles took the cane and made several halting, tottering steps forward until he stood by Kenton's wheelchair.

"Take the scissors—my friend," said Kenton.

Charles shook his head and turned to face the crowd of friends assembled in his living room. "The reason I wound up in the hospital with *this*," he said, pointing toward the bandage on his forehead, "was because I couldn't come to grips with *this*." He held up the cane for a moment, then leaned on it again. He put his hand on Kenton McCarthy's shoulder. "But that was before I met *this* man.

"Kenton has the same disease I have. But he hasn't let it stop him. In fact, I think that he keeps a busier schedule now than I did when I was working full time."

Everyone laughed.

"Kenton is a pastor," Charles continued, "but he's also a lifesaver. If it hadn't been for him, I probably wouldn't be here. So, if anybody's going to cut this ribbon, I think it should be him."

A crooked smile spread across Kenton's face as he shook his head. "I can't—lift them."

Charles was undaunted. "At every ribbon cutting I've ever seen," he said, "more than one person has his hand on the scissors. There's someone else I need to thank. A couple of someones, actually. Pam and David, shall we do this together?"

The Bachmans smiled and came up beside the wheelchair. Pam took one of Kenton's hands and put it on one of the handles and David took the other. Together they cut the ribbon.

———

Lori sat by the bay window in her sister's kitchen, sipping cappuccino and scanning *The Dallas Morning News* classifieds for a good deal on an apartment. She had wanted to get her own place for some time, just to get away from Kate's unrelenting attempts at matchmaking, but she had kept postponing the move. As aggravating as Kate could be, Lori didn't want to hurt her feelings. And she suspected that Kate wouldn't take kindly to her moving out. But now that she had decided to explore the Circle of Peace, she felt it would be better if she moved sooner rather than later.

Even so, she was beginning to wonder if the Circle had forgotten about her.

Nearly a week had passed since she had told them that she was in, but she hadn't heard a word. Maybe they had decided that she would not make a good candidate after all, and she *never* would hear from them.

She heard the front door open and close.

"Hey, Sis," Kate said as she came into the kitchen. She handed Lori a small bubble-wrap envelope, then tossed the rest of the mail on the table. "Must be your day," she said. "Two letters and a package. Not much else, though. Just junk mail and bills."

Lori looked through the pile of junk mail and circulars and found her two letters. The first was a small brown envelope. It had been hand-addressed, and the return address was a Dallas post office box. She held the envelope gingerly, afraid to open it. She wasn't sure how she knew but she suspected it was a letter from the Circle. And the bubble-wrap envelope was probably her prepaid cell phone. She set them both aside, unopened.

The second letter concerned her even more. The postmark was from Humble, Texas, her ex-husband's last known address. Although there was no name on the return address, the handwriting was unquestionably Philip's. Her stomach turned sour just thinking about what he might have to say.

Lori heard a series of electronic beeps as Kate popped a frozen dinner in the microwave.

"So who're the letters from?" Kate asked, sitting down at the table across from Lori. She popped open a can of diet cola and took a sip.

Lori laughed it off. "Probably from patients asking to pay in chickens and sheep."

"Aren't you going to open them?"

Lori shook her head. "No, I'll look at them later. They've got to be work related. Nobody *ever* writes me letters."

"That's because your social life needs some serious help, little sister."

Lori groaned inwardly but held her tongue.

The microwave emitted a long, loud beep. Kate got up from the table and pulled out the little plastic-encased dinner tray. She tore the plastic off the top and pulled a small fork from a drawer. "Diet lasagna," she muttered. "An oxymoron if I've ever heard one."

As she came back to the table, she looked over Lori's shoulder and raised her eyebrows. "The *classifieds*? What are you doing? Trying to find a beau through the personals? That's a lousy way to get a date, Sis." She sat down across from Lori again. "You might wind up with an ax murderer or some other kind of nut. Besides, with a gorgeous guy like Drew practically begging you to go out with him, why would you want to roll the dice with the personals?"

Lori heaved a weary sigh. "First, I am *not* looking for a date. Second, I went out with Drew. He's a nice guy, but that's as far as it's going to go."

Kate looked skeptical. "Then why are you reading the classifieds? Not looking for a new job, are you?"

"If you *must* know," Lori answered, "I'm reading the apartment listings."

"Apartment listings?" Concern tinged Kate's voice.

Lori hesitated. The moment of confrontation had come unexpectedly and she wasn't sure she wanted to go through with it. "Yes," she finally answered. She reached across the table and took her sister's hand. "Kate, I love you. I'll never be able to repay you for what you've done over this last year." She paused, searching for the right words. "But it's time that I took the next step in getting back on my feet. I need my space and you need yours."

"There's plenty of room here," said Kate.

"That's not the problem," Lori answered. "I need to get on with my life, Sis. As long as I stay here, I'm going to be your little sister."

Kate didn't answer right away, which worried Lori. Usually when her sister was silent, it was because she was upset. Some long moments passed. Finally she spoke up.

"You're right," Kate said, nodding. "Well, tomorrow's Saturday, and we'll start looking together. I know some great places where—"

"Uh, Sis," Lori broke in, "that won't be necessary."

Kate was startled. "Why not? Don't you want me to help you?"

"No, no, it's not that. It's just—" She fumbled for words, trying to think of a reason why Kate couldn't help her. She grasped at the first straw that came to mind. "Drew," she said. "Drew offered to help me. And, well, you *have* been wanting me to see more of him."

A look of resignation crossed Kate's round face. "Enough said. Three is definitely a crowd." She took a bite of her lasagna and made a face. "Cold. As usual, I've been talking too much." She got up to put the dinner back in the microwave.

Lori drained her cappuccino. She could only hope that Drew would be free tomorrow. Kate would be sure to find out whether Drew really *was* helping her. "I'm going to take a shower," she said, giving Kate a kiss on the cheek and putting her mug in the sink. As she left the kitchen, she scooped up her mail, desperately fighting the urge to throw it all in the trash.

———

Pam said good-bye to the last guest, closed the door of Charles's apartment, and leaned against it. She wiped her brow with a melo-dramatic flair. "Alone at last. I thought they'd never leave." Then she looked around the apartment and said, "This place now officially qualifies as a disaster area. There's a linguini spill behind the dinette table."

"I'll clean it up," said David. "You've done enough. Go keep Charles company."

"I won't argue with you," Pam answered. She sat down on the sofa opposite Charles's recliner. He looked weary but she thought she saw something else in his eyes.

"You look sad, Charles. What's wrong?"

He started, as if awakened from a dream. "What? Oh, it's nothing important."

"Judging by your expression, that's not true. It *is* something important."

He shrugged. "I guess my little friend decided to look for greener pastures after I disappeared. I just hope a car didn't hit him."

Pam jumped to her feet. "Oh, goodness. I forgot." She dashed down the hall to Charles's bedroom. Seconds later, a scruffy, tailless—and decidedly plumper—cat scurried into the dinette and began lapping up the spilled food greedily. Pam walked up behind the cat and leaned against the kitchenette doorway.

"I shut him up in the back bedroom because he's incorrigible around food. You can't eat a thing without him getting in your face, wanting a piece of the action. He'd have mooched off people all night."

Charles's face broke into a broad grin when he saw the cat.

Pam picked up the cat and set it in his lap. Charles scratched its neck.

"Have you named him?" she asked.

He nodded, still scratching the scruffy cat's neck. "I thought of a name when I was in the hospital. His name is Columbo."

The cat jumped down from Charles's lap and went back to cleaning the dinette floor.

"Why Columbo?" asked David. He was on his knees in the dinette with a sponge in his hand, scrubbing up linguine the cat had left behind.

"He looks like the TV detective," Charles said. "Rumpled and messy."

"But lovable," Pam added. "I think it's the perfect name for an investigator's cat."

"Okay, Columbo," David said, picking up the cat and handing it to Pam. "You're getting in the way now."

Pam plopped Columbo back into Charles's lap.

"Welcome to Hamisch Consulting Services, Columbo," said Pam. "You are now officially assistant number two."

"Number two?" said Charles.

"*I'm* assistant number one," Pam said, smiling.

Lori sat on her bed and tried to open Philip's letter, but her hands were trembling. The choice of which letter to open first had not been difficult. Philip never wrote long letters. True to form, his letter was scrawled in pencil on cheap notebook paper. It was simple and to the point.

Dearest Lori,

I've been miserable for the last year. I know we've had our differences but I'd really like to work things out. I've changed.

I'd like to see you again and show you how much. Can't we try again?

Love, Philip

She shook her head, crumpled the letter into a ball, and said, "No, Philip, we can't." Tossing the letter into the wastebasket by her night-stand, she picked up the second envelope.

A cold chill swept through her and she paused, staring at the envelope for a long time. Her tongue felt like it was glued to the roof of her mouth. She took a deep breath and tore one end of the envelope. She wiped her palms on the bedspread before pulling out the single sheet of paper.

The paper felt strange. Its coarse texture was like a napkin's, but the paper itself felt stiff and brittle. She unfolded it carefully, half afraid the paper might crumble to dust in her hands.

The note, written in black marker, was succinct, to say the least. It merely read, "Case #11085. Patient: Nina Ware. You will receive instructions later. Please burn this paper after you've read it."

Lori's heart sank. She would have to assist with the death of one of her own patients. She had hoped for emotional distance—a patient she did not know and had not treated. How Nina Ware had learned about the Circle, Lori did not know, but she had evidently requested an intervention. Nina would be her "commitment" case, the event that would seal her membership in the Circle of Peace.

She walked over to her nightstand. She had already lit a scented candle, so burning the paper would not be a problem. Finding some-thing safe to burn it in *would* be a problem. They had no ashtrays and all the dishes were downstairs in the kitchen. She couldn't very well waltz down there and ask Kate for a plate so she could burn up her letter.

The best solution was probably to light the paper over the can-dle, carry it into her bathroom, and let it finish burning in the sink. She could close the door and turn on the exhaust fan. Maybe Kate wouldn't smell the smoke.

She held a corner of the paper over the candle, ready to run into the bathroom with the burning note. But instantly—before she could blink—the entire sheet ignited with a brilliant orange flare. The blind-ing light so startled her that she dropped the paper.

It vanished in a smokeless flash before it hit the floor.

TWENTY-ONE

The sun flooded the sky with a deep red-orange radiance as it scraped the horizon. The high cloud cover picked up the glow, turning the world blood red. The buildings of the downtown canyon embraced the warmth, looking as if they had been pulled red-hot from a furnace. But soon the splendor would fade and shadows lengthen. The crimson sky would cool into the stark luminescence of a full moon.

In the shadowy recesses, the Angel would make his rounds.

Even though it had only been a few weeks since he had helped Shadowman escape his unbearable life, it seemed like an eternity since he had been able to release someone.

Much too long.

The Angel had decided long ago that he must not proceed reck-lessly. Typically it took months to win a new subject's trust. To hurry was to risk failure—and exposure.

But now he knew he had to take a chance. The hunger, the need, was unbearable.

His latest subject, Toby, had been particularly difficult. Despite his case history—perfect for the Angel's purposes—Toby was dis-trustful. Trust, of course, was a core issue with most homeless men. After all, they themselves were not trusted by others. How could they be expected to give what they never received? Most of them could be won over with consistent effort: A few meals. A few counseling sessions. Occasionally some cash. The sight of a friendly face was usually so welcome that it rarely took the Angel more than a few weeks to win a man's trust.

Toby had proved to be harder. Suspicious of the Angel's motives, he had pressed repeatedly for more information. He wanted to know the Angel's background, where he worked. Why did he spend time with the homeless? What other people had he helped? The man had practically asked for references. Even Odell Taylor, who had initially peppered the Angel with questions like the top-flight attorney he had once been, had not been as tough a nut to crack as Toby.

The Angel found Toby's persistence insulting and infuriating. Nevertheless, he'd maintained control, held his tongue, and offered answers that appeared to alleviate the man's concerns.

The Angel had been tempted to abandon Toby as too difficult a case. But he could not neglect his purpose. He had come to serve people from good backgrounds who had fallen on hard times. He helped those who had led productive lives but had made some mistakes. He was called to release these unfortunates from the prison of life. Toby fit the criteria.

So, despite his being unbearably distrustful, Toby would be rescued. The Angel would see to that. It was his calling.

The sun dipped below the horizon, and as the world progressed through ever-deepening shades of purple, the Angel climbed into his Toyota to begin his search for Tobias "Toby" Hutchins.

One of the problems the Angel had faced in dealing with Toby was that Toby's distrust made him secretive about where he spent his nights. The Angel had to be careful in making inquiries; he didn't want the man to become even more suspicious.

"Some evenings, I bring sack lunches around to the men who come to my therapy sessions," the Angel had said at the end of one session. "If I know where to find you, I'd be happy to add you to the list."

Toby shook his head. "I can look out for myself. Been doin' it a long time."

The Angel nodded toward the streets. "Most of the men out there have been looking out for themselves for a long time. That doesn't stop them from accepting help when it's offered."

"I don't like charity," Toby said. "What I get, I earn."

"But you're accepting charity right now, aren't you?"

"What do you mean?"

"I don't charge anything for these counseling sessions. Isn't that accepting charity?"

"I don't look at it that way," Toby answered. "You're just giving me a leg up. A chance to sort through my problems and get back on my feet."

"What's different about accepting a little food?"

"People who give you food want to control you. They want to tell you what to do and when to do it. They want you to follow them."

The Angel nodded. He understood. "What if I gave you the sack lunch with no strings attached? You don't even have to come to therapy if you don't want to."

Toby paused, thinking about the offer. Then shook his head. "No thanks."

He walked out the door and closed it behind him.

Under his breath, the Angel uttered a soft curse.

The Toyota turned down a back alley only a few blocks north of downtown. Toby Hutchins had been difficult to locate, but not impossible. The secretive young man had not taken into account the Angel's resources. Toby might have reservations about accepting "charity," but others were not so scrupulous. It was a small matter to enlist the help of Jones and Griffin. Griffin never talked to anybody, and Jones—his guardian—was loyal beyond question. The Angel had used them before when he had needed information.

After the last session, he tucked a few dollars into Jones's pocket and asked him to follow Toby and find out where he was staying at night, what he did for food, and anything else he could learn. A few days later, the Angel had his information.

Toby had managed to jimmy the back door of an abandoned storefront and was using the place as a private apartment. Although he did not like to accept charity, he apparently had no compunction about breaking and entering. As the Angel had suspected, Toby foraged for food. He hung around the back doors of restaurants in the evening, waiting for them to toss out their garbage. Depending on the restaurant, the pickings could be quite good. For someone like Toby, who didn't want to accept handouts from food kitchens, this was a workable alternative.

The Angel stopped his car a few hundred feet from Toby's door. He turned off the engine and sat quietly for a few minutes, letting the darkness envelop him. The only sound was the quiet ticking of the car's engine as it cooled. He had scoped out this location for several nights to make certain that Toby was staying in the same place every night.

Now he had to find a way to get his special sack lunch into Toby's hands. He couldn't just knock on the door and deliver it. As skittish as the man was, that might be enough to make him run. So he'd passed a few more dollars to Jones and Griffin and had them keep an eye on Toby, make notes about his patterns. Did he have a routine? What Dumpsters did he frequent? Did he hit a particular place at a certain time of day?

A few more days passed and the Angel knew where to place the sack—and what to put in it. Toby had an affinity for fast food for his evening meal, particularly cheeseburgers and fries. And the fare was especially good at Burger Shack, a downtown eatery specializing in "homestyle" burgers and fries.

With that in mind, the Angel had made a large purchase earlier that day. Four super-size burgers and a double order of home fries. He'd opened a bottle of cherry cola and dumped out a small portion, just to make it look used. Next, he crushed several Valium tablets and dissolved them in the cola. Finally, he repackaged the offering in a small plastic garbage bag and placed it in the Dumpster on top of the other garbage.

Then the Angel went to a coffee shop across the street that afforded a clear view of the Dumpster, ordered his own supper, and waited.

It wasn't long before Toby made his rounds.

The Angel watched as the homeless man rummaged through the trash and pulled a bag from the Dumpster. The Angel had placed some masking tape on the bag to help him identify it. There was no question. Toby had taken the right bag.

Got him!

The Angel sat in the darkness.
Waiting.
Patiently waiting.

Several hours had passed since Toby Hutchins had taken the bag of goodies back to his hideaway. Assuming he had eaten the food and drunk the soda right away, he should be peacefully snoozing somewhere inside the vacant store.

The Angel fingered the small ceramic figurine on the seat beside him.

A tingle raced down his spine, which always happened just before he delivered someone.

It was time.

He stepped out of the Toyota and closed the door silently. For a few moments he stood motionless in the nearly pitch-black alley, listening. He heard paper rustling as a gust of wind blew down the alley, scattering discarded newspapers against the wall.

The Angel pulled a small flashlight from his pocket. He had taped several layers of red theatrical gelatin over the lens. The soft, red light would be difficult to notice from a distance and it would provide him with enough light to navigate in the darkness. His eyes adjusted to the red light in the darkness faster than to the brightness of a flashlight beam.

Several doors lined the back of the empty building. Most were secured with heavy padlocks. Toby's door had no padlock and stood slightly ajar. The Angel walked soundlessly to the door, keeping the flashlight low and pointed toward the ground. A rat scurried along the edge of the building, disappearing into a crack in the wall.

Taking care to not make any sound, the Angel pulled the door open. He waited. Listened. Then he stepped inside.

The air smelled musty, like a place smells when it has been shut up for a long time. He picked up a faint whiff of death in the air, too. Probably a rat or cat had died nearby.

In the dim glow of the flashlight, he discovered that he was in the store's backroom. Several large clothing racks stood against one wall, remnants of a business long extinct. Not much was left. Several dust-covered wine bottles, lying on their sides told of someone else who had used the building long ago. He directed his flashlight toward some footprints on the floor. The trail led down a short hallway and into a side room, probably an office.

The door to the office was open. He walked carefully to the door and waited, motionless, for a few moments, just listening. He heard no unusual sounds. No creaks from the wooden floor. No cats fighting. No rats scurrying. The only sound to reach his ear was that of quiet breathing and an occasional snore.

He stepped through the office door and scanned the floor with his flashlight. Near the back of the room was a huddled mass. Toby Hutchins lay on his side with one arm thrown over his head. The empty bag and hamburger wrappers were near his feet. A few fries were scattered on the floor.

"Toby," the Angel said softly.

No response.

Good. The Valium was doing its job.

He already knew that finding a vein would not be a problem. He had observed Toby's arms during therapy sessions and saw no needle scars. He removed the red gelatin from the flashlight and set the flashlight on the floor, pointing toward Toby.

"Just relax, Toby," he whispered as he pulled on some latex gloves. "I'm going to fix you up. No worries."

Pulling a tourniquet and a prepared syringe from his jacket pocket, he gently lifted Toby's arm from over his head and began to wrap the tourniquet around the bicep.

Before he could tighten it, a hand caught his wrist in a viselike grip.

He looked down to see Toby's angry eyes glaring at him.

"What are you doing?" Toby demanded.

"Shhhh. Relax," the Angel said in his most soothing tone. "I'm here to help you."

"Strange way to help someone. Sneaking in on them at night. What's in *that*?" he asked, nodding toward the syringe on the floor. He tightened his grip on the Angel's wrist and shifted around. His foot kicked the plastic bag, sending a bottle rolling across the floor. A nearly full bottle of cherry cola caught the Angel's eye as it rolled past the flashlight. A cold draft of fear swept over him.

Toby was not sedated.

The Angel kept his cool and spoke softly. "Just some medicine. To help you with your addiction."

"I don't *have* an addiction."

The Angel tried to pull his hand free but Toby jerked it back.

"You know what *I* think?" Toby said. "I think you're trying to kill me. Just like you killed my friend, Artie Harris."

"I don't know what you mean," said the Angel.

"Yes you do," growled Toby. "Don't try to lie your way out of this."

"Mr. Hutchins, your mind is playing tricks on you. You need to trust me."

Toby's eyes narrowed. He was on his feet, still gripping the Angel's wrist. "You think we're stupid, just because we're homeless; you think we don't see things."

Toby towered over the Angel. Maneuvering the Angel's hand into a painful wristlock, Toby reached into his battered green trousers with his left hand and pulled out something shiny. Seconds later a switchblade gleamed in the flashlight's dim glow.

"Artie Harris was the only one who tried to help me when I landed on the streets. He had his problems, but he was a good man. Why'd you kill him?"

Sharp spasms racked the Angel's left arm and shoulder every time Toby twisted his wrist. But he would not give this piece of human refuse the satisfaction of hearing him scream. He leaned on his free hand, grimacing in pain. Toby twisted his arm again and the Angel lurched forward. His free hand slid across the floor and his fingers brushed against the syringe.

"You're going to answer me before I kill you," Toby said. "You'll beg for mercy or I'll rip your arm off."

This time the Angel obliged. He whined, "Why are you doing this? I'm only trying to help you." His hand closed around the syringe.

Before Toby could answer, the Angel swung his free hand in a broad arc, plunging the syringe into Toby's neck. Toby howled in pain and dropped the switchblade. He stumbled backward, clutching at his neck and trying to dislodge the syringe. As he floundered, blinded by pain, his feet became tangled in the plastic trash bag and he fell to the floor. He rolled onto his stomach, yanked the syringe from his neck, and began to push himself up.

The Angel was ready for him. He landed a savage kick to Toby's midsection, dropping him back to the floor. Losing no time, he put a knee in Toby's back, seized the tourniquet, wrapped it around the man's neck, and pulled. The tourniquet—now a garrote—did its job efficiently.

When Toby's body finally relaxed, the Angel released the tourniquet and fell back against the wall. For a long time he sat on the floor of the filthy, condemned building, leaning against the wall and breathing heavily. His heart thudded against his chest. He could feel his pulse pounding inside his head.

He had never known such exhilaration before. He looked at the scene around him. He would have to clean up and get out quickly. He palmed the tourniquet and scooped up the syringe, dropping them into his jacket pocket next to the ceramic angel he had planned to leave behind.

No angel would watch over Toby Hutchins.

PART THREE
LORI

TWENTY-TWO

"I don't know how I can help you, young lady, but I'm certainly glad for the company," Ruthie Jacoby said to Katherine Bainbridge as she poured some tea from a bone china teapot. "It's been awfully lonely here since Isidore passed away."

It had only been a few weeks since Kate had seen Ruthie, but she thought the old woman looked much more frail, more careworn than ever.

"Let me help you with that," she said as Ruthie tried to carry a tray with two cups of tea and a plate of cookies over to the table near the leather sofa where she was sitting. She stood up but Ruthie scolded her gently.

"Now, now. Sit down, young lady. I'm old but I'm not an invalid yet." She set the tray down on the table. "Do you take cream and sugar?"

Kate shook her head and smiled. "No thanks. I've got to cut down wherever I can." She took a sip from the delicate teacup. "This is a beautiful tea service."

Ruthie beamed. "Isidore gave it to me for our golden wedding anniversary." A melancholy look came into her eyes. "It wasn't long after that we found out he had Alzheimer's." She closed her eyes. A single tear traced its way down her cheek.

"That's what I wanted to talk to you about," said Kate, putting her teacup on the coffee table.

"About Poppie's Alzheimer's?"

Kate shook her head. "About the night before he passed away." She paused, searching for the right words. "Mrs. Jacoby, did anything *unusual* happen that evening?"

Ruthie looked puzzled. "I'm not sure what you mean, dear."

"I'm not completely sure, either," Kate replied, "but your husband had been a patient at Sentinel several times. I guess I'm just trying to find out if anything different happened that night."

"Why do you want to know?"

Kate hedged. She didn't want Ruthie to know what she suspected. "Your husband's death took us all by surprise. I just want to make sure everything was done properly. Does that make sense?"

Ruthie nodded, smiling. "You needn't worry. My Poppie received the best of care, just like always. Even better than usual."

Kate's teacup stopped halfway to her lips. "What do you mean?"

"Well," Ruthie said, "lots of people always stopped by, but this time that handsome young counselor came to visit."

"Counselor?"

Ruthie took a sip of tea and nodded. "Mmm-hmm," she said. "He was a good looking young man. He said he wanted to introduce himself and see how Isidore was doing. Now what was his name?"

"Drew Langdon?" asked Kate.

Ruthie nodded triumphantly. "That's it."

———

"Last one," Drew said as he lugged a heavy box through the front door of Lori's new apartment.

Less than a month had passed since she had told Kate that she was going to move out. After that, things had progressed—and changed—with dizzying speed. Kate was still not enthusiastic about the decision, but Lori had expected that. Lori hadn't expected Kate to become cool and uncommunicative, as if Lori had deeply offended her.

Kate had always been so unflappable and seemed virtually incapable of taking offense. Slams and criticisms about her weight, about the fact that she had never married, and even about her incessant cheeriness rolled off her like rain off the roof. But Lori's announcement that she was moving out had hit her sister with avalanche force. Lori didn't appreciate the depth of Kate's feelings until Kate had declared herself too busy to help with the move.

When she asked him in order to cover her initial lie to Kate, Drew Langdon had quickly offered to help Lori find an apartment. He was a bit surprised that she was moving out, and even more surprised that she wanted his help. But he had been more than happy to help. The first day of apartment hunting they found a comfortably sized two-bedroom place only about a mile from SHS. That would shorten Lori's daily commute considerably. It also was closer to the mall where Jackie Palermo held her self-defense classes. The neighborhood wasn't quite as nice as Kate's, but Lori was pleased with her choice.

Now, surveying the chaos of her new home, Lori sat down on a large box and put her head in her hands. "This place looks like a warehouse," she said. "It'll take weeks to find order in this mess."

They had stacked moving boxes in the center of nearly every room. Some of the boxes would have to double as furniture because furniture was one thing Lori didn't have.

"Don't feel bad," said Drew. "My place still looks like this most of the time." He sat on the floor and leaned up against a wall. Sweat streamed down his face. Then he flashed her a wry grin. "You could always ask your sister to come decorate."

"I don't think either of us is ready for that."

"How did she take your moving out?"

"About the same as Lincoln took the news about the South's secession."

"I was wondering why she made herself so scarce when we moved you out."

"She said she had to work," Lori replied. "Seems like she's been going over the top with that lately."

Drew got to his knees and tore open a box marked "Towels and Linens." He pulled out a thick, dark burgundy-colored hand towel. "Do you mind?" he asked, holding up the towel.

"Be my guest," Lori replied.

He sat back down and began wiping his sweaty face with the towel.

"At least I could have offered you something cold to drink."

"You haven't *got* anything cold to drink," Drew quipped. "Your refrigerator won't be delivered until tomorrow."

"How about some lukewarm tap water?"

Drew laughed. "I'll take a rain check."

Lori's face grew serious. "Drew, I want to thank you for helping me. I know we don't see eye-to-eye on everything, but—"

"Don't mention it," he interrupted. "Happy to help. And speaking of helping," he said, looking at his watch, "I need to return the rental truck by one o'clock or we'll get a late charge. I'd better hustle." He picked up his jacket from one of the boxes. "Oh, I almost forgot." He pulled several envelopes from his jacket pocket. "The mail carrier brought your mail by during our last box run."

"Everything's probably addressed to Occupant," Lori joked as she flipped through the mail. "I haven't been here long enough for anyone to—" She stopped cold when she came to a nondescript brown envelope. It was addressed to Dr. Lori Westlake, 3924 Savannah Way, Dallas, Texas. Her new address. The handwriting was unfamiliar, but Lori had no doubt that the envelope was from the Circle of Peace.

"What?" said Drew.

"Nothing," Lori said, tossing the pile of mail onto one of the boxes. "As I expected. All junk."

⁂

Charles Hamisch sat on a chair beside his bed, watching as Pam Bachman loaded his artist's brushes and oil paints into a box. He had tried to help her dismantle the easel and lay it up against the wall, but the effort had so exhausted him that he'd had to sit down and let Pam finish the packing. The bedroom was now littered with boxes of art supplies that Charles would never use again.

"We'll need to clear these boxes out of here before they deliver your new bed this afternoon," Pam said. "What do you want to do with all this stuff?"

"Who cares?" Charles snapped. "Throw it all out. I was a lousy artist, anyway." He had been cradling a bristle brush in one limp hand. Now he let it fall to the floor and nudged it toward her with his foot.

Pam paused for a second. "Charles," her voice was firm but kind, "don't hand me that line. I've seen your work. You could have been a professional artist if you'd wanted."

"Not anymore," Charles said. He lifted his withered hands. "All I could do now is finger paint." He sighed and hung his head. "And before long I won't even be able to do that."

Columbo strolled into the room and rubbed leisurely against Charles's foot. A second later, the cat hopped up onto the bed. He nuzzled Charles's arm for a moment, then discovered a sunny spot on the bedspread, plopped down, and began to give himself a bath. Charles lifted one arm and slid it toward the cat. He brushed the back of his hand against its soft fur.

"I'm sorry, Pam. I shouldn't have snapped at you."

Tears welled in his eyes. He looked toward the ceiling and tried to blink them away. "Every day I lose something else. A few weeks ago I could walk with a cane. Now I need a walker. Soon it will be a wheelchair."

Pam tried to change the subject. "Art seems like an unlikely hobby for a police officer. Why *didn't* you go into it professionally?"

Charles shrugged. "I thought about it when I was younger. But that would have turned it into work, taken all the fun out of it. Art has always been my escape. When the world didn't make sense, I could pick up a brush and leave for a while, or take my carving tools and shape the world the way *I* wanted it to be."

His eyes grew misty again. "It's all gone now. Nothing makes sense anymore, and I can't do a thing about it."

Pam picked up the brush that Charles had dropped. She placed it in the box with the others. "I'm sorry. It must be so hard for you."

Charles nodded but didn't answer. A tear streamed down his cheek and dropped on his trousers. "Look at me," he sniffed. "Crying like a big baby."

"It's okay." Pam pulled a tissue from a box on the nightstand and tucked it into his hand. His fingers, curled and stiff, squeezed the tissue like a clamp. Slowly, he lifted it to his face and brushed his nose.

"Can't even blow my own nose," he said with a little chuckle.

"Allow me," said Pam. She held the tissue to Charles's nose while he blew. "There you go," she said, tossing the tissue into a nearby wastebasket. "That wasn't so bad, was it?"

"I'm losing everything, Pam." His voice was quiet.

"Not everything," she said, taking his hands in hers. "You know that. You still have David and me. And you still have the Lord."

Charles nodded. "You know, from the day David led me to Christ, I've never doubted my faith. But now, I don't know; God seems awfully far away sometimes."

Pam nodded. "But he's still there."

Columbo looked at both of them, meowed, and returned to his bath.

Charles chuckled. "When all else fails, I still have this worthless cat."

Lori's hands trembled as she held her latest instructions. As with the previous letter, the anonymous author directed her to memorize the information and then burn it. But there was a lot more information to absorb this time. She already knew *whom* she would be assisting. Now she was being told *when, where,* and *how.* She had to hand it to these people. Security-conscious to a fault, they were also quite ingenious in planning interventions.

"Assistance is to be conducted," the letter read, "between 1:30 and 2:00 AM on Friday, November 9. Patient will be in the SHS Cancer Center preparing for surgery."

The surgery, of course, would never take place.

"Patient has agreed to the terms and will be expecting the intervention. Your task is to pick up and deliver the medication for the procedure."

Lori understood that the Circle of Peace did not have the luxury of doing business as Dr. Kevorkian had. They needed to maintain a veil of secrecy at all times. Ironically, this meant conducting business right under the noses of the medical community.

Autopsies, of course, posed the greatest danger of discovery, but those were the exception rather than the rule. When an intervention occurred in a hospital, the medical examiner would probably not be involved so long as there was a plausible explanation for the death. Assuming the patient's family was on board with the decision, there was not much danger of anyone requesting an autopsy.

She continued reading. "The patient and her family do not know who will be performing the procedure. They will have said their good-byes prior to patient's admission."

She nodded approvingly. This was one of the reasons she was willing to work with the Circle. They thought of everything. Most importantly, they valued the patient's wishes above all else. There was no malice here. No involuntary euthanasia. No murder. They were merely returning control to the patient, control that should never have been taken away in the first place. Lori was nervous about her role in the intervention, but she also felt at peace.

The final paragraph reminded Lori of what to do with the paper after she had read it. "Burn these instructions after you have memorized them. You will receive a text message with final instructions at 8:00 AM sharp on the day of the patient's admission."

She walked over to the stove where a cinnamon-scented candle burned. As she held the instruction sheet over the flame, the paper vanished with a brilliant orange flare.

She now understood how she would seal her commitment to the Circle. She would transport and deliver the materials the Circle would use in carrying out Nina Ware's intervention. It was a small thing, but if Nina's death was ruled a homicide, it would make Lori an accomplice.

———

"Are you ready to go back to the front room?" Pam asked.

Charles nodded and Pam rolled his walker over and positioned it in front of him. Unlike the walkers commonly used by the elderly, this model had large wheels, handgrips, handbrakes, and even a seat where Charles could rest if he got tired of standing. He placed his hands on the handgrips and slowly pulled himself to his feet. Pam stood beside him like a gymnast's spotter but was careful not to assist unless he really needed her help. After he stood up, Charles paused to catch his breath. Pam could see tiny beads of perspiration forming on his forehead.

"Not going to be able to do that much longer," he said between breaths.

"Take your time," said Pam. "There's no rush."

"That's good," he answered, "because I only have two speeds nowadays: turtle and snail."

As he inched his way down the hall toward the living room, the doorbell rang.

"Maybe that's your new bed," Pam said as she moved past him to answer the door.

"I hope so," Charles answered. "One more night on my old bed and I won't need a walker anymore. I'll need a wheelchair."

The doorbell rang again, followed immediately by a thumping sound.

"I know that sound," Charles said. "Better let him in or he'll break down the door with that chair of his."

Pam opened the door and Kenton McCarthy's powered wheelchair rolled in. Kenton's wife, Janice, brought up the rear. "I'm sorry," Janice said. "I've told him not to use his chair as a battering ram but he just won't listen. He's worse than a teenager when he's driving that thing."

Kenton grinned up at her. "Sheee's worth—zan my mother."

Janice flashed him an indignant look. "I am *not* worse than your mother."

Charles stopped where he was, staring at Kenton. It had only been a few weeks since he had last seen him, but he was shocked by how much ground Kenton had lost in such a short time. If Charles hadn't known better, he'd have thought that Kenton was malnourished. He looked as if he'd sunk through the bottom of his wheelchair. Limp flesh hung from sticklike arms. His hands had curled into claws. What Charles found most disturbing was Kenton's difficulty in speaking, a sign that his friend's bulbar symptoms were progressing. He knew that it wouldn't be long before Kenton would no longer be able to eat and would need a feeding tube to survive.

"Wh're you—ssshtaring at?" Kenton said, jostling Charles back to reality.

"I'm in awe of your marvelous machine," Charles shot back. He resumed his slow walk down the hallway. "Just you wait till I get mine. I'll race you."

Kenton let out a laugh and rolled the chair further into the living room. "I'll leave you—in the—dussht."

Janice rolled her eyes. "Boys and their toys. It never changes." She turned back toward the door.

"Would you like to stay for lunch?" Pam asked. "We'll be eating soon."

"Thanks, no," said Janice. "I've got some errands I need to run. Kenton wanted to stop by and visit while I hit the stores."

Kenton made a face. "Shopping's—boring."

"You've got that right," Charles said. "He'll be fine here with us. Take your time."

"I'll walk you out to your van, Janice," Pam said. She looked over her shoulder at Charles and Kenton. "You two behave while I'm gone." The two men responded with noncommittal expressions. Pam laughed and followed Janice out the front door.

As Charles eased himself down into his recliner, Kenton said "Sso—how're you—doing?"

Listening to Kenton's slurred speech, Charles understood why some early-stage ALS patients found themselves accused of being drunk. Kenton sounded like someone who'd had one too many. Add a little stumbling and tripping and you could definitely make a case for intoxication.

"Depends on the day," Charles answered.

"Me—too," replied Kenton. "My—F—V—C—was—forty—three—percent—today." Kenton spoke slowly, fighting to keep his voice understandable.

FVC was another one of those terms that Charles wished he'd never had to learn. It stood for "forced vital capacity" and was a measure of a person's ability to breathe. As an ALS patient's breathing muscles weakened, the FVC would drop. When it reached the thirty percent range, the patient would either need to be hooked up to a ventilator or risk death by respiratory failure.

The decision of whether or not to go on a ventilator was something Charles would rather not think about. Not yet, at least.

"Sssho—whash—*your*—problem?"

Charles shrugged. "I'm on an emotional roller coaster. One day I feel great. Next day I'm angry at the world."

Kenton nodded and listened.

"It's like one long grief process that never ends. Every day something else goes. Or I have to give something up. Or I lose another function. I'm wasting away and it scares me.

"How do you do it, Kenton?" Charles asked. "How do you stay so positive?"

Kenton's face screwed up into a wry grin. "You—aren't—with—me—all—the—time."

Charles laughed. "I'll take that to mean you have your moments."

"I—have—them," Kenton said.

"Don't you get angry or depressed?"

"Sometimes—but—I—keep—going."

"Why? You're a prisoner in your chair. I can still get around and some days I just want to stay in bed, pull the covers over my head, and die."

"Every—day—issh—a—gift."

"I don't understand."

Kenton smiled. "You—will."

Just then Columbo strolled into the room, stretched, and jumped up onto Kenton's lap. The shaggy cat stood nose-to-nose with Kenton for a few seconds, then turned in a circle and lay down.

"You've made a friend," Charles said.

"I'm—irresishtible."

The sound of the front door opening interrupted their conversation. Pam walked back through the door. She brushed at her eyes and walked down the hall toward the bathroom.

Charles could tell she'd been crying.

Lori surveyed the pile of boxes in her living room, wondering where she would begin the process of unpacking. Truth was, she didn't want to start *anywhere*. She just wanted to take a hot shower and go to bed. She knew where the towels were and Drew had set up the bed before he left. But she was awfully hungry and didn't have a clue of what to scrounge up for supper.

She was about to resign herself to going hungry and head back to the bathroom for her shower when the doorbell rang. She sighed and turned around to answer the door, but it opened before she got there. Drew stuck his head inside and said, "You really should lock this, you know." He pushed the door open wide. "Since your kitchenware isn't unpacked yet, I thought you might need something to eat." He had a large carryout pizza box balanced on one hand and a two-liter bottle of cola in the other.

Lori smiled and said, "Bless you."

Charles sat at the table, polishing off the tuna casserole that Pam had made. She had been strangely quiet ever since her conversation with Janice McCarthy, but he hesitated to ask her about it. Janice had taken Kenton home an hour earlier and neither of the women had been particularly talkative.

"Do you need help getting ready for bed?" Pam asked.

Charles blushed. The idea of somebody—and a woman, at that—helping him to change clothes, bathe, and go to the bathroom, embarrassed him deeply. He knew the time was drawing near when he would need that kind of help but he wasn't ready to accept it yet.

"I think I'll be okay," he said. "David should be home by now. Go spend some time with him."

"He knows I'm here. And he's more than happy to let me stay as long as you need me."

"Go on home."

Pam nodded weakly. "Maybe you're right." She took her purse from the dinette floor and got out her keys.

"Pam," Charles finally said, "what's wrong? What happened with Janice?"

"I don't want to burden you with it. You've got enough on your mind."

"Go ahead. Burden me."

Pam fumbled with her keys for a moment, then sat down at the table. "Kenton's losing ground pretty fast. He had an adverse reaction to the riluzole and had to stop taking it. Now it seems like ALS is taking him that much faster."

Charles nodded.

"Janice sees Kenton slipping away from her and she's powerless to do anything to stop it," Pam continued. "She wants to keep up a brave face for him but sometimes the grief has to come out. When it does, it helps to have an understanding shoulder to cry on. Today I was the shoulder."

Charles sat quietly, not wanting to tell Pam that he had also stopped taking his riluzole—not because of an adverse reaction, but because he *wanted* to die sooner.

———

Lori and Drew sat on the floor in her living room, leaning up against the wall. On the floor between them lay the nearly empty pizza box. A single piece of pepperoni remained.

"One slice left," said Drew. "Why don't you save it for a snack?"

"I'm stuffed," Lori replied. "But if you don't mind, I *will* keep it for tomorrow's breakfast."

"Cold pizza for breakfast? Is that from the FDA's official dietary guidelines?"

"If it isn't, it should be."

Drew stood up and offered Lori his hand. She took it and he pulled her up. They stood facing each other for a long moment, still holding hands. "I'd better be going," Drew said. "You're going to have a busy day tomorrow."

"What?" Lori laughed. "How do you know what kind of day I'm going to have?"

"You haven't had a *slow* day since I met you."

"You got me there." Lori smiled and looked up at Drew. "Drew, I just want to thank—" She didn't get to finish her sentence. Drew pulled her close to him and their lips met.

———

It took Charles nearly two hours to get ready for bed, something that might have taken twenty minutes only a few months ago. As he crept out of the bathroom using his walker, he couldn't help but notice how much his bedroom had changed.

Gone were the art supplies, the easel, the carving tools and wood blocks. His old bed was gone too. David had dismantled it earlier in the day and had moved it out. In its place stood a brand new hospital bed with all the whistles and bells. Charles was resigned but grateful. The remote control would give him the ability to raise and lower the bed, and it would be much more comfortable than his old one.

But it was one more concession to ALS.

One step closer to the grave.

His bedroom had once been a comfortable place where he could rest, work on his art, escape the troubles of the world.

Now it was a hospital room.

Soon, it would be a hospice.

———

Lori stood on the front steps of her apartment building, watching Drew drive away. She hadn't wanted him to leave, and he probably would have stayed if she'd asked. But she kept telling herself that she wasn't ready to get into another relationship.

Not yet.

When Drew's taillights disappeared around the corner, Lori breathed a quiet sigh and went back inside.

She groaned when she saw the continuing disarray. They had worked all day and still it seemed they'd made no progress on unpacking.

"It's all going to have to wait until tomorrow," Lori said to no one in particular, trying to break the silence. "I've done all the organizing that I'm going to do today. I just want to take a long hot—" She stopped when she noticed another envelope among the pile of mail that Drew had given her earlier.

She pulled it from the pile and examined it.

The plain business envelope was hand addressed and bore no stamp. All that was written on it was her name, "Lori."

"Maybe Drew was too shy to propose in person," she joked as she tore the end off the envelope and pulled out a small sheet of yellow notepaper. Her throat began to constrict in fear as she read the brief note.

Lori, I want to see you. Philip.

She looked at the envelope again. No return address. No stamp. The envelope had been hand delivered.

Philip was in town.

TWENTY-THREE

Quinn logged into the chat room. The others were already present.

> Quinn: Seems like we're having a lot of special meetings lately. What's this one about?

> Malachi: Your meeting, Zoë. Tell us about it.

> Zoë: The intervention in Case #11085 has been canceled.

> Quinn: Why? What happened?

> Zoë: The patient's mother had second thoughts. She persuaded the patient to cancel.

> Copper: Any details that need to be taken care of?

> Zoë: Servant needs to be told that the intervention is off.

> Copper: That's your responsibility, Malachi.

> Malachi: I'll notify Servant.

> Zoë: Very good, then. Meeting adjourned.

One by one the members signed out of the chat room. Quinn stared at the blank laptop screen for a few seconds. Servant would have to wait to seal her commitment to the Circle.

He hoped she wouldn't change her mind in the meantime.

————

David Bachman pulled on a pair of latex gloves, stepped under the yellow crime-scene tape, and entered the decrepit building. A flurry of odors assaulted him as soon as he stepped inside. Stale urine. Vomit. Feces. But overwhelming all the rest was the sickeningly sweet redolence of decomposition. A CSI team was already processing the scene but David wanted to take a quick walk-through. He was not the investigating officer on this case but he wanted to examine the scene to see if there were any similarities with the Death Angel killings. He covered his face with a handkerchief and continued inside.

The old storefront, abandoned for years, was scheduled for demolition. Once a posh clothing boutique, the building had spent the last decade as home to an assortment of rats, cats, and homeless people. For one homeless man in particular, the building had become a tomb.

Shredded newspapers were strewn everywhere. Empty syringes and drug paraphernalia littered the floor. David noticed piles of beer and wine bottles, most covered with a thick layer of dust, in various corners near boarded-up windows. A trail of footprints on the dusty floor led down a hall and into a small office. David followed the trail.

A body—white male—already well along in the process of decay, lay inside the tiny room. A crime scene technician was photographing the body. David peered through the doorway but did not go in.

The scene was similar to so many others David had seen in recent months: a homeless victim in a secluded location. But there were some obvious differences as well. The other deaths had all appeared to be overdoses of one thing or another. In this case, some nasty-looking ligature marks around the victim's neck pretty much ruled out an overdose as the cause of death. Violence didn't figure into any of the "angel" cases. They would have to wait for the autopsy report for final confirmation but the ligature marks certainly pointed toward strangulation.

The other striking absence in this death scene was that David saw no ceramic angel lying anywhere near the body. It was possible, of course, that the killer had put the angel in one of the man's pockets. But in most of the previous cases the murderer staged the scene so that the angel had been prominently displayed.

Is the Death Angel changing his MO? David wondered. *Or was this just a random act of violence? A turf dispute? A robbery?*

On the surface, there appeared to be no clear evidence linking this killing to the others. But David couldn't shake the notion that this case was connected. If so, it represented an escalation in the intensity of the killer's crimes. Was simply overdosing his victims no longer providing the thrill, the rush, that the killer needed?

We need to stop this guy, David said to himself. *And soon.*

TWENTY-FOUR

The Angel strolled through the gardens outside the Sentinel Health Systems complex as golden-red sunbeams streamed through the treetops. Early in the morning, the gardens provided a quiet place to think. He stopped and inhaled deeply, taking in autumn's cool aromas, trying to relax, to regain equilibrium.

Killing Toby Hutchins had been like pouring gasoline on a pile of smoldering embers. What had once been a controlled, methodical purpose had exploded into a voracious hunger. He now felt himself spiraling downward into a black vortex of compulsion. If he didn't find a way to regain control, he would lose himself—and his mission.

How strange it was that the need to serve people could become an obsession. It had started so simply. Merely helping one woman escape the prison of her body. Helping her husband to get on with his life.

There had been many others after MariBeth Wilson. Too many to count. But he had always been careful, circumspect, controlled. He hadn't wanted to risk his work by being sloppy.

Yet he *had* become sloppy.

His need had begun to cloud his judgment. He had tried to liberate Toby Hutchins before he had won his confidence. As a result, he'd had to kill him the way a common murderer would do it. He had endangered everything he lived for. It was imperative that he regain his poise.

But it felt so good.

No. He *must* master the need. Reestablish control.

But killing Toby had given him a surge of power, a thrill unlike anything he'd ever experienced.

The Angel leaned against an iron railing, watching the koi swimming in the pond. His knuckles were white, his fingernails digging futilely into the cast-iron railing. He could feel his pulse thrumming in his throat.

He remembered how it felt to pull the tourniquet around Toby's throat.

The Angel's mouth was dry.

His watch beeped.

He looked up at the four towers of the SHS complex.

Time to go to work.

TWENTY-FIVE

Lori, watch out for Drew."
Clutching her cell phone to her ear, Lori reached across the bed
and turned down her clock radio.

"Kate, what are you talking about?"

"I can't go into it over the phone, Sis. Just be careful."

Lori rolled her eyes. This was just like Kate.

"Kate, you amaze me sometimes. First you practically hold a gun
to my head to get me to date the guy. Now when it looks like he and I
might actually start a relationship, you want me to back off?"

"I know it sounds crazy, but please be careful. Don't go anywhere
alone with him," Kate replied.

Lori sat down on her bed and rubbed the sleep from her eyes.
"What? Why? Is he now some kind of serial killer?"

There was a pause on the line. When Kate spoke again, her voice
was quiet and composed. "Come to Dr. Galloway's office at seven thirty
this morning. I want you there when I tell him what I've found."

Lori glanced at her bedside clock radio. It was ten minutes
past six.

"I'll think about it." Lori snapped the phone shut and flopped
back on the bed.

"And thanks for the wake-up call," she grumbled.

The ninth of November began stuffy and warm with temperatures
in the mid-eighties. Never a big fan of air-conditioning—particularly

in November—she had slept with her apartment windows open. Now she wished she hadn't. Even after a shower the high humidity would make her skin feel sticky and dirty. Her clothes would cling to her body as if she'd just finished a long workout. It was one of those days where the air felt so heavy and oppressive that you wanted to carry a machete to cut your way through it. Lori thought she'd left this kind of weather behind in Houston.

WBAP's morning show advised that the first major cold front of the season was supposed to blow in sometime in the evening.

I'll believe that when I see it. Lori welcomed the news that the unseasonably stifling weather would finally be retired in favor of genuine autumn temperatures but she hoped the cold front's arrival would not be too dramatic.

Kate had warned her about North Texas weather, dramatic black skies and often near-instantaneous temperature drops of thirty or forty degrees. That didn't bother Lori but the possibility of killer tornadoes that sometimes accompanied those storms did. The idea of massive wind vortexes weaving through the storm front like barrel racers at a rodeo, destroying whatever lay in their path, chilled her more than any cold weather could.

Lori hated storms. But there were no twisters—at least not yet.

She had awakened at four thirty, uncomfortable and hot. Unable to get back to sleep, she had lain in bed, sweating and thinking about Nina Ware. She had convinced herself that she was at peace with what she was about to do. But a nagging uneasiness had been growing in the pit of her stomach since late yesterday. Had she still been living with Kate, she'd have been able to ignore it. Kate's constant conversation would have distracted her. But now that she was on her own, the silence magnified the echoes of her conscience like an empty room magnifies sound. But conscience wasn't the only thing bothering her. Another complication had arisen since she'd made her agreement with the Circle of Peace.

She was falling in love.

Despite Kate's out-of-the-blue warning about Drew, Lori found herself irresistibly drawn to him. She'd tried to avoid it, and certainly hadn't planned on it. Continuing her membership in the Circle of Peace would pose a serious problem.

Once she was a full member of the Circle, she would have to keep secrets from him, secrets that involved the most important details of her life. Common sense told her that she should break it off with him, that she should never have allowed a relationship to develop in the first place.

But she'd never met someone like Drew before. He was the very antithesis of Philip. Gentle and compassionate, he cared about Lori more than he cared about himself. She had not allowed herself the luxury of getting close to anyone since she had left Philip. But now she felt herself drawn to Drew as if pulled by a river's strong current.

Perhaps she would humor Kate and listen to her newfound fears about Drew. It might give her the willpower to break off the relationship before they became too involved.

But she needed a shower first.

TWENTY-SIX

E very day is a gift."
  Charles Hamisch lay in his new hospital bed, staring at the ceiling and repeating Kenton McCarthy's favorite saying. He had been awake for nearly two hours, ever since spasms and cramps in his hands and feet jarred him to consciousness. The simple phrase nagged at him. He'd been trying to make sense of it all. But he still found himself completely at a loss. This particular morning, all cramped and contorted, certainly didn't feel like a gift. More like a curse.

What rankled Charles more than Kenton's "every day is a gift" philosophy was his infuriating response when Charles told him he didn't understand.

Kenton had just smiled his crooked smile and said, "You will."

Charles wanted to ask, "How? When?"

Didn't the Bible say that "to live is Christ, and to die is gain"? If dying was gain, why was it wrong for him to want out of this life? What was wrong about wanting to go home and be with the Lord? As his life on earth was slowly becoming a living hell, why shouldn't he want to go to heaven? And why shouldn't he speed up the inevitable?

He had a head full of questions, yet all his ALS pastor-friend would say is, "You'll understand."

Charles lay on his bed, afraid to get up, wondering what new losses the day would bring. However, any designs he might have had about staying in bed were shattered when he felt a slight tremor. Gentle pressure moved up one leg, reached his stomach, and then his chest.

He found himself gazing into Columbo's face. The cat stared at him for a few seconds, then licked Charles's nose with his rough, sandpapery tongue.

"I suppose you want breakfast."

Columbo sat down on Charles's chest and purred.

"Guess it's time to see how well this new bed works."

The previous night he had clipped the remote on to the fitted sheet, near where his right hand would rest. His arm muscles responded sluggishly but he was able to get his hand on the remote. The only problem was that he hadn't taken time to memorize which buttons went with which functions. Sitting up by himself was not a great option; his arm muscles were becoming too weak to push his upper body upright. Trial and error would have to do.

He pressed a button. The motor under the bed whirred and Charles felt his feet being lifted.

"Not that one."

He pushed another button and felt like he was on an elevator, going up.

"Okay, I'm oh-for-two."

When he pressed the third button, his head began to lift up.

"Now we're cookin'." He held the button down until the mechanical bed had nearly raised him to a sitting position.

As the head of the bed moved up, Columbo jumped down and sauntered toward the doorway. Now that Charles was sitting up, he could see the remote. He pressed the button to lower his legs, then swung his legs out over the edge of the bed. His feet didn't touch the ground, but that was the whole idea with this new gadget. He could raise or lower the entire bed to make it easier for him to climb in and out. It was an expensive option but it might just buy him a little more time before he required around-the-clock help.

He lowered the bed until the bottoms of his feet touched the cold floor. Then, using the upraised mattress to support himself, he stood up. His walker was within easy reach and he pulled it to himself.

Several plaintive meows came from the hall, as if Columbo were saying, "I'm starving out here. Will you hurry up?"

Charles began pushing his walker toward the bathroom. "Don't be in such a hurry," he growled. "Just getting to the bathroom and back could take half the morning."

TWENTY-SEVEN

L ori grabbed a coat and headed for the door. She didn't need the coat at the moment, but if the weather forecasts were accurate, by night she'd be glad for it.

She glanced at her wall clock as she went out the door.

Five minutes past seven.

Enough time to take advantage of her new proximity to SHS and leave her Mustang behind. And it would give her some time to think. She decided to cut through the gardens to Dr. Galloway's office.

As she walked along the sidewalk, the gray, overcast sky added a touch of gloom. In the absence of strong sunlight, the air felt more oppressive than Lori had imagined possible for a November morning.

She was now regretting the decision to make her short commute to the hospital on foot. Less than two blocks from her apartment, perspiration was trickling down her cheeks. At this rate, she'd need another shower by the time she got there. It was hard to believe that by this time tomorrow she would need her heavy coat and scarf just to stay warm.

As she walked along the sidewalk, a flock of grackles burst out of the trees that lined the street, screeching and flapping like an evil, black cloud. A shiver passed down Lori's spine. She felt as if she had stepped into a scene from Alfred Hitchcock's *The Birds*.

Traffic along the street rolled at a sluggish pace as Lori neared the Sentinel complex. As she walked, she scanned her surroundings, just as Jackie Palermo had taught her in self-defense class. Maybe the dingy weather had her spooked or maybe it was Kate's cryptic warning about Drew, but she couldn't escape the feeling that someone was watching her.

"Shake it off, girl," she muttered. "It's broad daylight, and you're too old for ghost stories."

Brave talk notwithstanding, she pulled her keys from her shoulder bag. A small canister of pepper spray hung from her key ring. She flipped off the cap and placed her index finger on the nozzle release. The sensation of being followed might indeed be little more than her overwrought imagination at work. However, her new apartment was not in the best of neighborhoods. Several of the buildings were decorated with undecipherable graffiti, a mute testimony to persistent gang activity.

Another unpleasant possibility came to mind. She had been feeling strange ever since Philip's latest letter had come. If she took it at face value, then Philip was in town. Maybe nearby. And if he decided to make a case for renewing their relationship in person, there was no telling where he might be lurking.

Of course, Philip was a liar with a capital L. Lori would not put it past him to get a friend to hand deliver the letter just to frighten her.

Well, it wasn't going to work.

Or was it?

She swung around and looked behind her, half expecting to see someone dart behind a tree trunk, or for a car to suddenly speed up and pass her by. She saw nothing but the same stagnant line of cars, still creeping slower than she was walking in rush hour traffic. Nevertheless, the feeling of unease would not leave her. She stepped up her pace.

The final stretch of the commute took her away from the street, along a series of rock steps that led thirty feet down into the heart of the gardens and finally back up and into Sentinel's main atrium. If anyone *had* been following in a car, they would be stuck in traffic unless they decided to leave their vehicle in the middle of the road.

Apparently the waist-high cast-iron gate leading to the back entrance of the SHS complex was not used often. Lori had to wrestle with the latch before it would open. As she pulled the gate toward her, it creaked and squealed on rusty hinges.

Before going through, Lori risked one last quick glance behind her. She could see no one on foot—anywhere. No cars or SUVs swung behind her to cut off her escape. Everything was normal.

But nothing felt right.

She slammed the gate behind her and ran down the steps, wanting to put as much distance between her and the road as possible. At the bottom of the stairway, stone paths began to split off from the main trail toward various parts of the gardens. Lori allowed herself to slow down. About twenty yards down the path she saw the place where she'd had her conversation with John Doe, the place where the direction of her life had begun to change. A stone bench stood near the path. Lori sat down to catch her breath, still clutching her pepper spray.

She wasn't sure what was spooking her. Was she in genuine danger? Had Kate's call rattled her? Or was she haunted by phantoms generated by a nagging conscience, warning her not to assist in Nina Ware's death?

A distinctive metallic squeal and clang from thirty feet above jarred Lori into action.

Someone had followed her through the gate.

TWENTY-EIGHT

The Angel sat down at a computer terminal and entered his user name and password.

He accessed the SHS patient database and waited for the query window to come up.

Instead of the tiny animated hourglass that usually indicated the computer was processing, a miniature blood transfusion bag emptied and refilled as the computer did its work.

He rolled his eyes and breathed a sigh of disgust. *Some genius in IT has too much time on his hands.*

Seconds later, a search window opened.

The Angel clicked inside the input field and when the flashing cursor appeared, he typed "Ware, Nina" and hit *Enter*.

The little IV bag reappeared, emptying and refilling.

A few seconds later, Nina Ware's admission record filled the screen. Apparently she had taken advantage of Sentinel's quick check-in feature. All of her data was available, even though she would not be admitted until afternoon. The record gave the Angel all the information he needed. The patient would be admitted to D422 at approximately four thirty PM in anticipation of surgery for pancreatic cancer the next morning.

That surgery, of course, would never take place.

Nina Ware had contacted the Circle of Peace to request an intervention. Her family had apparently been on board with the request, and guardianship arrangements had been made for her child. The intervention had been approved. It was only because of her step-mother that Nina had developed misgivings. She had decided to fight her cancer and cancel the intervention.

So much the better.

Whether she liked it or not, today would be Nina Ware's liberation day.

TWENTY-NINE

L ori stood up, her muscles tense. The approaching footfalls sounded heavy, indicating a man, most likely. And he was running.

Not wanting to risk a confrontation, Lori dashed along the rough-hewn stone walkway that followed a switchback pattern up the nearly three stories to Sentinel's atrium. At midday she wouldn't have needed to run at all because the gardens would be teeming with tourists and several security guards. But at this hour, the tourists were still sleeping and the guards hadn't come on duty. Lori jogged up the walkway, trying to watch her footing on the uneven stones.

None of her self-defense classmates would have been disappointed that she was retreating instead of fighting. It's a common misconception that people with martial arts skills never run from a fight. In truth, the first rule of self-defense—drilled into Lori from day one of her training—had been "Run!"

Lori ran.

She knew the main path through the gardens well. She also knew a few shortcuts that might help. Steep concrete staircases periodically broke off, cutting across the zigzag pattern made by the walkway. The staircases served two purposes. Ostensibly, they were to provide little side excursions for the more adventurous tourists. The staircases also provided convenient shortcuts for groundskeepers and maintenance personnel.

Lori cut to her left and up one of the maintenance staircases, taking the steps three at a time. When she came to a landing about halfway up the stairs, she stopped for a quick look back. Whoever was chasing her hadn't made it to the steps—yet. But Lori knew that if she hesitated the pursuer could close the gap. She pressed on, following the ascent up to the walkway's next level.

Out of breath and with a painful side-stitch stabbing at her, Lori stopped at the top of the stairs. She bent over and held her right side, ready to run to her left and continue up the walkway if necessary. Another maintenance staircase was nearby, about two hundred feet ahead on the right. First she needed to catch her breath; she also needed to calm down and get control of her emotions.

It was entirely possible, even likely, that she had spooked herself, and the man behind her was nothing more than a businessman with the same idea she had of taking a shortcut through Sentinel's gardens.

Calm down, girl, Lori told herself. *You're too worked up.* She stood still, breathing in through her nose and out through her mouth, listening to the pounding of her heart. But then came the "click, click, click" of footsteps echoing as someone ascended the maintenance staircase.

Lori renewed her frenzied dash, trying to reach the next staircase before her pursuer could close the gap. But only a few feet from the staircase, her left shoe caught a corner of one of the paving stones and she turned her ankle. She lurched forward as her legs gave way, scraping her right knee on the way down. Her pepper spray canister flew from her hand and clattered to the walkway several feet ahead of her.

The footsteps came closer.

With her right knee screaming in pain and a cry of panic rising in her throat, Lori crawled forward. She desperately groped for the fallen pepper spray as precious seconds flew away.

Her fingers closed around the pepper spray as she heard the ticking of her would-be attacker's shoes just around the bend.

The ground was a terrible place to be in a self-defense situation because it severely limited your options. But Lori had no choice. Time and her injured ankle left her no alternative.

She put her thumb on the trigger and rolled around to meet her pursuer. A split second before she sent a stream of liquid needles into her pursuer's face, Lori relaxed and took her thumb off the canister.

"Lori! What's wrong? Why are you running?"

"Drew?"

THIRTY

Charles hummed a tune as he pressed the lever on the electric can opener. The dull, overcast sky visible through the dinette window stood in stark contrast to his mood. He was feeling good for the first time in weeks. In fact, he was feeling great. His arms and legs appeared to be working correctly and with minimal effort. It had not taken him nearly as long to dress and it was nice to feel at least somewhat strong.

He'd even left his walker in the bathroom and was using only his cane to steady himself. Charles knew that remissions in ALS cases are extremely rare but not unheard of. As good as he felt this morning, it was hard to suppress a glimmer of hope that he might be one of those rare cases.

The can opener whirred and ground its way around a small can of cat food that Pam had left the night before. "She must like you," he said to the cat. "This is expensive stuff."

Columbo sat expectantly on a step stool near the kitchen sink as Charles scooped the contents of the can into a small bowl. The cat put one paw on the counter and sniffed the approaching breakfast. When Columbo was happily eating his morning meal, Charles ambled over to the dinette window and pulled aside the curtains. "Looks pretty dreary out," he said. "But other than that, it's a pretty nice day. If you don't mind spending the morning by yourself, I think I'll go out for a little drive. Kenton has visited me a few times. Maybe I'll repay the honor."

Charles reached for the key rack on the wall near the telephone, but the rack was empty.

"That's strange," he said. "I'm sure I hung them here. 'Course, it *has* been a while since I drove." He pulled open a few kitchen drawers in case the keys had somehow found their way in there, but found nothing.

"Maybe Pam needed to borrow the car," he muttered. "Strange she didn't ask, though." He walked back over to the window and looked out again. His car was parked just where he'd left it on the night of his retirement party.

He picked up the phone and hit the speed dial button to connect to the Bachmans. Pam picked up. "Hello?"

"Pam? I was wondering—"

"Oh, hi, Charles," Pam said. "I need to run a few errands before I come over. Do you need anything?"

"I was just wondering if you know where my car keys are."

There was a long pause.

"Pam? You still there?"

"Yes," she answered quickly. "Yes, I'm still here."

Another pause.

"Is anything wrong?"

"No, nothing wrong. Umm, Charles, would you mind waiting just a bit?"

"Why can't you just tell me where my keys are?"

"Just hang in there, Charles. We'll be right over. Bye, now."

She broke the connection before Charles could respond.

He hung up the receiver. "*We'll* be right over? Who's *we*?"

⸻

With Drew's help, Lori made it the rest of the way up the walkway to Sentinel's main atrium. Her ankle, though sore, was not sprained. The scrapes on her knee and palms hurt worse than the ankle, but Lori suspected that a little soap and antibiotic ointment would take care of them.

They hadn't spoken much since Drew had found her sprawled on the walkway. At first, Lori had been too embarrassed to speak. Now Kate's warning had begun to nag at her.

"You know," she said as Drew helped her sit down on a sofa in the atrium, "you could have called my name a little sooner. It would have saved me a lot of pain and grief."

"I'm sorry, Lori," Drew replied. He knelt beside the couch and helped her put her leg up. "But I didn't expect you to go tearing off like a scared rabbit."

Lori winced as he rolled up her torn pant leg to reveal the scraped knee.

"That needs to be washed," he said. "Probably needs some kind of cream, too."

"Thank you, Dr. Langdon," Lori said, grinning. "You're so astute."

Drew laughed. "I'm sorry, Lori." His tone was soft and genuinely apologetic this time. "I promise to announce myself next time I decide to walk you to work."

"I'm sorry, too," she said. "I've been on edge ever since I got those letters from Philip."

"He won't come back," Drew said. "Not if he has any brains in his head. You've got three things working in your favor now."

"Three?" Lori said.

Drew held up a finger. "One, you've got a restraining order against him. Two," he said, holding up another finger, "you've got your self-defense training."

"And three?" asked Lori.

"You've got me to look out for you now."

Lori paused and looked into his eyes. She didn't care what Kate said; she felt safe and secure.

"I like that," she said.

"So do I," Drew replied as he leaned in and kissed her.

———

Detective David Bachman had just plopped down at his desk with a mug of coffee and a pile of file folders, ready to plunge into the day's work when his cell phone chirped.

He shook his head and looked across his desk to another officer, Jeff Mullins. "Going to be one of those days." He flipped the phone open and noticed the caller ID: Pam.

"Hi, babe. What's up?"

Pam's voice was clear but David could sense the tension. "Charles wants his car keys."

David heaved a sigh. "Want me to meet you there or pick you up?"

"Meet me there. It'll be faster."

David closed the phone and slipped it into his trouser pocket. He finished off his coffee with a long gulp. "Jeff, can you cover for me for about an hour?"

"What's going on?"

"I've got to go tell Charles that he can't drive anymore."

Jeff grimaced. "Better you than me."

"Be back as fast as I can." He grabbed his jacket and headed for the door. On his way past the sergeant's office, he heard a voice call out.

"Bachman," Sergeant Jackson said. "Need to see you a minute."

Glancing at his watch, David made a reluctant detour into his supervisor's office.

Sergeant Irvin Jackson, a rotund, balding man in his fifties, sat behind his desk with a file folder open before him. As David entered the office, Jackson closed the file and handed it to him. "Nice piece of work, Bachman, but no soap on your 'Death Angel' case. There's just no evidence that any of these vics were murdered. The little angels are the only thing you've got going for you, and that's not enough to go forward with."

David was dumbfounded. "You've got to be kidding. Surely it's worth digging a little deeper. What about exhuming the bodies and running some tox screens?"

"Ain't gonna happen. Nobody wants to go shouting 'serial killer' unless there's a good reason. Tends to upset the tourist bureau."

"But—" David protested.

Jackson shook his head. "Focus on your other cases. These stay closed."

David pursed his lips, holding back a reply that would only get him in trouble. "Yes, sir," he said as he turned toward the door.

"Where're you headed?" Jackson called after him.

"Gotta take Hamisch's car keys away from him. Want to ride along?"

"I'd sooner stick my hand into a fire-ant mound," Jackson replied. "Good luck."

～～～

Pam Bachman was waiting in the parking lot outside Charles's apartment when David drove up in his Ford F-150 pickup. She climbed out of her car when she saw him pull into a parking place. She had the grim, dread-stricken appearance of someone who was about to join the battle for the Alamo.

David kissed her. "Waiting for reinforcements?" he said.

"No way I'm doing this alone," she answered.

"What was it that Ben Franklin said? 'We must all hang together or we shall all hang separately.'"

"Something like that," Pam said.

"Let's go, then."

Pam rang the doorbell, then opened the door and called, "Knock, knock?" They had used this arrangement for some time in order to save Charles the unnecessary steps of walking over to the door and opening it. He had provided the Bachmans with a set of keys, just in case he forgot to leave the door unlocked.

The keys were not necessary today. Charles sat in his recliner, facing away from the door. He didn't answer their queries.

"Hi, Charles," Pam said in a cheery, singsong tone that sounded phony even to David.

"How you doin' today, man?" David added, giving Charles a pat on the shoulder as he walked by.

"I *was* doing fine," Charles said, looking straight ahead. "Where are my keys?"

David and Pam looked at one another somewhat sheepishly, as if each wanted the other to go first. "Well," David finally began, "we've been wanting to talk to you about that."

"And?" Charles said, raising his eyes to look at them.

"And—" David continued weakly, at a loss for words. "Look, I don't know how to say this." Charles just kept staring at him. He obviously had no intention of making this any easier.

Pam broke in. "Charles, it's time you stopped driving." She sat down on the sofa across from him. "It won't be easy to give up your mobility. It'll be like losing your freedom. We know that. But you can't drive safely. We don't want you to hurt yourself."

"Where are my keys?" Charles asked again.

"We have them," Pam admitted.

"I know how you must feel," David said, realizing his mistake as soon as the words were out.

"You couldn't possibly know how I feel," Charles shot back, his eyes smoldering. "Do you know what it's like to wake up each morning wondering whether you'll be able to get out of bed? Do you have any idea what it's like to watch yourself waste away, knowing there's nothing you can do about it?"

David broke in. "Charles, we're only trying to help."

Charles shook his head and looked at the floor. When he spoke again, his voice softened. "Some nights the leg cramps are so bad I can't sleep. I lie there looking at the ceiling, wondering what it's going to be like when I can't move at all, when someone has to get me out of bed and dress me. What it's going to be like when someone has to feed me or brush my teeth or take me to the bathroom." He looked at them again. "Or clean me afterward."

David and Pam sat silently.

"It takes a lot of trust to be that dependent on someone," Charles said.

"We were trying to help," said David.

"You'd have helped more if you'd talked to me *before* you took my keys."

"We're sorry, Charles," said Pam. "We'll bring them back."

Charles shook his head. "Keep 'em. Keep the car. I don't care anymore."

"Charles," David said, "don't—"

Charles motioned toward his new computer desk. "You can take all that computer stuff, too. It was stupid to think I could still do anything productive."

"That's not true," Pam said. "There's a lot you can do. You'll see. I'll be back later today to help you get started."

"Don't bother," Charles said. "I called the hospice service. They'll be sending someone to take over. Leave the apartment keys on the dining room table."

Tears filled Pam's eyes. "Charles, don't do this."

Charles pushed himself to his feet. He stood for a few seconds, steadying himself with his cane. "It's already done," he said. "Thanks for your help. Now, if you'll excuse me, I have to use the bathroom." He took a few steps down the hallway, then paused and looked over his shoulder. "I can still do *that* by myself."

<hr>

Lori cleaned up in the employee's locker room, changed into hospital scrubs, and put on her lab coat. Not her usual uniform, but she didn't have time to go back home for a fresh set of clothes. As she entered the atrium, she spotted Dr. Galloway walking toward the hospice facility. She ran to catch up to him.

Dr. Galloway probably wasn't over fifteen or twenty years her senior, although Lori had never asked, and it was difficult to guess. Thick, wavy silver-gray hair and a full, salt-and-pepper beard made him look older than he was. But whatever his age, Dr. Galloway possessed a bedside manner that Lori envied.

She had watched him at the beds of dying patients, acting as if he had no other patients or duties on earth. Lori had seen his schedule and knew better. But when a patient or family member needed him, Dr. Galloway would always be there.

Lori had already decided that if she ever needed hospice care, he would be her physician of choice.

Dr. Galloway broke into a broad smile when he saw her coming. "Lori," he said, "how are you doing? I heard you're out on your own now."

She nodded and fell in step with him. "Much to my sister's chagrin, I'm afraid."

He laughed and put his arm around her shoulder. "Don't you worry. She'll get over it. There's just too much mother hen in her. Now, what can I do for you?"

"Kate invited me to sit in on her meeting with you."

Dr. Galloway raised an eyebrow and nodded. "Can you enlighten me on the mystery?"

Lori shook her head. "She's playing her cards pretty close to the vest on this. Wouldn't tell me anything over the phone."

"Your sister has a flair for the dramatic. Come on, then," he said, stepping out with such an energetic stride that Lori practically had to run to keep up. "We don't want to keep her waiting." He glanced at Lori. Now, what's *your* trouble?"

"Trouble?" said Lori. "What makes you think there's trouble?"

"Your face, Lori. I haven't seen you looking so grim since you first moved here."

"When I first moved here? Oh, with my ex-husband? No, nothing like that."

"What then?"

"Well, maybe you can give me some advice: Did you and Mrs. Galloway disagree on many issues?"

He stopped and looked at her. "We disagreed all the time. Of course, she usually won."

Lori laughed and they started walking again. "I mean about big things."

"Like which car to drive or what house to buy?"

"No, things that have to do with your basic convictions about life."

Galloway cocked his head and looked at her quizzically. "Lori, I can't give an answer without knowing what you're asking."

She shook her head. "I'm making a mess of this. Look, I think I might be falling in love with someone."

"And you're already fighting?"

"No. But under the surface, I think there are some major points of disagreement between me and this person—how we look at life. Do you think a relationship can still work with those kinds of issues?"

"It might help if I knew who this person is—"

"Not yet," Lori interrupted, smiling.

"—or the specifics of the disagreement?" Galloway added, looking hopeful.

Lori shook her head.

"Then I suppose you have to ask yourself whether your beliefs are nonnegotiable."

"What do you mean?"

"Well, if you and this person can agree to disagree, then you might get along. Otherwise—" He made a seesaw motion with his hand.

"In other words, can I compromise what I believe in for the sake of the relationship?"

They stopped at the entrance to the hospice facility. Dr. Galloway turned and faced Lori. "If what you believe in is truly non-negotiable, you won't be willing to compromise—even for the sake of a relationship."

Lori sighed.

"Sounds like I didn't help much," Galloway said.

"Actually you did. Just because I don't like the diagnosis doesn't mean I'm going to shoot the doctor."

"I hope not." Dr. Galloway smiled. "You know, if you told me more, I might be able to give you more useful counsel."

Lori shook her head. "Can't do that. Not yet, anyway."

"Well then," he said, "we'd better go see what Katherine has dug up."

Lori paused at the doorway. "Dr. Galloway?" Lori said.

He turned around. "We aren't talking business. You can call me Barnabas," he said gently.

"Barnabas. How far would you go—in living out your belief system, I mean?"

"Lori, are you *sure* you don't want to tell me what's going on?"

She shook her head.

He looked thoughtful for a moment. "If I really believed something and was committed to it, I suppose I'd follow that path to its conclusion—no matter *what* the consequences. Come on." He motioned her into the hospice.

Lori looked at her watch again. It was now 7:32. In less than half an hour, she would receive her final instructions from the Circle. She checked her cell phone and made sure the ringer was set to "vibrate."

David and Pam Bachman stood in the parking lot outside Charles's apartment. Tears streamed down Pam's face as she leaned up against David's truck.

"What are we going to do?" she said. "We can't just leave him like that."

"Give him some space and some time," David answered. "He'll cool down eventually. When he does, he'll realize what he's done. I've worked with Charles long enough to know how his mind operates. He's got a short fuse but he gets over things pretty fast."

Pam brushed the tears away with the back of her hand. "He's not angry, David, he's quitting."

"At the moment, he's quitting because he's angry." David pulled his keys from his pocket. "But he's really depressed, too."

"That's the worst thing for him," she said. "When someone with ALS is depressed, the disease progresses faster."

"Maybe he's right," David said. "Maybe it's pointless to fight it."

"I'm not talking about fighting it," Pam said. "I'm talking about looking at things differently. Right now Charles thinks he's dying of ALS. He needs to learn that he can *live* with ALS."

"You think it would be worth it to have Kenton drop by one more time?"

Pam took her cell phone from her purse and flipped it open. "That's exactly what I think." She keyed in Kenton's office number.

David said, "It sure can't hurt to see if Kenton can break through Charles's—"

Pam held up a finger. "Hello, Kenton? Oh he's not in?" She silently mouthed the word *secretary* to David. "Do you know where I could reach him? It's kind of an emergency."

Pam paused a moment, listening. The longer she listened, the more serious her expression became. "Oh," she said, "I'm so sorry. Tell her we'll be praying. Bye now." She closed the phone and turned to look at Charles's front door. When she looked back at David, tears had begun to well in her eyes again.

"Kenton's in the hospital. He developed pneumonia a few days ago and isn't responding to treatment." Pam embraced David and rested her head on his shoulder. "They don't expect him to make it."

———

Kate was sitting at her desk when Lori and Dr. Galloway entered the hospice office area. Her solemn expression shocked Lori, but Dr. Galloway seemed not to notice.

"Come into my office, ladies," he said, leading the way.

Kate picked up a thick file folder and followed Dr. Galloway. Lori trailed after her sister, thinking she hadn't seen Kate look this somber since their mother's funeral.

"Close the door," Dr. Galloway said, motioning to Lori to pull the door closed behind her.

A plush leather sectional sofa occupied one corner of the office. The doctor gestured toward it. "Let's sit down over there."

Kate sat down on the comfortable sofa with the file folder in her lap, looking decidedly *un*comfortable. Lori sat at the end of the sofa. Dr. Galloway was in between.

"What have you brought me, Katherine?" he asked.

For a few moments, Kate looked as if she didn't know where to start. Or didn't *want* to start. Finally, she took a deep breath and said, "Someone's killing patients. I have proof."

For the next thirty minutes she presented her case. Although the evidence was mostly circumstantial, it was, nevertheless, compelling.

Dr. Galloway apparently thought so, too. His face grew more serious with each case Kate discussed. And Lori came to the disturbing guess that her sister was laying out the activities of the Circle of Peace in detail. She was not privy to the Circle's history so she couldn't be certain. But as Kate tallied up a list of nearly twenty "unexpected" deaths, Lori realized that the Circle's secret operations might not be as secret as they thought.

Dr. Galloway never said a word, but his body language telegraphed a growing interest. He leaned forward, resting his arms on his knees, never taking his eyes off Kate.

But through the presentation, Lori was puzzled that Kate had made no mention of Drew Langdon.

"What about Drew?" Lori asked. "You said that I should be careful around him."

Kate nodded. "I asked Ruthie Jacoby if anything was different about treatment of Isidore on the night he died. The one difference was that Drew came by."

"And?" said Lori.

"And there was no *reason* for him to visit Isidore Jacoby. He wasn't on the list of staff who were supposed to check on the patient. And he had no prior relationship with the Jacobys."

Lori was incredulous. "That's it? Your whole reason for suspecting Drew is that he didn't have a reason to visit?"

Kate closed her file folder and fixed her sister with a cool gaze. "Why would a grief counselor stop in to visit a patient who was not supposed to die?"

Lori threw up her hands. "That's ridiculous."

Dr. Galloway apparently didn't think so. When Kate had closed her file folder, he had leaned back in his seat. Now *he* was the one who didn't know where to start.

"Katherine," he said, "I don't know what to say. To be honest, I was just humoring you when you brought your suspicions to me earlier." He shook his head as if in self-recrimination. "I'm embarrassed to say that I didn't even keep your first report. But after seeing what you've got here, I'm convinced that you're on to something." He paused for a moment, looking as if he were weighing options. Finally he spoke. "We have to take this to Dr. Johnston."

He stood up and went over to his desk.

Lori couldn't believe what she'd just heard. "Why Dr. Johnston?" she asked.

Dr. Galloway looked back at her as he picked up the phone and began to type in the number. "The news hasn't been announced, but Dr. Johnston is the new chief of staff. He'll decide if there's to be a formal investigation."

Now Kate was incredulous. "Shouldn't we go to the police?"

"That's Dr. Johnston's call."

Lori's heart sank. Of all people to be named chief of staff, it *had* to be the one person on staff who had it in for her. As if to punctuate her sense of dread, she felt her cell phone vibrating in her lab coat pocket.

Her instructions from the Circle had just come in.

———

The digital clock on Lori's desk read 8:28 AM.

Dr. Galloway had not reached Dr. Johnston, but he had told Lori and Kate that he would set up a meeting as soon as he could.

After leaving Galloway's office, Lori toyed with the idea of going to the coffee shop on the west end of the atrium, ordering a latté, and not checking her messages. But she'd already gone too far and knew too much. There was nothing to do but follow through with what she'd started.

And hadn't Dr. Galloway said to do precisely that? If you really believe in something, follow it to its conclusion, no matter what the consequences.

She flipped open her cell phone and worked through the menu options until she came to her messages. The message was brief, another IP address and a time: 8:30 AM. She would have to visit a chat room again to receive her instructions for the evening.

She turned to her computer and clicked on her Internet browser icon. She typed 241.31.5.165 in the address field. The familiar deep-blue page appeared, containing two form fields: one for user name and the other for password. She entered "Servant" in the user name field and "Goshen" in the password field.

She swallowed, noticing how dry her throat and mouth had become.

She clicked the *Submit* button.

The screen flickered for a moment and a chat room window opened. A small information square at the bottom of the window indicated who was in the room. So far, she was the only one logged in.

Lori waited for what seemed like an eternity. Finally, a line appeared:

> Malachi has entered.
>
> Malachi: Hello, Servant.
>
> Servant: Hello, Malachi.
>
> Malachi: Are you ready to fulfill your commitment?
>
> Servant: Yes.
>
> Malachi: Wonderful.
>
> Servant: What do I do?
>
> Malachi: Go to the staff locker room. Locker number 1035. The combination is L23, R2, L46. Memorize it.
>
> Servant: Done.
>
> Malachi: Inside the locker you will find a man's tan jacket. Your materials will be in the jacket's right pocket. Deliver those materials to the patient's room.
>
> Servant: Where do I put them?
>
> Malachi: There will be a small roll of tape with your materials. Go into the bathroom and tape the package to the underside of the toilet tank lid.
>
> Servant: Got it.
>
> Malachi: Under no circumstances discuss the intervention with the patient or a family member. As far as they are concerned, you know nothing about it. Do you understand?
>
> Servant: Yes.
>
> Malachi: Thank you for your help.

A new line popped up in the information window at the bottom of the screen:

Malachi has left.

Lori closed the chat room window and shut down her browser. She noticed a small icon, looking something like a medical chart, in the lower right corner of her monitor. The title underneath the icon read, *Patient Records*. Lori clicked it, bringing up the hospital's database. At the search prompt she typed "Ware, Nina."

Instantly, the screen filled with Nina Ware's medical records, many of which Lori had personally entered. Lori clicked on a button labeled *Admissions*. Nina Ware's early admission record came up. She was due to arrive at the hospital at 4:35 PM and would be assigned to room D422.

The surgeon who would be operating on her was Isidore Jacoby's old family friend and chief of staff-elect, Dr. Terrence Johnston.

The Angel shut down his computer. He wouldn't need it anymore today, and it was a sin to waste energy. He was pleased with himself, pleased with how nicely his plan was progressing.

Dr. Lori Westlake had checked in. He knew she would. The Angel had passed on the Circle's instructions to her. Of course, the Circle's instructions were irrelevant now that the intervention had been canceled, but she didn't know that.

Soon she would be implicated in Nina Ware's death. She would implicate the Circle, but there was no evidence to support her claims. The police would consider her a lone wolf. She would be tried, convicted, and sent to prison.

The Circle would have to lie low for a while, but eventually they would be able to resume their activities.

And they would fulfill their most noble purpose, bringing stability and balance to the Angel's life.

The sacrifice of Dr. Lori Westlake would guarantee that the Circle—and the Angel—would be undisturbed for years to come.

Part Four

NINA

THIRTY-ONE

Nina Ware took one long drag from her half-finished cigarette and crushed it under her foot. Her stepmother, Sara, looked at her as if she had just set fire to the American flag. She pointed at the butt, still smoldering on the otherwise immaculate asphalt parking lot. "You aren't gonna just leave that there, are you?"

Nina rolled her eyes. "Mama, they don't care. It's not like this is a museum."

"They might not care," Sara retorted, "but I do. Look at this place. If it's not a museum, it oughta be." Sara bent over to pick up the cigarette butt.

Nina pulled on her stepmother's arm. "Mama, don't do that. You're gonna hurt your back again."

Sara straightened up, holding the crushed butt triumphantly between her thumb and forefinger. She tossed it into a nearby trash can. "I taught you better than that, child. Now, let's go. It's about time for you to check in."

At precisely four thirty, Nina and Sara strolled through the sliding glass doors into the Sentinel Health Systems atrium. Sara gazed at the opulent surroundings in slack-jawed wonder as Nina approached the reception desk.

Tony Garcia smiled warmly and said, "May I have your room pass, please? He looked at it briefly and then stamped it. "Very good, Ms. Ware. You'll be in D422. Follow me and I'll escort you to your room."

"Mama, come on!" Nina called back to her stepmother as Tony began walking toward the bank of elevators that served the D building.

Sara caught up to Tony and Nina as they passed the fountain that served as the atrium's centerpiece.

"Sorry to hold you up, but this place is *amazing*," Sara said.

"You've never been here before?" asked Tony.

Nina answered for her. "No, this is my stepmama. She lives in Lubbock. She just come up for my operation."

"I wish I'd have known. I could have had you come in a little early and given you a tour. I'll just have to give you the abbreviated version on the way up." Tony pressed *Up* on the polished brass plate by the elevator door. The door opened instantly and Tony motioned them inside the glass-walled elevator. "The Sentinel complex is made up of four main buildings, all joined by a covered atrium. Surgical cases are in Building D, also known as the Travis Building." He pointed across the atrium. "Medical cases go to Building B, the Houston Building. Building A houses our professional building and administrative offices."

"What's it called?" asked Sara.

"It's the Austin Building," Tony answered.

"What about Building C?" Nina asked.

"That's the Crockett Building. It houses our maternity center and hospice facility."

"What's a hospice?" asked Nina.

"Our hospice is a facility for terminally ill patients who have no family and can't be cared for at home. They come here to live out the last stages of their illness. We provide a comfortable, homelike atmosphere and palliative care—we make them as comfortable as possible. We like to think of our hospice staff as a family for those who have no family."

"You only admit patients who don't have families?" asked Sara.

Tony shook his head. "If caring for a patient at home is too much for the family, we'll take them in. They did that for my mother, as a matter of fact. She was dying of breast cancer and I was the only family she had left. I'd have had to quit work to care for her, so she lived out her last few months here at SHS."

"I'm sorry," said Nina.

An expression of deep pain flashed across Tony's face, then was gone. "Me, too," he said.

A bell chimed as the elevator stopped at the fourth floor.

"This way," Tony said as they stepped off the elevator. "Your room is just down the hall."

THIRTY-TWO

It had been a long, quiet day since David and Pam had left. Charles hated to be so unkind to them but he really couldn't see any other way. After they left, he had made his way to the bathroom and pulled out a bottle of pain medication that was leftover from his back surgery a few years earlier. He wasn't sure how many pills he would need for an overdose, but judging by the size of the bottle he figured he had enough.

He dumped some cat food into a cereal bowl and set it on the floor. As Columbo greedily lapped up the food, Charles sat down at the table in his dinette. He preferred his recliner, but the soft chair was beginning to give him back problems.

His father's old Bible lie on the table in front of him. He flipped through the pages until he found the place marker that had been in the Bible since he was eleven years old. The marker, a laminated news clipping, only slightly yellowed, was a bit larger than a three-by-five-inch card. He picked it up and ran his fingers along the edges. It was amazing how after so many years the paper appeared untouched by time.

He scanned the familiar headline: "Officer Cited for Bravery." The article told the story of how Officer Bradford Hamisch—Charles's father—had rescued fifteen people from a hostage situation at a Dallas-area hamburger joint:

"Officer Hamisch was off duty at the time, enjoying a meal at Hamburger Heaven with his wife, JoAnn, and their three children,

when an armed gunman held up the local fast-food establishment.
Officer Hamisch was escorting his eight-year-old son to the restroom
when he heard the gunman ordering all the customers into the back
of the restaurant."

Charles could still hear the hushed urgency in his father's voice.
Dim light reflected off the blue steel of his father's service revolver.

"Lock yourself in the restroom, son."

"Daddy, what are you gonna do?"

"Don't ask questions," his father had whispered as he pushed
Charles into the small room. "Lock the door and don't open it till I
come for you, y'hear?"

"Yes, sir."

Then the door had closed, leaving Charles in the confines of the
dim, windowless restroom. He had turned the lock on the doorknob
and sat down between the sink and the toilet, leaning against the wall.
His eyes had traced the greasy black stains on the white paint around
the doorknob. The room was smelly and Charles wasn't hungry anymore. He just wanted to go home.

He had waited for what seemed like days in that dark room. And
then he'd heard a quiet knock. His throat had felt like it was swell-
ing shut, and he'd sat motionless, as silent as a dead person, afraid to
answer.

The knock had come again.

Charles had held his breath.

Then he'd heard his father's strong voice, "It's okay, Charlie.
Everything's okay now."

Charles had leaped to his feet, thrown open the door, and jumped
into his father's arms.

The memories grew fuzzy after that. All Charles could remember was a lot of officers standing in formation and saluting while
the police chief gave his daddy some kind of medal. He remembered
having to wear his scratchy, mothball-smelling church suit that day.
It had made his neck itch.

He remembered shaking hands with the police chief and hearing
the man ask in a booming voice, "Well, son, what do you think of your
father?"

Charles had shrugged.

"Don't you know? He's a hero."

Later, Charles learned just how *much* of a hero his father was, how he had started a dialogue with the gunman—who was as panicked as everyone else. He had talked the gunman into giving up and saved fifteen people's lives. He had saved Charles's life.

Years later, when Charles was old enough to understand the scope of his father's heroism, he'd vowed he would live as his father had lived. He'd vowed to become a police officer.

He flipped the card over to a second article. A small picture of poor quality in one corner showed Bradford Hamisch in his dress uniform and cap. The photo had been taken the day of the award ceremony. The headline beside the picture read, "Decorated Officer Loses Battle with Cancer."

The article was dated only one year after his father had received his medal for bravery.

A cloud of unease had begun to grow over little Charles as his father took off work for a seemingly endless round of doctor's appointments. His father had tried to reassure him that it was "just routine," but something in his face had told Charles that it wasn't at all routine. He remembered how dark and cold the living room had seemed the night his father called a family meeting.

"I've got to go to the hospital for an operation."

They had all asked what was wrong.

"Oh, got some spots on my right lung, that's all. But the doctor said he's going to take them out and fix me right up." His father had smiled, but the smile didn't reach his eyes.

After that came a whirlwind of memories and images, most of which Charles would've gladly erased from his mind. His father and mother had tried to "protect" him and his sisters. They'd never told them that the doctor had said his dad's case was hopeless. They'd never mentioned that his father would die.

An "everything is normal" optimism was maintained around the children while they were watching their father slide from a robust 220 pounds to a skin-clad, eighty-four-pound skeleton. Everything was still "normal" when Brad Hamisch lost all his hair to chemotherapy and his skin became jaundiced and leathery.

More and more often, the children were shooed outside or sent to neighbors' and friends' houses for meals and unexpected overnights. Then one day when Charles came home from one of those overnights, his parents were not there. His Aunt Ethel had flown in from Arizona and was bustling about the house, cleaning.

"Where's my dad?" Charles had demanded, fear rising in his throat.

"Don't you worry about it, honey," Aunt Ethel had said. "Everything will be all right soon."

Charles had noticed her wiping something away from her eyes.

"I want to see my dad! Where is he?"

His aunt had looked like she didn't want to answer the question. But finally she said, "He's in the hospital, sweetie."

"I want to go see him, now!"

"You can't, Charlie. You're not old enough. Now come help me fix dinner. People will be coming by." She had put her hand on his shoulder, but he had wrenched free from her grasp. She'd looked angry, like she was about ready to hit him, but the phone had rung and she had turned to answer it.

"Hamisch residence." Her voice was formal, businesslike. "No, she's at the hospital with him. Room 302. You can call there directly."

Charles had begun to edge toward the front door. His aunt had paused, keeping an eye trained on him. "What's that?" She had lowered her voice. "No, it won't be much longer."

Charles had just eased the screen door shut when he heard his aunt's shrill voice. "Charles Hamisch, you come back here!" He'd ignored her as he hopped on his bike and pedaled out into the street.

The hospital was nearly two miles away, but it was a warm summer evening and the sun wouldn't go down for another two hours. No one had paid any attention to the ten-year-old boy riding his bicycle across town.

He had chained his bike to a parking meter, sauntered through the front door of the hospital, and joined a group of people waiting for the elevator. Ten people were already waiting for the next car. He had noticed a sign between the elevator doors that read, "No one under fourteen allowed on the floors." He'd stood self-consciously, looking at his shoes and hoping no one would notice.

When the elevator doors had opened, he had inserted himself into the middle of the group. He had almost gotten on when he heard someone call out, "You there, in the yellow shirt. Wait a minute." Charles had looked around. He was the only one wearing a yellow shirt. A security guard was motioning him out of the elevator.

"Sir?" Charles had said, lowering his voice and trying to sound older.

"Can't you read?" the guard had said, pointing at the sign.

"My dad's up there." His voice had quavered slightly.

"I'm sorry, son. Rules are rules." The guard had pointed toward the lobby. "You can wait out there."

Charles had nodded and walked out to the lobby, where he had sat down on a chair. He was trying to figure out what to do next when he heard a door open to his left. In the next few moments, everything had happened like lightning. A large group of people came in the front door and went up to the information desk. They were all talking in Spanish and the volunteer receptionist couldn't understand a word. She'd called the security officer, hoping that he could make some sense out of things.

Charles had seen his chance and had sneaked through the stairwell door before the officer saw him. The poor lighting in the stairwell made it feel like a dungeon. He'd run up three flights of stairs and stopped at a heavy metal door with a large 3 painted on it. Pausing for a moment to catch his breath, he had eased the door open.

After looking up and down the hall to make sure nobody would catch him, he had crept down the deserted hallway. When he'd passed room 306, he had frozen. He'd heard a woman's wrenching sobs coming from a nearby doorway. He hadn't needed to see the number on the door. He'd recognized his mother's voice.

Walking unsteadily to the door, he had looked in. At first, no one noticed him. His grandparents stood on the far side of the bed, holding each other and crying. A minister was at the foot of the bed, praying.

His mother was resting her head on the bed, caressing his father's hand with her cheek and sobbing.

Charles had forced his eyes from his mother to the figure on the bed. His father's mouth was open, as if he were in a deep sleep. His eyes were open, too, but they stared blankly at the ceiling.

"Charles!" his grandfather had gasped. Everyone had turned to look at him. His mother's hair was a mess and black streams of mascara trailed down her face.

He had stood frozen in the doorway, his lower lip quivering. When his mother stretched her arms toward him, a wave of grief had washed over him like a torrent through a broken dam. He had run to her and melted into her embrace.

Years later, when he was old enough to understand the agony his father had endured, he had vowed that he would *not* die as his father had died. He would go out on his own terms. Now he sat alone in his tiny apartment, having driven away his two closest friends so that he could keep his vow.

THIRTY-THREE

Lori stepped off the elevator on the fourth floor of the Travis Building. The digital wall clock read quarter to six. Nina Ware should have been admitted more than an hour ago.

She had found the "materials" in locker 1035, exactly where Malachi had said they would be. Inside the locker she'd found a small plastic bag containing an empty syringe and a vial of insulin.

Her only task was to place the syringe of insulin in Nina Ware's room. In so doing, she would demonstrate her commitment to the Circle's values and work. She would also be committing a crime and making herself an accomplice in Nina's death.

She had almost changed her mind, almost decided not to go through with it. Now that her own sister was on the verge of leading a crusade against the Circle of Peace, it didn't seem to be an opportune time to join the group.

But deep down, Lori believed in what the Circle was doing.

These people were not murderers as Kate thought. They were regular people who were risking their careers, their reputations, and their freedom to give dying people some small measure of dignity.

She didn't know who the other Circle members were, but she respected their courage.

And she wanted to be part of them.

Outside the door of room D422, Lori took a deep breath and knocked. "Come in," Nina called in her thick Texas drawl.

Lori peeked inside and said, "Is this a good time?"

"Dr. Westlake," Nina said, "Thanks for stoppin' by." She was sitting on the bed, looking like she had just come from the shower. She wore a pink terrycloth robe and fuzzy white slippers and had her hair wrapped up in a thick towel. "I want you to meet my stepmama, Sara Ketchum."

A thin, bony woman with stiff gray hair and a wrinkled face that looked like tanned leather stood up and shook Lori's hand. "Pleased to meet ya."

"So," Lori said, "how are you doing, Nina?"

Nina's face darkened. "Some days better'n others, but Dr. Johnston said I gotta 'spect that."

"I suppose he's right," Lori said.

"Wanta see what I really hate?" Nina pulled the towel from her head. Except for hints of some peach-fuzzy growth, she was completely bald.

Horror shot through Lori like a seismic shock wave. "You're on chemo?"

Nina nodded. "Done for a while. They quit it 'cause they want me strong for the surgery. After I get better, I'll have to do some more."

Lori's mouth went desert dry. "I thought you said you weren't going to have chemotherapy."

Sara looked up from her *People* magazine and chimed in. Her voice sounded gravelly. "She got to thinkin' about it. Realized she had a lot to live for. A beautiful baby. A family that loves her. I told her, 'Y'all can't just think about yourself. What you do affects lots of other people.'"

Nina said, "I know I prob'ly won't see Dakota grow up, but maybe I can hang on long enough to watch his first tee-ball game."

Lori couldn't speak. Conflicting thoughts fired through her mind like lightning bolts. This was probably all part of the act. They were just trying to put off anyone who might be suspicious. That had to be it.

"Know what else, Dr. Westlake?" said Nina.

"What, Nina?"

"My daddy couldn't be here for my operation, but he bought me a video camera. Once I get to feelin' better, I'm gonna make a bunch of videos for Dakota. When he's older, he can look at them and get to know his mama."

Lori's body felt like a limp dishrag. When she spoke, her voice was weak and distant. "That's great, Nina. Well, I just wanted to offer my best wishes."

"Thanks for telling her not to quit," said Sara.

"Hmmm?" Lori looked at her, puzzled.

"You're the one got me thinking," Nina said. "When y'all said I shouldn't give up without no fight."

Lori managed a weak smile, nodded, and left the room.

About halfway down the corridor toward the elevators, Lori had to stop and close her eyes. She leaned up against the wall, bracing herself against a water fountain. Her head was reeling.

She couldn't come out directly and ask Nina if she wanted the euthanasia procedure without exposing the Circle and herself to great risk. After all, what if there were some mistake and Nina *hadn't* requested an intervention? Nina's mother would certainly talk to the authorities. On the other hand, it was entirely possible that all Nina's talk was nothing more than a cover story to protect the Circle.

But there was no way to know without asking *someone*.

"Dr. Westlake, are you all right?"

Lori opened her eyes. Faye Renaud stood beside her, looking concerned. "I'm fine," Lori replied. "Just a little dizzy. I think I might be coming down with something."

"There's a bad virus making the rounds right now," said Faye. "You'd better get home and get some rest."

Lori nodded. "I'll do that. Thanks."

Faye continued down the hall and went into Nina Ware's room.

Lori looked at the wall clock. It was 6:00 PM. Only seven and a half hours until the intervention was supposed to happen. She decided to head for her office and try the chat room again. Maybe there was still time to sort all this out.

THIRTY-FOUR

Columbo had finished his supper and was dutifully removing the last molecules of cat food from the bowl. Charles still sat at the table, looking at his father's Bible. His grandfather had given the Bible to him a few weeks after the funeral.

"You're the man of the house now, Charlie," Grandpa had said. "So it's only right that you have this." He'd handed him the leatherbound Bible. "I gave this to your father on his sixteenth birthday. He left it with us when he went into the navy and never picked it up again. He didn't seem to have much use for it. That's why it still looks new."

He remembered standing beside his grandfather, running his fingers over the soft leather and flipping through the delicate pages. The Bible had fallen open and an envelope had dropped out. When Charles had opened the envelope, he'd found his father's obituary and the laminated card that held the news clippings.

The Bible had opened to the book of Hebrews, where his grandfather had underlined his favorite verse. It said, "I will never leave you nor forsake you."

Charles had lost count of the times his grandfather had looked him in the eye and said, "Never forget, Charlie, God will always be with you. Even when everyone else has gone."

Now Charles sat alone and murmured to himself, "If God is really with me, why do I feel so alone?"

"God," he prayed softly, "I don't want to die slowly. Not like my dad. Is that so wrong?"

He sat stiffly, lost in the past until the persistent buzzing of the doorbell jarred him back to the present.

The doorbell stopped—and the pounding started. Then he heard Pam Bachman's voice calling.

"I'm coming," he shouted.

He took his cane and made his way over to the door as the pounding continued.

Why doesn't she just open the door herself? Then he remembered. He'd told her and David to leave the apartment keys on the table.

He pulled the door open. "Pam, what's wrong?" Her face was drawn and sad.

"I need to get you to the hospital right away," she said. "Kenton McCarthy is asking for you."

THIRTY-FIVE

Lori stepped off the elevator and walked out into the atrium. The early evening sunlight that normally streamed through the west-facing atrium windows had been supplanted by charcoal black clouds. She could hear low rumblings of thunder. Distant lightning flashes periodically accented the skyline. A stiff wind whipped through the silver maples and Bradford pears near the garden entrance, dislodging a discarded grocery store bag that rolled past the sliding doors like a West Texas tumbleweed.

She was thankful she didn't have to go outside to get to her office.

Pedestrian traffic in the atrium had slowed to a trickle. The reception desk and most of the shops had closed. A handful of people huddled around a table near the fountain, watching the approaching storm.

Lori hurried over to the Austin Building. Now that it was after business hours, the office elevators were locked. However physicians and staff members had key cards to summon the elevators twenty-four hours a day.

She slid her card into the slot, punched in her PIN, and the elevator doors opened. As she stepped inside and the doors closed behind her, she heard a sharp pop, followed instantly by a deafening explosion, followed by darkness. She tried to stifle her panic as she stood in darkness. A second later, the lights came back on and Lori heaved a sigh of relief. She was not claustrophobic, but she did not relish the idea of being stuck in an elevator during a power outage.

Not wanting to wait for a second lightning strike, she quickly pressed the fifth floor button and felt the welcome surge in her stomach as the elevator whisked her to the fifth floor.

As she expected, the corridor lights had dimmed and virtually all of the offices were closed. She swiped her key card through the electronic lock on her office door, went inside, and sat at her desk. Grabbing the mouse, she double-clicked a desktop icon to bring up her Web browser. As soon as it loaded, she clicked in the address field and typed in a series of numbers: 241.31.5.165.

"Come on," she said under her breath. "Please. Someone be there."

As if on cue, her computer emitted an electronic chime and a small alert box appeared in the center of the screen.

241.31.5.165 not found. Please try again.

She retyped the numbers, hoping she had just made a mistake.

241.31.5.165 not found. Please try again.

She tried a third time.

241.31.5.165 not found. Please try again.

She slammed her fist on her desktop. "No!"

The clock on her computer screen now showed six thirty. There was still time to clarify Nina's wishes, but not if she couldn't find someone with whom to consult.

This is a definite weakness in the Circle's system if you can't get someone in an emergency.

She put her head in her hands, on the edge of despair.

Then she remembered.

Maybe there is a way.

THIRTY-SIX

Streaks of lightning lit up the sky, and huge raindrops pounded Pam's windshield until she pulled under the overhang outside the Sentinel Health Systems reception area.

"Do you want a wheelchair?" She had to shout to be heard over the storm.

"It'll be faster," Charles replied. Pam nodded and waved to a young parking valet, who promptly rolled a wheelchair out to her. Aligning the chair with the side of the car and setting the wheel brake, Pam helped Charles stand up and ease himself into the seat.

A strong gust of wind blew chilly vaporized raindrops through the covered drop-off area. Charles shivered and hunkered down in the chair. "I think I should have worn a heavier jacket," he said. "I don't have quite as much insulation as I used to."

"We'll be inside soon," said Pam. She gave the valet a five-dollar tip and allowed him to park her car. "Let's go," she said, wheeling Charles up the ramp in the sidewalk and into the atrium.

———

Charles hated hospitals. He hated the smell, the atmosphere, the way everyone walked around hushed, as if in a library. Most of all, he hated hospitals because it was like being thrust into a time machine and rushed back to his father's deathbed. The fact that he was probably on his way to another deathbed scene didn't make it any easier.

As Pam wheeled him down the hallway toward Kenton McCarthy's room, Charles wished for some way to escape what he knew was coming. But no matter how difficult these next few minutes might be, he knew he had to endure them—for Kenton and Janice's sake if for no other reason.

Charles saw Janice standing near the head of Kenton's bed with her back to the door. A short, balding African-American man stood at the foot of the bed, holding a large black Bible. His head was bowed in prayer. Janice was the first one to notice Charles and Pam at the door. She smiled and motioned for them to come in. She embraced Pam and leaned over to kiss Charles on the cheek. "I'm so glad you came, Charles. Kenton has been asking for you." She motioned toward the man with the Bible. "This is our pastor, Bobby Siles."

The pastor extended his hand to Charles, "Pleased to meet you."

Charles took his hand and nodded. He couldn't manage to clear the lump that was rapidly forming in his throat.

Kenton's bed was set at an incline and he was wearing an oxygen mask. His eyes were closed and he appeared to be asleep. Charles could hear him wheezing with each labored breath.

"How is he doing?"

"He's been resting a little easier this evening," said Janice. "Kenton," she said, brushing his cheek with the back of her hand, "Charles is here."

Kenton opened his eyes slightly. One corner of his mouth curled up in a hint of a smile. He mumbled something, the noise of which went no further than his mask. He tried to move his hands to his face, but he couldn't lift them off the bed.

Janice understood what her husband wanted and removed the oxygen mask. "Just for a few minutes," she said. Kenton nodded weakly.

Pam handed Charles his cane and helped him to his feet. He shuffled over to Kenton's bedside and stood for a moment, not quite sure what to say.

Kenton struggled to speak. "Hhhhhhowrrrre—youuu—doooing?"

Charles nodded. "Okay."

Kenton smiled and shook his head. "Reeeallly?"

Charles gritted his teeth, driving back boiling emotions that threatened to overflow. He choked out the words. "I've been better."

Kenton nodded. Then his expression grew serious. "Doooo—yooouu—unnnnerrrstannd—yyyyet?"

Charles shook his head, not sure what Kenton meant. "Do I understand?"

"Efffffrrrreey—tthhhaay." Kenton coughed, and the cough quickly became a labored hacking.

Charles looked around for help and realized for the first time that the others had left him alone with Kenton. He leaned over and helped his friend put on the oxygen mask. "Settle down, now," he said. "Don't try to talk. Just relax and breathe."

Kenton nodded and closed his eyes.

"Good," said Charles. He lifted the oxygen mask once more. "Now, what were you trying to say?"

"Effffreey—thhday—gghhhivvt."

"Every day's a gift?"

Kenton nodded.

Charles shook his head. "Sorry. I still don't get it."

Kenton smiled. "Tssss—ohhh—khhhhay. Yooouuuu—wiiiill." He leaned back and closed his eyes. His breathing was growing more labored. Kenton nodded toward his hand. "Fvvurrr—yoooou."

"For me?" Charles looked at Kenton's hand and noticed an envelope underneath it. The envelope was addressed to him. Charles picked it up. "Should I read it now?"

Kenton closed his eyes and shook his head.

Charles felt a hand on his shoulder and turned to see Janice standing beside him. "I think he needs to rest a bit. Thank you so much for coming."

Charles eased himself back into the wheelchair. "I think I need to rest, too. Take me home, Pam."

Janice tried to put the oxygen mask back on Kenton's face, but he kept shaking his head, preventing her from covering his mouth. He opened his mouth and spoke weakly, "Shhhhhaarrlls."

"I'm still here, Kenton." Charles answered.

"Nehhhffr—ghhhiff—uhhhpf."

Charles shook his head and glanced up toward Janice. "I'm sorry. I can't make out what he said."

Janice smiled. "He said, 'Never give up.'"

THIRTY-SEVEN

Lori stepped off the elevator and into the SHS staff exercise facility and locker room. When she'd changed clothes earlier, she had left the Circle's prepaid cell phone in her own locker. She'd noticed that some numbers had been preprogrammed into the phone. If one of those numbers would put her in contact with Malachi or another member of the Circle, she could find out whether Nina Ware still wanted to go through with the intervention.

The lockers were located in the basement of the Austin Building, along with a spa and workout room. The workout room included a sauna, Jacuzzi, and state of the art exercise and weight training equipment, all available free to SHS employees. Unlike the rest of the building, this room enjoyed a fair amount of traffic until late in the evening.

Lori frequently used the workout room, so her presence there wasn't unusual. She only hoped she didn't run into anyone she knew. SHS employed more than fifteen hundred people at this complex alone, so the odds of being recognized were relatively small. But she preferred that nobody be able to place her at the scene, so to speak.

The shower-room air felt clammy as she walked down the long row toward her locker. She could hear some conversations taking place in the women's showers but didn't recognize any of the voices.

Not wanting to remain "visible" any longer than necessary, she quickly opened her locker and slipped the cell phone into her lab coat.

The spacious atrium was nearly deserted, so she claimed a small table off in a dark corner and took out the cell phone.

The prepaid cell phone was a nice touch. Like everything else the Circle did, it was simple and virtually untraceable. Malachi had warned her against using it except in a real emergency, but if this wasn't an emergency, she didn't know what would be.

She turned on the phone and toggled through the menu options. Selecting "Saved Numbers," she found a single telephone number in the phone's memory. She highlighted the number and pressed *Send*.

One ring. Two. Three.

"Come *on*. Somebody be there."

A fourth ring.

Then a message, curt and succinct. "Leave your message at the tone and hang up." It was a man's voice. Perhaps Malachi's?

Lori heard the tone.

"This is Servant. I need to confirm that the patient in question has genuinely requested intervention."

She pressed the *End* button and set the phone on the table in front of her. The wall clock now read 7:15. Still plenty of time, but Lori hoped it wouldn't take long for Malachi to get back to her. Until then—

"Lori?"

Lori looked up to see Drew Langdon approaching. So much for not seeing anyone she knew.

"What are you doing here? I thought you had self-defense class tonight." He leaned down and kissed her.

She felt the pit of her stomach sink to her feet. She was so focused on Nina and the Circle that she had completely forgotten about self-defense class. Jackie Palermo would miss her *and* she would ask about it. On top of that, now Drew could place her at the hospital. She'd never make it as a career criminal.

"Hi, Drew," she said. "I'm not feeling that great tonight. I decided to skip the class. What about you? Why are you here so late?"

"There's a patient upstairs who probably won't last much longer. The wife already has pastoral support, but I like to check in, just to let them know I'm available. I probably won't be up there very long. Will you be here a while?"

Lori shook her head. "Probably not, Drew. I think I'm going to head home and get some rest."

"Who's taking you?"

Lori's forehead wrinkled. "What do you mean?"

"You walked here this morning. Don't you remember?"

"Yes, but what difference does *that* m—" A thunderclap interrupted her. She looked out toward the crystal entrance. It was pouring.

"I don't think you want to walk home in *that*," Drew said.

Lori rubbed her forehead. She had the beginnings of a terrible headache. "I forgot all about getting the car."

"Don't worry about it. After I heard the weather report at lunchtime, I went home and got mine. I won't be long; I'll come back and take you home." Drew paused for a second, looking at the cell phone, then at Lori. "Aren't you going to get that?"

"Get what?"

Drew nodded toward the cell phone.

It was flashing and vibrating.

THIRTY-EIGHT

The ride home from SHS was silent and uncomfortable. Pam drove carefully through the downpour and Charles quietly fingered the envelope that Kenton had given him. By the time Pam pulled into the handicapped space by Charles's apartment, the downpour had eased to a gentle drizzle. She switched off the ignition and headlights and turned in her seat.

"Charles, David and I are so sorry we didn't trust you. We shouldn't have taken your keys. We should have talked to you."

He dismissed the apology with a wave. "I'm the one who should apologize. I was a jerk."

"Not a jerk," Pam said. "If I were in your shoes, I hope I'd handle all this as well as you have."

She got out and came around the car.

"Would you like me to stay and fix you some supper?"

"No, thanks. I need to be alone tonight. Just get me to the door, and I'll be fine."

Charles gave her the envelope to hold. Then she helped him swing his legs out of the car, handed him his cane, and eased him to his feet. Using the cane on one side and with Pam steadying him on the other, Charles walked up to his front door. He handed Pam the key to his apartment. "It's hard for me to turn it," he said.

She opened the door and stepped back as he stepped inside. Instantly, Columbo was rubbing up against his feet and meowing.

"I see your welcoming committee is here," Pam said with a laugh.

"If I could just teach him to cook and clean. . . ." Charles took Pam's hand. "Thank you. And tell David I'm sorry for this morning."

"He understands—and we're praying for you."

Charles flashed a grim smile. "I need it."

"Oh," she said, "I almost forgot." She handed him the door key and Kenton's envelope.

"Keep it," he said.

Pam looked puzzled. "But Kenton gave it to you," she said.

"I mean the door key," Charles said. "Keep it. And come see me tomorrow. Please."

THIRTY-NINE

Lori stared at the cell phone as it continued flashing and vibrating on the tabletop. She didn't want to answer it with Drew standing right there, but she might not get another chance to find out exactly what was going on with Nina. As she picked up the phone she heaved a sigh, rolled her eyes, and said, "A doctor's work is never done."

Drew took the hint. He pointed at his watch. "I'll be back in ten or fifteen."

Lori nodded and pressed the *Answer* button as Drew walked away.

"Hello?"

"Servant, why are you calling?"

The voice was vaguely familiar but Lori couldn't place it. "Is this Malachi?"

"Don't worry about who I am. *Why* are you calling?"

"I have a problem."

"What is it?"

"I went by to see Nina—" Lori said.

"*Don't* use proper names!"

Lori felt her face grow hot. "I'm sorry. I went by to see the patient and she doesn't act like someone who expects—expects an *intervention* to be performed."

"Did you deliver the materials?"

"No, but—"

"*Tsk.*" There was a long pause on the line. When the voice spoke again, it was cool and controlled, but tinged with suppressed anger.

"Every case is fully investigated and cleared *before* it comes to this point. You have endangered our work and your own position. Complete the delivery as scheduled and do *not* call again."

"But—"

The connection was closed.

Lori turned the phone off and slipped it into her lab coat pocket. The ball was back in her court, but she was no longer certain she wanted to finish the game.

FORTY

Charles sat down at the dinette table and tried to open the sealed envelope. He was tired, and his fingers were sluggish. He had to retrieve a knife from the silverware drawer as a letter opener. He pulled a typewritten sheet from the envelope, and a small bracelet fell out of the envelope. Setting it aside, he unfolded the sheet.

Dear Charles,

It's too difficult to talk anymore, so I dictated this letter to Janice. I wish I could tell you these things face-to-face, but maybe this is better.

When I learned I had ALS, I was angry with everybody. I was angry with God because He let me get this awful disease. I was angry with other people because they didn't understand what I was going through. I was even angry at Janice because she was so strong about it. I think I'd have felt better if she'd yelled or broken a few things.

I couldn't imagine what it would be like to be completely paralyzed and dependent on others for everything—not able to feed myself or talk. I thought of ways to take my own life and make it look like an accident. But then something strange happened.

I had a dream one night. I'd mostly been having night-mares about ALS and about being paralyzed. But this dream was different. I was walking down a trail in the woods, and

*Jesus was there. He asked me why I was so angry, and I said,
"I've dedicated my life to serving you. Why did you let me get
ALS?"*

*Jesus just smiled and said, "If I want you to glorify me
through ALS while others are healthy, what is that to you?
You follow me."*

*I told him that I didn't understand but He just kept smil-
ing at me. Then he said, "Redeem your suffering."*

*I thought about that dream for a long time. I still don't
know whether it was real. But I do know that its message
was true.*

*Charles, you can burn yourself out in your anger over
ALS. You can check out early—on your own terms. Or you
can realize that ALS is just a way to glorify God. I know
you're afraid of becoming totally dependent on others. Have
you ever considered that God wants to use you in other people's
lives? And the best way he might be able to do that is through
ALS?*

*I sound like a preacher now. Just think about it. "What-
ever you do, do all to the glory of God."*

I'll be waiting for you in heaven.
Your brother in Christ,
Kenton

Charles sat for a long while, reading and rereading Kenton's
letter. He kept coming back to the last phrase: "Whatever you do, do
all to the glory of God."

He flipped over the bracelet that had been in the envelope. On it
were inscribed the words, "Never Give Up!"

FORTY-ONE

Lori sat at the table in the atrium, staring off into space. When Drew returned, he waved his hand in front of her face. "Earth to Lori. . . . Earth to Lori."

Blinking as if awakening from a hypnotic trance, she looked up at Drew and offered a weak smile. "Oh. Hi, Drew. Sorry. I was lost in my thoughts."

"Something on your mind?"

Lori paused for a second. Perhaps the best way to handle the situation with Nina was to walk away from it. If she didn't deliver the insulin, then the intervention could not be performed. If she was wrong, and Nina was following a script, no harm was done. The intervention could be rescheduled. But if Nina had really changed her mind, Lori would be preventing a terrible accident from taking place.

Of course, she was probably also blowing whatever chance she had of becoming a member of the Circle of Peace. But she preferred that to allowing someone to be euthanized by mistake.

She looked up at Drew. "Yes, there is something on my mind. But I don't want to talk about it here. You have time for dinner—a nice *long* dinner? I'm buying this time."

"Sounds like an offer I can't refuse," Drew said.

"By the way, how's the patient and his family?" Lori asked.

"He slipped away while I was up there. It was a blessing though. He had advanced ALS. Definitely not the way I'd like to go out."

Lori nodded.

In the same quiet corner of Tony's Italian Cuisine where they'd shared their first meal, Lori sat across the table from Drew, looking at him over a pasta sampler platter. He had almost finished his lasagna, but she had only picked at her food.

"You ready to talk about it?"

"About what?"

"About whatever's on your mind."

Lori shook her head. "It's something I've got to work out myself. I just thought it would be nice to have some company tonight to keep my mind off—" Lori stopped in mid-sentence and took a sip of wine.

"Off what?"

"Something I thought I believed in, but now I'm not so sure about."

Drew reached across the table and took her hand. "Sure you don't want to talk about it? It might help you sort out your feelings."

"You're helping more than you know, just by being here," Lori said.

"Can't you at least give me a hint about what's bothering you?"

"Do you remember Nina Ware?"

"Your cancer patient who wants to die?"

Lori nodded. "She's decided to fight. She's scheduled for surgery tomorrow and is already on chemo."

"That's good, isn't it?" Drew asked.

"Yes, but—"

"But what?"

Lori looked at her watch. It was ten after ten. "You know, Drew, I'm really tired. I think I'd like to go home now."

The rain had stopped and the thunder had moved off to the east when Drew pulled up in front of Lori's apartment. Lightning flashes on the western horizon foretold the approach of more rain, but for the moment the storms had passed.

Drew came around to the passenger side and opened the door. As Lori stepped out, she wrapped her arms around herself. "I left my jacket at the office." She edged close to Drew, and he placed his arm around her shoulder.

"Are you sure you don't want me to stay?" he asked as they stood in front of his car. "You look like you really don't want to be alone tonight. I don't understand what's going on but I'd like to help."

Lori shook her head. "I have to work through this one by myself, but it was sweet of you to ask." She turned her face up toward his, and he kissed her. "I'll see you tomorrow," she said as she took out her keys. At the door, she turned and gave a half wave to Drew. She heard his car pull away from the curb as she inserted the key in the lock.

As soon as she stepped into her apartment, she sensed that something was not right—but she wasn't certain. Automatically her fingers felt for the pepper spray canister on her key ring.

She flipped on the lights and scanned the room. If someone had ransacked her apartment, it would have been difficult to tell. She still hadn't finished unpacking and the place was a wreck.

Then she realized what was wrong: It wasn't what she was seeing; it was what she smelled, a scent she had once loved but now detested.

Cologne.

Philip's cologne.

Her ex-husband had been in her apartment very recently.

In fact, he might *still* be in there.

FORTY-TWO

Charles sat at the table, flipping through his Bible and rereading Kenton's letter. Columbo had jumped onto the table and was curled up in a ball, sleeping. Charles ran his hand absentmindedly over the cat's fur as he read out loud, "For to me, to live is Christ, and to die is gain."

How do you die for the glory of God?

Charles wasn't a theologian, but in the past few years he had learned enough about the Bible to think of some answers to that question. He knew people went into dangerous places to tell others about Christ, and some died. Christians sometimes were killed because they confessed Jesus. What they did could be described as dying for God's glory.

But he wasn't a missionary. He wasn't a martyr.

He was a weak man who was slowly dying from a disease. It wasn't his choice to sacrifice himself. He would gladly get rid of it if he could. How could he possibly glorify God through his ALS?

Nor could he dismiss Kenton's letter as the insensitive platitudes of someone who didn't understand what he was going through. But Kenton was also a pastor. You kind of expect a pastor to have that perspective. Charles was just a cop.

"I'm sorry, Kenton," he said out loud. "I don't know if I'll *ever* figure it out."

Columbo lifted his head and yawned. Charles looked at the wall clock. "I guess it's time we hit the sack, Columbo. It's almost ten thirty, and at my current pace, it'll be midnight before we get there."

He took his cane and stood up, but before he could begin his slow trek down the hall, the phone rang. A sinking feeling developed in the pit of his stomach. He didn't get many telephone calls, and none at ten thirty at night.

"This is Charles," he said.

"Charles?"

It was Pam. He could hear the sadness in her voice.

"Yes, Pam?"

"Kenton's gone. He passed away a little while ago. Janice wanted me to make sure you knew."

Charles didn't know what to say. He never knew what to say in these situations. "Tell Janice that I'm sorry, and that I'm very glad I got to know Kenton."

"Janice told me to tell you that Kenton had one last message for you," she said.

Charles could feel his throat thickening. "What was that?" He managed to choke out the words.

"He said, 'No regrets.'"

"Thanks for calling, Pam."

No regrets.

As he hung up the phone, tears blurred his eyes. He looked up toward the ceiling and said, "See you in heaven, Kenton. Save me a good spot."

FORTY-THREE

Lori sat down on her bed and breathed out a shuddering sigh. Her hands were ice cold and she was trembling.

Philip had been in the apartment. She was certain of it. But after turning on every light, looking behind every stack of boxes, and investigating every closet, she was equally certain that he was no longer there.

There was no sign of forced entry. How had he gotten in?

She had a restraining order against him and considered calling the police, but what would she tell them? The unmistakable scent of Philip's cologne was already dissipating, and as far as she could tell, he had touched nothing, taken nothing, and left nothing.

He had merely *been* there.

The scent of his cologne was not exactly hard evidence. If she called the police, they would just think she was crying wolf. Then if she really needed them, they might not respond quickly enough.

There was only one thing to do.

She got up and tore into the nearest box. "Now where did I put that thing?" There was a box near her bed labeled "Towels." Lori got up and tore the box open. She dumped the contents of the box onto her bed. A pile of plush towels—and nothing more—fell out.

She ripped open another box, this one labeled "Linens," and dumped it on the floor. Only linens.

With an urgency bordering on panic, she began to attack the other boxes, dumping the contents of one after another onto the floor.

Sweat formed on her brow and trickled down into her eyes, burning them.

"Where *is* it?" she growled.

Finally, she tore open a box labeled "Junk" and dumped its contents. Out tumbled a hodgepodge of old makeup, earrings, dead batteries, and a .22 caliber pistol.

She hadn't used it since she'd gotten her license to carry a concealed weapon.

She hated guns, but if Philip was stalking her again, she wasn't going to take a chance.

Now, Lori thought, *I just need to remember where I packed the bullets.*

———

At precisely 1:12 AM by the digital wall clock on the Travis Building's fourth floor, the Angel stepped out of the stairwell and into the corridor. Room D422 was on the far end of the floor from the nurses' station and there was no sign of traffic.

The door to Nina Ware's room stood ajar. Only a dim incandescent fixture over the sink illuminated the room. Nina's vitals would have been checked by now, so there would be no unexpected interruptions.

The young cancer patient appeared to be resting peacefully.

Her stepmother, stretched out on a recliner and snoring loudly, left no doubt as to *her* status.

The Angel pulled on a pair of latex gloves and withdrew a syringe from his lab coat pocket. Carefully removing the cap, he injected the contents into Nina Ware's IV tubing. After recapping the syringe, he dropped it into the red biohazard receptacle on the wall.

One last thing to make it complete. He took a ceramic angel from his pocket and placed it on the bedside table.

Now everything was in place.

His work done, the Angel looked up and down the corridor. No one was in sight. He made his way back to the stairwell and left the way he had come.

Balance would soon be restored.

Very soon.

Part Five

THE ANGEL OF MERCY

FORTY-FOUR

Lori awoke to the sound of the telephone ringing. She looked at her clock through sleep-blurred eyes. It was just after six, and the sun was barely peeking over the horizon. She reached for the phone on her bedside table.

"Hello?"

"Dr. Westlake?" a woman's voice asked.

Lori rubbed her eyes. "Uh-huh."

"This is Dr. Johnston's secretary. He needs you in his office as soon as possible."

"It's six in the morning—what's up?"

"I'm sorry, I can't go into that. All I can tell you is that it's urgent."

"An emergency?"

There was a short pause. "Not directly."

"Okay," Lori said, sitting up and yawning. "I'll be in shortly."

She hung up the phone, wondering what Terrence Johnston could possibly want so early in the morning. If it had been Dr. Galloway, she'd have gone over in a heartbeat. She wasn't in as big a hurry to accommodate Dr. Johnston, even if he *was* going to be the new chief of staff. Whatever bee he had in his bonnet could wait until she'd had a shower and a cup of coffee.

At 7:15, Lori walked into Dr. Johnston's outer office and waiting

233

room. "I'm Dr. Westlake," she told the receptionist. "Dr. Johnston wanted to see me?"

The receptionist motioned toward the door. "Go right in. They're waiting for you."

"Nice of you to finally join us, Dr. Westlake," Dr. Johnston said as Lori walked through the door. "I'd like you to meet Detective Bachman." He motioned toward a man who was sitting in a chair in front of the desk. Detective Bachman stood up and offered his hand.

"Pleased to meet you, ma'am," he said.

"Detective Bachman would like to ask you a few questions," Dr. Johnston added.

"What is this about?" Lori asked.

"Please," Detective Bachman said, motioning toward a chair. "Have a seat."

Lori sat down. She felt a cold chill creeping into her fingers.

The detective took out a small notebook and opened it. "Do you know a Nina Ware?"

"Yes. She's one of my patients."

"Not any longer," interjected Dr. Johnston.

Detective Bachman shot him a not-too-subtle glance that told the doctor to hold his peace.

"What are you talking about?"

"Ms. Ware was found dead at about four this morning," the detective said.

Lori felt like someone had just punched her in the stomach. For a few seconds, she sat stunned.

"When was the last time you saw Ms. Ware?" Detective Bachman asked.

Lori's head was spinning. She couldn't think.

"Dr. Westlake?"

"I—I'm sorry." She rubbed her forehead as if warding off a headache. "I stopped by to see her yesterday evening."

"Do you remember when that was?"

Lori closed her eyes. "It was about six or seven o'clock. I don't remember exactly."

"That's fine," said the detective. "What did you talk about?"

"Uh, her surgery. She was going to have a procedure this morning."

"Were you supposed to perform it?"

Lori shook her head. "No. I'm not a surgeon."

"So you were just checking in to see how she was doing?"

"I'm her primary care physician, and she'd been pretty despondent. I wanted to make sure she was in a good frame of mind."

"Fine," said Detective Bachman, making some notes in his notebook. "Is that the only time you went to her room last night?"

Lori nodded.

"Where'd you go after you visited Ms. Ware?"

"I went out to dinner with a friend, Drew Langdon. He's a grief counselor here. We ate at Tony's Italian Cuisine. We were there until around ten."

"Will he verify that?"

"Yes, of course. What's going on? Why are you asking me all these questions?"

Dr. Johnston interrupted. "Ms. Ware did not die of natural causes."

Lori's voice was almost inaudible. "What happened?"

"We won't know until we get the medical examiner's report," answered Detective Bachman. "Now you're sure that you didn't go to her room again, maybe after you finished dinner?"

"No, I went straight home. Ask Drew, he drove me there."

Detective Bachman closed his notebook. "That's all I need right now." He handed Lori a business card. "If you think of anything else, I'd appreciate it if you'd give me a call at this number."

"Certainly," Lori said, still in a daze.

The detective shook hands with Dr. Johnston. "Thank you for letting me use your office."

"Happy to be of service," said Dr. Johnston.

"Pleased to meet you, ma'am," Detective Bachman said to Lori as he left.

Lori stood to follow him out.

"Dr. Westlake, I'm not through with you," said Dr. Johnston.

Lori was not in the mood for a lecture. She needed time to think. To figure out what had happened. But she couldn't afford to offend Terrence Johnston. She took a deep breath and turned around. "Yes, doctor?"

"I'm going to recommend to the disciplinary committee that you be placed on paid leave and your privileges temporarily suspended until this is all sorted out."

Lori was incredulous. "What?"

"Dr. Westlake, a patient—*your* patient—was murdered last night. Or, some might say, euthanized. You were seen leaving that patient's room."

"That was early in the evening," Lori protested. "The nurses would have been in to see her several times after I left."

"You were seen leaving the patient's room at *one thirty* in the morning. She died not long after."

Lori shook her head. "That's impossible. I was nowhere near the hospital at that time. I was at home in bed."

"And who can verify that?" Dr. Johnston challenged.

"Who said that they saw me here in the middle of the night?"

Dr. Johnston walked behind his desk and sat back down. "There are a lot of unanswered questions surrounding this death, Dr. Westlake. Until we sort it all out, I think it's better that you not be treating patients."

"But you can't—"

"The disciplinary committee meets at three this afternoon. You'll know something by the end of the day."

"But—"

"That will be all, doctor." Terrence Johnston had a satisfied smirk plastered on his face.

———

Lori stepped outside the office and stood in the hallway, numb and reeling.

Nina. That poor young thing. What happened? Did Malachi make other arrangements? Did he know she didn't intend to go through with it? And why was somebody lying about seeing me there just before Nina died?

Lori felt like she was walking in a fog. Nothing made sense. Why would the Circle try to frame her? They could only harm themselves by doing that.

Lori had less than seven hours to find some answers, for her own sake and for Nina's. If she were placed on paid leave, her access to information would be cut off. She pulled her cell phone from her pocket and speed-dialed her office.

Her receptionist's voice came on the line. "Dr. Westlake's office, may I help you?"

"Shelley, this is Lori." Her voice was shaky. "Something's come up. I need you to cancel all my appointments for the day."

"Dr. Westlake, are you all right?"

"I'm fine," Lori lied. "Can you cancel those appointments for me?"

"You're going to have a lot of unhappy campers."

"It can't be helped. If they need to see somebody today, see if one of the other doctors can squeeze them in."

"Will do."

"Thanks." Lori hung up the phone. *Next stop, the Travis Building.*

When Lori stepped off the elevator on Travis Four, she knew she'd made a tactical error. The floor was crawling with police taking fingerprints and photos, reviewing files, interviewing witnesses. D422, Nina's room, had been cordoned off with yellow crime scene tape. A uniformed officer guarded the entrance to the room.

Lori decided to do an about-face and find another way to get the information she needed when she heard a man's voice call to her. She turned to see Detective Bachman approaching.

"I'm glad you came up, doctor," the detective said. "I was just about to send for you. Just some routine procedural stuff."

"Sure," Lori said, her voice filled with a phony cheeriness. "Anything to help."

"Come on down to Ms. Ware's room with me for a minute," he said, leading the way.

Lori followed the detective to D422. The door was open. "I'm sorry I can't invite you inside," he said. "But I wanted you to check from here and tell me if anything looks unusual. You know, if you see something out of the ordinary."

Lori hesitated when she got near the door. As a doctor, she'd seen more than a few dead bodies. It went with the territory, so to speak. Nevertheless, she found herself reluctant to look at Nina.

"Don't worry, doctor. She's not in there anymore."

Lori flushed with anger and embarrassment. She looked into the room for a few seconds, then shook her head and withdrew. "Everything looks exactly the way it did last night."

"And what time last night did you say you were here?" Detective Bachman pressed.

Lori would not be baited. She gave him a cordial smile. "I hope you find your killer, detective. Now if you'll excuse me, I need to get back to work."

"You'll be around here all day?" the detective asked. "Just in case I need to run something else by you?"

"All day." Lori smiled and headed back to the elevator. She pressed the button, hoping the doors would open quickly.

She heard Detective Bachman call to her again. "Dr. Westlake?"

Lori turned around. "Yes?"

"Aren't you forgetting something?"

"I'm not sure what you mean," said Lori.

"You must have come up here for a reason," the detective said.

Lori tapped her head like she was trying to remember something. "Must be a senior moment," she said. "I forgot."

The elevator doors opened. "Ciao," she said, waving at Bachman.

"Doctor?" Bachman called again.

Lori stopped, holding the elevator doors open.

"I'm sorry to hold you up, but would you mind going over to the nurses' station for just a few minutes?"

"Why?" Lori asked.

"We need to get your fingerprints." Bachman shook his head and waved it off. "Just routine."

"What do you think *now*?" Dr. Barnabas Galloway leaned forward in his chair as Dr. Terrence Johnston sat at his desk and reviewed the file folder containing Katherine Bainbridge's latest report. The color drained from the hospital chief's face as he flipped page after page.

He started to speak, but then riffled through the papers one more time. "I wouldn't have believed it. Not before this morning." He looked across the desk at Galloway. "We've got to do something." Resignation was evident on his face.

"Not a great way to begin your tenure as chief," said Galloway.

"I can think of a lot of other ways I'd have preferred," Johnston responded.

"Think we could deal with it in-house? Keep it quiet?" Galloway asked.

Johnston's expression soured. "Not with half the police department running around Travis Four." He closed his eyes and shook his head. "When the press gets wind of this—"

"P.R. department's already working on a response," said Galloway.

Johnston nodded. "They're supposed to give me a statement to release to the press any time now." He stood up and began to pace around his office. "But a response to the Nina Ware case is child's play compared to *that*," he said, jabbing a finger toward the file folder on his desk.

Terrence Johnston lowered his voice. "Barnabas, we've got a *serial killer* operating in this hospital."

"Do you still think it's Lori Westlake?" Galloway asked.

"I did until I read that file folder. Now I'm not so sure," Johnston replied. "Not sure she acted alone, at least."

Galloway raised his eyebrows. "A team of killers?"

"It's either that or separate, unrelated incidents. And I find that difficult to believe," said Johnston.

"So what do we do?" Galloway asked.

Johnston sat back down at his desk. "We've got to confront the principals. Get them all in here. Get Katherine Bainbridge in here, too. Let's get this thing on the table and sort it out."

"What about Detective Bachman?"

Johnston shook his head. "Not yet. Not until we have some idea of what we're dealing with."

"I'll notify everyone," Galloway said.

———

Back on the main floor, Lori still clutched the paper towel the officer had given her to wipe the ink from her fingers. She quickly made her way across the atrium to the Austin Building. Her heart was pounding like a bass drum. She needed to track down Faye Renaud but had no intention of going back up to the fourth floor of Travis. She wouldn't risk another unplanned encounter with Detective Bachman. This time she used the stairs instead of the elevator and ran up to Drew's office on the second floor.

"Is Drew in?"

"Yes," Drew's secretary replied. "As a matter of fact, he's been looking for you, Dr. Westlake. Go on in."

Lori ran through the door and into Drew's office. He was on the phone but hung up the instant he saw her. "Lori," he said, "I've been looking all over for you."

Lori fell into his embrace.

"Are you all right?" he asked.

"Drew, something strange is going on," she said, "and I need your help."

He led her to a chair. She sat down and he took the chair across from her. "I've heard. The police have been asking me questions about what we did last night, what time I dropped you off, what I saw. Lori, did you come back here last night?"

She shook her head. "I never left the apartment after you dropped me off. Somebody on the floor is lying. I need to find out who and why. Could you check it out for me?"

"No need to," said Drew. "I already know—sort of."

"You *know*?" said Lori, horrified. "How?"

Drew shrugged. "The grapevine. Hospital scuttlebutt. Word has already spread about what happened last night and that you've been implicated."

"Who said they saw me here?"

"I don't know the 'who' part. But someone phoned in an anonymous tip and suggested that Nina Ware's death should be investigated. The tipster said that you came in about one-fifteen, and that you entered through the stairwell door and went directly to Nina's room."

Lori stood up and walked to the window. "It doesn't make any sense."

Drew came up behind her and put his arms around her. "Have you talked to Kate? Does she know anything about this?"

Still looking out the window, Lori sighed and shook her head. "Today's her day to visit home hospice patients. She probably won't even be in."

"She won't be out *all* day," Drew replied. "There's some kind of meeting later this morning that she and I are supposed to be at."

"What meeting?"

Drew shrugged. "I don't know. I just know I was summoned to a meeting at Dr. Johnston's office at ten thirty, and Kate's supposed to be there, too."

Lori felt her stomach sink. Was it possible that Drew was about to find himself in the same boat she was in?

"Drew, I think we should talk. There's something you should know."

Drew smiled. It was a warm smile, Lori thought. Reassuring.

"I'd love to more than anything," he said. "But I've got a patient waiting as we speak."

"Guess that'll give me time to track down that anonymous caller," Lori said as she turned toward the door. Drew put his hands on her shoulders and gently turned her around to face him.

"Be careful," he cautioned. "I've only met this Detective Bachman once, but I don't think he'll look kindly on any interference."

"What else can I do?" Lori replied. "I've got a feeling that sitting around and waiting for Detective Bachman to finish his investigation is not going to be particularly helpful to me."

Drew cupped her face in his hands and brought her lips up to meet his. "Just be careful," he said.

FORTY-FIVE

As far as Charles was concerned, one of the most frustrating things about having ALS was that every day was different. You never knew until you got up whether you were going to have a good day—with muscles that were somewhat responsive and had some energy. On a bad day nothing worked, you were achy and tired, your muscles were spastic and cramping, and you felt like you couldn't move out of your chair if someone offered you a million dollars to do it.

Then there were days like today. Physically, he felt pretty good. His hands were more responsive than usual and his legs not so wobbly. However, the emotional drain of last night's hospital visit and Kenton's death had taken its toll. Charles was depressed, and depression aggravated his symptoms. It had taken him a full two hours to get out of bed, shower, shave, and get dressed. He knew that he could not go on much longer without some kind of help.

On top of that, he was feeling particularly rushed this morning, which tended to make everything more difficult. David Bachman had called just after eight to tell him that Pam would be by to drive him to Sentinel Health Systems around lunchtime. David wouldn't elaborate on what he wanted, but whatever it was appeared to be urgent. All he would say was that something big had gone down last night, and he might need Charles's help.

Now dressed in comfortable khaki slacks, a navy pullover shirt, and slip-on shoes—he hated slip-ons, but shoelaces were a thing of the past for him—he guided his walker down the hallway. A loudly meowing Columbo led the way toward the kitchen. "Yeah, yeah," Charles muttered. "I hear you. Be patient. You could still be living out on the streets and dining on rats, you know. Did you ever think of that?" The cat ignored him and ran ahead into the kitchen.

Charles pulled open the refrigerator and took out a plastic-wrapped bowl of cat food. He had asked Pam to fix a bowl in advance because he didn't always have the strength to pull the tab to open the can. He carried the bowl to the dinette and set it on the tabletop. Columbo obligingly hopped up on a chair and then onto the table to retrieve his breakfast.

"It's a good thing my mother didn't live to see this," Charles said as he pulled the plastic wrap off the bowl. "She couldn't abide animals in the house, let alone on the table. If she saw me letting you eat up here, she'd throw us both out." He ran his hand down Columbo's shaggy tan and white fur.

Columbo ignored Charles and crouched down by the bowl to eat his food. "Of course," said Charles, "bending down to the floor and getting back up aren't exactly the easiest things to do, so you get special privileges. Now it's my turn to get some breakfast."

Before he could get back to the refrigerator, the doorbell rang. Thinking it was Pam, he didn't move to answer the door. He'd already unlocked it; besides, she had her own key.

The doorbell rang again.

"She's being awfully formal this morning," Charles said as he maneuvered his walker over to the door. "It's open, Pam," he called out.

Still no one came in.

Charles turned the knob and tugged on the front door. Fortunately, it opened easily for him this time. "Why the decorum?" he asked as he opened the door. He paused when he saw a short, black-haired woman standing there. "I'm sorry," he said. "I thought you were someone else."

The woman's voice was cheerful, and Charles liked her at once. "I'm Katherine Bainbridge, from Sentinel Health Systems' Hospice Facility. Are you Mr. Hamisch?"

"I'm sorry. I forgot that I'd called you," Charles said. "Please come in." He moved back from the door and allowed the woman to enter his apartment. "You'll have to excuse my rudeness in not answering the door," he said. "I thought you were my caregiver."

Katherine followed Charles into the living room and sat down on the sofa across from his recliner. "That's not a problem," she said. "I just wanted to stop by and introduce myself. You called our service a while back and applied for residency in our facility."

"Yes," said Charles, "but I didn't expect you here quite so soon."

Katherine laughed. "Don't worry. I didn't come to take you there today. I just wanted to tell you that your application has been approved. Dr. Galloway likes me to go around and meet prospective patients in person and answer any questions you have."

"Dr. Galloway?"

"Dr. Barnabas Galloway is the head of our facility. I'm his executive assistant. Between the two of us, we aim to make Sentinel's hospice facility the best in the country. So, do you have any questions?"

Charles thought a moment. "I can't think of any right now but I'm sure there will be some."

"Do you know anything about hospice care or do I need to give my prepared speech?" There was a twinkle in Katherine's eyes as she handed him a folder with a glossy green background and gold lettering that read, "SHS Hospice Service."

Charles glanced at the folder and set it on the table by his recliner. "Hey, that's why you make the big bucks. Go ahead and give me your spiel."

"All right then." Katherine picked up the folder, opened it to the first page, and pointed to a picture of a woman. "The modern hospice movement started in 1967 with Dame Cicely Saunders, the founder of Saint Christopher's hospice in England.

"From the beginning, the focal point of hospice care has been to provide pain and symptom management for terminally ill patients, while also addressing their psychological and spiritual needs. Most hospice care in the United States is done in homes because the cost of inpatient care is too high.

"However, there are a small number of inpatient hospice facilities, primarily for those who have no family to assist with their care. Part of our corporate mission at SHS is to provide inpatient hospice care for any qualifying member who requests it.

"You know our slogan," she said with a smile: "'Quality health care for all of God's children.'"

"So I've heard," Charles replied, a wry grin spreading across his face.

"Our facility," Katherine continued, flipping to a glossy color picture of a hospice room, "provides a homelike atmosphere for all its residents. Each patient is assigned his or her own living quarters, which they are free to decorate as they please."

Katherine glanced around the room. "I'm sure you'll want to bring along some of these marvelous carvings and paintings."

"Maybe," Charles replied.

"The living quarters are similar to small efficiency apartments or motel suites. Each room comes with a kitchenette, a handicapped accessible bathroom, cable Internet, satellite television, and twenty-four-hour access to medical care, counseling, and pastoral care.

"Those who are still in good enough health, and who wish to, can prepare their own meals in their rooms. Do you cook, Mr. Hamisch?"

"Nothing edible."

Katherine laughed. "Well, if you don't cook, you have nothing to worry about. Our chef is very good, and if you desire some community interaction, you can eat in a common dining room with other patients."

She turned another page in the folder. This one had a photo of a distinguished-looking man with graying hair and a beard. "Dr. Barnabas Galloway, the head of our facility, is also one of the architects of the program. He takes great pride in his accomplishment because he considers it his way of leaving a legacy. In fact, there has already been discussion—albeit hushed—about the possibility of someday renaming the Crockett Building in Galloway's honor when he retires."

Katherine closed the folder and handed it back to Charles. "That's the end of my speech," she said. "You can read the rest on your own. This is our patient guidebook. It will tell you everything you need to know. It also has my office number and my cell number. Feel free to call me anytime, day or night, if you need something or have a question." She stood to leave and Charles began to get up with her. She motioned for him to sit back down. "I can let myself out."

As she turned toward the door, she saw the plaque that Charles's fellow officers had given him at his retirement party. "You're a police detective?"

Charles had seen the look before. She wanted to ask him something, or tell him something.

"Retired," he said.

She paused a second longer, as if considering whether to bring up what was on her mind. Then she looked at her watch and appeared to decide against it. "I bet you have some interesting stories to tell," she said.

Charles smiled. "I've got a few eye-openers."

"Unfortunately I'm going to be late for an important meeting if I don't leave now to see the rest of my patients. But I may just come back when I have more time and listen to some of your stories. Would you mind?"

"It would be my pleasure," Charles answered. "Drop by anytime, Ms. Bainbridge."

"Please. Call me Kate," she said as she left.

⸻

Lori sat at her office desk, rifling through the drawers. Her first hurdle was to figure out how to discover the identity of the anonymous tipster who had cast suspicion on her. The most logical place to start was with the Circle of Peace.

Whoever phoned in the tip *had* to be a member of the Circle. Based on the limited knowledge Lori had, only Circle members would have known that Nina Ware had been scheduled for an intervention. Only a member would have known the planned date and time of the patient's death. And only a Circle member could have had any reason to implicate her in Nina's death.

But why?

Was this the Circle's retribution for her failure to fulfill her part of the bargain? Or did someone in the Circle want to carry out a personal vendetta? Her last conversation with Malachi had been less than amiable, but she couldn't think of anything that would have motivated retaliation on his part.

The problem was, the only way to contact the Circle was with the cell phone they had given her—and Lori couldn't find it.

She slammed a drawer closed and pulled open the one below it. No phone.

She sat back in her chair and closed her eyes, trying to remember the last time she had used the Circle's phone. *Where did I leave it?*

And then it came back to her. When she had used the phone to call Malachi, she had been in the atrium—and she had slipped the phone into her lab coat pocket when Drew had came along.

She sighed and put her head in her hands.

She had left her lab coat at home.

———

Lori's tires screeched as she swung the Mustang around the corner and onto Savannah Way. If there was ever a day when every minute counted—when she *didn't* need a delay—this was it.

As she drew nearer to her building, she muttered a quiet curse, realizing that a delay was now the *least* of her problems.

Two police cruisers and an unmarked car were parked in front of the building. A uniformed officer stood watch at the building's entryway.

She briefly considered flooring it and driving by the building but she knew that it wouldn't do any good. If Bachman wanted her, he knew where to find her. At least if she went up to her apartment she might find out what was going on.

And there was always the possibility that the police were there on some other call.

Not likely.

She parked near one of the cruisers and jogged up the steps to the building.

The uniformed officer stepped forward to intercept her. "May I help you, ma'am?" he asked.

"Yes," Lori answered, trying to sound casual. "I live in apartment number two. I'm Dr. Westlake."

The officer stepped aside and motioned her into the building. "Go right in."

Lori stepped inside the door that led into her building, and her heart skipped a beat. Her apartment door stood wide open and she could hear people moving around inside. When she looked inside the front door, her heart all but stopped.

"What's going on?" she demanded.

She knew perfectly well what was going on but the sight before her was so shocking that she couldn't help feeling angry and violated. Although her apartment in its semi-unpacked state had certainly not been neat, it had been a model of cleanliness compared to what it was now.

The police officers had unpacked the rest of Lori's boxes and the contents lay scattered around the apartment in total disarray.

Down the short hallway near her bedroom door stood a man wearing crisp new slacks and a tweed sport coat. When he turned around, Lori immediately knew she was in for trouble.

"Dr. Westlake," Detective Bachman greeted her as if she were an old friend, "it's good to see you again."

Lori did not feel particularly sociable but she didn't dare let down her guard around this man. "You've been busy, I see," she said.

"Never let grass grow under your feet," Detective Bachman retorted. "One of my grandfather's favorite sayings."

"May I ask what you're doing?" Lori questioned, trying not to sound overly antagonistic.

Detective Bachman pulled some folded papers from the inside pocket of his sport coat. "As a matter of fact," he said as he handed her the papers, "this should explain everything. It's a search warrant for your apartment. The warrant will explain what we're looking for."

Lori bit her lip, trying to hold back the words that wanted to flow out. Finally she spoke with a quiet, controlled voice. "Will you be here long?"

"Actually," Detective Bachman replied, "we're just about finished. We found what we came for."

Lori felt a surge of panic. Surely they weren't looking for the Circle's cell phone.

At that moment another uniformed officer came out from the bedroom. He was holding a plastic zipper-seal bag. Lori recognized the contents immediately. It was the syringe and vial of insulin that she had been told to deliver to Nina Ware's room.

She had forgotten about it after she'd decided not to deliver it.

Detective Bachman held up the bag. "We found these little items in your lab coat. Strange thing to go walking around with, isn't it?"

"Not for a physician," Lori said, trying to bluff her way through it.

Bachman flashed a toothy smile. "I wouldn't go anywhere if I were you, Dr. Westlake. I might want to have another talk with you. Soon."

Bachman motioned toward the other officers. "Let's go," he said.

He paused in the doorway and looked back at Lori. "Sorry about the mess."

Lori raced to the door and locked it behind the departing officers. They hadn't taken her lab coat with them, only the vial and syringe. Maybe the prepaid cell phone was still in the pocket.

She found the lab coat on her bed, along with a pile of other clothes, but the police had emptied the pockets. Lori began tearing through the pile of clothes, tossing things on the floor haphazardly. "It has to be here. They didn't take it."

When she was just about to give up, she saw the phone sitting on her nightstand.

Her hands felt clammy as she turned on the phone and tried once more to contact Malachi. The line was ringing, but no one answered.

"Come on. Somebody answer. Please."

Lori's heart sank when a sterile-sounding voice came over the line. "We're sorry. The mobile customer you are trying to reach is not available. Please try your call again later."

She pressed the power button and turned off the phone, biting her lip and trying to blink back the tears that were forcing their way into her eyes.

She was on her own.

———

Kate gave herself a pep talk as she jogged into the atrium. "Come on, Bainbridge, move those legs. Can't be late." She glanced at the giant digital clock above the reception desk: 10:25.

She knew she shouldn't have spent so much time at Charles Hamisch's apartment. Now she was going to come bustling in to Dr. Johnston's office looking harried and out of breath. Not a way to inspire confidence.

She was about to head toward the elevators when she saw Tony Garcia standing behind the reception desk. He was waving and motioning for her to come over.

She groaned. "Not now." Nevertheless, she smiled broadly and trotted over to him.

"Hi, Oscar," she said, using her nickname for him. "Can I talk to you later? I've got to get over to—"

Tony cut her off. "I was just wondering if there was any more news about Dr. Westlake."

Kate stopped in her tracks. "What are you talking about?"

"You don't know?" Tony said.

An icy hand gripped her heart. "Know what?"

Tony flushed and fumbled for words, apparently not prepared to deliver bad news.

"Look, Kate, I'm sorry," he said, looking across the atrium, avoiding eye contact. "I thought you'd heard."

Kate grabbed his shoulders. "Tony, what's happened to my sister?"

Tony looked at the floor. "One of her patients died last night. They think Dr. Westlake killed her."

Kate couldn't speak for a moment. She felt as if someone had punched her in the stomach and knocked the breath out of her. She heard Tony's voice, but as from a distance, from a fog.

"Kate. Are you okay?"

"Hmm?" She looked toward the voice.

"Do you need a chair or something?"

She shook it off. "No. I—I'll be all right." She patted his shoulder and turned toward the elevators. "Thanks, Tony."

It wasn't possible. Lori couldn't be the one. It simply wasn't possible.

Still in a daze, Kate made her way to the elevator bank for the Austin Building. As she stepped into the elevator, she heard a familiar voice. "Hold that elevator, please." Barnabas Galloway came running toward the elevator.

"Thank you, Katherine," he said as he breezed through the door. "It looks like we're both going to be late for Terrence's meeting." He pressed the button for the seventh floor and the elevator surged upward.

"Dr. Galloway, did you know about this? About Lori?"

He nodded. "I'm sorry."

"I just can't believe it," she said.

"Don't give up hope yet. Let's see what Terrence has to say."

FORTY-SIX

The atmosphere in Dr. Johnston's office was that of a court of inquisition, with the new chief of staff as Grand Inquisitor. But, Kate observed, the subject of the inquisition was not present. Apparently only she, Dr. Galloway, and Drew Langdon had been invited to the party. Lori had been left out.

"It goes without saying," Dr. Johnston began, "that everything said in this room *stays* in this room." He looked around, surveying the faces of the others. "Is that understood?"

They all nodded.

Kate spoke up. "I have a question," she said. "Why isn't Lori here?"

Dr. Johnston looked put-upon. "Dr. Westlake's situation is not under review here. Her case is now a matter for the police."

"But this discussion has a bearing on her situation," Dr. Galloway said. "Shouldn't she be here?"

"I agree," said Drew. "Without Lori here, this has the appearance of an inquisition. What's next, a lynching?"

Dr. Johnston's eyes flashed at Drew and he clipped his words. "We are treading on very thin ice here, as it is. Any discussions we have with or about Dr. Westlake are now subject to subpoena. If we refuse to cooperate, or interfere with the police investigation in any way, we could all be subject to obstruction charges."

Regaining his calm, he continued, "Our purpose here is to review Ms. Bainbridge's findings and formulate a response."

"Then why am I here?" Drew asked.

Dr. Johnston paused for a moment before replying. "That, Mr. Langdon, will become apparent as we proceed. Now, Ms. Bainbridge, if you would review your research and conclusions for us."

Drew's presence at the meeting unnerved Kate. She had not expected him to be there. Granted, the accused had a right to face his accuser, but that was in court, not face-to-face in an office.

"Ms. Bainbridge?" Dr. Johnston broke into her thoughts. "Whenever you're ready." The sarcasm that edged his voice unnerved her further.

"Yes," she said, fumbling with her folder. "Of course."

She began with the earliest case, and for the next half-hour, she worked forward, briefly sketching out each unexplained death and her reasons for suspecting that it was a mercy killing. She finished her summary by recounting Isidore Jacoby's unexpected—and as yet unexplained—death, but held back the details of her interview with Ruthie Jacoby.

Drew Langdon, the only one present who had no previous awareness of Katherine's investigation, listened in stunned silence. She had barely finished speaking when he broke in. "You don't believe that Lori did all of this, do you? That's crazy."

Kate didn't reply.

Dr. Johnston answered for her. "Actually, Mr. Langdon, we were wondering about *your* possible involvement."

Drew jumped to his feet, his fists clenched. "What?" He looked at Kate. "Kate, what is this?"

"Elaborate, please, Ms. Bainbridge," Dr. Johnston said.

She cleared her throat and looked at her papers. Her voice shook when she spoke. "I visited Ruthie Jacoby and asked her about the night her husband was admitted." She glanced at Drew. "She said that you came by and visited Mr. Jacoby the night before he died."

"And that's a crime?" Drew asked.

"Drew, sit down," Dr. Galloway urged quietly.

Drew ignored him and faced Kate, "Does Lori know about this?"

Kate nodded.

Drew glared at Dr. Johnston. "This *is* a lynching." He turned and stormed toward the door. "Well you can do it without my help." He slammed the door behind him as he left.

The crisp air stung Charles's cheeks, but it felt wonderful to be outside on one of the first genuinely cool days of autumn. The sky was completely clear and the intense blue almost made his eyes hurt. There was a smattering of color in the trees as well. Not much, to be sure, but a little. North Texas was not the greatest place to enjoy fall colors. When cool weather arrived, the trees went straight from green to shades of brown. However, certain species, such as Japanese maples and silver maples, could still put on an impressive show of reds and yellows. As Pam wheeled Charles along the path leading into the Sentinel Health Systems gardens, the drab colors of the trees along the perimeter gave way to an intensity of color rarely seen in a North Texas landscape. The designers had selected the mix of trees for just such an effect.

"Isn't it beautiful?" Pam said.

"Awe inspiring," Charles replied.

Pam rolled the wheelchair over to a small picnic table, not far from the entrance to the gardens. "David said to wait here," she said. "He'll join us for lunch soon."

"On a day like today, I don't mind the wait."

"How are you doing today?" asked Pam.

"Physically or emotionally?"

"Both."

"Physically, just so-so. It's getting harder and harder to stay on my feet for very long. And my arms are getting too weak for the walker. I don't think it's going to be too long before I need one of these things permanently," he said, tapping the armrest of his wheelchair.

"And emotionally?"

Charles didn't respond for a few seconds, and when he did, his voice was thick. "Last night was difficult. I'm going to miss Kenton, but I'm happy for him."

"What did he mean when he asked you if you understood?" said Pam. "I heard him say that just as Janice and I were leaving the room last night."

"When we first met, he told me that every day was a gift. I told him I couldn't understand how an ALS patient could say that. After that, every time he saw me he asked if I understood yet."

"Do you?"

He shook his head. "No, not really. Kenton gave me a note last night that spelled it out. I've got to be honest, though. I see what he means, but I don't think it's made it to my heart yet."

"What did he tell you?" Pam asked.

"Hey, there!" a voice broke in. "What are you doing running around with my wife?"

They turned to see David coming down the walkway. He kissed Pam and turned to address Charles. "Looks like I'm going to have to put you under twenty-four-hour surveillance, my friend."

"What can I say?" Charles laughed. "She kidnapped me."

David sat down on one of the picnic table benches and Pam sat across from him. She opened a small cooler filled with chicken salad sandwiches and bottled water. She had cut Charles's sandwich into small pieces to make it easier for him to handle and chew.

"So, why did you summon us down here?" Charles asked.

"I need help, partner," said David, taking a bite of his sandwich. "It's amazing how quickly attitudes change downtown, just because of the discovery of one little angel."

"They believe in your serial killer now?"

David nodded as he washed down his sandwich with a swig from the water bottle. "This time the vic isn't just some burned-out derelict, so they're on board big time. That's why I need your help. You think Hamisch Consulting is ready for its first case?"

"I've *been* ready," said Charles. "Bring me up to speed."

David recounted for Charles the details of Nina Ware's death and the discovery of her body.

Charles nodded. "She had terminal cancer?"

"Yep."

"Think it's a mercy killing?" asked Charles.

"That's what it looks like," David replied.

"How's this fit in with your homeless murders?"

"Right now, the only thing that ties them all together is the little angel. We're going to try to get court orders to exhume the bodies of the homeless men for detailed tox screens."

"It's quite a jump from killing some homeless guy to mercy killings in a hospital," Charles said.

David shrugged. "Like I said, I'm not sure how the cases are related, but if they are, maybe the perp was perfecting her technique on the streets before moving uptown."

"*Her* technique? You think your killer is a woman?"

"I know, I know," David said. "Serial killers are usually male. But we have a tip that this woman was seen leaving the victim's room just minutes after the fatal dose would have been administered."

"Anything else linking her?"

"We do if the medical examiner's report comes back as acute insulin poisoning. And that's where you come in. They haven't assigned me a new partner yet and I need help on this one. I need you to find out whatever you can about a doctor named Lori Westlake. She's on staff here at SHS."

———

Quinn was surprised to find that all the members had responded so quickly to his call for an emergency meeting. Meetings during business hours were dicey at best, and sometimes members would ignore the summons, either because they didn't want to take the risk or because they were occupied.

The fact that all had logged in to the chat room so quickly was a testimony to the seriousness of the situation.

> Quinn: You all know what has happened.

> Copper: The question is, what do we do about it?

> Malachi: We proceed as if nothing happened.

> Zoë: How is that possible? Two times now a patient has been euthanized who was not supposed to be.

> Quinn: Don't use specific terms, Zoë. Speak in generalities.

> Malachi: We must see this as an opportunity.

> Quinn: In what way?

> Malachi: Servant is obviously a loose cannon. We must allow her to be prosecuted.

> Quinn: Agreed. She doesn't know enough about us to be a threat.

> Zoë: You haven't addressed my question.

Copper: What question?

Zoë: We're dealing with two unauthorized interventions, not one.

Quinn: And your point is . . . ?

Zoë: Even if Servant performed the intervention last night, she couldn't have done the other one.

Malachi: Both were Servant's patients. How do we know Servant didn't freelance?

Zoë: I don't believe she would do that.

Copper: You're only one voice here.

Malachi: Servant must be cut off.

Quinn: What if she tries to expose the Circle?

Malachi: Even if she tries, there's no way to make a connection.

Quinn: So we let her take the fall?

Malachi: And the side benefit is that after she is convicted, the authorities will not be looking for anyone else.

Zoë: We can't do this.

Copper: Any talk of the Circle will be dismissed as a conspiracy theory.

Zoë: Is anybody listening? It's wrong.

Malachi: I believe you've been outvoted, Zoë.

Copper: Agreed.

Quinn: Same here.

Zoë: I won't be a part of it.

Seconds later, a small prompt appeared at the bottom of Quinn's screen:

Zoë has left.

Quinn: I believe our business is concluded, then.

Copper: What about Zoë? Will she be a problem?

Malachi: She's just upset. I'll take care of Zoë.

———

"You've got to hold it together, girl," Lori said to herself. "You've *got* to hold it together." But she wasn't holding it together. She was coming apart at the seams.

She sat on her sofa with a tissue in her hand, surrounded by piles of clothing, knickknacks, and half-emptied boxes. She needed to be proactive, to do *something* to clear her name, but she didn't have a clue about what to do or where to start.

"One step at a time. I still need to find out who made that call."

Maybe she could talk to someone who worked the night shift. She could call Travis 4 and find out who was on duty. It might not solve her problem, but it was a *start*.

Wanting to avoid any possibility of the call being traced to her, Lori decided to use the prepaid cell phone. She dialed SHS's main number and asked the operator to transfer the call.

"Travis Four, may I help you?" a woman's voice answered.

"I need to speak to Faye Renaud."

"May I ask who's calling?"

Lori hadn't expected this. They *never* asked who was calling. She lied.

"Just a minute, please." There was a pause on the line. Then someone picked up.

"This is Detective Bachman, may I help you?"

Lori muttered a curse under her breath and hung up. She could look up Faye's home address *if* she could find her phone book. The other possibility would be to access the personnel records on the SHS computer system. She looked at her watch. It was 12:36 PM. If the disciplinary committee suspended her, she would lose access to the system.

As she considered her options, the cell phone chirped.

At first she wasn't sure if she should answer it, but her curiosity won out. She pressed the *Answer* button. "Hello?"

"Listen carefully. I can only say this once." The voice was a woman's voice, but it was soft and muffled. "He's setting you up. I don't know why, but he's setting you up."

"Who's setting me up? Who is this?" asked Lori.

"This is Zoë. I can't talk about this over the phone. Can we meet?"

"Name the place," Lori said.

"I have something to show you. Come to my house as soon as you can. The address is 11311 Bois d'Arc Lane."

"But—" Lori protested.

The line went dead.

The specified house was a gray, two-story American Foursquare house in one of Dallas's older neighborhoods. It was not a particularly upscale part of town, but neither was it rundown. Most of the houses and yards were well kept, although Zoë's house looked as if it could have used a fresh coat of paint about five years ago. Tall live oak trees shaded the neighborhood and testified to its age.

Lori parked her Mustang a few doors down from number 11311 and waited, trying to see if she could spot any activity—or any police surveillance. The house looked quiet. Lori couldn't see any cars parked nearby.

She climbed the front porch steps and knocked on the screen door. The slightly warped wood made a thumping sound against the doorframe. It was loud enough to alert half the neighborhood to her presence, but no one came to the door. Lori opened the screen door to try knocking on the inside door. Rusty hinges squealed as the door opened.

Someone had left the front door open a crack. Lori nudged it open further and knocked on the inside of the doorframe.

"Hello? Zoë?"

No answer.

Alarm bells were going off in Lori's mind. Her instinct was to get out of there as fast as she could. But she knew Zoë might be her only chance to clear herself, to find out who was setting her up, and why.

She stepped inside the house. Her shoes clicked on the hard-wood floor. The wailing and shouting of a heavy metal band was coming from a radio somewhere inside the house. She called out again, "Zoë?" Just as a precaution, she placed her finger on the trigger of her pepper spray canister as she walked down the short hallway to the kitchen. An open pizza box—minus two pieces—sat on the kitchen counter. She touched the pizza with the back of her hand. It was still warm.

She called louder, "Zoë, are you all right?"

Still no answer.

She stopped and listened. The radio music sounded muffled, like it was coming from upstairs. She detoured through the dining room and living room. A plate with two pieces of pepperoni pizza sat on a coffee table, facing an old console television. The TV was on but the sound was turned down. Whoever had been in the room had also taken a few bites from one of the pizza slices. The other piece was untouched. Lori went back out to the front hallway and shouted up the stairs. "Zoë, do you need help?"

Her gaze fell on a pile of mail that lay on a side table near the staircase. Among all the junk mail addressed to Occupant, she saw one that caught her attention.

The letter was addressed to Faye Renaud.

Faye is Zoë.

Lori made her way slowly up the stairs. The old steps groaned and squeaked under her weight. At the first landing, she stopped and called again. "Faye? It's Dr. Westlake."

No answer. The sound of the radio was louder but she couldn't tell which room it was coming from.

"Talk to me, Faye."

Lori came to the top of the stairs. All four doors were closed.

She could still hear the radio.

Lori opened the first door.

Just an empty bedroom.

The second bedroom was empty, too.

The next door opened to a small bathroom. It was empty.

Only one room left.

Lori gently turned the knob and opened the door a crack. "Faye?" She pushed the door open further, bracing herself against what she might find.

The master bedroom was empty.

A clock radio beside the bed still blasted out its angry music. The bedclothes were rumpled, as if someone had made the bed hastily, but otherwise nothing appeared out of the ordinary.

Lori switched off the radio and sat down on the bed, trying to figure out what to do next.

The instant she sat down, she knew that something was wrong. The bed felt hard.

Pulling back the covers, she found a thin hardcover journal, the type of diary you could purchase for a few dollars at any Wal-Mart.

She flipped through the book and found pages and pages of records in Faye Renaud's spidery handwriting. The final entry caught her eye.

Case #11085

Client: NW

Intervention request by: Patient

Referral: Physician #236

Decision: Request withdrawn

Intervention: Not assigned

Results: Patient expired (rogue member?)

Lori's hands felt clammy. These were Faye's notes about Nina Ware's case. She had evidently been keeping copious notes of all of the Circle's interventions, perhaps for her own protection. If she were ever indicted, this would be a powerful bargaining chip.

Lori flipped back a page and read the preceding entry.

Case #11034

Client: IJ

Intervention request by: Wife's nephew

Referral: Physician #124

Decision: Request denied

Intervention: Not assigned

Results: Patient expired (suspicious)

A chill ran down Lori's spine.

IJ. *Isidore Jacoby.*

The book had to be what Faye had wanted to show Lori. The problem was, without Faye, most of the entries would be meaningless. No doubt she had intended it that way. It was her personal ticket to freedom—or a lesser sentence.

And *somebody* didn't want Faye sharing the information.

As Lori sat reading the journal, an overwhelming sense of her own vulnerability swept over her.

Zoë—Faye—had been afraid even to leave her house. She'd ordered a pizza delivery.

The pizza was still warm, but Faye was nowhere to be found.

And Lori was now standing on the second floor of her house. No exit. No escape route.

She had to get out of there. Now!

She took the journal with her and rushed down the stairs and out of the house. Wherever Faye was, Lori couldn't help her now.

As she walked briskly back to her car, trying not to run, not wanting to attract any attention from the neighbors, her mind was a jumble.

What am I going to do now? I need to be somewhere public—someplace where the Circle wouldn't dare try to harm me.

But I also need help. I can't try to do this on my own anymore. I need to talk to Drew.

The journal fell to the sidewalk as Lori fumbled for her keys.

"Settle down!" she muttered to herself as she opened the car door. "Panicking is not going to help anything."

Taking a deep breath to settle herself, she started the car and headed for Sentinel Health Systems.

FORTY-SEVEN

"What have we got so far?" Charles asked Pam. He had tried working at his computer for a while, but had quickly become fatigued. Pam was now doing the online research as Charles directed her from his recliner.

"Not much, I'm afraid," Pam said. "Lori Westlake is thirty-five years old and has lived in Dallas for about a year. Divorced. No children. It was apparently a messy divorce, though. She's got a restraining order on the ex, a Philip Westlake. He stalked her and made some threats after they split up. That's apparently why she moved up here—to get away.

"She's a staff physician with Sentinel Health Systems," Pam continued. "Until last month she lived with her sister, Katherine Bainbridge, also employed by Sentinel. Recently moved to an apartment complex close to Sentinel.

"She lived in Houston before she moved up here. Worked at Hermann Hospital. Good work record. No complaints. No criminal history. Spotless driving record. This lady's so clean she squeaks."

"And the only thing tying her to Nina Ware's death is an anonymous tip saying that she was seen leaving the room about the time the drug would have been administered?" Charles asked.

Pam nodded.

"Pretty thin. What about the other cases? The street people. Any witnesses who can place her downtown when those deaths occurred?"

"You've read the files," Pam said. "Not one."

"Then why is David so focused on this one suspect?"

"Ever since he made the connection between the homeless deaths and the ceramic angels, he's been obsessed with this case. He can hardly stop thinking or talking about it. I practically have to threaten him to get him off the subject. It just about killed him when Sergeant Jackson told him to leave the cases alone and move on."

"David's always been one to look out for the underdog. Maybe that's why these killings haunt him," Charles said.

"I'm worried about him. He can't let it go."

"That obsession is narrowing his focus," Charles added.

"So what do we do?" asked Pam.

"Try to open up his eyes to other possibilities."

FORTY-EIGHT

Drew Langdon threw a file folder into his briefcase and slammed it closed. A burly security guard stood by, making sure that Drew didn't remove anything from the office that wasn't his own property.

He had barely been back in his office before the guard had arrived with the notice of his suspension. Johnston hadn't even bothered to place him on paid leave pending an investigation. He'd just suspended him outright.

It was Kate's fault. Associating him with one of the unexplained deaths was bad enough. What really hurt was that Lori had known and hadn't warned him. She'd let him walk into an ambush without a word. He'd thought that they had something going. Evidently not.

He picked up his briefcase and headed for the door.

The rent-a-cop held out his hand. "Your cell phone and key card, please."

Drew slapped the card into the guard's outstretched hand, unclipped the phone from his belt, and handed it over.

"Don't forget to turn the lights out," he snapped as he brushed by the guard and out the door.

———

After being connected to Drew's voicemail for the fifth time, Lori decided to stop trying to call him and just stop by his office to show him Faye's journal. But when she got there, she found the door open and a security guard inside.

"May I help you?" the guard asked.

A pang of fear shot through Lori. "Where's Mr. Langdon? Is he all right?"

"He's been suspended."

"Suspended? Is he still in the building?"

"Not if he knows what's good for him," the guard replied.

Stunned, Lori continued on to her own office, but when she arrived, she found Dr. Johnston waiting. He had a large brown envelope in his hand.

"Dr. Westlake, I need to have a word with you."

Lori braced herself for what was coming. "Yes?" she said, smiling but speaking through gritted teeth.

Terrence Johnston handed her the envelope. "Here is the disciplinary committee's decision. We are putting you on an indefinite paid leave until this business with Nina Ware is resolved. You will not have access to your office during that time and your patients will be reassigned.

"If criminal charges are filed against you, your leave will become an unpaid suspension. Should you be convicted, your employment here will be terminated immediately. You have the right to appeal all this, of course."

Lori took the envelope and turned it over in her hands. "Which," she said, "will do me absolutely no good, I imagine."

Dr. Johnston's gray eyes fixed on her with a disdainful coldness. His eyebrows bobbed up and down. "Nevertheless, you do have that right." He turned on his heel and walked away. After a few strides, he paused and turned back to her. "One more thing, doctor. One of the terms of your leave is that you refrain from being on hospital grounds."

"Do I at least get to clean out my desk?" she asked.

"I'll notify security. They'll send a guard around to assist you."

"To *watch* me, you mean."

"That's your choice of words, doctor, not mine."

"You're enjoying this, aren't you?" Lori challenged. "You opposed my coming on staff, and now you feel justified." She walked up and stood toe to toe with him.

Dr. Johnston's face reddened. When he spoke, his tone was patronizing. "Dr. Westlake, don't be melodramatic. My concern—and the committee's—is for the reputation of Sentinel Health Systems. We can't have a loose cannon running around our hospital killing patients, now can we?" He turned on his heel and walked down the hallway toward his office.

You already do, Lori thought. *You have at least four loose cannons. And you almost had a fifth.*

She decided that she would clean out her office by herself rather than suffer the indignity of having a nosy security guard looking over her shoulder the whole time. She would not give Terrence Johnston that satisfaction. If she acted quickly, she might still be able to get in and lock the door before the guard arrived.

She took out her key card and inserted it in the electronic lock. The tiny LED light at the top of the lock flashed red.

They had already changed her code.

She felt a rising tide of anger, frustration, and grief. She tried to put her key card back in her wallet, but her hands were shaking so much that she couldn't hold the card still. Clutching the card in her hand and blinking away tears that threatened to blur her vision, she headed toward the one person she hoped would still help her.

———

Kate was at her computer when Lori entered her office, but the instant she saw her younger sister, she rushed over and embraced her. "I've been so worried about you," she said. "How are you holding up?"

Lori clung to her as the tears began to flow. "Not very well," she managed to say, struggling to keep her emotions in check. This was not the time for a meltdown. She had to pull herself together and stay strong until she could uncover the truth about what was going on.

Gathering her resolve, she stepped back from Kate's embrace, brushed a stray tear from her cheek, and sat down on the sofa across from her sister's desk.

"Lori," Kate began tentatively, her voice quiet and somber, "we've had our differences over the years, but you've never lied to me. You didn't do it, did you?"

"No, but . . . " Lori didn't finish the sentence.

"But what?"

Tears glistened again in Lori's eyes. "I *almost* was a part of it."

Kate's eyes narrowed. "*Almost?* What do you mean?"

Lori couldn't keep her secret bottled up any longer. The whole story tumbled out as Kate listened in horrified silence. Lori told her everything—about John Doe; about the Circle of Peace; about Malachi, Quinn, Copper, and Zoë; and about Nina Ware's *procedure*, the euthanasia she was supposed to have participated in to seal her commitment.

Kate's eyes filled with tears as she listened to her sister's story.

Lori paused, expecting her to break in at any moment and tell her how disappointed she was. But Kate surprised her.

"Oh, baby, I'm so sorry," she said. "I wish we could have stopped them before they got to you. But you said you weren't involved last night. What happened?"

"I stopped by to visit Nina earlier in the evening," Lori said. "I was supposed to hide a vial of insulin and a syringe in her bathroom. Whoever was going to euthanize her would know where it was hidden and use it. But when I talked to Nina and her mother, they didn't sound or act like people who were expecting any kind of intervention." She dabbed her eyes with a tissue. "Just the opposite. Nina had gone from totally giving up to being one of the most optimistic cancer patients I've ever talked to. She acted like she was going to beat the thing."

"So what happened after that?" Kate asked.

"I tried to contact someone in the Circle and finally got Malachi. He told me that everything was set, that Nina's attitude was just part of the cover story."

"And?"

Lori shrugged. "I didn't believe him. So I decided not to go through with it. I went out to dinner with Drew. Then I went home and went to bed."

Kate stiffened at the mention of Drew's name. "Do you think they sent someone else to do it?"

"It's the only explanation I can think of that makes sense."

"But why would someone lie about it and say that they saw *you* there?" Kate's eyes narrowed as she pondered her own question. "Retaliation? Punishment?"

Lori handed the journal to Kate. "I don't know, but I think the answer's in here. Faye Renaud is part of the Circle of Peace. She called me and said she had something to show me, but when I got there she was gone and her front door was open. I found this journal up in her bedroom. It has to be what she was talking about."

Lori put her head in her hands. "Kate, I've made such a mess of things. What am I going to do?"

Kate sat silently for a few moments, flipping through Faye's diary. She held up the little book. "First, we're going to make a copy of this," she said. "Then I'm going to introduce you to someone who might be able to help."

FORTY-NINE

Charles Hamisch had never been one to take naps. He was a classic type-A workaholic, and proud of it. His work ethic had served him well as a detective, but as ALS had exacted its toll on his body, he'd found himself sleeping longer and taking more naps. It was almost as if weariness was part and parcel of this disease.

He was sound asleep in his recliner when the doorbell rang. He fought his way to consciousness, but still felt more than half-asleep as his eyes opened and he reoriented himself to his surroundings. He tried to get up but his arms and legs were not responsive. His mouth felt like a desert, and phlegm stuck in the back of his throat as he called out, "It's open." The sound came out as little more than a gurgle.

He felt tentacles of panic clutching his throat. He tried to call out again, but with the same result.

Again, the doorbell rang, this time followed by knocking.

His heart thrashed against his chest. Droplets of sweat formed on his forehead. He tried once more to push himself out of his chair, but his arms and legs felt leaden. He managed to squeak out another gurgling cry for help, but this time when he inhaled, the phlegm at the back of his throat made its way to his windpipe. He began hacking violently. He couldn't catch his breath.

For the first time since his diagnosis, he thought he was going to die. Blinded by tears brought on by the choking spell, he felt detached from the world around him. All that registered in his mind was the terrifying, claustrophobic sensation that he was suffocating.

"Quick, get him up and lean him forward."

The voice—a woman's voice—sounded like it was coming from a long way away.

He felt hands grabbing his shoulders and heard the metallic *twang* of the recliner being returned to an upright position. Someone was bending him forward. Pounding on his back.

The hacking eased. The suffocating feeling began to dissipate.

"Relax, Mr. Hamisch," the voice said. "Just relax and take a deep breath."

Eyes closed, Charles tried to obey the voice.

"That's good." The voice was soothing. "You're going to be all right."

When Charles finally opened his eyes, he saw two women, one on either side of him, holding him upright. Katherine Bainbridge and someone he didn't know.

Charles tried to thank them but all that came out was a raspy sound.

"Don't try to talk," the other woman said. "Just breathe as deeply as you can. Do you have an oxygen tank or generator?"

Charles shook his head.

She nodded. "That's okay. You're doing great."

"Should we call the EMTs?" Kate asked.

Charles shook his head again. This time he managed to croak out a response in between gasps for air. "No," he said. "I'm—okay now."

The two women helped him ease back into his chair.

Kate fanned herself with her hand. "Whew. That's enough excitement for *my* day," she said.

"Sorry," Charles said, his voice still hoarse.

"No problem," the other woman said, extending her hand. "I'm Dr. Westlake."

Charles almost choked again. "Doctor *Lori* Westlake?"

"Yes. How did you know?"

Kate broke in. "Lori is my sister. She needs some advice and we were wondering if you might be able to—"

Lori shook her head and held up her hand, signaling for Kate to stop. "No. I don't want to bother Mr. Hamisch. He needs to be resting, not helping me sort out my problems."

"Trust me," said Charles, still trying to catch his breath. He motioned toward the sofa. "It'll be no bother. I'd really like to talk to you."

"Why?" asked Lori.

"Let's just say I want to hear *your* side of the story."

With Charles's encouragement, Lori told her story one more time, leaving out no details. When she finished, she handed him the journal. Kate backed her up by explaining how she had been investigating the deaths and what she'd found.

After Kate had filled in her part of the story, Charles sat quietly for a few seconds, carefully paging through the diary. Finally he said, "You say that this nurse who called you—Faye, was it?—that she seems to have disappeared?"

"I don't know if *disappeared* is the right word," Lori said. "She wasn't at her home when I went to see her. But she called me, and it looked as if she—or somebody—had been there a few minutes before I came. And the way the radio was blaring in her bedroom, it's almost as if she *wanted* me to go upstairs and find the journal.

"Look at the two most recent entries," she continued, motioning toward the journal, which lay in Charles's lap. "Faye is suspicious of someone, but why she didn't write it down, I don't know."

Charles picked up the journal, thumbed to the pages that pertained to Isidore Jacoby and Nina Ware, and read the sketchy entries silently. Finally, he looked at Lori and Kate. "We have to find her. Without Faye, it's doubtful these notes are going to be of any use to you. She's definitely the key. Find Faye and you're likely to get some answers."

"Any suggestions as to *how*?" Lori asked.

"Kate, go back to Faye's house and see if she's back. But if nobody's home, *don't* go inside—even if the door's wide open. Check with the neighbors and ask if anyone has seen her in the last few hours. Tell them you're a coworker and you're concerned about her."

"What can *I* do?" asked Lori.

"You need to keep the journal and lay low," Charles answered. "Any suspicious activity on your part only makes your situation worse. You will have to turn the notes over to the police, and soon. But let's at least wait a few hours to see if we can track Faye down. In the meantime, go home and try to relax. Read a book. Watch a DVD.

Do something to take your mind off your situation. Let Kate and me handle this for you."

"Then you believe I'm innocent?" Lori asked.

"I believe you are telling the truth about the Circle of Peace and about Nina Ware. That doesn't mean you're out of the woods, legally speaking. Even the little bit that you did with the Circle opens you to a conspiracy charge. But we don't need to worry about that right now. First we need to take care of the more serious matter. Let's find out what Faye knows and why the Circle is lying about you."

FIFTY

Lori decided to take the detective's advice and do something to take her mind off her situation. On the way back from Charles's apartment, she and Kate stopped by the video store and rented a copy of *Singing in the Rain*. "I need a sappy, sentimental love story tonight," she told her sister.

Their next stop was SHS, so Kate could pick up her car.

Lori swung the Mustang into the parking garage and pulled up beside Kate's Civic.

As Kate stepped out of the Mustang, she said, "I'm going to go look for Faye. *You* go home like Charles told you to."

"I'm on my way," said Lori. "I'm going to go home, take a hot shower, order a pizza, try to call Drew. I haven't been able to reach him all day. He needs to know about Faye's diary."

"Stay away from him, Lori," Kate said. "I never quite trusted him, and I'm definitely not sure of him now."

Lori was incredulous. "Never quite trusted him? Kate, you practically twisted my arm out of the socket to get me to go out with him."

"Never mind that," Kate said as she turned toward her car. "Just stay home and be careful."

"I will," said Lori, rolling up her window. "After I call Drew," she added when Kate couldn't hear her.

As soon as she got home, Lori left a voicemail message for Drew, then took a long, hot bubble bath. Wearing a soft terrycloth bathrobe over a pink flannel nightgown and fuzzy pink slippers, she curled up on her sofa and started the movie.

The opening credits had barely finished rolling when the phone rang. She considered ignoring it but decided to answer in case it was Drew.

"Hello?"

The voice was quiet and cautious. "Dr. Westlake?"

"Yes."

"This is Faye."

Lori sat straight up. "Faye, where are you? I came to your house but you weren't there."

"He's stalking me. I had to run." Faye's words were clipped, nervous.

"Faye, I found the diary. We need to talk."

There was a long pause on the line.

"Faye?" Lori said, "Are you still there?"

"I'm at the Deluxe Inn, on I-30 East. Room 155. Come as soon as you can. I can't talk anymore."

"Faye, wait. Don't hang up," Lori said. But it was too late. She had already disconnected.

The Deluxe Inn did not live up to its name, at least on the outside. Bright orange neon letters promised a rate of nineteen dollars for a single room. The trash-strewn parking lot held a handful of cars, and most of them looked like they were held together with duct tape and wire. Lori hoped the Mustang would still have its wheels when she came back out.

Room 155 was at the far end of the lot near a huge trash bin overflowing with an assortment of garbage bags. Apparently someone hadn't paid the collection bill, because the stench from the overstuffed bin was overwhelming.

Lori parked and turned off her lights. She couldn't see any light coming from the window of 155. The only sounds were coming from three young Hispanic boys riding their scooters around the parking lot.

She knew she shouldn't have come. She should have called Charles Hamisch or tried to get a hold of Kate. But she had gotten herself into this mess, and she felt she should bear at least some responsibility for getting herself out. As she walked to the door of 155, she scanned the lot to make sure no one was waiting in ambush for her. All she could see were the boys.

When she reached the door, she looked over her shoulder one more time and then knocked lightly.

No response.

Not this again. She tried the knob. The cheap handle turned easily and the door popped open. By the heavy, metallic scent in the room, Lori knew instantly that something was wrong. She stepped inside and flipped on the light switch. The room remained cloaked in darkness. In the blackness, she could barely make out the silhouette of the undisturbed double bed. Beyond it sat a limp figure in a large stuffed chair.

Lori couldn't make out a face, but she didn't need to. She knew it was Faye. Who else would it be? She carefully made her way to the bathroom and turned on the light. The bathroom's light reflected off the walls, giving her enough light to see that Faye was dead. She had been bound to the chair, and duct tape had been placed over her mouth.

Lori pressed her fingers to Faye's neck, feeling for a carotid pulse. Nothing. No respiration either. Faye's eyes were closed and her hands were crossed neatly in her lap. Her wrists had been slashed, but apparently her killer had left before she was dead. In her last moments of consciousness, Faye had scrawled three letters in blood on the back of her left hand. Lori couldn't make out the first letter—maybe a *W* or an *M*?—but the next two were definitely *A* and *L*. The *L* trailed off her wrist and into her lap.

"W-A-L . . . or . . . M-A-L," Lori whispered. "Malachi!"

She turned her eyes from Faye's corpse and saw something that froze her heart.

A small ceramic angel stood on the table beside the chair.

FIFTY-ONE

Y ou're *what?*" David Bachman exclaimed in disbelief.
"I'm turning down your contract offer," said Charles. "I can't work for you on this case."

David sat down at the dinette table across from his former partner. Pam set a piping hot bowl of vegetable soup in front of him. Charles was already working on his soup. He was still able to feed himself but had been forced to start using special large-handled utensils that were easier to grasp.

"Why not?" David demanded a little too loudly.

Pam put a hand on her husband's shoulder. "Honey, lower your volume."

Charles took a sip of his soup. "I don't believe Lori Westlake is your killer." He nodded at Pam. "Good soup, Pam."

"I didn't ask you to draw conclusions, pal," David said. "I only asked you to gather information."

"And I did what you asked," replied Charles. "I gathered information. I even interviewed the suspect."

David was incredulous. "You did *what?* You weren't supposed to—"

"Calm down and eat your soup, partner," said Charles. "It's getting cold and you're getting on my nerves."

David's face went beet red. He got up and stormed out of the apartment. Pam called after him. "Honey, come back and relax."

Charles shook his head. "Help me up."

Pam handed Charles his cane and helped him walk out the front door, which was standing wide open. David was leaning against his truck, smoking a cigarette. He exhaled an angry burst of gray smoke and the wind whisked it up and away in a mini-whirlwind.

"You gave those things up years ago," Charles said as he shuffled across the parking lot.

David looked at the cigarette and took another drag. "I started again," he said, blowing another quickly dispersed stream of smoke in the air.

Charles leaned against the pickup bed and rested his arm along the edge. "You've got tunnel vision, my friend," he said. "You're so desperate to pin this on Dr. Westlake that you're missing some gaping holes in your case."

"Such as . . . ?" David flicked the cigarette onto the asphalt and ground it out with his heel.

"If she killed all those homeless men, why didn't somebody see her down there? The only scene she's been placed at is the last one, and that's by an anonymous tip. There are no fingerprints, or any other physical evidence for that matter, linking her to the crimes."

"There are the angels," said David.

"Which link the *crimes* together, not the suspect," Charles shot back. "You don't have anything tying the angels to *her*."

"What about the vial of insulin and the syringe?"

Charles nodded. "Unusual, but given that she's a physician, it's not compelling. Not without something else."

David's cell phone chirped, interrupting the conversation. He flipped the phone open. "Bachman. When?" David nodded. "Anything else? Mm-hmm. I'll be right there."

He closed his phone and turned back to face Charles. "An SHS nurse was just found dead in a sleazy motel on I-30. A female caller made the 9-1-1 call from a pay phone about a half-mile away." He yanked open the door of the truck and climbed in. "Oh," he said, "they found a ceramic angel at the scene. And a blue or green Ford Mustang was seen in the parking lot less than a half an hour before the 9-1-1 call came in. Dr. Westlake drives a Mustang."

David slammed the door. As the engine roared to life, he rolled down the power windows. "I hope you're right about her, Chuck," he said, shouting to be heard over the truck's powerful engine. "She seems like a nice lady. But if I find so much as a hair in that motel room that belongs to her, I'm bringing her in."

He gunned the engine and drove off.

Charles's heart sank. If the SHS nurse turned out to be Faye Renaud, the journal Lori found would be worthless.

FIFTY-TWO

Dr. Westlake, please tell me you didn't go to that motel room," Charles said. "You *promised* you wouldn't go out tonight."

Lori sat down on the sofa in Charles's living room and looked at the floor. "Faye called me again and said that someone was following her and that she needed to talk to me. She was going to tell me who phoned in the tip. I know it was stupid for me to go there, but what else could I do?"

"You could have called me," Charles said, irritated. "You could have called your sister."

"She couldn't have called me. My cell phone was turned off," Kate said. "I hate that thing." She came in from the kitchen, carrying three mugs, followed closely by Pam holding a carafe full of strong coffee.

Pam set the carafe on the coffee table. "If you don't mind, Charles, I think I'm going to bow out now," she said. "You may be able to work against David, but *I* still have to live with him. If I stay here and help you, it could be detrimental to my marriage."

"I understand, Pam," Charles said with a smile. "Besides, I have a personal physician and a hospice nurse here with me. I think I'll be well cared for."

Pam went over to Lori and took her hand. "Lori, I just want you to know that I'll be praying for you."

A strange expression—almost of amazement—came over Lori's face, as if the idea of someone praying for her was inconceivable. She

stood up and hugged Pam. "Thank you," was all she could manage
to say.

"I'll see you tomorrow," Pam said to Charles. She patted him on
the shoulder as she left.

Kate poured mugs of coffee for herself and Lori. She poured
Charles's coffee into a stainless steel mug with a lid. "So where do we
go from here?" she asked.

"We're back to square one," Charles said, "though the stakes
have definitely been raised. Someone must have felt threatened by
Faye. And she was our best chance to clear your name, Dr. Westlake.
Without her, we can try to use her journal and whatever knowledge
you have to identify one of the other members of the Circle. Bringing
one of them in the open is your only chance, I'm afraid."

He thought for a moment and then said, "Dr. Westlake, how did
you communicate with the Circle?"

"Text messaging and online chat rooms," Lori answered. "They
gave me a prepaid cell phone. When we were supposed to meet, they
would text message me with an Internet address. I'd log on to the
chat room."

"Was that the only way?" Charles asked.

"Sometimes they'd contact me through the mail, but I had to burn
every message."

"They didn't give you any emergency numbers?"

Lori nodded. "There was a contact number programmed into the
phone. When I couldn't get through to the chat room one time, I used
the cell phone to call Malachi."

"Do you still have it?" Charles asked.

"It's locked in the trunk of my car, along with the diary, but I
don't know how much good it will do. I tried the number earlier today
and it was disconnected."

"Get them both."

Lori ran outside, leaving the door standing open. Columbo took
the opportunity to come inside and hop up onto Charles's lap.

"What do you have in mind?" asked Kate.

"I'm not completely certain," Charles said as he stroked the cat.
"But somehow we've got to bait the other members of the Circle, get
one of them to show himself."

Lori came back in with the cell phone and gave it to Charles.

He turned it on and checked the stored numbers.

"We might be able to track down whoever these numbers were assigned to," he said. "If there's some way we can coordinate the numbers with the journal entries—"

"That's very helpful," a voice broke in from behind Charles. "Thank you."

David Bachman stood in the doorway along with two uniformed officers. He walked over to Lori. "Dr. Lori Westlake, I'm placing you under arrest for the murders of Nina Ware and Faye Renaud." He nodded to one of the officers. "Cuff her and Mirandize her."

As the officers took Lori into custody, David turned to Charles and held out his hand. "I'll take those, thank you."

Charles handed him the phone and the journal. "David, she's not your killer."

David ignored the comment. He patted Charles on the shoulder. "We've got enough to hold her, partner. I'm sorry for you, but Lori Westlake is going down for these killings. Now, you'll have to excuse me, but I've got an interrogation to conduct." He nodded toward Kate, who had been standing there, speechless. "Ma'am," he said as he turned and followed Lori and the officers out of the apartment.

FIFTY-THREE

To say that the ride to Kenton McCarthy's memorial service was tense would be a gross understatement. There had been a time when Pam Bachman couldn't get David and Charles to *stop* talking. Now it was all she could do to get them to say two words to each other. However, because Charles could not drive himself to the service, it was her job to try to maintain some kind of peace as David drove the trio toward Oak Park Baptist Church.

"Now I expect both of you to be on your best behavior during the service," Pam admonished from the backseat. "I don't care what your differences may be, you will *not* add to Janice's grief by bickering, either at the service or at the reception. Are we clear on that?"

Charles and David both nodded.

"Truce?" said Charles, lifting up his left hand.

"Truce," David replied, taking Charles's hand.

David pulled the truck into a handicapped parking space close to the church's front entrance. He hung Charles's parking permit from the rearview mirror. "You know, it's a plus driving you around now. I never get to park this close when I'm by myself."

"It's nice to know I'm still good for something," Charles replied without rancor.

David got out and pulled Charles's wheelchair from the truck bed. Pam sat in the backseat, waiting with Charles. "I hate to see you and David at odds like this," she said.

"Don't worry about it," Charles replied. "It'll blow over. This isn't the first time we've butted heads over a case. It's just tougher this time around because we can't exactly leave it at the office."

David opened Charles's door and offered him his hand. "Come on, partner," he said, "we can't keep them waiting."

———

Charles's mind raced with thoughts about how to draw out the Circle and prove Lori Westlake's innocence. He was so preoccupied that he was having a difficult time focusing attention on Kenton's memorial service. He needn't have worried. From the moment that David guided the wheelchair through the door, Charles was captivated by the service. He had been to a lot of funerals over the years, but this was the first one for someone who had died from ALS. His own struggle with the disease made him alert to the presence of other PALS at the service. He had never seen so many in one place. A special section at the front of the church had been reserved for wheelchairs.

At his own request, Kenton's coffin was not present. Instead, as people came in and took their seats, a video projector flashed a continuous slide show on two large screens, mounted on either side of the platform, while hymns played softly in the background. Pictures of a healthy Kenton cross-faded to photos of the wheelchair-bound Kenton that Charles knew. The slide show gave those assembled a silent but powerful testimony to the courage of this man who would not give up. No flowers decorated the front of the church, again at Kenton's request. He wanted all the money that would have been spent on flowers or plants to be given instead to further research for a cure for ALS.

Pastor Bobby Siles was the lone figure on the platform. He wore a navy pin-striped suit with a white carnation in his lapel and held a large black Bible in his lap. He sat with his eyes closed and his dark brown hands resting quietly on the Bible. Charles noticed that his fingers occasionally tapped along in rhythm with the music.

When the music and slide show finally ended, Pastor Siles walked to the pulpit and opened his Bible. In his gravelly deep voice he said, "I trust in You, O Lord; I say 'You are my God.'" He paused a moment then said, slowly and eloquently, "My times are in your hands." He closed the Bible, looked out over the group of assembled mourners, and said, "Let me tell you about my friend, Kenton McCarthy":

> Just over three years ago, he got the worst news that a person could possibly receive. The doctors told him he had ALS—Lou Gehrig's disease—and that he might have three years to live. That was bad enough, but the worst part was that ALS would slowly leech away Kenton's ability to function normally. Eventually he wouldn't be able to walk, or feed himself, or even move.
>
> Now, as you know, Kenton was a pastor. He was used to being the strong one. He was used to taking care of other people. The idea that someone would have to take care of him was more than he could handle. So he called me and asked me to come preach for him that first Sunday, and he took off for a little cabin in Colorado.
>
> Now understand me, he wasn't running away. That wasn't Kenton's style. But he needed time to think, time to work through what he'd just been told. He didn't even take Janice with him.

Janice smiled at the memory. A wry grin creased the pastor's face. "He didn't invite *me* either. I don't know why. I coulda *used* a vacation." The congregation laughed.

> Since I didn't get to go with Kenton, I can't tell you everything that happened. I can only tell you what Kenton told me when he came back.

He leaned forward on the podium, held up a finger, and dropped his voice to almost a whisper. "Kenton McCarthy went to those hills to wrestle with God."

His voice rose to a crescendo.

> Kenton McCarthy went to the Rocky Mountains because he knew that out there—where nobody but God would hear him—he and God could have it out. And he let God have it with both barrels. He shouted. He complained. He cried. And he prayed.

And do you know what God did?

God took it. All of it.

And then he led Kenton to his book, to the Bible. And Kenton read these words: "Peter turned and saw that the disciple whom Jesus loved was following them. When Peter saw him, he asked, 'Lord, what about him?'"

The pastor peered out at the congregation over his half-frame glasses.

Now, you have to understand the context here. Jesus had just told Peter how Peter was going to die.

Wouldn't you like for him to drop *that* bomb on you? Then old Peter decides that it's not enough to know how he is going to die. He wants to know how *John* is going to die, too. He wants to get a competition going. So he says, "Hey, Lord, what about that one over there? What about John? How's he going to check out?"

Now listen to what Jesus says to Peter. "If I want him to remain alive until I return, what is that to you? *You* must follow me." In other words, Jesus tells Peter to mind his own business.

And when Kenton McCarthy wrestled with God in the mountains, that's what God told *him*, too.

Kenton complained, "But God, it's not fair."

"Follow me, Kenton."

Kenton shouted, "I can serve you better and longer if I'm healthy."

"Follow me, Kenton."

Kenton pleaded, "Lord, I don't want to die this way."

"I'll carry you through it," Jesus answered. "You just follow me."

And when all of Kenton's energy was gone, when he'd run out of arguments, when he'd run out of complaints, when he'd run out of tears for the moment, God reminded him of these words from the Psalms:

"I trust in You, O Lord; I say, 'You are my God.' My times are in Your hand."

Kenton came back from Colorado a changed man because he knew that his times—his life *and* his death—were in God's hands. And Kenton's only responsibility was to faithfully walk the road that God had chosen for him.

Pastor Siles gestured toward the ALS patients assembled on one side of the auditorium.

A lot of you here are walking that same road.

Then he motioned toward the congregation.

Maybe some of you out there will be on that road someday. One thing's for sure. We're all going to die. But our times are in God's hands. You can walk that road by yourself or you can walk it—as Kenton did—with God's son, Jesus Christ, as your savior and your friend.

The pastor's voice became very quiet, almost weary. He took off his glasses and laid them on his Bible.

You want to know why so many people today are killing themselves? Why so many want doctors to help them do it? Why so many even want doctors to do it for them? Its because we've turned away from God, and without God life has no value.

Kenton McCarthy knew different. He understood that he was made in God's image, and that God infused every second of his life with meaning. Every day he lived—even with ALS—he considered a gift from God.

Kenton preached until he couldn't preach any longer. Then he stepped aside and asked me to come out of retirement to take over for him. But he never stopped ministering. He never quit serving God.

His times were in God's hands.

And on the last day of his life, in the last seconds of his life, do you know what he said?

Pastor Siles paused for a moment, struggling with emotion. When he spoke, his voice was husky.

His last two words were, "No regrets."

He fixed his eyes on the congregation.

What will *your* last words be?
Over the last three years, Kenton touched many of your lives. We've set up some microphones on the floor. Come share with us something about Kenton.

Charles watched as the pastor sat down and wiped his face with a handkerchief. There was a brief, uncomfortable silence as the congregation waited for someone to be the first to speak. Finally he heard an electric whirring sound coming from the front of the auditorium as a red motorized wheelchair made its way to one of the microphones. Its occupant—a woman who appeared to be in her forties—looked like she had melted into the chair. The chair itself was slightly reclined and a cushioned headrest supported the woman's head. She maneuvered the chair by means of a joystick. As she pulled up to the microphone stand, an usher lowered it so it was near her chair. She spoke through an electronic voice synthesizer. To Charles she sounded like a female version of Stephen Hawking.

"Thank you, Kenton," the electronic voice said in a generated monotone. "No regrets." That was all she said. The whirring sound began again as she maneuvered her chair back to the special PALS section.

One by one, the assembled PALS—members of Kenton's support group, Charles assumed—made their way to the microphone. Some spoke longer than others, but most of their speeches were brief. Many were difficult to understand. But each one, without exception, finished by saying "No regrets" or "Never give up."

As Charles listened to the testimonies, he suddenly turned and whispered to David. "Wheel me up there." David obliged and rolled the wheelchair up to the front. When Charles's turn came, David took the microphone and handed it to him.

He tried to grip the mike but his hand wasn't cooperating and it fell into his lap. He looked up at David, who took the microphone and held it near his mouth. Strong emotions seized him, and for a few moments he couldn't speak. His jaw muscles worked as he fought for control. Finally a single tear traced its way down his cheek.

He looked up and said thickly, "I understand, Kenton."

———

"There's one thing I just can't figure out." David was at the wheel of his truck, driving Charles back to his apartment.

"What's that?"

"You say that Kenton made an impact on you, but you're helping someone who stands against everything he believed in. Lori Westlake is already on record as an advocate of euthanasia and physician-assisted suicide. It's not a huge leap to believe that she was putting her beliefs into practice. In fact, most of the people I've interviewed at the hospital have no trouble at all believing she's guilty. So why are you supporting her?"

Charles smiled and said, "I think God understands."

"What do you mean?" Pam interjected.

"I don't agree with Dr. Westlake's position. But that doesn't make her guilty of murder. I don't believe the evidence points to her, that's all."

David said, "If it doesn't point to her, who *does* it point to?"

"I don't have an answer to that."

"*I* do," said David as he pulled into the handicapped parking space in front of Charles's building. "And I have that person in custody."

FIFTY-FOUR

"So, what're y'all in for?"

Lori lay on a solid steel bed in her jail cell, staring at the ceiling and wishing she could just ignore the question and go to sleep. Incarceration brought with it unimaginable feelings of humiliation and hopelessness. It wasn't just the embarrassment that came along with being arrested. It was the total loss of privacy and control, the indignity of being strip-searched, the feeling of being less than a person.

In fewer than twenty-four hours, her world had been reduced to a nine-by-twelve-foot living space with two beds, a combination sink-toilet, bars instead of a door, and one cellmate—a middle-aged strawberry blonde woman named Brenda Dodds. Lori hadn't said much since being arrested, but that hadn't been a problem. Brenda Dodds seemed content to talk enough for both of them. That's how Lori learned that Brenda's husband had been having an affair, that she was serving a twenty-year sentence in Gatesville on a second-degree murder conviction for killing her husband, and that her court-appointed attorney was appealing the conviction. Lori also learned that Brenda had been brought to the Dallas County Jail for a hearing on her appeal and that she was enjoying the change of scenery—although she preferred Gatesville's food to County's. That's also how Lori learned that in jailhouse slang, Brenda was her *cellie*, not her cellmate.

Lori found Brenda's gabbiness somewhat annoying, but at least it had kept her from having to talk. Now the dreaded "What are you in for?" question forced Lori to confront a situation she would rather forget. She couldn't imagine how she had landed in such a fix, and she had no idea how she could ever get out.

Her eyes filled with tears. She tried to answer Brenda. She tried to say the word *murder*, but all that escaped her lips was a choked sob. As the tears began to stream down the sides of her face, her carefully constructed defenses crumbled like a sand castle at high tide. Unable to stem the flood of grief, she covered her face with her hands and wept uncontrollably.

"Oh, honey, I'm sorry," Brenda said. She got up from her bed and came over and knelt by Lori's side. She stroked Lori's hair. "It's okay. Just let it all out." Brenda tore off a few sheets of toilet paper and handed them to Lori. "Here, honey. Blow your nose."

After a few minutes, Lori's sobbing subsided and she sat up. She could feel that her eyes were puffy. Her hair felt matted and greasy. She brushed it back out of her eyes with one hand. "I must look like a wreck," she said.

"Don't worry about it, honey," Brenda answered.

"Lori. My name's Lori Westlake."

"Pleased to meet you, Lori," said Brenda, moving back to sit on her own bed. "I'm sorry I got you so upset. You don't have to tell me why you're in here if you don't want to."

"No. It's okay," Lori said. "I want to." She unfolded the whole story as Brenda listened sympathetically. When Lori ran out of words, she said, "I don't know what's going to happen now."

They sat quietly for a few minutes before Lori asked, "How long have you been in prison, Brenda?"

"Next month it will be five years."

"And how long do you have to go?"

"I have to serve out half my sentence before I'm eligible for parole. So, unless my appeal is accepted, I've got at least five more years to go."

Lori shook her head. "How do you cope?"

"It was hard at first," Brenda said. "I was mad. Really mad. It all seemed so unfair, you know? But I changed."

Lori nodded. "What changed you?"

"In prison, loners don't survive long. You need somebody to watch your back. Some people get in gangs, others just become good friends with strong people. I linked up with the Christians."

Lori's jaw dropped. "Christians? In prison?"

Brenda laughed. "I know, most people think 'jailhouse religion' when they hear about Christians in prison. There *are* some phonies. I guess I was one—for a while. But a lot are real."

"So why did you join up with them?"

"They were safe. They didn't hurt anybody else. But after I hung around with them for a while, I realized that they really were different. They had somethin' I didn't have."

"What was that?" Lori asked.

Brenda looked her straight in the eye and said, "Not a *what*, honey. A *who*." Brenda smiled, and her smile was radiant. "They had Jesus."

Charles lay on his bed and stared at the ceiling. The faint red glow from the digital clock on the nightstand gave the room an eerie atmosphere.

It was 11:30 PM and he was nowhere near falling asleep.

Columbo pressed tightly against his thigh, apparently determined to shove him off of the bed by morning. He moved his hand over the cat's thick fur and gently stroked its head. A quiet purr emanated from Colombo's throat and escalated to a contented thrum.

The events of the day replayed like a TiVo recording in his mind. Over and over again he heard Pastor Siles ask, *"What will your last words be?"*

Juxtaposed against the pastor's deep voice was his own voice saying to Lori Westlake, "Faye was our best chance of finding someone who can clear your name, Dr. Westlake. Without her, we have to try to identify one of the other members of the Circle. Bringing them out in the open is our only chance, I'm afraid."

There had to be a way to get the Circle of Peace out in the open.

Then in the recesses of his conscience he heard Kenton's voice, *"No regrets."*

"I have something for you," Brenda Dodds said in a hushed voice.

Lori wasn't sure what to expect as Brenda reached underneath her mattress. Now that it was past lights out, she couldn't see much. She wasn't afraid that her cellie would pull a shank or some other kind of homemade weapon. Even in the brief time she had known Brenda, she understood that, murder conviction notwithstanding, Brenda was not a violent woman—at least not any longer. Lori had no doubt that at one time she had been. Brenda's face was etched with lines that only come from a hard life. No doubt this woman bore deep scars, both physical and emotional. But something deep inside Brenda had changed. And the change intrigued Lori.

"Here it is," said Brenda. "It got pushed back farther than I thought." In Brenda's hand was a small, palm-sized book with a brown cover. "It's a New Testament," she said as she offered it to Lori.

Lori shook her head. "I can't take your Bible, Brenda. You need that."

"It's okay," Brenda replied. "My Bible's waiting for me back at Gatesville. They came around passing these out yesterday. I didn't get to bring my Bible with me when I caught the chain bus, so I took this one so I'd have one here. But I'd really like you to have it. I'll probably be going back tomorrow anyway."

"I wouldn't know where to start reading it," Lori said.

"Just about anywhere is good," Brenda replied. "But they told me to start reading the gospel of John."

Lori took the small New Testament and opened it. Brenda had written a note on the inside cover: "For Lori. Remember: God is good—all the time. I'll be praying for you. Love, Brenda. 2 Corinthians 5:21."

"Thank you, Brenda," Lori said. She lay back down on her bunk and opened the little book to its table of contents. It wasn't easy to read in the darkened cell, but if she held it just right she could catch some light filtering in from the corridor. She found the page number for 2 Corinthians, then flipped over to chapter five. Running her finger down the page over the tiny black print, she found verse twenty-one, and read these words: "God made him who had no sin to be sin for us, so that in him we might become the righteousness of God."

———

As he lay in the quietness of his bedroom, Charles knew that there was really only one way to draw the Circle of Peace out from hiding.

And it would be dangerous.

No regrets. The phrase echoed in his mind as if it had been shouted across the Grand Canyon.

Charles scratched the cat absentmindedly. Columbo rolled on his back to give Charles access to his ample belly.

"If you want to catch a bear, you've got to have honey," Charles said quietly.

His decision made, he closed his eyes and went to sleep.

———

Lori and Brenda talked long into the night. Brenda intrigued Lori. Here was a woman who had led a rough life, who had every reason *not* to believe in God. In fact, here was a woman who had every reason to hate God. If God had ever given anyone a raw deal in life, Brenda Dodds was that person.

Raised in an abusive household, Brenda had run away at fifteen to escape her father. Alone on the streets of Dallas, she had turned to prostitution to stay alive. Prostitution led to drugs, and addiction led to more prostitution. By the time she was eighteen, she had been treated for almost every STD imaginable except AIDS. By some miracle, she had not turned up HIV positive.

When a counselor at a drug clinic challenged her to clean up her life before she wound up dead on the street, she had decided to accept the challenge. She checked in as a permanent resident, came through detox with flying colors, enrolled in some business training programs, and graduated a year later with a new outlook on life.

Within two months of graduation, Brenda was hired on as a secretary in a large accounting firm. Two months after that, she was assigned to be the personal secretary to Shawn Dodds, an up-and-coming young accountant with the firm. She didn't last long as his secretary because they fell in love and were married after a four-month courtship.

Brenda thought she had died and gone to heaven.

Her joy lasted exactly two years.

Prince Charming turned out to be a womanizer who had a nasty tendency to run around with his secretaries. Eventually he started working later and taking long business trips about which he would provide no details. Brenda suspected that Shawn was having an affair but she couldn't bring herself out of denial long enough to do something about it. Life had turned out too good for something like this to happen. So she pressed on blindly and refused to acknowledge what was almost certainly going on.

Reality came crashing in when she had to have a medical exam for a new life insurance policy. Part of the exam involved a blood test. She had been shocked when the insurance agent called and told her that she was being turned down for the policy because of health problems that showed up on the exam.

It took a while for her to get the results sent to her, but when the envelope came, she recoiled in horror at the news. She was HIV positive. She knew it couldn't have come from her earlier lifestyle. She had been clean too long, been tested too many times. The only way she could have gotten HIV was if Shawn had given it to her.

Something inside her snapped. Shawn was a gun enthusiast, and Brenda—in the spirit of being a good wife who shared her husband's interests—had learned how to handle guns. That night she loaded Shawn's 9 mm pistol, sat down on the sofa in a corner of the darkened living room, and waited for him to come home.

When he stepped through the door, she didn't even wait for him to turn the light on.

She shot him in the head.

A jury convicted her of second degree murder and sentenced her to twenty years. By passing the HIV virus on to her, her husband had probably sentenced her to an early death. Yet this remarkable woman was upbeat about the future.

"With everything you've gone through, everything you're facing, how can you be so happy?" Lori asked.

Brenda just shrugged and said, "I know where I'm going when I die. After you've settled that, there's not much else to worry about."

"Quiet down in there," said a voice from the corridor.

Lori mouthed the words "thank you" to Brenda, and lay back on her bunk.

Lori silently replayed her conversation with Brenda again and again. It almost sounded too good to be true. Forgiveness just through trusting in Jesus? Just through God's grace? She paged through the little New Testament and found the gospel of John. By holding the little book just right, she could still read it in the weak light that trickled in through the bars. Eventually her eyelids grew heavy and she nodded off.

———

The cell door slid open, jarring Lori out of a sound sleep.

"Inmate Dodds," an officer's voice called out, "time to take a ride."

"What time is it?" Lori asked, momentarily disoriented.

"Time for me to catch the chain," Brenda answered, stepping out into the hallway.

Lori sat up and tried to blink the sleep out of her eyes. "Catch the chain?" she asked.

"My bus back to Gatesville."

The cell door rolled back into position and clanged shut.

"Brenda," Lori said, looking through the bars. "Thank you."

"You just remember what we talked about," Brenda said.

"I will," said Lori. "And Brenda?"

"Yes, hon?"

"I believe."

Brenda broke out into a broad grin. "Atta girl."

"Come on, inmate. Let's go," the officer said, and Brenda led the way down the corridor.

Lori watched until Brenda was out of sight, and then slumped down on her bunk. She still didn't know what lay ahead, but whatever it was, she could face it now.

FIFTY-FIVE

Lori didn't know how much longer she slept, but it felt like only a few minutes before an officer came by and opened her cell.

"Get your things, Westlake," she said. "Time to go."

"Where?" Lori asked, once more trying to shake off the drowsiness.

"Home—for now," said the officer.

Lori didn't understand. "What?"

"Someone bailed you out," the officer said. "But don't worry, we'll see each other again."

Lori didn't have any "things" to get, except for the New Testament that Brenda had given her. Clutching the little book in both hands, Lori followed the officer out of her cell, wondering who could have bailed her out.

Certainly not Kate, Lori thought. Lori's bail was set at a million dollars. Kate didn't have that kind of money, even if she did only have to pay ten percent to make bail.

After Lori was processed out, her questions were answered. Kate was waiting for her, along with Barnabas Galloway.

Lori's throat tightened as she saw the smile on Dr. Galloway's face. She worked hard to hold back her tears. After all she'd been through in the last twenty-four hours, she was beyond fragile, treading on emotional eggshells.

Kate rushed over and took her in a motherly embrace.

Lori felt a hand on her shoulder, and she turned toward Barnabas Galloway.

She looked at him through reddened, tear-blurred eyes. "Dr. Galloway, I don't know what to say."

Galloway looked disappointed. "It's Barnabas, Lori."

Lori nodded and wiped the tears away with the back of her hand.

Barnabas Galloway put his arm around her shoulder and led her toward the exit. "And you don't have to *say* anything. It's my pleasure to get you out of this place. And if I have anything to say about it, we're going to *keep* you out. Let's get back to my office and talk about getting you a lawyer who isn't paid by the state."

A blast of cool, refreshing air washed across Lori's face as they stepped out of the building. "I didn't know fresh air could feel this good," she said.

Kate laughed and waved her hand in front of her nose. "If you think *this* air is fresh," she said, "you might need to have your head examined—literally."

Lori inhaled deeply. "After a night in *that* place," she said, "even exhaust fumes smell great."

As they walked across the parking lot toward Dr. Galloway's Cadillac SUV, Kate's cell phone buzzed.

"No rest for the weary," she said as she pulled it out. "This is Katherine Bainbridge. May I help you?"

As she listened, Kate's expression grew serious. "Certainly," she said. "I'll be right over."

"Who was it?" Dr. Galloway asked. "Anything I need to know about?"

Kate shook her head, looking puzzled. "That was Charles Hamisch," she said. "He wants me to come see him right away. He said that he wants to be admitted to the hospice."

"Do you want us to come with you?" Dr. Galloway asked.

"No," Kate answered slowly. "I'll take care of it."

FIFTY-SIX

"Charles, are you *sure* you want to do this?" Pam asked.

"Pam, we've got to face reality." Charles sat in his wheelchair, stroking a purring Columbo and directing Pam as she packed his clothes and possessions to take with him to the hospice. "I'm almost at the point where I need twenty-four-hour care. I appreciate all that you and David have done for me, but I have to be realistic. You can't be here twenty-four seven, and that's what I'm going to need. You have a husband and a home. Since I don't have any family, I qualify for admission in Sentinel's hospice facility. I'll be comfortable there, and I promise I won't try to check out early."

"Then you're not giving up?" Pam asked.

"No, Pam. I'm not quitting. And as far as I'm concerned, I can operate Hamisch Consulting right from my room. As long as you're willing to keep helping me, that is."

"Absolutely," said Pam. She folded one of Charles's shirts and put it in the suitcase.

"I do have one request, though," said Charles.

"What's that?"

"Well, my number two assistant will not be welcome at the hospice. And I've kind of grown attached to him. Do you think you could take care of Columbo for me?"

Pam cringed. "Charles, I don't know. David *hates* cats."

Charles smiled. "So did I, before *he* showed up." He scratched Columbo and the cat stood and arched its back under his fingers.

"Easy there, boy," Charles winced as Columbo dug his claws into Charles's thigh. "Just because the legs don't work doesn't mean they can't feel anything."

Pam closed up the suitcase. "Well, that's about it. David will come by to help me pack up the computer later. We'll bring that over tomorrow, if that's all right."

"That will be just fine. I'll probably want to spend a few days adjusting to the place before I get back in a work routine, anyway."

"Well, let's go and get you set up at your new home."

Charles raised his eyebrows. "What about Columbo?"

Pam heaved a sigh. "David will probably have a cow about it, but Columbo can stay with us—temporarily."

Charles nodded. "I can't ask for more than that."

"Hello-o-o. Anybody home?" a voice called from the front room.

"Back here, Kate," Charles answered.

Katherine Bainbridge stepped into the room. "Packing already?" she said. "Don't you think we should *talk* about this before you pack?"

"My sentiments exactly," Pam said. "Don't you think he's rushing things?"

"Well," Kate said, "we don't generally admit patients into the hospice facility until they're in the final stages of their disease."

Pam nodded in agreement. "Now that you're here, Kate, maybe we can talk him out of this craziness."

"Now, now," Charles said, "I can't have you two ganging up on me. Actually, Kate, I'd like to talk to you alone for a few minutes."

"Uh-huh," Pam said, "I know this routine. Divide and conquer." As she walked past Kate, she patted her on the shoulder. "Hang tough, girl. Talk him out of this."

Kate closed the door to Charles's bedroom as Pam stepped into the hall.

Charles nodded toward the bed. "Turn me around and have a seat on the bed," he said.

She turned the wheelchair so that it faced the bed, and then she sat down across from him. "Charles," she said. "I know you're discouraged, but we can't admit you to the hospice yet. You can still function; you can still get out there and enjoy life."

Charles held up his hand, stopping her. "Kate, I need your help."

"I know that, Charles, but this isn't—"

He interrupted her again. "Kate, listen. There's only one way to penetrate the Circle of Peace. We have to give them a reason to come out of hiding."

Seeing her look of incomprehension, Charles spelled it out for her.

"Kate, we need to bait them, and I'm the perfect candidate."

Kate's look of confusion morphed to one of horror. "Charles, I can't let you do that. Think of the risk you'd be taking."

Charles laughed. "Kate, remember who you're talking to here. I'm a tough old cop, and I took greater risks than this in my years on the force. Besides, what's the worst that could happen? I die? That's going to happen anyway. And I can't think of a better reason to risk my life than to put these people out of business."

"I'll need to get Dr. Galloway's approval."

"No," Charles countered. "This has to stay between you and me. We can't tell anybody."

"But Dr. Galloway is the head of hospice. He'll have to approve it."

"Then we'll need to get creative. We'll have to find a way to convince him *without* telling him what we're doing."

"But why?" Katherine asked.

"Kate, we don't know who is involved in the Circle. That means we can't trust anybody. Not even Dr. Galloway."

"What about Lori?" She looked hopeful.

"Don't you think Lori has enough on her plate?"

Kate gave a reluctant nod of agreement. "But how are you going to get in touch with them? It's not like they advertise."

"When Lori showed me Faye's journal," Charles replied, "I noticed that Isidore Jacoby's intervention had been requested by his wife's nephew. I got Pam to do some research and track down the nephew. This morning I placed a call to Chicago and talked to him. I told him that I have ALS and that I want out."

"And he believed you? Just like that?"

Charles shook his head. "Nothing's ever that easy. He did a lot of verbal tap dancing at first, said he was sure he didn't know what I was talking about."

"So how'd you persuade him?"

"Simple. I just had to convince him I was suicidal." A look of deep weariness creased Charles's features. "That was a role that wasn't too difficult to play. We talked a bit longer and finally he gave me a telephone number. I called them and put in my request just before Pam got here." Charles fell silent and looked down at his lap.

Katherine took Charles's hand.

"Charles, you aren't secretly hoping that the Circle will be successful, are you? Because if that's the case, I won't have any part of this."

Charles chuckled. "I'd be dishonest if I told you the thought never crossed my mind." Katherine looked at him sharply, but Charles quickly added, "That's *all* it did, Kate. I'm in for the long haul."

Katherine stood up. "All right then. I'll see what I can do to get you admitted today."

"What are you going to tell Dr. Galloway?"

"The same thing you told Ruthie's nephew." Katherine walked around to the back of the wheelchair and pushed Charles toward the door. "I'll tell him you're suicidal."

———

It took Kate a few days of persuasion and paperwork, but Barnabas Galloway finally agreed to admit Charles to the hospice center, if only to prevent him from taking his own life.

Pam Bachman wheeled Charles through the sliding glass entryway into Sentinel Health Systems' atrium.

"Beautiful place," said Charles. "I didn't really take the time to appreciate the surroundings last time I was here."

Pam didn't answer. She just continued rolling Charles toward the reception desk.

"Still mad, Pam?"

"Not at you as much as I am at Katherine Bainbridge," she said. "I can't believe she's agreed to admit you. It's like you've just decided to give up and wait to die. You're not even trying anymore."

In a way, Charles *wasn't* trying anymore. If he was to convince the Circle to intervene in his case, he had to make his ALS symptoms look worse than they really were. That was the easiest acting job he'd ever had. He hated keeping Pam in the dark about it, but there was no choice.

She pointed to his hands, which lay curled in his lap. "It's like you've shriveled up overnight. Look at your hands. If you don't do your range-of-motion exercises, you'll lose what movement you still have."

That *was* a concern for Charles. He hoped that the Circle didn't take too long to act. Exercise couldn't stop the onslaught of ALS, or even slow it down, but the range-of-motion drills helped keep muscle atrophy at bay. This little bit of undercover work could hurt him if it went on too long.

Pam stopped at the reception desk and handed Charles's room pass to the desk clerk. A name plate on the desk identified the clerk as Jennifer. She reviewed Charles's pass and entered his information in her computer. "Welcome to Sentinel, Mr. Hamisch. All your paperwork looks to be in order, so we'll just get someone to show you to your room." She waved across the atrium toward a handsome young man, dressed in the same blue and gold colors she was wearing. "Tony? Your guest is here."

"Guest?" Charles asked.

"Tony will explain," Jennifer said with a knowing smile.

Tony jogged up to Charles and Pam. "Hi, I'm Tony Garcia. Katherine Bainbridge told me to be watching for you and to give you VIP treatment when you arrived. Now, since all we give around here is VIP treatment, that part's taken care of. But I do want to make sure that all of your questions are answered."

He took the room pass from the receptionist.

"Looks like you'll be in room C21. All of our hospice suites are on the first floor. The floors above it house maternity, the newborn nursery, and neonatal ICU." He began wheeling Charles toward the Crockett Building.

When the wheelchair rolled into suite C21, Pam whistled in amazement.

"Whoa," said Charles. "This is nicer than my old digs. Maybe not as big, but definitely nicer."

"I'm *impressed*," Pam echoed. "I'd heard that this facility was something to see, but I had no idea it was this nicely done."

Decorated in pastel yellow with a large west-facing picture window, the suite was bright and cheery. A sofa and an electrically powered recliner, both upholstered in rich forest green colors, were on the far end of the room near the large window. A small kitchen nook on the left provided a place for fixing meals. "See that, Pam?" Charles said, nodding toward the kitchen. "I don't have to eat hospital food all the time. You can come over anytime to fix me some linguine and clam sauce."

"I'll be sure to bring some over," Pam said, smiling for the first time since they'd arrived. "Charles, if you don't mind, I think I'll leave you with Tony. David will be getting off work soon and I'd like to be there when he gets home."

"That's fine, Pam," Charles said. "I think Tony's got things under control."

She kissed Charles on the forehead and said to Tony, "Take good care of him."

"Looks like you've got some good support," said Tony after Pam exited the room.

Charles smiled. "The best."

"Well then, let's continue with the tour, shall we?" Tony said, maneuvering Charles's wheelchair through a large open doorway on the right. "This is your bedroom. It has an electronically operated hospital bed and a bathroom with a large, wheelchair-accessible shower. As you can see, our hospice facility is state-of-the-art."

He picked up a remote control and pointed it toward the wall opposite the bed. A moveable panel rolled upward, revealing a brand new plasma screen television on the wall, facing the bed. A DVD player was built into the bedside table and tiny surround sound speakers had been mounted in each corner of the room. "I'd like to have this entertainment system at home," Tony joked. "But I could never afford it."

"Now I see where all my HMO premium dollars are going," Charles said, only half kidding.

"Wait, there's more," Tony said without missing a beat. "An emergency communications system has been incorporated into the bed rail and the remote control. Three buttons on the rail will summon whatever kind of help you need." He pointed out three buttons—green, yellow, and red—arranged in a triangle near the bottom of the remote. Then he showed Charles three corresponding buttons on the bed rail. "The green button is for calling a nurse on the intercom. The yellow button is to call an aide to the room, such as when you need help moving, going to the bathroom, whatever. The third button—the red one—is a panic button. Don't press this one unless you need help ASAP. It's like dialing 9-1-1." He lowered his voice to a conspiratorial whisper. "If your call isn't legitimate, they get pretty testy."

"One question," said Charles. "Is living here going to be like being in a hospital? Are they going to wake me up every three hours to poke and probe?"

Tony laughed. "Not to worry. You don't get that kind of attention unless you're pretty bad off. Someone will check on you at shift change. Other than that, you're not even going to know the staff's here . . ." he handed Charles the remote, "unless you call them, of course."

It was a good system, Charles thought, although he noticed that the buttons on the bed rail were placed too far up to be of use to him if his ALS progressed much further. Lifting his hands was becoming more and more difficult, though not impossible. To push the buttons, Charles would have to reach across his body and bring his hand almost all the way up to his shoulder. Fortunately the handheld remote control performed all the same functions. That would work fine—at least until his fingers could no longer press the buttons.

"Do you want to go to the recliner or your bed?" Tony asked.

"I'm kind of tired," Charles said. "Would you mind helping me get ready for bed?"

———

Tony had just helped Charles into bed and pulled his covers up when Dr. Galloway and Katherine Bainbridge came into the room.

"I hope we're not interrupting anything important," said Dr. Galloway.

"Nope," said Tony. "I'm all finished here."

"Did you give him VIP treatment?" Kate asked.

Tony grinned and motioned toward Charles. "You'll have to ask him."

Charles gave a weak thumbs-up. "He did great."

Dr. Galloway put his arm around Tony's shoulder. "Anthony is a special friend to the hospice service patients."

Tony looked uncomfortable. "Well, I'd better get back out front. Let me know if you need anything, Mr. Hamisch." He winked at Kate as he left.

"Thanks, Oscar," she said.

Charles exchanged glances with Dr. Galloway. "Oscar?"

Kate laughed and waved it off. "That's just my nickname for him. He's named after a famous actor but won't tell anyone who it is. Says we have to guess it. I'm no good at guessing games so I call him Oscar. I figure that I've got all the bases covered that way." Her expression softened. "He's a good kid."

Dr. Galloway nodded. "He's had a rough time of it. His mother was one of our first patients."

"When she died," Kate said, "Oscar—Tony—was left with four younger brothers and sisters to support. Dr. Galloway convinced the human resources department to hire him on."

"And I haven't regretted it for a moment," Dr. Galloway said, glancing at his watch. "Mr. Hamisch, I hate to introduce myself and run, but I've got some prior commitments. I just wanted to welcome you and let you know that I am at your disposal anytime."

"Thank you, doctor."

"Katherine, I believe you can take it from here and get our new patient oriented."

"I've got it under control," she answered.

As soon as he was sure that Dr. Galloway had gone, Charles said, "Kate, close the door."

"I've got it," she said.

After the door was closed, Kate stepped up close to the side of Charles's bed and lowered her voice, "Charles, are you absolutely certain you want to go through with this?"

Charles nodded. "I think it's our best—maybe our *only*—chance to draw the real killers out."

"How long do you think it will be before they send someone?"

"I don't know, Kate. Based on the brief explanation I received, it's usually fairly soon after a patient is admitted. But since I'm supposed to be a long-term patient, they've got more flexibility."

"And what is your plan when someone *does* show up?"

Charles grinned and held up the remote. "See that red button?"

"So now we wait," said Kate.

"Now we wait," Charles agreed.

FIFTY-SEVEN

Lori sat at her dining room table trying to read the New Testament that Brenda had given her, but she couldn't concentrate to save her life. She gazed out the undersized dinette window, watching the late afternoon light diminish to a dusky autumn sunset.

I hate waiting.

In some ways, this was worse than jail. Her paid leave had become an unpaid suspension after the DA filed murder charges, and paying bills would soon be a concern. She was persona non grata at SHS; in fact, she was under a court order not to come within one thousand yards of the hospital. She had nothing to do but meet with her lawyer and sit around to wait for the court system to set a trial date. Even if she *did* have something to do, there were reporters hanging around outside the apartment. Going outside generally meant risking a gauntlet of questions that she'd rather not have to answer.

The only good thing to come from all of this was that she now had time to get her apartment organized. It had been bad enough before the police search, but they had managed to eliminate what little bit of order she had established.

She didn't have much outside support, either. Kate was working night and day and didn't have much time for her. And to make matters worse, Drew had disappeared from her radar screen just when she most needed his encouragement.

Despite Kate's suspicions, the district attorney hadn't filed any charges against Drew. In fact, he didn't even seem interested in considering Drew as a suspect. According to Kate, Dr. Johnston would have lifted Drew's administrative leave and restored his position, but Drew hadn't shown up for work since the day Lori had been arrested.

She had tried calling his home and his cell phone, but both were disconnected.

So, with nothing better to do, Lori sat and waited.

And she hated waiting.

———

Quinn sat with his laptop open, quietly fuming. The screen displayed a familiar—but empty—chat room. The meeting had been set for 6:00 PM and he had been waiting for nearly ten minutes. Still no one else had signed in.

Quinn wondered if this was a portent of the Circle's future. Zoë was dead, and by all indications Servant was the guilty party. Had the other members decided enough was enough? Because their security rules prohibited face-to-face conversations about Circle business, it wasn't easy to find out what was going on.

Just as Quinn was about to leave the chat room, a prompt appeared at the bottom of the screen.

> Malachi has entered.
>
> Malachi: We'd better start the meeting now. I don't believe Copper will be able to join us.
>
> Quinn: We're not supposed to meet unless everyone's present.
>
> Malachi: Copper knows what's going on and he supports our actions.

Quinn was hesitant, but Malachi generally had the last word in Circle discussions.

> Quinn: All right. What about the new case?
>
> Malachi: The patient has been admitted and evaluated.

Quinn: Do you think it is advisable to take on a new case?

Malachi: It has never been "advisable" to take on any case.

Quinn: Granted. But due to current circumstances, perhaps we should wait.

Malachi: This patient has waited long enough. The case proceeds.

Quinn: When?

Malachi: Immediately. The materials have been placed in the locker. You may proceed at your convenience.

Quinn: Has the patient been notified?

Malachi: He will be.

The Angel logged out of the chat room and closed his laptop. Zoë's treachery had changed everything.

He had regained control of himself and had allowed the Circle to become his stabilizing force—his balance—again. But when Zoë had broken ranks and nearly revealed his identity to Lori Westlake, he'd had no choice but to kill her.

And then it all came surging back. The power, the rush, the sheer pleasure of taking a life. And he had nearly lost control again.

For the first time in many years, the Angel was afraid. If he lost control again, he would lose himself entirely. He would become a killing machine, not an angel of mercy.

The only answer to his problem was discipline. Control. For that reason, if for no other, the work of the Circle must continue unabated. But for his own sake, the Angel must forgo the pleasure of assisting with the latest case.

He must allow Quinn the privilege of assisting the cop with ALS.

Besides, unless he missed his guess, he would have to run interference for Quinn.

Katherine Bainbridge was getting too close. Much too close.

The Angel had ignored Katherine Bainbridge's investigation of the Circle for a long time because he didn't consider it a threat. But now his opinion had changed. The woman displayed an uncanny knack for uncovering the truth. And that couldn't be allowed to continue.

It's time to pay Katherine a little visit.

———

"If I don't get out of this apartment," Lori said out loud to the empty room, "I'm going to go stir-crazy. I've got to go somewhere, do something. Even if it's just a movie."

She looked out the window. The sodium vapor lamps illuminated the street with pockets of yellow-orange light. She didn't see any TV news vans outside. As dark as it was, she might be able to sneak out without being seen.

She put on a green and black windbreaker and was about to step outside when the phone rang. She groaned and turned back into the apartment. She *so* wanted to ignore the ringing and let it go unanswered, but as soon as she did, it would be something important.

"Hello?"

A muffled voice came over the line. "Lori? It's Drew."

Lori's heart skipped a beat. "Drew where have you *been*? Are you all right? Why haven't you called?"

"I need to talk to you," he said. "Can you meet me?"

"Where?"

"Over at Sentinel."

"Drew, I can't go over there. I'm under a restraining order."

"Meet me down in the gardens. Twenty minutes."

"But Drew, I—"

He had already broken the connection.

She hung up the phone. *Drew, what are you thinking? You picked the one place I can't go. What am I going to do?* She zipped up her jacket and stepped out into the night.

FIFTY-EIGHT

Quinn glanced around before he opened the locker. He heard some other voices in the staff locker room, but nobody was near enough to see him. He entered the combination and opened the locker. As Malachi had promised, the materials were there.

Quinn smiled.

Sometimes the simplest solutions were the best.

———

The rusty gate clanged shut behind Lori. As she looked down the dark staircase leading from the back entry into Sentinel's gardens, she was already regretting the decision to come down here.

"Drew," she complained to herself, "if you had to meet me somewhere, why couldn't it have been at the Italian restaurant?"

Every few feet a pathway light cast an off-white semicircle on the steps. Lori would have preferred the kind of lighting usually found in car dealership parking lots. Virtual daylight.

Quietly, she made her way down the steps and into the gardens, stopping every few steps to listen. So far, at least, she had avoided a repeat of her previous excursion into the gardens. Nobody else had come through the back gate.

As she reached the bottom of the path, the heart of the gardens, she scanned her surroundings, looking for Drew. But even though her eyes had adjusted to the darkness, she couldn't see him anywhere.

He hadn't specifically said that she should meet him in this part of the gardens, but she was hesitant about ascending the stairs near the buildings. At this distance she was *technically* still obeying the restraining order. She was more than a thousand feet away from the hospital building.

She had turned to go back up the stairs toward the gate when she saw someone standing on the third step. It looked to be a man about Drew's size, but she couldn't be sure. All she could see was a shape.

"Drew?" she said softly.

The man stepped forward.

"Lori."

Lori smiled and ran to him. She couldn't see the face but she knew the voice.

Drew kissed her, and Lori melted into his embrace. "Where have you been?" she asked.

"Hiding," he said.

"From what?" Lori said, trying her best to sound uninformed.

"It's a long story. I confronted Kate the night you were arrested. It took a while, but once I convinced her that I didn't have anything to do with Mr. Jacoby's death, she showed me a copy of Faye's journal and asked me to help her expose the Circle of Peace."

"How'd you convince her?"

"A good alibi helped. The night that Mr. Jacoby died, I'd been called to a private home to counsel a couple whose daughter had just been killed in a car accident. I was nowhere near the hospital, and the couple could verify my story. After that, I guess Kate felt she could trust me again, because she told me a detective was trying to railroad you, and she asked me to help her find out the truth. I didn't have anything to lose, and I wanted to help you any way I could. Since then, I've been trying to lay low and follow up on whatever leads we get."

"So did you turn up anything?" Lori asked.

"Maybe. That's why I called you. I need your help."

"Doing what?"

Drew looked up toward the Sentinel complex. "We've set a trap. Charles Hamisch was admitted to the hospice, and he's asked the Circle to euthanize him."

Lori was incredulous. "Charles?"

Drew waved her off. "He's not serious about it. He's just making himself the bait."

"So what do you need from me?" Lori asked.

"Kate thinks the Circle will move tonight. She was supposed to be staked out in an empty room across from Charles's, but her car's not in the parking lot and she's not answering her cell phone."

"She might have been called out to a patient's house," said Lori.

"That's why I need your help. We've got to get up there and make sure nothing happens to Charles."

"Drew, neither of us are supposed to be on the SHS complex."

"Lori, if nobody's up there watching him, Charles could be in danger."

Lori paused a moment. "What room is he in?"

"C21."

Lori nodded. "Let's go."

"Stay right where you are," a voice broke in. "Don't move."

Someone stepped out of the shadows less than twenty feet from them. Whoever it was had a gun.

Again, Lori couldn't see the face, but she definitely knew the voice.

FIFTY-NINE

A rustling noise by Charles's bedside roused him out of a deep sleep.

For a few seconds, he couldn't remember where he was. He looked around, but everything was hazy. He tried to rub the sleep out of his eyes, but his arms were under the covers and felt like they'd been encased in lead. He blinked, trying to focus on the blurry silhouetted figure standing beside his bed.

"I locked the outside door so we wouldn't be disturbed," the man said softly. He pulled a pair of latex gloves from his front pocket and put them on. Then he pulled something from his back pocket.

Charles blinked again, trying to clear his vision in the darkened room. "Who—who—?"

"Shhhhh. I'm with the Circle of Peace and I'm here to help you."

Charles squinted and looked at the man's face. He recognized him immediately.

Garcia. Tony Garcia, the young man who brought me to the room. Said he wanted to show me the "VIP treatment."

"Tony?"

Tony smiled. "In the Circle I'm known as Quinn. Anthony Quinn Garcia. My mother liked Greek actors."

Tony opened up what looked like an oversized shower cap.

Charles squinted again. *No, it's too big to be a shower cap.* The bag was easily large enough to fit completely over someone's head, and it appeared to have an elastic band around one end.

Tony put his hands inside the bag and pushed his fingers outward, expanding the plastic.

"This is how I helped my mother."

Charles's mouth went dry.

"We agreed that when the pain got too bad I'd help her end it. But we had to be careful how we did it. She didn't want me to go to jail or anything. I rigged up the bag and had it ready."

Charles moved his fingers under the covers, trying to find the remote control for the bed. It had to be there. It had been in his hand when he fell asleep but he couldn't feel it now.

Tony evidently noticed Charles's panicked expression. "Don't worry," he said in a reassuring voice. "This *can* be kind of scary, particularly if you're claustrophobic. But I'll talk you through it."

Got to keep him talking, Charles thought as he continued to move his sluggish fingers around under the weight of the blankets.

———

"Hello, Philip," Lori said in a voice that was quiet but tinged with fear.

Philip Westlake stepped further into the open. "You never answered my letters." His thick Texas drawl was hard and cold as dry ice. Even in the gardens' dim light, his eyes burned with rage. "I *told* you I'd changed. I wanted us to try again."

He came nearer to Lori and Drew but stayed out of reach.

Salt and pepper stubble covered his chin. He smelled like he'd bathed in whiskey.

"And what do I find?" he demanded. "I find you sneaking out at night to meet *him*."

"Philip," said Lori, "we're divorced."

"*You're* divorced," he screamed back at her, pointing the gun at her head. "I never agreed to it."

Lori tried to keep her voice even. "Philip, if you leave now, I won't have you prosecuted."

Philip broke into hysterical laughter. "You won't have me prosecuted? Well thank you, ma'am. I guess I'll just leave now."

Lori sensed Drew's muscles tensing as if he were getting ready to jump Philip. She reached a hand sideways to hold him back.

"Keep your hands to yourself, woman," Philip bellowed. He stepped in and backhanded Lori to the face, knocking her to the ground. When she fell, she cracked her head against the pavement. Her vision dissolved into a mass of white and black sparkles.

As Lori lay dazed on the ground, she felt Drew lunge toward Philip. As the two men struggled only a few feet from her, Lori knew she needed to get up and help Drew. But she couldn't will her legs to move.

The next sound she heard was the sharp *pop* of the handgun firing.

—

"How will you—do it?" Charles asked.

Tony opened his hand, revealing a small pill. "This is Halcion. It won't raise any eyebrows if it's found in your system. You have a standing order for it."

"Why do I need a sleeping pill?"

"It'll help you relax. As soon as you're drowsy, I'll slip the bag over your head. The elastic will seal off the air flow. It won't take long after that."

"Will you leave the bag there? Is that how they'll find me?"

Tony shook his head. "No. I'll take it with me when I leave.

"Now here," he said. "Let's get started."

"My arms are too heavy today," Charles protested.

"No problem," Tony replied, "I'll help you. Just like I helped Mom."

He brought the tablet to Charles's lips.

SIXTY

Lori rolled onto her side and looked in the direction of the gunshot, just in time to see Drew slide from Philip's grasp and onto the ground.

Philip began shouting nonsense at Drew and brandishing the gun like he might take another shot.

"Philip, no!"

Lori's ex-husband turned in her direction and pointed the gun at her. "Stay out of this or you'll be next!"

Philip turned back toward Drew and pointed the gun at his head. Lori knew she had to do something fast. She grabbed an egg-sized rock from the edge of the path and hurled it at Philip. It caught him right between the shoulder blades.

He let out a scream of rage and rushed toward her. She knew she'd only have one chance to stop him. She rolled on her back in a defensive posture and waited for him to get within range.

Come on, Philip, one step closer.

As soon as he was close enough, she landed a well-placed heel kick to his groin. He doubled over, screaming in agony, but maintained a firm grip on the gun.

Before he could recover, Lori rolled sideways and trapped his shins between her legs. Quickly rolling in the other direction, she caught him behind the knees and threw him face forward into the concrete. The gun flew from his hand and skittered across the walkway.

Lori bounced to her feet, ready for another round, but Philip was unconscious. Blood puddled beneath his shattered nose.

Lori ran over to Drew, knelt by his side, and felt for a pulse. It was thready, but at least it was there.

"Come on, Drew, hang on," she pleaded.

His eyes fluttered open.

"Drew, are you with me?"

He nodded weakly. A thin trail of blood traced its way from his mouth and down his cheek. His breath came in labored wheezes.

"I've got to get help, but I'll be back. Do you understand?"

His lips curled up in a hint of a smile. His words were barely audible, but Lori understood every one. "Not—going—anywhere."

Lori kissed his forehead. "I love you," she said, blinking back tears.

He nodded and closed his eyes.

Before leaving Drew, she picked up Philip's gun and hurled it into the bushes, then sprinted up the walkway toward the Sentinel atrium.

"I need some water," Charles said. "I can't swallow the pill without it."

"Of course," Tony said, looking around for Charles's water pitcher.

"It's over by my sink," Charles said. He willed his sluggish fingers to move as Tony went to pour a glass of water. The "panic button" remote had to be within his reach.

It's got to be here. It was in my hand when I fell asleep.

"Here we go," said Tony. "Here, let me help you again."

Charles allowed Tony to put the pill in his mouth, but before he took the water, he rolled the pill under his tongue. Soon after he swallowed the water, his mouth was flooded with the bitterness of the Halcion as it dissolved under his tongue. At the same instant, his fingers found the remote.

Tony pulled a chair up beside the bed and sat down. "The sedative will take effect soon," he said. "Then I'll finish up for you."

Charles had practiced with the remote in the dark in anticipation of just such a moment. He gently pulled it closer and ran his fingers over the buttons. The panic button was larger than the others and had conveniently been marked with a Braille dot. He found it with his index finger and pressed it as firmly as he could.

Nothing happened.

SIXTY-ONE

Lori burst through the emergency room doors shouting, "A man's been shot! I need help. Stat!"

Two EMTs came out of the break room on a dead run. "Where is he?" they shouted in unison.

Lori pointed out the doors toward the gardens. "In the gardens. All the way down."

The two men grabbed their cases and raced out the doors. Lori started to follow but a tall man in a lab coat stepped in front of her. His name tag read Dr. Nathan Young.

"Hold on, Dr. Westlake," he said. "You're not going anywhere." He signaled for a nurse to bring a wheelchair. Lori tried to push past him but he blocked her way.

"Drew's been shot," she said. "Get out of my way."

Dr. Young gently held her shoulders. "Don't you think we should take care of you first?"

Lori paused and looked down at the deep red stains on her jacket. All at once she felt her head throbbing. She'd seen the blood on her jacket but had assumed it was Drew's.

"I've got to go help Drew," she said, trying again to push past the doctor, but not as forcefully this time.

Dr. Young shook his head. "Look, we've called 9-1-1, so the police will be here soon. And the EMTs will be more than halfway down there by now. If you go trying to help, you'll just get in the way. And if you collapse down there," he turned her head and examined the cut, "which is very likely, you'll just draw help away from Drew."

He pointed toward the wheelchair. "Now get in that chair."

Grudgingly, Lori obeyed.

———

Rolling the Halcion tablet under his tongue wasn't the brightest idea Charles had ever had. But he hadn't planned on keeping it there for long. He was just trying to avoid swallowing it long enough to press the red button.

The panic button was broken but the Halcion was working just fine.

He bit the inside of his cheek, trying to drive off the feeling of drowsiness that was quickly overtaking him. But he knew he was fighting a losing battle. The Halcion would soon take over, and then Tony would "help" him exit this life peacefully.

Got—to—stay—awake.

Charles looked over at Tony, who was sitting quietly by the side of his bed. The plastic bag was in his lap.

Tony smiled at him.

———

Lori sat fuming in ER treatment room number three. Dr. Young had personally ushered her into the examining room, but before he could do anything he was called away to a more urgent case. Since then, Lori had been forced to sit and wait for word about Drew.

She hated waiting. It gave her too much time to think. And Drew was all she could think about. How reluctant she had been at first to even go out with him. The recollection of how she'd met him at the door in jeans and a Dallas Cowboys sweatshirt brought a hint of a smile to her face. Now, the thought of losing him made her throat tighten.

Her mind flashed back to the gardens, to Drew's urgent warnings about what was going on at Sentinel.

"Charles could be in danger. We've got to get up there."

Lori's heart skipped a beat.

In the race to get help to Drew, she'd forgotten all about Charles Hamisch. She had to send somebody over there.

She hopped down from the examining table and instantly regretted it. Even that small of a movement sent sharp arrows of pain through her body. A flurry of black dots danced across her vision like a host of migrating birds. Her head felt like it would explode.

She leaned on the table and paused, fighting for control. A wave of nausea swept over her. Her head was swimming.

Gathering her resolve, she stumbled over to the wall intercom and hit the emergency button: "Code Blue. Crockett 21," she said.

Then everything went black.

Charles was floating. He felt like a passive observer. Detached. Disinterested. Sluggish.

He couldn't keep his eyes open another second.

"It's time, Charles," a gentle voice broke through the clouds that filled his head.

Who was that? Tony?

Charles opened his eyes a crack. He had a vague impression of a man slipping something over his head.

What are you doing? Charles tried to understand, to force himself to think, but he couldn't concentrate.

He just wanted to sleep.

Somewhere in the distance he thought he heard a banging sound and someone calling his name.

Tony had just secured the bag over Charles's head when someone started hammering on the door and rattling the handle.

"Mr. Hamisch? Mr. Hamisch, open the door."

More voices.

Strong hands pounding on the door.

"Get a key," someone shouted.

Tony glanced at his watch and mouthed a quiet curse. Something was wrong. The nurse wasn't due to check on Mr. Hamisch for at least another half hour. Nevertheless, he remained calm. Circle protocol required that every interventionist have an escape route prepared. Tony's plan—out the window—might not have been creative, but it was functional. Since all of the hospice suites were on the first floor, he merely had to slip outside and follow the maintenance walkway back to the front of the building.

"Sorry, Mr. Hamisch," he said. "Looks like we're going to have to abort." He started to pull the plastic from Charles's head when he heard a commanding new voice at the door.

"Police. Open the door."

Tony broke into a cold sweat. The police wouldn't be here unless this was some kind of setup. Which meant his so-called escape route might already be covered.

The door shuddered under a renewed attack from the other side.

Tony ran to the window and looked out. Safety lamps mounted on the side of the building cast a pale luminescence on the surrounding landscape. The area outside the window appeared unoccupied. If the police were there, they were doing a good job of concealing themselves. He still had a chance.

He yanked on the latch but the window wouldn't open.

Another thud resonated through the door. This time the whole wall shuddered.

No time to be delicate.

Tony grabbed a nearby chair and slammed it through the window. Glass exploded outward, showering the walkway with tiny shards that sparkled in the whitish light.

As he stepped through the window he looked back and saw the bag still covering Charles's face. He couldn't risk going back to retrieve it, but maybe it was for the best. If the posse took long enough breaking through the door, the patient might just slip away after all.

"Police! Down on the ground. Now!"

Tony looked behind him. Fifty yards away, two officers were rounding the corner with guns drawn. They began running toward him.

Apart from the dim light cast by the safety lamps, it was dark behind the Crockett Building, and the terrain was a maze of Dumpsters and huge air conditioning compressors. Tony knew that both the darkness and the terrain were in his favor. With any luck at all, he could make it to the gardens and disappear.

He darted into the shadows. The officers shouted at him to stop but he paid no attention.

He dodged a compressor and cut behind a Dumpster.

He could hear the officers shouting to one another. They sounded confused. They would have to move carefully, slowly. Not knowing if he was armed, they couldn't risk running blindly after him.

Got to keep moving.

Staying low and close to cover, Tony made his way quickly and silently toward the far end of the building. He peered around the corner, making sure no one was coming. No sign of flashing lights or sirens.

From this location, he would have to traverse a parking lot and one street to get to the gardens. He'd be exposed for a few seconds, but once he made it to the garden entrance, he'd be home free.

No time like the present.

He broke into a run.

As he rounded the corner of the building and cut across the parking lot, he heard more shouting behind him. It sounded like they were getting closer. He kept running, but risked a quick glance over his shoulder to check on his pursuers' progress.

I'm going to make it.

A split-second later, Tony heard the ear-shattering blast of a truck's air horn. He heard tires squealing and smelled burning rubber. He looked around in time to see the onrushing headlights.

Then he saw no more.

Lori dreamed. And the dreams were dark and unsettling. She saw Philip and Drew. Charles. And someone else. Someone shadowy and unknown. Someone very dangerous.

The acrid odor of smelling salts ripped through her dream like a razor.

At first, all she saw was the hand that held the small vial beneath her nose. She pushed it away. For a few seconds, her gaze roamed around the room. She was still in the ER examining room, and since she couldn't feel the cold floor beneath her, she assumed she was back up on the examining table. Then her eyes slowly focused on Dr. Terrence Johnston.

His face was tired and drawn. "Dr. Westlake, are you all right?"

Lori groaned inwardly. Johnston was the last person she wanted to see right now.

"I've been better," she said.

"Don't try to sit up just yet."

Defiant to the last, Lori sat up anyway. She immediately wished she hadn't. Her head throbbed, spears of fresh pain lancing through her skull with every heartbeat.

"Excuse me," a man's voice interrupted from the doorway. "I need to speak to Dr. Westlake for a moment."

Lori looked past Dr. Johnston and groaned again. Detective Bachman, the other person competing for first place on her "most disliked" list, entered the room. But this time, there was something different in his demeanor. His expression was haggard. Sad, even.

Doctor Johnston moved toward the door. "I'll step out while you two talk."

Detective Bachman caught the doctor by the arm as he turned to leave. "I think you'd better stay," he said.

"What do you mean?" Dr. Johnston asked. "What's wrong?"

Lori knew. Call it intuition or a good read on Bachman's face, but she knew. And all at once her blood ran cold.

"Charles? Is he—"

Detective Bachman shook his head. "Charles is okay. A little sleepy, but he'll be fine."

"And the man who was in there with him?" Dr. Johnston asked.

"He's dead."

Lori's eyes searched Detective Bachman's face. She still saw sadness there.

"It's about Drew, isn't it?" she asked.

Bachman heaved a sigh and nodded. "I'm sorry. He didn't make it."

Lori clenched her teeth together and squeezed her eyes tight, desperately trying to hold back the tears. Her breath came in short hitches.

Fight it back. Not now. Fight it!

It wasn't that she didn't want to cry in front of these men; she was just afraid that if she started crying now, she might never stop. But as she thought about Drew, about those last few moments with him, sorrow swept over her like a tsunami.

SIXTY-TWO

The cold, ice-blue digits on David Bachman's dashboard displayed 12:23 AM as he wheeled his truck onto Katherine Bainbridge's street. The street, lined with wizened live oak trees, was quiet and dark, except for the tiny pockets of soft orange light cast by the streetlamps.

"Thank you for bringing me all the way over here," Lori said. "I just can't be alone tonight."

"Don't mention it."

Kate's house came into view on the left. Her Civic sat dark and quiet in the driveway and the house was shrouded in gloom. Lori was relieved to see Kate's car there

"That's odd," said Lori. "Kate usually parks in the garage."

Bachman pulled into Kate's driveway and shifted into park. "I'd feel better if I went up there with you," he said.

Lori shook her head. "No, that's all right. As crazy as everything has been today, I'm sure she just forgot."

Bachman walked around to the passenger side of the pickup and opened the door for Lori. She picked up the small bag of pain medication the ER doctor had sent home with her, and held out her hand. Bachman took her hand and helped her step down from the cab.

"Can I at least help you up the steps?"

Lori shook her head. "I'll be all right," she said. But deep inside she didn't think she'd be all right for a long time.

"Dr. Westlake, I'm very sorry about Mr. Langdon."

Lori choked back tears and replied thickly, "So am I."

The detective waited in the truck as Lori carefully made her way up the steps to Kate's front door. She took out her key and unlocked the front door, then turned and waved. Bachman flicked his brights on and off and backed out of the driveway.

Lori closed the door behind her and locked the double-key deadbolt.

The only light came from a host of tiny green night-lights, placed in various electrical sockets in the front room. The phosphorescent glow gave the house a creepy, Halloween-like feel. And it was deathly quiet. Kate usually left a radio on in the kitchen, just to create background noise. Tonight all Lori could hear was the ticking of the antique clock on the fireplace mantle.

She had hoped her sister might be waiting up for her, that she might have gotten one of the three messages Lori had left on her answering machine. But Kate had evidently turned in early. That wasn't particularly unusual, given her crazy schedule.

Lori needed to talk, but she decided not to bother Kate. At the moment she needed sleep more than conversation anyway. Her head was pounding again, and now her arm and leg ached from where she had landed on the concrete after Philip backhanded her.

She decided that one more pain pill might make for a better night's sleep.

As she started down the hallway toward the kitchen to get a glass of water, she thought she sensed movement behind her.

She swung around.

No one was there.

She shook her head. "You're getting spooked, kiddo. Time to get some serious rest."

She turned back toward the kitchen and her heart nearly stopped.

The doorway was no longer empty.

SIXTY-THREE

Barnabas Galloway leaned casually against the doorframe, pointing a gun at Lori. The night-lights in the hall painted his face a ghoulish green. Fear shot through Lori like a lightning bolt. Every hair on her body felt like it was standing on end. She took a step backward.

"Dr. Galloway, what are you doing here? Where's Kate?"

"Don't make this difficult, Lori."

"Make *what* difficult?"

"Come now. Surely you're not that dense."

The truth hit her like a freight train. She took an involuntary step backward. "Malachi?"

"Very good. You're a regular Einstein." His voice dripped sarcasm.

"I started out the same way you did, you know," Galloway said, still pointing the gun at her. "It felt so good to be able to *help* people. To end their suffering. I've lost count of how many I've assisted over the years. It could run in the hundreds." He looked at her and smiled. "There's a great sense of power that goes along with taking a life, Lori." He took a step closer to her. "Did you know that?"

"What did you do to Kate?" Lori fought to keep the tremor out of her voice.

Galloway cleared his throat. "Katherine's fine—for now."

Lori's mind raced. There were only two exits. One went past Galloway toward the garage; the other was back the way she had come—out the front door.

"Katherine should have left well enough alone," Galloway said. "Everything was operating quite smoothly before she began to stick her nose in the Circle's business."

"Where is she? Tell me!" Lori demanded.

Galloway smiled. "You're not exactly in a position to be making demands," he said. "But there's no reason you shouldn't know. Katherine is out in the garage, in my SUV. Under sedation."

Lori's heart surged with a mixture of hope and fear. But she couldn't think about Kate right now. She couldn't lose focus. She had to buy some time, keep Galloway talking.

"Why didn't you just kill her outright like you did Faye Renaud?"

Galloway expelled a short, derisive laugh, as if Lori had asked, "Why is the sky blue?"

"I had someone to take the blame for Nurse Renaud's death," he said.

Lori's stomach began to churn when she realized he was talking about *her*. But now her fear began to turn to anger. She edged imperceptively back toward the doorway of the living room. In the semi-darkness, Galloway appeared not to notice.

"Explaining Katherine's death, on the other hand, will be more problematic," he said with ice in his voice. "And your coming here has complicated things immensely."

He took a step forward and motioned toward the kitchen with the gun. "Please step this way, nice and slow."

Lori didn't move.

"As for why Katherine is still alive," Galloway continued, "that's simple pragmatism. Corpses decay; living bodies don't. As long as I keep her alive and under sedation, I have time to plan for the proper disposal of her body—and now yours, as well."

He motioned again with the gun toward the kitchen door. As the barrel rose toward the ceiling, Lori saw her chance and broke for the hallway. As she darted into the living room, her hands went reflexively up to her ears, expecting a gunshot. But the only sound was the squeak of her shoes on the hardwood floor. The rest of the house was enveloped in silence.

When she reached the front door, she twisted the knob and pulled with all her might. The knob turned freely, but the door didn't open.

The double-key deadbolt!

She fumbled in her coat pocket, trying to find her keys.

"There's no way out, Lori." Dr. Galloway's calm, almost soothing voice echoed in the quiet room.

She turned to face him, pressing her back against the front door. *Stay calm*, she told herself. *If you panic, it's all over.*

In the dim light, she could see that Galloway was now holding a syringe in one hand and the pistol in the other.

As he approached, Lori edged forward, away from the door. If Galloway reached for her, she needed room to maneuver.

When he was about ten feet away, he stopped, as if trying to decide the best way to approach her. They stood facing each other. Two shadows in a darkened room, both standing their ground.

"It's up to you," said Galloway, nodding first toward the pistol and then the syringe. "We can do this easy or we can do it hard."

Lori took a deep breath and let it out. She needed to sound relaxed. Confident.

"If you want to kill me, you're gonna have to shoot me."

"I don't want to make this painful for you," Galloway said.

"Don't lie," Lori said, her voice filling with contempt. "You need to keep me alive until you can work out your little plan. You're not concerned about my pain. You're a selfish coward who gets his kicks from killing people."

Galloway snorted in disgust. "And how does that make me different from you? We're both taking another person's life, but you and your Circle friends are so pious, so sanctimonious about it. *You* have no problem killing people as long as you have their *permission*. How dare you look down on me! We're both taking the place of God. At least I'm honest about it." A wicked grin distorted his features. "I enjoy killing people."

In one fluid movement, he flipped the pistol around in his hand and lunged toward Lori, swinging the butt of the gun in a wide arc toward her head. She ducked, but not quickly enough to avoid a glancing blow that sent a fresh blast of pain through her already throbbing head. She fought to retain her balance.

One chance.

Ignoring the racking pain, Lori stepped forward, scraping her heel down Galloway's shin and driving it into his instep.

He screamed in pain and raised his arm to strike her again, but she didn't give him the chance. Clasping her hands together, she drove her elbow backward, catching Galloway solidly beneath the point of the sternum. He doubled over, gasping for breath.

Lori seized the advantage, grabbing both of his ears and wrenching them as hard as she could.

With a shriek of pain, Galloway dropped the gun and crumbled to his knees.

Maintaining her grip on one of his ears, Lori retrieved the gun from the floor, and then she released him. He fell on his side and curled up into a protective position. Lori kept the pistol trained on him.

"Remind me to thank Kate for insisting I take that self-defense class," she said.

EPILOGUE

Charles Hamisch's Apartment
Two Months Later

Charles Hamisch took a long sip from a straw as Lori held the mug for him. Columbo lay curled up in his lap, fast asleep. Charles's hand was resting on the sleeping cat.

"How is it?" Lori asked.

Charles made a noncommittal face. "I guess I can get used to drinking coffee through a straw," Charles said, "as long as it's not too hot."

Lori put the mug back on Charles's dinner tray.

"Have you taken your riluzole?" she asked.

"Yes ma'am."

"Do you need anything else?"

"Just an answer to a question."

"And what would that be?" she asked.

"Something's bothering you. What is it?"

Lori didn't answer.

"Is it the hearing with the medical board tomorrow?"

Lori shook her head. "Considering all I've done, I'm happy that I'm only losing my *job*. I could be losing my freedom."

Charles nodded. "It could have been a lot worse. If you lose your license, do you think you'll move back to Houston?"

"Well," Lori said with a smile, "with Philip going to prison, that's an option. But I don't think I'll go there. I need a fresh start."

"Well, Columbo and I took a vote and you've got a standing invitation to be my personal care-giver."

Lori laughed. "Much as I enjoy taking care of you and Columbo," she said, "I don't think I could make a career of it. Actually, I'm thinking of following in Drew's footsteps and becoming a grief counselor."

"So what's bothering you?"

Lori's face clouded over. She sat down on a chair beside Charles's recliner. "I'm still trying to sort things out."

"Such as?"

"I don't know. I just feel so stupid. How could I be so gullible? To think that Galloway was setting me up to take the fall for his killings. I feel so violated."

"Well, you can be sure he won't be using anybody else, and neither will the Circle. David Bachman told me yesterday that Dr. Galloway has been *very* cooperative. With his assistance they have been able to track down your mysterious John Doe. Turns out he was the one known as Copper, the fourth member of the Circle. His real name is Douglas Cox. He's the administrator of an SHS facility in Cincinnati. Evidently the Circle liked to keep one "off campus" member in the loop with each one of its groups. Sort of as a monitor, I imagine."

"In the interest of keeping the death penalty off the table, Mr. Cox has been naming names left and right. Adding in your testimony, the entire Circle of Peace network will be shut down very soon."

Lori gave him a wan smile. "That's good—I guess."

"Do you still think the Circle of Peace was a good thing?" Charles asked.

Lori shook her head. "I used to. Now I just don't know anymore."

"What changed your mind?"

"Dr. Galloway, believe it or not," said Lori. "He said that we were both taking the place of God by choosing to take a person's life as we saw fit. Maybe it was the way he said it, but I guess I'd never looked at it that way before."

Charles smiled. "You thought that by helping people end their suffering, you were doing God's work, not taking his place?"

"Exactly," said Lori.

"When I first learned I had ALS, I would have agreed with you. In fact, I probably would have been one of the Circle's willing customers if I'd known about them. I couldn't face the idea that I was going to become totally helpless. And I definitely couldn't imagine that a good God would want me to exist like that."

"What changed your mind?" asked Lori.

"Kenton McCarthy helped me see things in a different light."

"How?"

"It's not about me."

Lori looked perplexed. "I don't understand."

"My ALS. It's not about me. Who knows what God is doing through my suffering? For all I know, he might just be using my illness to teach someone else how to serve, and love, and care for a person who is utterly helpless. If I decide to end my own life, I take away that opportunity."

"In other words . . . ?" Lori said.

"In other words, my times are in God's hands. And I can't think of a better place to leave them."

"Knock, knock?" Kate Bainbridge cracked open Charles's front door. Pam Bachman stood right behind her.

"Uh-oh," Charles said. "Party's over."

"Are you ready to get to work?" asked Pam.

"I don't know," said Charles, winking at Lori. "I'm pretty tired today. I don't think I'll be able to get around very well."

"No more excuses," Kate said. She turned toward the door. "Bring it in, David."

Charles heard the sound of an electric motor whirring. A few seconds later, David Bachman came rolling through the door riding a bright red, motorized wheelchair.

"What's this?" Charles asked.

"Your new wheels, partner," said David. "And after taking it for a test drive, I must say that this baby is *sweet*."

"Where'd you get it?" asked Lori.

"It was Kenton's," said Pam. "Janice said that he wanted Charles to have it after he was gone."

Charles smiled. "Thank you, my friend," he said with a glance toward the ceiling.

"OK, everybody out," Pam said. "It's after nine AM and it's time for Hamisch Consulting to open its doors. Charles and I have work to do."

"So much for retirement," said Charles.

Columbo hopped up into the wheelchair, settled himself, and went to sleep.

GENETIC RESEARCH...
CLONING...HUMAN LIFE...
LIFE AND DEATH DECISIONS...

Lethal Harvest
By William Cutrer and Sandra Glahn

The present and the future collide in this riveting medical thriller torn from today's headlines. Personal faith is forced to confront a lethal combination of blind ambition, scientific risk, and political intrigue. Guaranteed fiction!

Deadly Cure
By William Cutrer and Sandra Glahn

The explosive sequel to the CBA best-seller, *Lethal Harvest*. Around every turn in the story lies a blinding matrix of complicated motives and challenges to the sanctity of life. Guaranteed fiction!